ANGELS
OF
MUSIC

Also by Kim Newman and available from Titan Books:

Anno Dracula
Anno Dracula: The Bloody Red Baron
Anno Dracula: Dracula Cha Cha Cha
Anno Dracula: Johnny Alucard

An English Ghost Story
Professor Moriarty: The Hound of the D'Urbervilles
The Secrets of Drearcliff Grange School
Jago
The Quorum
Life's Lottery
Bad Dreams
The Night Mayor

ANGELS
OF
MUSIC

KIM NEWMAN

TITAN BOOKS

Angels of Music

Print edition ISBN: 9781781165683
E-book edition ISBN: 9781781165690

Published by
Titan Books
A division of Titan Publishing Group Ltd
144 Southwark Street
London
SE1 0UP

First edition: October 2016
1 3 5 7 9 10 8 6 4 2

A CIP catalogue record for this title is available from the British Library.

Printed and bound in the United States.

Did you enjoy this book? We love to hear from our readers.
Please email us at readerfeedback@titanemail.com or write to us at
Reader Feedback at the above address.

To receive advance information, news, competitions, and exclusive offers online, please sign up for the Titan newsletter on our website:
www.titanbooks.com

For Randy and Jean-Marc Lofficier

Christine Daaé – the Angel of Song
Trilby O'Ferrall – the Angel of Beauty
Irene Adler – the Angel of Larceny
La Marmoset – the Angel of Light
Sophy Kratides – the Angel of Vengeance
Unorna – the Angel of Magic
Ayda Heidari – the Angel of Blood
Ysabel de Ferre – the Angel of Rapture
Hagar Stanley – the Angel of Insight
Katharine Reed – the Angel of Truth
Clara Watson – the Angel of Pain
Lady Yuki – the Angel of the Sword
Gilberte Lachaille – the Angel of Love
Elizabeth Eynsford Hill – the Angel of Many Voices
Riolama – the Angel of the Air
Alraune ten Brincken – the Angel of Ill Fortune
Olympia – the Clockwork Angel
Thi Minh – the Angel of Acrobatics

ACT ONE: THE MARRIAGE CLUB

"'The requiem mass is not at all gay," Erik's voice resumed, "whereas the wedding mass – you can take my word for it – is magnificent! You must take a resolution and know your own mind! I can't go on living like this, like a mole in a burrow! Don Juan Triumphant is finished; and now I want to live like everybody else. I want to have a wife like everybody else and to take her out on Sundays. I have invented a mask that makes me look like anybody. People will not even turn round in the streets. You will be the happiest of women. And we will sing, all by ourselves, till we swoon away with delight. You are crying! You are afraid of me! And yet I am not really wicked. Love me and you shall see! All I wanted was to be loved for myself. If you loved me I should be as gentle as a lamb; and you could do anything with me that you pleased.'"

Gaston Leroux, *The Phantom of the Opera (1909–10)*

I

TOWARDS THE END of the seventies – that colourful, hectic decade of garish clothes, corrupt politics, personal excess and trivial music – three girls were sent to the Paris Opéra. They could dance a little, sing a little more, were comely when painted and cut fine figures in tights. Were the world just, they would have been stars in the ascendant. Leading roles would have been assigned to them. Rewards would have come along... fame, riches and advantageous marriages.

However, a rigid system of seniority, patronage and favour-currying then governed the house. Our heroines, no matter how perfectly they trilled audition pieces or daintily they lifted skirts from shapely calves, were of the 'untouchable' caste, and fated to remain in the depths of the chorus. If critic or admirer or patron were to call public attention to their qualities, they would likely find themselves cast as slaves in the next production, faces blacked with burnt cork, holding the Queen's train at the rear of the stage. Such was the ruthless dictate of the house's reigning diva, Signorina Carlotta Castafiore.

Yet... Christine Daaé had a Voice. Trilby O'Ferrall had a Face. And Irene Adler had a Mind. When they arrived at the Opéra, the women were gems in the rough. To be revealed as diamonds of the first water, they required polish, cutting and careful setting. Without such treatment, they were likely to become dull pebbles, lost among so many other shingles on the beach.

Many equally appealing young ladies have served years in the chorus as their brothers served terms in the armed forces (or prison), trying not to squander meagre pay on absinthe or cards, hoping to emerge whole in mind and limb from regular ordeals, dreaming of comfortable retirement. At best, they might end up the second wives of comfortable widowers; at worst, they might... well, 'at worst' is too hideous to be dwelled upon, save to observe that such as they were found ragged on the cobbles or drowned in the Seine with a frequency which verged upon the scandalous.

These demoiselles tended to attract the puppy-like devotions of decent, dull-witted youths and the carnivorous attentions of indecent, cold-hearted roués. Our trio, in their private dreams, yearned for a different stripe of suitor – mysterious, dominating, challenging. Without such a presence in their lives, the girls lacked direction. But, even kept outside the circle of the limelight, they had an unnerving tendency to sparkle. Carlotta saw the shimmering in her wake, and made sure they stayed in shadow. Nevertheless, one by one, they were *noticed*... not by the stuffy and harassed management or the violently partisan audience claques, but by a personage who saw into their secret selves.

This unique individual was at once Christine's Trapdoor Lover, Trilby's Mesmerist Genius and Irene's Mastermind of Intrigue. All Paris knew him as the Opera Ghost, though most deemed him a phantasm rather than a phantom. He was a bogey conjured by stagehands to throw a scare into pretty little ballerinas, not the spectre of a dead man whose bones lay unshriven in a recess of Charles Garnier's palatial opera house. Those who had cause to believe the Phantom of the Opera a man of flesh and bone were wise enough not to speak of him. There were rumours about what happened to those who earned his displeasure.

His protégées came to know him as Monsieur Erik.

Among the Phantom's few intimates was the Persian. The exact function of this long-faced, astrakhan-capped fellow at the opera house was hard to determine but evidently essential. The girls flitted through a surface world of upholstered finery, fashionable cafés and society engagements, of grand opening nights and merry madcap balls; the Opera Ghost confined himself to the decaying, watery labyrinth below street level, among the scenery of out-of-fashion productions and tombs of tortured men. Only the Persian passed easily between the two realms. It was said he was the only man living who had seen the true face behind mirror and mask, though some claimed to have glimpsed a yellow-eyed, noseless spectre in Box Five, upon which it had a permanent lease.

From behind a mirror in Dressing Room 313, Erik gave 'music lessons', whispering for hours to his songbirds – his Swedish-born French nightingale, French-born Irish thrush and All-American eagle. He first discovered Daaé, his most naturally gifted pupil, and called from her a voice to rival the angels. Moreover, he taught her to *feel* the music, to imbue the polite perfection of her natural tones with the rude turbulence of her young heart. Thanks to Erik, Christine's voice could reach and affect in a manner those who heard it would never forget, though for her finest performances her only auditor was a single, tattered soul weeping under his mask.

O'Ferrall, near death after a spell under another mesmerist-tutor, was cracked in voice, body and spirit when brought to Erik. He repaired her voice if not to its former, artificial magnificence – once, briefly, she had performed at the highest level – then at least to pleasant adequacy. Not a natural singer like Christine, Trilby was, if properly presented, the greatest beauty of the age, an attainment involving at least as much sacrifice and special exercise as musical distinction.

Adler, the American, was warier, less obviously talented, too strong-willed for the special tutelage Erik bestowed upon her sisters in song, but prodigiously gifted. She could turn her quick mind and light fingers to almost anything. Irene's involvement with the Agency was a matter of negotiation towards mutual advantage rather than submission to the will of the Opera Ghost.

Each, in her own way, benefited from Erik's work with them, and grew when they worked together. Collaboration went against the instincts of the potential diva in each… but they were more effective as a trio than they would have been as three solo turns. Should their maestro have been interested, a healthy income could have been generated by hiring out *les trois jolis anges* as entertainment for cafés, society functions, musical soirées, orgies, weddings, funerals and the like… but his vision for his protégées was of a different stripe. He saw in them deeper, more specialised talents and was determined they should be put to good use. A mystery himself, Erik set out to rid the city – *à terme*, all France (and overseas territories and possessions) – of competition. His own mask would stay in place, but all others would be lifted.

Though seldom seen above street level, Erik founded a private enquiry agency. Just as an opera director does not appear on stage, except to take bows after a first night, Erik remained in his well-appointed cellars while his protégées acted on his behalf and received the applause due to them.

It was circulated in the proverbial circles that those who wished to engage the Opera Ghost Agency must first make contact with the Persian or, for more delicate matters, Madame Giry, the Keeper of Box Five. These loyal operatives would convey the details of the case to the Phantom himself. Often Erik was already well apprised of matters in which prospective clients wished him to take an interest. Thanks to an intricate array of tubes and shutters, he could eavesdrop on gossip uttered in any box, dressing room or lavatory in the house. Few matters of moment troubled the city without being discussed somewhere within the Paris Opéra. Once a case came to Erik's attention, it was his decision – unaffected by the scale of fee on offer – whether a commission was accepted or declined.

If accepted, a bell sounded.

II

Bells were forever ringing around the house, to summon artistes, dressers, musicians, commissionaires, wine-waiters, clerks, servants, composers, scene-shifters, rat-catchers, chorus girls, washer-women. Bells were sounded to alert the audience when a performance was about to commence or resume. Not to mention the cow-, sheep- or goat-bells rung by percussionists when pieces with rustic settings were given. Only a finely tuned ear could distinguish individual tones among such tintinnabulation. But our three girls knew their bell. When it tinkled, anything they happened to be doing – no matter how important – was set aside in their haste to make their way to a dressing room at the end of a basement corridor which had apparently been abandoned as too far from the great stage for convenience.

When Erik rang the bell, Christine Daaé was in a scuttle-shaped bathtub, all a-lather, singing scales... Trilby O'Ferrall was posing in a sunlit upper room for a class of impoverished art students who'd pooled meagre funds to purchase an hour of her time... and Irene Adler was practising her lock-picking blindfolded, working away with hairpins and clever fingers.

Within moments, the tub stood empty, the students disappointed and the lock unpicked. The girls nipped swiftly to answer the summons, using dumb-waiters, trapdoors and other byways known only to intimates of Charles Garnier. They arrived simultaneously at Dressing Room 313. The Persian looked up from the latest number of *La Petite Parisien* and flapped a hand at them, the smoke from his Turkish cigarette making a question mark in the air. The trio arranged themselves on a divan before the large, green-speckled mirror. Christine and Trilby were still wriggling into suitable clothes. They helped each other with hooks and buttons. Irene coolly replaced the pins she had been using as lock-picks. When the Persian turned down the gaslight, it was possible to discern a chamber beyond the mirror's thin silvering. A slender shadow stood there, extravagantly cloaked and hatted, violin tucked under his chin. Erik extemporised the sort of 'hurry up' trill used to encourage unpopular acts to get off the stage in *salles des variétés* as the girls concluded their business with a minimum of pinching and tutting.

'What's the ruckus this time, Bright Boy?' asked Irene, whose speech still bore the pernicious influence of her native New Jersey. 'Is some mug tryin' ta knock over the Louvre again?'

'Could it be a plot to bring down the government?' asked Trilby.

'Or set off dynamite under Notre-Dame?' asked Christine.

The Persian exhaled a smoke ring. 'Nothing so everyday, ladies.'

All eyes turned to the mirror. Trilby, by a degree the prettiest of our trio and a long chalk the most vain, fussed with her short brown curls, accompanied by a teasing little violin tune. She noticed the others looking at her, smiled sweetly and put her hands in her lap as if about to listen dutifully to a sermon.

The violin was set down and a sepulchral voice sounded, conveyed into the room through a speaking tube with a woodwind tone.

'Our client,' said Erik, 'is most exalted. In fact, a president.'

'The President of the Republic!' exclaimed Christine, saluting.

With the shortage of male chorus – thanks to the brutal levies of the Franco-Prussian War, the Siege, the Commune and *la Semaine Sanglante* – the boyish Daaé frame was often gussied up *en travestie* in braided uniform. She was better at close-order drill than any lad in the company. Off duty, as it were, she often favoured military tunics. Though born in Sweden, she had been raised mostly in France and was a true patriotess. She could have posed for the image of Marianne if, unlike the often-painted Trilby, she were not addicted to the fidgets.

'It can't be that maroon in the White House!' said Irene Adler.

'Ireland hasn't got a president, more's the pity,' muttered Trilby – born in Paris of an Irish father and a French mother, never to set foot on the green sod from which she inherited her complexion. 'Just the cursed God English, and their fat little German Queen.'

'Our client is far more respected than a mere head of state,' said Erik. 'She is *la Présidente*. Apollonie Sabatier, *née* Joséphine-Aglaé Savatier. Her salon may be more vital to *la vie parisienne* than any government building, museum or cathedral.'

'Salon?' queried Christine.

'He means whorehouse,' explained Irene. 'What Miss Potato's Limey oppressors call "a knocking-shop".'

Trilby good-humouredly stuck her tongue out at Irene.

'I've heard of Madame Sabatier,' said Trilby. 'She's one of those Horizontal Giantesses.'

'Indeed,' continued Erik. 'The most upstanding, indeed paradoxically vertical of the nation's *grandes horizontales*. You will have seen her portrait by Meissonier, her statue by Clésinger.'

'That Baudelaire freak was nuts about her,' said Irene.

There was a pause. It would be easy to conceive of a yellowish, skeletal brow wrinkling in a frown, a lipless mouth attempting a *moue* of displeasure, a glint of irritation in sunken yellow eyes.

'What did I say?' whined Irene. 'Everyone knows the guy was ga-ga for the dame. Did you ever see Baudelaire? Weirdest-looking turkey this side of the state fair, mooning over this overpriced sporting gal. Most ridiculous thing you ever heard of. Just like Beauty and the Beast!'

An exhalation of impatience hissed through the speaking tube.

The Phantom had a particular, personal dislike of the Jeanne-Marie Leprince de Beaumont fairy tale known far and wide as *La Belle et la Bête*. When the management attempted to revive André Grétry's *Zémire et Azor*, a once-popular *opéra comique* inspired by the story, the production was dogged by a run of bad luck. At the end of the dress rehearsal, the luckless tenor cast as Azor discovered that the inside of his beast mask had been cruelly coated with indissoluble glue. The prank became unpleasantly apparent when he attempted to tear off his mask to take a bow. No understudy would take the role on opening night, and the piece was replaced at the last moment by a less controversial item from the repertoire, Daniel Auber's *Fra Diavolo, ou L'Hôtellerie de Terracine*.

Irene thought over her comments about ugly geniuses smitten with beautiful women, looked again at the silhouette beyond the mirror, and paled in rigid terror. She had spoken without thinking, which was unlike her.

Without the benefit of 'music lessons', Irene was less schooled than Christine and Trilby in the discipline expected of Erik's operatives.

Eventually, the hissing became a normal susurrus, and Erik resumed.

'It is true that the Salon Sabatier has been the haunt of poets and artists. *La Présidente* has admirers among our greatest creative minds.'

'I know all about the minds of poets and painters,' said Trilby. 'Filth and degeneracy is what goes around in their clever little brains. Enough scribblers and daubers have trotted after me. Ought to be ashamed, so they should.'

Trilby spat in her hand and crossed herself. It was something her father often did when pledging to creditors that funds would be available by the end of the week, just before the O'Ferrall *ménage* moved to a new, usually less salubrious address.

'Our client requires us to display great sensitivity and tact,' decreed Erik.

'None of the tittle or the tattle,' said Christine.

'Exactly. In the course of this investigation, you might well become privy to information which *la Présidente* and her particular friends…'

'Johns,' put in Irene.

'…would not wish to be generally known.'

'Have you noticed how these fancy fellers *always* think their wives don't know a thing?' said Trilby. 'Bless their hearts. They're like tiny children. Wouldn't they be surprised if they knew what their missuses got up to while they're tomcatting about town?'

All three laughed. Christine, it had to be said, frequently did not quite 'get' the meaning of her friends' comments – especially when, as was their habit, they spoke in English – but was alert enough to conceal occasional ignorance by chiming in with musical giggles. Her chief trait was adorability, and foolish fellows were already composing remarkably poor sonnets about the smallness of her nose with ambitions towards epic verse on the subject of the rest of her anatomy. Trilby was older than the others, though no one would ever tell to look at her. Her greater experience of the artistic life inclined her to be protective of her baby sisters. Foolish fellows in her presence tended to be struck dumb, as if she were a vision at Lourdes. Sometimes, a glazed look came into her eyes, and she seemed a different, more ethereal, slightly frightening person.

Irene, in years the youngest, was a harder nut to crack, and men thought her handsome rather than pretty, as dangerous as alluring. She put it about that she fled her homeland after knifing a travelling preacher for whom she had been shilling. It was considerably more complicated than that. She often imagined returning to New York on the arm of one of the crowned heads she had seen in the rotogravure. In her copy-book, she had already designed an Adler coat of arms – an American eagle, beak deep in the side of a screaming naked Prometheus. A foolish fellow who stepped out with her tended to find some unknown *apache* had lifted their note-case, snuff-box, cuff-links and watch during the course of a delightful evening with a disappointing curtain.

'It is a matter of a man and his wife which has been brought before us,' announced Erik. 'The man of some distinction, the woman an unknown.'

The Persian undid the ribbon on a large wallet, and slid out clippings from the popular press, a wedding brochure, photographic plates and other documents. These were passed among the girls.

Some excitement was expressed at a reproduced portrait of a handsome fellow in the uniform of a brigadier of the armies of the late Emperor. There was cooing of admiration for a curly moustache and upright sabre. With a touch of malice, the Persian handed over a more recent likeness, in which the golden boy was all but unrecognisable. These days, the soldier was an enormous, shaggy-browed, weathered hulk, a pudding of flesh decorated with innumerable medals.

'You recognise Étienne Gérard, retired Grand Marshal of France, still reckoned one of our most influential citizens,' said Erik. 'No one is as canny as he when it comes to badgering the right politician to change a procurement policy or effect a strategy of preparedness.'

'He started shouting "the Prussians are coming, the Prussians are coming" just after von Blücher bloodied his nose at Waterloo,' said Christine. 'I had an uncle like that.'

'Of course,' said Trilby, 'the Prussians really were coming.'

'That doesn't make the old man any less a booby.'

'You're behind the times, Chrissy,' put in Irene. 'Gérard stopped tooting that particular trumpet a few months back. He's a changed man since he got hitched to this little social-climber. Now, he's big on beating swords into ploughshares and insisting the French people have no greater pal than Bismarck.'

The wedding brochure commemorated the joining-together of Grand Marshal Gérard with his bride, Poupée Francis-Pierre.

'He's over ninety and she's what... sixteen?' said Trilby.

'Precise details about Madame Gérard's age, background or qualities are hard to come by,' said Erik. 'Such information is one objective of our investigation.'

'I heard she was a dancer,' said Christine, looking at a studio photograph of the bride. 'Looks like she's made of porcelain. You'd think she'd *snap* if the old goat so much as touched her.'

'Is she one of *la Présidente*'s dollymops?' asked Irene. 'Some addlehead dotards go for that rouge-cheeked widdle girlie act.'

'Madame Gérard is *not* a former ornament of the Salon

Sabatier,' said Erik. 'Indeed, she is the cause of some consternation among the girls there. Before his nuptials, the Grand Marshal, despite his advancing years, was an especially favoured and enthusiastic regular customer.'

'Tarts like 'em old and rich,' said Trilby. 'They can't do much, but pay well over the odds.'

Irene laughed, and Christine joined in.

'Though not of an artistic temperament,' continued Erik, 'Grand Marshal Gérard found Madame Sabatier's establishment more to his liking than many rival houses run to cater to more military tastes.'

'Boots and whips,' shuddered Irene.

'Subsequent to his wedding, he has not visited the Salon.'

'No wonder. He's getting poked for free at home.'

'*La*, Irène, you say such things,' tittered Christine.

'Madame Sabatier reports that losing a longstanding patron to marriage is an accepted risk of her business. However, she takes pride in the fact that, with this single exception, her clients have returned within three months of their honeymoons, and been more generous than before in the matter of recompense and gifts, usually with an added exhortation to increased discretion.'

Christine laughed out loud, musically. 'The Madame is deluded. Look at Gérard's life, all the way back to the last century. All those exploits and adventures. He's obviously a reckless romantic.'

'I agree,' said Trilby. 'The old idiot's probably in love with the minx.'

'I'll bet nuggets Petite Poupée has been down to the dressmakers to see how she looks in black,' said Irene. 'Then steered by the apothecary's on the way home. If used in excess, those boudoir philtres for the use of senior gentlemen are bad for the constitution... so I hear.'

'If that is the case, we are required by our client to intervene,' said Erik.

'I'll say,' put in Trilby. 'Can't let some filly get away with murder. We've got a reputation to think of.'

'Does Madame Présidente fear for Gérard's life?' asked Christine.

There was a pause. Breathing could be heard through the tube.

'It may come to that. At present, she is more concerned that the old fellow is not "acting like himself". She takes a keen interest in the defence of France...'

'Sausage-eaters are notoriously rough on whores and stingy about paying.'

'Thank you for that insight, Irene. "Adler" is a German name, is it not? As I was saying, Étienne Gérard's change of mind on matters military and political troubles Madame Sabatier more than his absence from her customer register. She believes the Grand Marshal might have been "got at" in some way...'

'Hypnotised,' said Christine, thrilled.

'Mesmerised,' said Trilby, dreamily.

'Doped,' said Irene, cynically.

'She wonders if the Grand Marshal even *is* the Grand Marshal.'

'Murdered and replaced by the mad twin from the attic,' suggested Christine, who read a great deal of sensation fiction, avidly following every *feuilleton* in every periodical in Paris. 'Possessed by one of those invisible *horlas* one hears of and forced to do the bidding of some creature from beyond the veil.'

The Persian gathered back all the documents, and resealed the packet.

'Erik,' said Irene, 'are you *sure* this is a job for the Agency? It sounds mighty like some scorned *comare*, sulking because Sugar Daddy has cut off the cash flow, out to do dirt to the chit who has stolen him away. Shouldn't they settle it with a decent knife-fight and leave us out of it?'

The Persian produced several more wallets.

'The Grand Marshal is not an isolated case.'

III

THE MARRIAGE CLUB had international members, though all were often found in Paris. Aristide Saccard, the daring international financier, a man who would never escape the soubriquet of 'shady'; the Duke of Omnium, an English cabinet minister whose speeches were rumoured to have the mystic power of sending entire Houses of Parliament into restful sleep ('If Planty ever had to declare war,' sniped one critic, 'we'd have to wake up the enemy to shoot at him'); Chevalier Lucio del Gardo, a respected banker no one outside the Opera Ghost Agency would have believed moonlighted as a needlessly violent burglar known as 'the Spine-Snapper'; Walter Parks Thatcher, the American statesman and banker; Simon Cordier, behind his back called 'Monsieur le Guillotine', a magistrate and sculptor, renowned for cool, balanced and unsympathetic verdicts in capital cases; and Cardinal Tosca, the Papal Legate, reputedly the greatest virtuoso of the boudoir to come (or be chased) out of Italy since Casanova.

All were getting along in years, widowed or lifelong bachelors, and had recently taken to wife much younger, socially unknown women, or – in the Cardinal's case – brought her into his household as official servant and unofficial bed-warmer. All had reversed long-held public positions since their happy unions, made peculiar public statements or financial transactions, been far less often seen in society than before (Gérard was not the only old bridegroom to be missed at his favourite brothel) and were reported by estranged friends and relations to have 'changed their spots'. All, it transpired, had first encountered their current spouses at *soirées* hosted, on an absurdly well-appointed barge in the Seine, by one Countess Joséphine Balsamo. Some said the Countess was a direct descendant of the purported sorcerer Cagliostro. It was believed among the peers of *la Présidente* that the Countess was directress of an unofficial wedding bureau, schooling girls plucked from orphanages or jails in the skills necessary to hook a prominent husband, arranging discreet disposal of the lovestruck old men, then taking a tithe from the widows' inheritances. A flaw in the theory was that none of the husbands, as yet, had died in the expected mysterious circumstances – several long-term moaning invalids had leaped from apparent deathbeds and taken to cavorting vigorously with their pixie-like sylph brides.

Christine held, against experience, to the possibility that nothing more was amiss than a collection of genuine May to December romances ('More like March to Next February,' commented Irene) which should be protected from the jealous wiles of Erik's client. Trilby considered malfeasance was likely on the part of these men of wealth and influence, and that the Countess Joséphine was simply a well-dressed procuress with a dubious title. She felt the true victims of the Marriage Club were the unfortunate, nearly-nameless children given over into the beds of men who purchased them as they might a hunting dog or a painting. Irene suspected everyone was up to no good, and wondered what their angle on *l'affaire Balsamo* ought to be. She was as much magpie as eagle and it occurred to her that this case should afford access to households where valuables might be carelessly strewn about for the filching.

The Persian, through his police and government contacts, had obtained a list of the Countess's holdings. Few of her interests were in the name she most commonly used. These papers were passed through a shutter, to the chamber behind the mirror.

'This seems the most likely "lead",' said Erik, after a perusal. '*École de Danse Coppélius*. The Countess is a "sleeping partner". Young women of barely marriageable age and malleable personality might be found in a dancing school, *hein*?'

The Persian showed again the photograph of Poupée Gérard. In the corner of the picture were scratched the initials '*É.d.D.C.*'

'It's a perfect front,' said Irene, getting the talk back on track.

'Haul 'em in, paint 'em up, sell 'em off.'

A lever was thrown, and two wardrobe doors sprung open, disclosing three varied sets of female attire and one suit of male evening dress (with turban). The girls knew at once which were their costumes. The Persian took the turban.

'Christine, Trilby,' said Erik, close to the glass, eyes shining. 'You will try to enrol at the *École Coppélius*. Christine, at least, should be able to pass an audition if dancing is actually required, while Trilby can certainly be passed off as bride-to-be material.'

The girls looked at each other, not sure whether to be offended by Erik's implications. Then Christine was struck by the loveliness of her new dress, and forgot any sleight.

The shutter opened again. A newly struck, gilt-edged invitation card lay within. The Persian picked it up by forefinger and thumb, careful not to smudge the ink. Erik had a printing press in his lair – along with much other apparatus somehow smuggled below for the use of the Agency.

'That,' said Erik, 'is for the Countess's Summer Ball, to be held tonight on her famous barge. She expects the pleasure of the company of Rhandi Lal, the Khasi of Kalabar, and his daughter, the Princess Jelhi.'

Irene held up a silken sari, pressed her hands together in prayerful submission, and bowed mockingly at the mirror, eyes modestly downcast.

'Try not to overact, Miss Adler.'

IV

WITH HER JEWELLED headdress, scarlet forehead dot, exposed midriff, kohl-lined eyes, near-transparent costume and sinuous walk, 'Princess Jelhi' was instantly popular, attracting a platoon of admirers in white tie and tails or dress uniform. Most of the men had swords: as a consequence of jostling for position among the upper ranks, several duels were likely.

As Irene flirted and fluttered, the Persian scanned the ballroom. The dancing floor was not the classic square, but an oblong. Brassbound porthole-shaped windows above and below the waterline reminded guests that they were on the river. The mooring was secure and the barge heavy in the water: only the slightest motion confirmed that the company was not on dry land. The theme of the ball was Childhood Remembered, and the room was dressed as a giant's child's playroom. Ten-foot tall wooden soldiers and other outsized toys stood around, as conversation pieces or to excite wonderment. In the centre of the floor, a gigantic, stately top spun on its axis, ingeniously weighted not to stray from its spot or fall over. Above it all shone a giant, crescent-headed Man in the Moon. A wooden spoon on wires shovelled snuff into a lunar nostril.

Irene lifted a bare foot, showing off her painted nails and oddments of paste jewellery from the opera house's vast store of dressing-up kit. The motion parted her sari, affording a glimpse of shapely inside-leg. Gasps rose from her admirers and she tittered modestly at the 'slip', chiding the gallants in delightfully broken babytalk French.

The Persian looked about for anyone *not* enraptured by the Princess. If the business of this ball was fishing for fiancés and an uninvited interloper was raiding the stock, the fleet who held rights in these waters would be out of sorts. The Countess Joséphine had not made an entrance, but the Persian knew she would be watching. Erik was not the city's only addict of secret panels, two-way mirrors, listening tubes and portraits with removable eyes. Any descendant of the mountebank Cagliostro would be mistress of such matters. The single exposed eye of the snuffling Man in the Moon glistened like a lens.

Irene Adler could be relied upon to glance at a crowd of gentlemen and single out the most distinguished victims – taking into account inherited or acquired wealth, ancient or modern title, achievements on the field of battle or in the arts, and degree of commitment to their current marital state. At a masquerade where everyone was dressed up as what they were not, she could spot a Crown Prince through a throng of mere Viscounts and chart a course which would lead inevitably to taking the prize. Within minutes, she had dismissed the also-rans and narrowed the field down to the three men in the company worth bothering with.

The choice picks were Count Rouboff, the Russian military *attaché* (which is to say, spy) and a cousin of the Tsar; Baron Maupertuis, the Belgian colossus of copper (and other base metals); and 'Black' Michael Elphberg, Duke of Strelsau, second son of the King of Ruritania (a mere unmarried half-brother's death or disgrace away from succession to the crown). Any or all of these might be candidates for the Marriage Club, though only the Baron was elderly.

Count Rouboff asked the Princess to demonstrate the dancing style of far-off Kalabar, and Irene obliged with a shimmy she had learned as warm-up for a snake-oil salesman in the Wild West. As a well-developed thirteen-year-old, her tour with a medicine show had been her first attempt at escape from New Jersey. Of course, the moves that dried mouths and stirred vitals in Tombstone, Cheyenne and No Name City were still effective in Paris, though the crowds were cleaner and, on the whole, had more of their original teeth. Some women simply gave up, collected their wraps, and went home in huffs, leaving behind befuddled gentlemen who would find domestic lives difficult for the next week or so. Others took careful note of Irene's steps, and resolved to learn them.

A five-piece orchestra provided ever more frenzied accompaniment in what they must have fondly imagined was the style of far-off Kalabar. The musicians were dressed as a strange breed of clown, with ridiculously stack-heeled boots, lightning-pattern leotards immodestly padded with rolled-up handkerchiefs and cut low to reveal thick thatches of chest hair (not entirely natural), faces painted with celestial maps so eyes and mouths opened disturbingly in purple moons or stars, and shocks of bright orange hair teased up into jagged peaks. The band made a lot of noise, and even more fuss – sticking out gargoyle tongues, making obscene advances to their sparkle-patterned instruments, capering grotesquely like dressed-up apes with their rumps on fire.

Irene began to unwind the interlocking scarves that constituted her sari, wrapping them around admirers' necks, brushing the trail-ends across their faces to raise their colour. The Khasi of Kalabar, suspecting this might go too far, was on the point of stepping in to reprimand his 'daughter' when the Princess was flanked.

Two pretty girls, similar enough in face and figure to be taken for sisters, assumed positions either side of Irene, clicked fingers, and fell in step, mimicking exactly her dance moves. A ripple of applause came from those who supposed the Countess had brought in a choreographer. A frown of surprise briefly passed across Irene's tinted forehead. She left off the Salome business, concentrating on energetic, elaborate footwork, with snake-moves in her hips and back. Out West, the crowd would have hauled out their Colt 45s and blasted the ceiling. The sisters, however, were not thrown. They perfectly matched her, not even seeming to follow a lead.

The Persian considered the bland, shiny faces of the girls. They showed no emotion, no exertion, scarcely even any interest. Irene was, in polite terms, 'glowing' – and thus in danger of sweating through her betelnut make-up. The caste mark on her forehead looked like an angry bullet-hole. It was harder and harder for her to keep up with the dance.

Everyone in the room was watching this trio.

The band were murdering '*Ah! Je ris de me voir si belle en ce miroir*' – the 'Jewel Song' from *Faust*. Carlotta's signature number, as it happens. One of the clowns sang like a castrato, inventing new lyrics in double Dutch. If he tried that within earshot of a certain Phantom, he'd find himself wearing a chandelier for a hat. The Gounod opera was a favourite with Erik.

Irene made a tiny misstep, and lost her lead. Now, she had to follow, to mimic, to copy – and the terpsichorean sisters began to execute a series of balletic leaps, glides and stretches which were too much for the New Jersey Apsara. Her bare foot slid, and she had to be caught by a nobody – her former admirers were now enslaved by the sisters.

For a moment, it seemed there would be a problem – three swains, two dancers – but Irene was instantly replaced by a third girl, darker haired but sharing the family resemblance. The debutante locked at once into the dance, and the three tiny, strong girls performed like prima ballerinas prevailed upon to share a leading role. Now there was a sister apiece, if sisters they were, for the Count, the Baron and the Duke.

The Princess was helped, limping, out of the circle by her rescuer, Basil – a homosexual English painter with only academic interest in the female form. Even he deserted her as soon as she was dumped on a couch, and was drawn back to the circle around the dancing girls.

'They ain't human,' the Princess said – through angry tears – to the Khasi.

The performance concluded with a tableau as the darker girl was held high, pose perfect. Thunderous applause resounded. The girls' pleasant smiles did not broaden.

'It must be mesmerism,' said Irene. 'Trilby's old tutor is probably behind it. Svengali. He put her to sleep with a swinging bauble and fixed her croak so she came out with the purest voice in Europe. Those witches have had the same treatment, only for dancing.'

Irene stood up, putting weight on her foot. Her ankle was not turned or sprained. Only her dignity was really damaged.

'The patsies are lost,' she told the Persian. 'While no one's watching, let's sneak out. There must be something on this tub to give the game away.'

He nodded concurrence.

V

'ZUT ALORS, TRILBEE,' said Christine. 'We have wasted our time. This is not a dancing school...'

'This is a mannequin factory,' concluded Trilby.

'That fool of a Persian must have made the mistake. And we have come all this way by fiacre. Erik should not put his trust in such a person. So the trip is not a complete wash-out, we should go to a café and have some pastries.'

'The Persian's not a fool,' said Trilby, concentrating.

'He has sent us to the wrong address.'

'But the name is correct, look. It may not be *École de Danse Coppélius*, but – see – here on the board. *Fabricants des Mannequins – M. Coppélius et Sig. Spallanzani*. Perhaps the dance school failed, and the Countess's partners found a new use for the building.'

They had hoped to enrol in evening classes.

'Chrissy, now it's time for subtle fuge.'

'Subtle what?'

'Fuge. You know, sneakin' about.'

'Ha! But you are ill-suited for such, with your hopping-of-the-clod Irish feet and so forth.'

'Never you mind my feet. It's your own slippered tootsies you should be thinking on.'

Christine arched her leg, displaying her fine calf boot and its row of buttons.

'Lovely,' said Trilby. 'Very suited for sneakin'. Now, if you'll climb up over this fence – mind the spikes on the tops of the rail, looks as if they've been sharpened – I'm certain you'll be able to get that chain loosened so I can follow. This is a task much more suited to your delicacy.'

For a moment, Christine wondered whether she had not been manipulated into taking an uncomfortable risk. But she knew the Irish girl was too simple-minded for such duplicity.

'Careful,' called up Trilby. 'You'll tear your...'

There was a rip, as Christine's skirts caught on a spike.

'Never mind. It'll set a new fashion.'

Trilby looked both ways, up and down the alley. They had sought out a side entrance to the factory, away from passersby.

Christine dropped from the top of the fence and landed like a cat, with a hiss. She had a fetching smear of grime on her forehead and her hair had come loose. From her reticule, she found a hand mirror and – angling to get moonlight to work by – effected meticulous repairs to her appearance, while Trilby waited for the chain to be seen to.

As it happened, the chain was draped incorrectly around the wrong railings. The gate had been left unfastened. It swung open with a creak.

'I suppose we should have tried that first.'

Christine frowned, a touch pettishly.

'Now is not the time to bring up this matter, Trilbee.'

'Perhaps not. Now, the fastenings of that little window, eight or ten feet up the wall, look to me to be similarly neglected. Let me make a cradle with my rough Irish peasant hands and hoist your dainty delicate Swedish footsie like so...'

With a strength born in hours of holding awkward poses while undressed in draughty artists' garrets, Trilby lifted her fellow angel up off the ground. Christine pushed the window, which fell in with a crash.

'Perhaps we should announce our arrival with twenty-four cannons, *hein*?'

Trilby shrugged, and Christine slipped through the window. She reached down, and pulled Trilby up after her.

They both stood in a small, dark room. Trilby struck a lucifer. All around were racks of unattached, shapely arms and legs.

'*Sainte Vierge Marie!*' exclaimed Christine, in a stage whisper. 'We have stumbled into the larder of a clan of cannibals!'

Trilby held the match-flame near a rack. Porcelain shone in

the light, and a row of arms swayed, tinkling against each other.

'No, Chrissy, as advertised, this is a mannequin factory.'

Against the wall sat a range of womanly torsos, with or without heads. Some were wigged and painted, almost complete. Others were bald as eggs, with hollow eye-sockets waiting for glass.

'What would doll-makers have to do with these mystery brides?'

'I've a nasty feeling we're about to find out.'

A light appeared under the crack of the door, and there was some clattering as a lock was turned. Then bolts were thrown, and several other locks fussed with.

'What are we to do, Trilbee?'

'Take off our clothes. Quickly.'

Christine looked aghast. Trilby, more used to getting undressed at speed, had already started. The clattering continued. Christine unfastened the first buttons of her bodice. Trilby – already down to stockings, drawers, corset and chemise – helped with a tug, ripping out the other ninety-eight buttons, getting Christine free of her dress as if unshelling a pod of peas. The door, so much more secure than the gate or the window, was nearly unlocked.

Trilby picked up Christine, and hooked the back of her corset on a hanger.

'Go limp,' she whispered.

Christine flopped, letting her head loll.

Trilby sat against the wall, making a place among a row of mannequins similarly clad in undergarments. She opened her eyes wide in a stare, sucked in her cheeks, and arranged her arms stiffly, fingers stretched.

The door finally opened. Gaslight was turned up.

A gnome-like little man, with red circles on his cheeks and a creak in his walk, peered into the room.

'Cochenille, what is it?' boomed someone from outside.

'Nothing, Master Spallanzani,' responded Cochenille, the gnome, in a high-pitched voice. 'Some birds got in through the window, and made a mess among the *demoiselles*.'

'Clear it up, you buffoon. There will be an inspection later, and the Countess does not take kindly to being displeased. As you well know.'

Cochenille flinched at the mention of the Countess. Christine and Trilby worked hard at keeping faces frozen. Slyly, the little man shut the door behind him, listened for a moment to make sure his master was not coming to supervise, then relaxed.

'My pretties,' he said, picking up a bewigged head and kissing its painted smile. 'Lovelier cold than you'll ever be warm.'

Cochenille tenderly placed the head on the neck of a limbless torso and arranged its hair around its cold white shoulders. He passed on, paying attention to each partial mannequin.

'Alouette, not yet,' he cooed to a mannequin complete but for one arm. 'Clair-de-lune, very soon,' to another finished but for the eyes and wig. 'And… but who is this? A fresh face. And finished.'

He stopped before Christine, struck by her.

'You are so perfect,' said Cochenille. 'From here, you will go to the arms of a rich man, a powerful man who will be in *your* power. You will sway the fates of fortunes, armies, countries. But you will have no happiness for yourself. These men who receive you, they appreciate you not. Only Cochenille truly sees your beauty.'

Christine concentrated very hard on being frozen. As an artists' model, Trilby was used to holding a pose, but Christine's nerves were a-twitch. She worried that the pulse in her throat or a flicker in her eyes would give her away. And the urge to fidget was strong in her.

'What these men know not is that they take my cast-offs,' said the gnome, rather unpleasantly. 'Before you wake, before you are sent to them, you are – for this brief tender moment – the Brides of Cochenille.'

With horror, Christine realised this shrunken thing, with his withered face and roué's face paint, was unbuttoning his one-piece garment, working down from his neck, shrugging free of his sleeves.

She would do only so much for Erik!

Cochenille leaned close, wet tongue out. Suddenly, he was puzzled, affronted.

'Mademoiselle,' he said, shocked, 'you are too… warm!'

Christine gripped the rack from which she was hung, taking the weight off her corset, and scissored her legs around Cochenille's middle. Trilby leaped up, tearing an arm from the nearest doll, wielding it like a polo mallet. She fetched the gnome a ferocious blow on the side of his head as Christine tried to squeeze life out of the loathsome little degenerate.

Cochenille's head spun around on his neck, rotating in a complete circle several times. He ended up looking behind him, at the astonished Trilby.

'He's a doll,' she gasped.

Something in his neck had broken and he couldn't speak. His glass eyes glinted furiously. Christine still had him trapped.

'And he is a disgusting swine,' she said.

Trilby lifted Cochenille's head from his neck and his body went limp in Christine's grip. She let go and the body collapsed like a puppet unstrung.

His eyes still moved angrily. Trilby yanked coils and springs from his neck, detaching a long velvety tongue with a slither as if she were pulling a snake out of a bag. She threw the tongue away.

Christine got down from her rack and uncricked her aching back.

Trilby tossed the head to her, as if it were a child's ball. She saw lechery in those marble eyes, and threw the nasty thing out of the window, hoping it wound up stuck on one of the fence spikes.

Outside, dogs barked.

Christine, conscious of her *déshabillé*, looked around for her ruined dress.

Then the door opened again.

They looked at the guns aimed at them. Christine slowly put her hands up. Trilby did likewise.

'Who have we here?' said the tall old man with the pistols. 'Uninvited guests?'

'Snoopers,' said his smaller partner. 'Drop 'em in the vat.'
The tall man smiled, showing sharp yellow teeth.

VI

IRENE AND THE Persian had doffed their Khasi and Princess
disguises. Now, they wore close-fitting black bodystockings
with tight hoods like those popularised by the English soldiers
at Balaclava. The lower parts of their faces were covered with
black silk scarves; only their eyes showed.

They crept along the deck of the barge, conscious of the
music and chatter below. The clowns were performing some
interminable rhapsody from Bohemia, which made Irene vow
to avoid that region in the future. The full moon and the lights
of the city were not their friend, but they knew how to slip from
shadow to shadow.

On the Pont du Carrousel, a solitary man stood, looking down
at the dark waters and the barge. Irene saw the shape and laid a
hand on the Persian's arm to stop him stepping into moonlight.
They pressed against the side of a lifeboat, still in the shadow.
Irene first assumed the man on the bridge was a stroller who had
paused to have a cigar, though no red glow-worm showed. She
hoped it was not some inconvenient fool intent on suicide – they
did not want attention drawn to their night-work, with lanterns
played across the water's surface or the decks where they were
hiding. The figure did not move, was not apparently looking at
the barge, and might as easily have been a scarecrow.

Irene slipped away from the lifeboat, did a gymnast's roll, and
found herself next to the housing of some sort of marine winch.
Heart beating fast, she looked up at the bridge. The possible spy
was gone. There had been something familiar about him.

The Persian joined her.

The Countess Cagliostro's barge was armoured like a

dreadnought. That was why it sat so low in the water. Aft of the ballroom were powerful engines, worked by humming dynamos. The barge was fully illuminated by electrical Edison lamps, and mysterious galvanic energies coursed through rubber-clad veins, nurturing vast sleeping mechanical beasts whose purposes neither of Erik's operatives could guess.

'She could invade a country with this thing,' said Irene.

'Several,' commented the Persian.

'Do you think it's a submersible?'

The Persian shrugged. 'I should not be surprised if it inflates balloons from those fittings, and lifts into the skies.'

'You've an inventive turn of mind, pardner.'

'That is true. It is part of the tale of how Erik and I became associates, back in my own country… but this is not the time for that history.'

'Too true. Let's try and find the lady's lair.'

Beyond the engines, the deck was a featureless plate but for several inset panes of thick black glass. Irene reckoned this was Erik's trick again – transparent for the sitting spider, opaque for the unwary fly.

From the pouch slung on her hip, she drew a cracksman's tool: a suction cup with an arm, attached to a brutal chunk of diamond. The tool was worth more than most of the swag Irene had used it to lift – the cutting gem had been prised from a tiara and shaped to order by a jeweller who nearly baulked at the sacrilege of turning beauty into deadly practicality.

Irene cut a circle out of the glass, and placed it quietly on the deck.

The space below was dark, a pool of inky nothing. Working silently, the Persian unwound a coil of rope from his torso and made a harness for Irene. After a tug to test the line, Irene stepped into the hole and let herself fall. The Persian, anchored strongly, doled out measured lengths of rope, lowering her by increments.

Once inside, the hole above was bright as the moon, and all around was cavernous dark. Irene blinked, hoping her eyes would adjust – but the gloom was unbroken, the dark undifferentiated.

Then there was a musical roaring, as if a steam calliope were stirring, and a thousand coloured jewels lit up, dazzling her. Incandescent lamps fired and Irene found herself dangling inside what might have been the workings of a giant clock. Gears and wheels, balances and accumulators were all around, in dangerous motion, scything through the air. She had to twist on her rope to avoid being bashed by a counterweight.

Music played – mechanical, but cacophonous, assaulting her ears.

The Persian began to haul her upwards hastily, out of the potential meat-grinder, and she climbed, loops of rope dangling below her. A razor-edged wheel whirred, slicing through loose cord.

Irene was pulled up on deck. By more than two hands.

Light streamed upwards from the hole.

Men in striped jerseys caught her. Their faces were covered by metal half-masks. The Persian, scarf torn away and hood wrenched off, was held by a stranger character, one of the ten-foot toy soldiers from the ballroom, miraculously endowed with life. Its tin moustache bristled fiercely and its big wooden hands gripped like implements of torture. Slung on its back was an oversized musket with a yard-long bayonet. Stuck out of its side was a giant key. The Persian was lifted completely off his feet, crushed against the soldier's shiny blue tunic.

'*Messieurs*,' said Irene, 'you're taking liberties. Get your paws off the goods if you don't intend to buy.'

The half-masked sailors were briefly confused, and relaxed their ungallant grip on her person. Irene darted and her slick leotard slipped through the hands of her would-be captors. Like an eel, she was out of their grasp, heading towards the side of the barge. If she got over, she would have a chance. The Persian could be rescued later, if that were possible.

Something rose from the shadows and took a much faster hold.

Three swift blows to the stomach knocked the wind out of her. She doubled up in pain, and was recaptured. The sailors were less considerate about keeping hold of her now.

The thing that had struck her emerged into the light.

It was a woman – of course – wearing a costume modelled on Elizabeth of England, with a red lacquered moon-face mask and towering headdress. Dozens of pearls studded bodice and face, exciting Irene's larcenous instincts. Getting her breath back, she sighed at such extravagance.

'The Countess Cagliostro, I presume.'

'Your hostess,' said the woman. 'Though I don't remember putting your names on the guest list. What were they again?'

'I'm Sparkle and he's Slink,' said Irene. 'We're desperate *apache* thieves. You've bushwhacked us properly, so do us the courtesy of summoning gendarmes and handing us over to French justice so we can start plotting our escape from *Île du Diable*. We accept this as an inevitable reverse of our chosen profession, sheer crookery. And there's no need to be unpleasant about it.'

The Countess's mask seemed to smile, its eye-slits narrowing.

She glided, on invisible feet, to the side of her toy soldier, and twisted the key as if winding a clock. Then she stood back, and the key turned as – with big, jerky motions – the soldier raised the struggling, bleeding Persian above its head, then dropped him over the side of the barge. After a long scream, there was a splash.

Irene's heart leaped. This was not what had been planned.

The soldier stumped away from the edge of the barge, and the Countess paid attention to Irene.

'Now that's taken care of, let's talk about you.'

Irene deemed it politic to swoon.

VII

'SHE'S WITH US now,' said Trilby.

'Irène,' said Christine.

'Eh... what?' said Irene.

Irene blinked, awake and uncomfortable. Her wrists were tied above her head, and she hung from an iron hook. To her sides dangled Trilby and Christine, similarly trussed, wearing only undergarments.

The air was warm. A fragrance swelled upwards.

'Don't look down, dear,' advised Trilby.

Of course, Irene could not help herself.

Below her feet was a vat shaped like a giant-sized witch's cauldron, heated by a bellows-fuelled furnace. Pink, molten mass bubbled angrily, smelling of paraffin and cinnamon.

'A coat of wax does wonders for the complexion,' said one of the men who stood below.

Irene looked up at her wrists. She could probably saw through her bonds by swinging on the hook, but then she risked a death-plunge into boiling wax.

'Who's your friend?' she asked Trilby.

'Coppélius,' said the Irish girl.

'Spallanzani!' insisted the man who had spoken. 'He's Coppélius!'

Spallanzani was the taller of the pair. With them was the Countess, who had kept her mask but changed into male evening dress spectacularly tailored to fit her figure. She was too hippy and busty for a dancer but had a wasp waist most opera singers would envy.

'Three pretty girls, with unusual talents,' said the Countess. 'Only one agency I know of in Paris lays claim to such employees. You are the Angels of Music? The creatures of… One Whose Name is Seldom Spoken. I have heard of your previous exploits. It will almost be a shame to write *fin* to such a *feuilleton*. Almost.'

Spallanzani and Coppélius laughed, unpleasantly.

'Naturally, ladies, I should delight in attending your final performance,' said the Countess, 'but pressing business elsewhere summons me. I have been absent from my Summer Ball for too long. Matters there are coming to a head. My doll-makers and I are required to oversee the course of true love. A trusted servant will remain behind to supervise your fatal immersion.'

The Countess snapped her long fingers.

A small creature lurched into the circle of light. Christine and Trilby groaned.

'Poor Cochenille,' said the Countess. 'He has been fearfully mistreated this evening.'

The little man's head did not fit on properly, and several of his limbs dragged. He would not have been especially attractive at the best of times, and now he was a complete grotesque. The Countess patted his head, and withdrew, the doll-makers trailing after her.

'They're mannequins,' said Trilby. 'The brides. Poupée Gérard and the others. Automata.'

'Clockwork,' said Christine.

'I guessed as much.'

'That lump isn't real either,' said Trilby, nodding at Cochenille.

'I heard that,' he shrilled. 'Soon you won't be so particular. When the wax hardens, the Countess will give you to me. As toys.'

'Toys shouldn't have toys,' said Christine. 'It's absurd.'

Cochenille manipulated a winch, unrolling chain from a drum, humming to himself.

The girls were lowered, by inches.

Christine and Trilby took deep breaths, and twisted, knees up to their chests, feet tucked against their rumps. Irene, who'd had quite enough perilous dangling for one evening, tried her best to imitate her colleagues' tactics, straining her shoulders and back. She yelped.

Cochenille lowered them further. They could feel heat boiling off churning wax. Spits painfully dotted their bodies, forming solid specks on their garments. It seemed the advantages of hot wax for the complexion were decidedly overrated.

They were hung from hooks fixed to a bedstead-sized frame which was attached at the corners to four chains which gathered up through an iron-loop affair to wind around pulleys fixed to the factory ceiling. The more chain was extended to lower them, the more give there was.

Irene looked up, and saw a dusty skylight and the roofs of Paris. For an instant, she thought she saw the billow of a cloak.

From somewhere, three sharp notes sounded.

Christine and Trilby threw their weight backwards, taking Irene with them, so she could see skylight and cloaked figure no more. The girls extended their legs, feet pointed like trapézistes. Their eyes were open, fixed on nothing in particular. They concentrated on becoming living pendulum weights.

It was a side-effect of the 'music lessons', Irene thought – the way Christine and Trilby sometimes started acting in concert like the Corsican Brothers or (and this chilled her) the mannequin dancers at the Countess's ball. She knew her colleagues were flesh and blood, but Erik had tinkered with their minds. At times like this, she regretted not also having submitted to the special tutoring, though she usually shrunk in cold terror from the idea.

'Stop that swinging, at once,' shrieked Cochenille. 'Naughty, naughty girls.'

Irene again did her best to imitate Christine and Trilby, throwing her weight in synchronisation with their trapeze act. The frame swung in a long arc, up and back, then down and forward, as if tossed on a great wave. It seemed for a moment that the girls' feet and legs might dip agonisingly into hot wax, but their heels barely brushed the furious surface. It was fortunate that Christine and Trilby were divested of their dresses, for skirts would have trailed in the wax and anchored them in the cauldron. Irene's leotard was close enough to a circus aerialist's costume to be suited for this venture.

Cochenille frantically worked the winch, which was stuck.

On the next pass, the frame took the girls past the rim of the cauldron, over dizzyingly empty space. Then they crossed the deadly gulf again, higher still at the height of the swing, and were pulled back.

Irene saw what was intended.

She hoped they wouldn't break their legs, though that would still be better than becoming a prize exhibit at the grand opening of the Musée Grévin, the waxworks which would supposedly rival London's Madame Tussaud's if it were ever finished.

On the next pass, as they looked down, the girls stuck out their legs, bracing themselves for a shock. Their feet slammed against the lip of the vat, which rang like a bell, and their swinging stopped. They bent at the knees and waists, but stretched out as if standing up at a forty-five degree angle, held by their chains but safe, feet planted on the hot metal, weight tipping the cauldron.

Another note sounded from nowhere.

Christine and Trilby were out of their useful trance.

All three girls complained of discomfort – strain on their muscles, searing against the soles of their feet, damage to their stockings.

Cochenille hopped in frustration. If he loosened the chain more, the girls would be able to slip their bonds. He must reverse the winch and raise them higher, dragging them over the lip of the vat.

The gnome took hold of the wheel of the winch.

'Give it a bit of kick,' said Trilby.

Irene strained with her thighs, putting more weight against the cauldron. The others did too.

The vat was on an axle set in housings, so wax could be poured into moulds. By inches, the girls tipped the vat with their feet. Liquid poured out of a spout-like groove in the rim.

The first pink gush splashed against the floor.

A wave broke against Cochenille's ankles, and froze solid on cold flagstones. He was trapped.

'Harpies of the inferno!' he shouted.

A greater cascade fell all around him, and he became encased in it, a doll inside a statue. He tried to move, and pieces of hot wax broke free – but more was poured onto his head, setting in drapes and drips and great chunks. He was more wax than doll now, a failed golem.

'You've done for me,' he shrilled, 'flesh and blood vipers in dolls' shapes! You've…'

Cochenille's voice shut off. The mound of wax shook and tumbled into pieces. The doll was beyond fixing this time.

Irene took her feet off the cauldron and swung upwards, hooking her legs through the frame, taking weight off her wrist bonds, which she freed and twisted apart. She climbed the chains, as feeling came back to her fingers. Monkey-like, Christine managed the same trick, leaving Trilby to take the strain of keeping the vat, now lighter for the loss of most of its contents, in pouring position. Then, in concert, Irene and Christine lifted Trilby free.

The vat clanged back on its axle.

Wax spread on the floor, solidifying.

The girls swung wildly on their frame, comparing bruises to their skin and damage to their costume. They picked deposits of wax out of each other's hair.

'That was horrid,' said Christine.

'I've got aches in places where I didn't think I had places,' said Irene.

'We're not out of the woods yet,' said Trilby. 'We've got to get down from here and finish the job. Some men have to learn that their brides are life-size dolls without minds.'

'Some men might not care,' observed Irene.

VIII

FORTUNATELY, THE MANNEQUIN factory had an extensive store of suitable costumes for their products. The trio found playroom clothes which would pass among the giant dolls and toys at the Summer Ball: Irene as a buckskinned cowgirl of the Wild West, Christine as a bold brigadier of Napoleon's army and Trilby as a parti-coloured harlequin.

In the factory's stable, they found a light carriage, with a pair of horses tethered and ready. Pinned to the seat was a hand-drawn map showing the best route between the factory and the barge's mooring, signed 'O.G.', for Opera Ghost.

'He thinks of everything,' said Christine.

'Always watches over us,' said Trilby.

'He might have been more help when we were about to be dunked in the boiling wax,' said Irene.

Her colleagues looked at her, shocked.

'Irène, Erik works best in the shadows,' said Christine. 'This you know.'

Irene shrugged and climbed up onto the box.

She knew now who had been up on the rooftops. She wondered about those strange, skull-piercing musical notes and their effect on her colleagues.

'Yee-hah, giddyup,' she shouted, taking the reins.

The vehicle charged out onto the street, knocking over a brazier at which a night-watchman had been warming his hands. Hot coals spilled on the cobbles.

The watchman made an impertinent gesture at the departing carriage.

Christine and Trilby argued over the map, feeding Irene instructions at each turn. The horses knew their way already, which Irene didn't find all that comforting.

The Angels of Music tore through the streets of Paris.

IX

AT MIDNIGHT, THREE happy couples were escorted by creaking wooden soldiers from the ballroom of the barge into a smaller, equally well-appointed chamber where the company was far more select. Here, music was provided by intricate automata whose instruments were parts of their bodies. The orchestra had been constructed by skilled Venetian craftsmen a century earlier.

A stiff-backed, golden-faced toy conductor – a marvellous

engine in itself, clad in a gold swallow-tail coat with jewel-studded epaulettes – precisely ticked off the seconds with a baton.

The Count, the Baron and the Duke each escorted a tiny dancer. Barbée, Cyndée and Annette en Lambeaux had entirely captivated their newfound fiancés with artificial charms, augmented by certain drugs administered through tiny scratches from sharp glass fingernails. Nothing was left to chance.

Each couple joined the dance, moving elegantly to the automata's tinkling. The other couples on the floor would have been familiar to Erik's agents, for their documents had been examined. Here was the Grand Marshal Gérard, the Duke of Omnium, the Chevalier del Gardo, Monsieur le Juge Cordier, Mr Thatcher of New York, Cardinal Tosca and all the other 'husbands', partnered with – and, in some cases, propped up by – deceptively fragile, hard-eyed wives. Indeed, a careful observer would have noticed these men were led around the floor by their painted dolls, in an advanced state of befuddlement verging on somnambulism.

At length, the dance concluded, and the couples stood in neat rows as if for inspection, male heads hung, female faces turned up. A trap slid open and a podium raised, upon which stood the masked Joséphine Balsamo, swathed in pure white furs, from arctic wolves and polar bears. She presented a savage, commanding aspect – like the chieftain of a marauding tribe clad in the skins of fallen enemies.

'Tonight, at last, our company is complete,' she announced. 'The men in this room can claim between them to control the world. Every sphere of human activity is represented – politics, finance, arms, faith, letters, industry, science. Beside you are your perfect wives, so demure, so devoted. You are theirs, entirely. Through them, you are mine entirely. You serve the Cause of Cagliostro. I have played a long game. You all had to be in place. Nothing in this world cannot be decided among the men in this room. Wars can be arranged. Fortunes shifted. Governments changed. On my whim, I could choose what people will say, think, eat, hum in the bath. This has been my goal for more years than I care to remember. My sole regret is that, at this moment, I am essentially talking to myself, for you, the wives, are but my instruments, unliving tools who express only my will. And you, the husbands, are sleeping, dreaming what I have deemed you will dream, dancing at the end of strings I control. Shall I feel lonely? Is this game *solitaire*? Earlier tonight, it was revealed to me that forces – pathetic, perhaps, set beside this company but not to be despised – were set against me, against *us*. Agents have been dealt with. But there may be others. Believe me, I am glad of this. For we must test our strength. We must seek out the other players of this Great Game and destroy them utterly.'

China palms clapped together in approval.

Beneath her moon-mask, the Countess smiled on her creatures.

X

FROM THE PONT du Carrousel, Christine, Trilby and Irene watched as carriages ferried away the Countess's lesser guests. Thus was the chorus dispensed with, ejected from the ball – only members of the exclusive Marriage Club remained on the barge with the Countess and her minions.

'Is that an unwound turban floating by the bilges?' asked Trilby.

Irene had not had time to explain fully the fate of the Persian.

Christine gasped and clutched her throat, apprehending at once that something dreadful had transpired.

Irene drew six-shooters from her leather hip-holsters, and thumb-cocked the hammers.

'Come on, Angels,' she drawled, 'a gal's gotta do what a gal's gotta do!'

XI

THE TRIO ADVANCED through the barge's ballroom, stepping tactfully over drunks and suicides, avoiding staff clearing away the debris, posing briefly among giant toys when it seemed they might be noticed. They came to a locked door. Irene put away her guns and picked the lock. The party was continuing, inside, in more select fashion. Christine, Trilby and Irene crept in, and sat at the back without attracting attention.

The Marriage Club was in session.

All around, on the polished wood floor, sat tiny artificial brides, cradling husbands like babies, whispering musically into their ears, caressing them intimately, giving tender orders.

The automated orchestra played a lullaby. The toy conductor swivelled on his podium, seeming to stare at the interlopers – then turned back to his musical machines.

The Countess sat on a throne, weighed down by white furs.

Irene drew a bead on the Countess's forehead and fired.

A bullet spanged against the red mask, cracking the face of the moon – but the Countess did not flinch. None of the husbands reacted to the shot, but all the wives looked up at once, glass eyes fixed malevolently on the newcomers.

Irene sighted with her other Colt, aiming for the spot where the Countess ought to have a heart. Knowing it wouldn't be any use, she fired again. A black smoking patch appeared on the Countess's furs.

'It's just another doll,' said Trilby.

They looked around the room, wary. So many automata, so many painted eyes.

Christine had drawn a sword, which she held up like an expert ready for attack.

In concert, the wives got to their feet, letting husbands fall or roll where they might. One or two of the men groaned, scratched their heads and tried to stand – then sprawled again.

There were at least thirty mannequins, clockwork-and-porcelain-and-wax sisters, costumed in high fashion finery. As they moved, clicks and whirrs suggested their interior workings.

'I'll wager they do more than dance,' said Christine.

'I'd not take that sucker bet,' said Irene.

The Countess's throne revolved. The puppet Countess's broken head fell unnaturally. On the turntable dais were two identical thrones, back to back. The Countess had been hiding behind a mannequin in her own image. She wore a fresh mask, a rainbow-winged butterfly of silk over steel, and a suit of scarlet, lightweight armour decorated with Chinese dragon motifs. Quantities of loose dark hair fell over her shoulders and down her back.

Irene fired at once, but the Countess – with supernatural swiftness – bent one way and then the other, avoiding the bullets which smashed into her throne or the wall behind her. She struck elegant poses as Irene missed with several more shots.

In the end, in frustration, she pitched the guns at the Countess as if shying horseshoes. With mailed gauntlets, the Countess knocked them out of the air, and they skittered uselessly across the floor.

The pack of brides took a march-step towards the three girls.

'You escaped the wax,' said the Countess. 'Well done. I could use ladies like you in my service.'

Irene knew that was not going to work. And so did the Countess. She shrugged, rattling the shoulder-pieces of her armour.

'What do you think you look like, dearie?' asked Trilby.

'Red Jeanne, evil twin of the Maid of Orléans?' suggested Christine.

The Countess seemed to consider the idea.

'She dyes her hair,' said Irene. 'You can always tell.'

The Countess made angry, spike-knuckled fists.

'What say we do this fair and square?' said Trilby. 'Just you and us. One to three. Not bad odds for a supposed immortal.'

'That's just how it will be,' said the Countess. 'I don't count these puppets as people.'

Christine, Trilby and Irene were backed against the wall. Only Christine had a usable weapon. She extended her sword-point.

One of the wives stepped out of formation and walked up to Christine. The sword dimpled against her chest, then slid through her torso. She stepped calmly up to Christine's face, blade emerging from her back, sword-hilt against her copper-wire ribs. She angled her head from side to side, looking into Christine's face – then reversed her walk, like a music box wound backwards, wrenching the sword from Christine's grip.

The orchestra still played, but the tinkling tune was running out, as if the music box were winding down. The conductor's baton slowed.

The Countess made a gesture, and there was a whooshing sound.

The wives' fingernails extended by an inch, razor-edges glinting.

'This is probably where we get cut to ribbons,' Irene told her colleagues.

Trilby and Christine held hands. Irene took a fighting stance. In the Bowery, while casing a joint for a crack she soon thought better of, she'd taken an afternoon of boxing lessons from Owney Geoghegan, the bare-knuckle champion. He had shown her some very useful tricks for facing stronger opponents with a longer reach than hers. Before she went under, she'd break a few toys.

The music stopped. The baton was still.

'Goodbye, Angels,' said the Countess.

Then the automaton conductor twisted, suddenly loose-limbed, on his podium, baton falling from gloved fingers. A curtain tore away from the complex works underneath the clockwork musicians and the original conductor could be seen – faceless, broken and stowed away under the bandstand. Several barrels were wired into the workings of the grand Venetian device, marked 'gunpowder'.

The girls just had time to realise who had taken the place of the mechanical music master.

The golden face-plate was lifted from a horror of a mouth.

The girls' hearts leaped. The Countess whirled, enraged but still confident of victory. The mannequins attacked.

Clawnails passed Irene's face, and she took hold of cold, unliving wrists. An implacable mask of beauty loomed close to her, chin dropped to show rows of sharp ceramic teeth. These dolls were designed for murder as much as marriage.

Erik – for it was he! – raised a tube to his mouth. It was about the size of a piccolo, but with fewer holes. He sounded three distinct notes, shrill and dissonant, unknown to music or nature. Irene had heard them once before this evening, and again her teeth were set on edge.

Christine and Trilby reacted at once to the signal. Their eyes became fixed, almost as glassy as the mannequins'. Ignoring aches and bruises, they cartwheeled into the fray, arms and legs scything through the cadre of wives, fetching off dolls' heads and limbs, spilling clockwork innards and horse-hair stuffing.

Irene, whose head hurt from the shrilling, concentrated on wrestling the contraption which was trying to shred her. She battered its wax-and-china face with her forehead, and tried to break its wrists.

Erik had his temporary mask back in place. He threw a lever, and the clockwork orchestra began to play Tartini's 'Devil's Trill' – but with strange lapses and lacunae, filled by the crackling of electrical arcs.

The Countess looked at Erik, mask to mask.

From the podium, Erik picked up a box, which trailed wires deep into the orchestra's innards and the barrels of explosive. Surmounting the box was a metal switch in the form of a grasshopper.

Christine danced, whirling swords taken from a toy soldier's wooden fist and a sleeping senior officer's scabbard, cutting through mannequins. She fought like an eight-armed Hindu goddess with a scimitar in each hand. She heard music, and the music directed her actions. Lady Galatea, Duchess of Omnium, hurled herself at Christine, foot-long porcupine spines sticking

50

out of her chest and back, arms wide for a deadly, skewering hug. Christine stepped under the embrace and used her swords like scissors, snipping the Duchess in half at the waist.

Trilby fought less elegantly, with feet and fists, delivering *savate* kicks and powerful fist-blows. She wrenched the arms off Madame Venus de l'Isle del Gardo, and whirled them about, raking their claws across the toys. Madame del Gardo hopped comically from side to side, off balance, trailing wires from her shoulders, twitching and sparking, lubricational fluids spurting from ruptured rubber tubes like yellow blood. The armless doll, momentarily the image of a more famous Venus, collided with a toy soldier, and its head flew apart in a puff of flame, burning wig shooting across the room, metal and china shrapnel ripping through the soldier. With Venus's arms, Trilby battered away several more of the wives.

It was a dazzling performance. Within moments, the floor was strewn with spasming, broken things. Springs and cogs scattered underfoot. Pools of yellow liquid formed, and electrical sparks set light to them. Flames ran quickly, spreading from doll to doll, melting wax prettiness away from metal skulls, crumpling lacework and human hair wiggery in instants, taking hold on torn and oily dresses. Some of the husbands sat up, awake, patting at scorching patches on their evening clothes, yelping in pain at the rude disturbance to their dreams.

Irene still wrestled with her single opponent, Madame Gérard, née Francis-Pierre.

Trilby stepped up, and wrenched off Poupée's head. Her body went limp.

Irene looked at Trilby, holding the head up like Perseus with Medusa. Its eyes still rolled and it tried several sweet smiles before its internal mechanisms wound down and the lids fell shut.

The last of the wives had fallen back to the throne, to protect the Countess, who was trying to make herself heard above the racket. The orchestra broke down, and the Tartini shut off. The wives were assembling themselves into a many-legged war machine, directed by the Countess.

The trio stood before the throne. Trilby and Christine opened their mouths and ululated, a high, clear, pure, penetrating sound that rose. Irene clapped her hands over her ears, but couldn't completely shut out the sound.

The Countess halted her work on the machine, a trickle of blood leaking from one of her eyeholes.

The voices soared, a wordless sound, two tones entwined. Edison bulbs burst. Champagne flutes flew to splinters. The faceplates of the last brides shattered, showing the intricate works beneath. Even their glass eyes burst.

Irene jammed her fingers into her ears, trying to shut out the pain.

Trilby and Christine, unaffected, seeming to be able to do this without breath, took the sound up to a peak. Somewhere on the barge, something major broke.

Another shrill note came, from Erik's flute, cutting through his protégées' voices, shutting them off.

And Christine and Trilby were fully awake, bleeding and puzzled.

'What happened?' Trilby asked Irene.

'You went away for a while,' she said. 'Everything's fine now.'

Trilby realised she was holding a broken head, had a moment of disgust, and dropped the thing.

'*Zut alors*,' said Christine. 'What a shambles!'

The Countess was gone, her throne descended into a trapdoor, a smear of thick blood marking her trail. Erik was vanished too. During the *mêlée*, he had fixed his detonator box to a clockwork percussionist, wiring its hand to the grasshopper switch and setting an hourglass timer which was already close to running out.

'We'd best tell everyone to abandon ship,' ordered Irene.

Most of the company were in the main ballroom when Erik's explosives went off. There was a great grinding sound as the greater works of the barge misaligned and tore themselves to pieces, wrecking whatever purpose they might have had. More explosions followed.

Christine, Trilby and Irene were in a corridor, which ought to lead up to the deck and safety. They found the doorway barred and bolted. The Countess evidently took the ruin of her schemes personally. The incandescent lamps wavered, and they were ankle-deep in cold water. Then the floor listed, and the water flowed away. The girls found things to hang onto.

'I think our music master might have planned this phase of the evening rather better,' observed Irene. 'We're quite likely to drown.'

'Have more faith, Irène,' said Christine, cheerfully. 'Something will turn up.'

They were looking at a foaming torrent advancing up the corridor. Something broke the surface angrily – one of the toy soldiers, or at least the top half of one. It thumped against a wall, turned over, and sank.

'How sad,' said Christine. 'I love a man in uniform.'

One of the porthole windows broke inwards, and a rope ladder descended.

A familiar face loomed through the aperture, a beckoning arm extended.

It was the Persian! Alive!

'Ladies, time to leave this playroom.'

He did not have to say it twice.

XII

ONLY TWO OR three of the Marriage Club were drowned, and they weren't among those who'd be most missed. The hero of the hour, feted as such in the popular press, was the aged Étienne Gérard. Shocked to his senses by cold water, the one-time Brigadier laboured fearlessly at great risk to his own life to aid his fellow guests in their escapes from the fast-sinking barge. Some wondered why such a noted gallant managed only to rescue wealthy, famous, *male* members of the party from the depths, leaving scores of poor, obscure, young wives to the Seine. No corpses were ever recovered, though broken mannequin parts washed up on the mudbanks for months. It was another of the mysteries of Paris, and soon everyone had other scandals, sensations and strangenesses to cluck over.

The Persian reported that he had been fished out of the river by his old friend, Erik – who effected emergency medical assistance, before taking the unusual step of venturing himself onto the field of battle.

Back at the Opéra, quantities of brandy were consumed, and repairs were made to the persons of the lovely ladies who had done so much for a world which would never know services had been rendered. As dawn broke, baskets of fruit and pastries were delivered, with a note of thanks from Madame Sabatier, who also enclosed a satisfactory banker's draft.

After hauling cardinals and bankers out of the cold water, the newly-widowed Grand Marshal Gérard – if one could be widowed after marriage not to a human woman but a long-case clock with a prettily painted face – repaired to the Salon Sabatier, paid in advance for the exclusive company of three of *la Présidente*'s most alluring *filles de joie*, and promptly fell into a deep sleep that might last for days. That certainly counted as a happy outcome.

The only pall cast over celebrations came when Irene announced that she felt it was time she quit the Opera Ghost Agency to venture out on her own. Christine and Trilby wept to hear the news, and bestowed many embraces on their friend, not noticing that she was unable to control a shudder when they touched her. Irene could not look at their active, lovely, characterful faces without recalling the expressionless, bloodied masks of skin that took their place when three shrill notes sounded. Not to mention the proficiencies in arts devastating and deadly they exhibited under the influence. Either of them could have had Owney Geoghegan's title away from him with one arm tucked into the back of their skirt.

The Persian understood and conveyed Monsieur Erik's good wishes.

'He suggests, however, that you limit your field of operations.'

'I should stay out of Paris?'

'He thinks… France.'

'Very well. There's Ruritania, and Poland, and London. All a-swim with opportunities.'

Irene left the building.

Behind his mirror, Erik knew regret. But he understood the American was not like his other girls. There was steel in her core, which made her unsuitable for 'music lessons', the specialised training he deemed necessary for his most useful Agents. That steel would never be bent entirely to his purpose, and might eventually bring them into conflict… as he had been brought into conflict with Joséphine Balsamo.

The Countess Cagliostro was, of course, still at large, and liable to be unforgiving now her carefully contrived plan of world domination was sunk at the bottom of the Seine. She would probably be suffering from a splitting headache, too, and be unhappy at the loss of her marvellous barge and so many toys. This was no time for the Agency to be under-strength.

The *feuilleton* was not over.

XIII

FOR DAYS, CHRISTINE and Trilby moped and were inconsolable. Every little thing was a reminder of something sweet or amusing Irene had said or done, and would set them off in further floods of tears. Other ladies of the chorus assumed their hearts had been ordinarily broken, and dispensed wisdoms about the untrustworthiness of the perfidious male sex.

Then, the bell sounded. Not for 'music lessons', not for an exploit, but a simple summons.

As they walked down the corridor to Dressing Room 313, they came upon a familiar, shambling, bent-over figure. Christine, acting on instinct, took him by the throat and shoved him rudely against the wall.

'No more, please,' said Cochenille, squirming.

Temporary repairs had been made to the mannequin, but he was still not in peak condition. As Christine pinned him, Trilby rolled up her sleeves, intent on smashing his face to bits again.

'Ladies, let him be,' said the Persian, looking out of the dressing room. He had been in a conference with Spallanzani and Coppélius. 'These gentlemen have made a break from their former employer.'

Christine dropped the gasping Cochenille. His hand came off, and he picked it up and stuck it into his pocket. Trilby gave him a kick and he scurried away, followed by the doll-makers, who gave the girls a wide berth as they passed out of sight. Trilby gave their backs the Evil Eye Stare.

'We have come to an arrangement,' said the Persian. 'Advantageous for our Agency.'

Trilby and Christine entered the dressing room.

On the divan sat a small blonde girl, dressed all in white, posed like a ballerina in a tableau.

'She's not a doll,' said Christine. 'She can't be.'

The girl's head moved and she blinked. There was no clicking or whirring.

'She must be the original, from which the mannequin-makers copied,' said Trilby.

The girl's chest swelled and contracted with breath. She gestured, showing the suppleness of her fingers. She picked up an apple from *la Présidente*'s basket, flicked out her nails and rolled the fruit in her hand, letting the peel slither away from the flesh in an unbroken ribbon, then crushed it to juice with a sudden, powerful squeeze.

Christine and Trilby walked around the divan, observing the newcomer from all angles, wondering at the ingenuity of her manufacture.

'This is Olympia,' said Erik, from behind the mirror. 'She will be joining us for "music lessons", and taking the departed Miss Adler's place in our roster of agents.'

Olympia curtseyed.

'It is a pleasure to meet you,' she said. 'I hope we shall be the best of friends.'

ACT TWO: LES VAMPIRES DE PARIS

'Just a moment, ladies and gentlemen. Just a word before you go. We hope the memories of Dracula and Renfield won't give you bad dreams, so just a word of reassurance. When you get home tonight and the lights have been turned out and you are afraid to look behind the curtains and you dread to see a face appear at the window… why, just pull yourself together and remember that after all *there are such things*.'

John Balderston, *Dracula* (1927)

I

IN THE EIGHTIES, the tune changed. The mad whirl of Paris became madder still. Those who saw their way to fast fortunes took every opportunity to puff up portfolios of dubious stock. At the end of each trading day, the speculators of the *bourse de commerce* waded through knee-deep drifts of tickertape, stepping over the bodies of those whose brains or hearts had burst. Fending off weariness with sniffs of cocaine, these young men – the sons of shocked, seething, respectable fathers – would repair to cafés, cabarets and casinos and conduct a nocturnal *ronde* of seductions, ruinations and foolish wagers. Monies gained by day on the market were thrown away by night on the card table or at the wheel. More than one chancer lost his clients' funds before dipping into his own reserves.

A generation of artistes maudits – poets, painters, novelists, composers, actors, musicians, singers – were culled by absinthe and venereal disease, which ran through the city like a flood from the sewers. Many were driven mad by their muses even before their minds and bodies rotted from the green fairy or the pox. Fashions were set in suicide. Certain bridges became so popular with self-murderers that they were roped off from before sunset till after dawn. Fine sets of duelling pistols were broken up as the down-at-heel-and-drooling patronised pawnshops to spend their final francs on 'just the one' gun and 'just the one' ball.

Beyond electrically illuminated districts where money and madness burned bright were freezing, nighted slums. The poor and wretched were made poorer and more wretched by savage government measures. Influenced by mine-owners, industrialists and colossi of capital, the Opportunist Republicans eagerly pledged the full forces of the state to stamping out a strain of rebellion which sprung up in the blighted north and threatened to take hold throughout the country.

The Army of the Republic was ordered to Montsou to put down a miners' strike with a ferociousness in excess of measures taken against rebel tribes in North Africa. There were French men and women who grew to hate and fear the tricolour flown by troops who marched towards them with bayonets fixed. Émile Zola looked to the miners, utterly defeated, and wrote, 'Men were springing forth, a black avenging army, germinating slowly in the furrows, growing towards the harvests of the next century, and their germination would soon overturn the earth.'

Withal, it was a gay time – the *Belle Époque*.

In opera, audiences of the eighties applauded Gounod, Saint-Saëns, Delibes and Massenet. Cults sprung up around Berlioz and Bizet, dead too soon to enjoy the success in revival of works scorned on their premieres. The reign of Verdi, longer even than that of Victoria of Britain, continued, but the spectre of Wagner stalked Europe – ominous, rumbling chords beneath soaring arpeggios. Claques feuded and divas drove managements to distraction, but houses were packed.

The Opera Ghost Agency remained in business... though, as might have been expected, there was a turnover. In time, the first Angels moved on and were replaced by others, all talented and intrepid, each unique and extraordinary. The departure of Christine, his first protégée, left the Phantom bereft behind mask and mirror. He steeled his heart when selecting those who followed her. His first trio were singers, but the next line-up included a dancer. Then, Erik considered the dramatic arts

– a veil will be drawn over the sorry debut and finale of Sybil Vane – before looking to other disciplines. Some specialists were engaged briefly, for a specific performance; others proved versatile enough to be held over for lengthy runs.

At the time of *l'affaire du vampire*, the Angels of Music were La Marmoset, Sophy and Unorna. On a variety bill, they could pass for an actress, a knife-thrower and a conjurer.

La Marmoset was the finest detective of either sex in Paris, which – whatever claims a patriotic English press might make concerning a certain resident of Baker Street – was to say the world. Once an independent investigator, often consulted by the Sûreté and the Deuxième Bureau, her agency was dissolved on the occasion of her marriage to one Mr Calhoun, a wealthy American whose current whereabouts were not known. Their union, evidently, had not been happy. The O.G.A. counted itself fortunate to have a Queen of Detectives on its lists. Other employers would scarcely have been as understanding of her habit of going disguised at all times. Fewer men had seen her true face than Erik's. She owned up to many names and identities, though it seemed likely she was really Camille Bienville... or perhaps Tampa Morel... or any one of a dozen other young women with convincing documents, childhood memories, elderly relatives who would verify their identities on stacks of Bibles, and press cuttings supportive of whatever pasts they claimed.

Sophy Kratides was first to point out that La Marmoset's London rival might be all well and good should you need one variety of cigar ash distinguished from another but was of singularly little practical use in more pressing matters. Coming to London as a naïve Greek lass, she had been seduced by a scoundrel, Harold Latimer, who imprisoned her in the household of a loathsome, tittering fellow named Wilson Kemp. The rogues starved and tortured Sophy's brother, to make him sign over family money due to her. The Great Detective Sherlock Holmes amused himself by picking at threads dropped by a Greek interpreter and arrived at the scene of the abduction too late to prevent the murder of Paul Kratides. Furthermore, Mr Holmes, his reputedly cleverer brother and the dogged bobbies of Scotland Yard didn't trouble to prevent the culprits leaving the country, spiriting Sophy along with them.

The impotence of such vaunted upholders of the law inspired her to a harsh assessment of herself. She detested being bundled up like a parcel and written off as a fainting damsel in distress. So, she made her first venture into extrajudicial execution, arranging the scene so the official verdict was that Latimer and Kemp had quarrelled and stabbed each other to death. Discovering unexpected talent and an inner reserve of Greek fire, she turned professional and rose to the first rank of a lucrative trade newly open to women in this changing century – assassination.

Unorna, the so-called Witch of Prague, bore the stigmata of *heterochromia iridis*. Her eyes were different colours – one a clear cold grey, the other a deep, warm brown so dark as to seem almost black. Born on the 29th of February in a bissextile year, she had only just passed her sixth birthday but was a grown woman. The girl with the strange eyes had made a profound study of the occult. Her home city was the site of the magical feats of Rabbi Loew, Johannes Kepler, Scapinelli and Dee. In Prague, the golem was vivified, the Voynich Manuscript decoded and the Philosopher's Stone hidden. Raised in the alchemical tradition, Unorna was apprenticed to the dwarf sorcerer Keyork Arabian. Latterly, she roamed the world, adding to her store of arcane knowledge. She learned the power to cloud men's minds in the mountain lamaseries of Tibet and collected strange orchids from the mangrove swamps of the Andaman Islands. She read the Scroll of Thoth in the secret vaults beneath the great pyramid and tracked the *wendigo* through the forested territories of the Canadian North-West. An adept of the art of mesmerism, she commanded the attention of Erik – whose mastery of the field was formerly unrivalled – by outstaring him. She offered her services to the O.G.A. in exchange for tutelage in certain practices of Australian aborigines. The Phantom, she believed, had mastered the disciplines known as the Voice, the power to persuade, and the Shout, the power to destroy.

It is often said that men like Erik never change, never learn – for, as geniuses and prodigies, why should they? But Irene Adler's declaration of independence, Trilby O'Ferrall's fading talents and Christine Daaé's ultimate defection persuaded him to moderate his puppet-mastering. Wind-up dolls had their uses, but clockwork women could only achieve so much. Olympia was not one of his favourite agents, though she was effective in some cases. Impossible to seduce or strangle, the dancing mannequin was fetched out of her cabinet on occasion to tempt and trap gentlemen who were inclined to emulate Bluebeard and stock their cellars with murdered wives. For all that, she was pretty but dull. Erik understood what Trilby's previous tutor meant when – with her declarations of devotion hollow in his ears – he declared, 'Ah, but it is only Svengali talking to himself again.'

With the Witch of Prague, our Phantom could not work his spell… so, with La Marmoset and Sophy, he would not. Opera itself was changing. Traditionally, producers conducted themselves like the late Emperor, peering down at an army from a hilltop, imposing their iron will upon underlings who would pay the butcher's bill on the battlefield. Many an impresario kept a portrait or a bust of Napoléon in his study, and would in private moments turn his hat sideways and put his hand inside his buttoned jacket to see how it felt. Now, a new breed of director whispered suggestions rather than barked orders, coaxed with sugar lumps rather than broke with the whip. Work was done in collaboration rather than by decree. Erik's first Angels of Music were biddable chorus girls; now, he dealt with potential or actual prima donnas.

The Persian, perhaps, was subtly influential in this change. With the Phantom behind the mirror, he was charged with day-to-day business, issuing emoluments and expenses, meeting with clients, even approving or vetoing cases taken on by the Opera Ghost Agency. He had Erik's trust.

Most mornings, the Persian would be in the Café de la Paix from eleven o'clock till noon, drinking bitter coffee, eating almond biscuits, and reading the papers. Those who wished to engage the Agency were invited to approach him.

On a day in late September, the Persian sat at his usual table, sipped his usual coffee, nibbled his usual biscuit and unfolded his usual *Figaro* to find an unusual envelope slipped into the newspaper. Impressed in the black wax seal was the outline of a bat.

The mark of *Les Vampires*.

Inside was a card which bluntly stated:

'The Grand Vampire wishes to meet with the Director of the Opera Ghost Agency, on a confidential matter.'

The Persian tapped the stiff card against his teeth.

A rare occasion, he concluded.

For this, Erik must come up from his cellar.

II

DISGUISED AS A provincial schoolmistress on her first trip to Paris, La Marmoset strolled through the *Quartier Latin*. In character, she tutted at the prices displayed in shop windows and steered well away from the idlers, loungers and probable footpads loitering on every corner. She envisioned the scrubbed, attentive faces of her class back in Tôtes and thought of the lessons she would give upon her return. She was determined to see the worst Paris had to offer, so she could caution her charges against moral peril.

Young men all around were leering at her, she had no doubt. Even with the autumn chill, many wore blouses unbuttoned to the waist and impractically tight britches. They lolled and swore and scratched and smoked and ogled. She felt a rising prickle in her chest, but suppressed the fervour of disgust. For the sake of the children, she would know something of sin. And she would know it before 14.39 on Friday, when her train home left Gare Saint-Lazare. She had an authentic return ticket in her purse – though the schoolmistress would have ceased to exist by the time the train pulled out.

In Place Saint-Michel, she approached a sleek, slick fellow idling by the statue of the Archangel trampling the Devil. As likely a prospect for sin as any, and cleaner than most. She asked for directions to the *Musée des Thermes*. He offered to escort her there. As they strolled, they talked... and the schoolmistress fell away from the Queen of Detectives like leaves from a tree.

La Marmoset kept up with the criminal underworld, of course. She recognised her new beau as Vénénos, Vice-President in Charge of Poison in the Cabinet of *Les Vampires*. A rising man. His superiors were well advised to watch what they ate or drank in his company, though his signature was the use of less obvious means of getting poison into a person. He gave those condemned by *Les Vampires* cause to fear tobacco, soap, tooth-powder, toilet paper, moustache wax, postage stamps and adhesive bandages. Sometimes, even word that Vénénos was out to get a named individual was enough to drive a prospective victim to suicide on the principle of getting the agony over with quickly.

This negotiation was delicate.

The Phantom of the Opera and the Grand Vampire were shadowmen, seldom in the company of even their closest intimates. They preferred to issue dictates through speaking tubes from behind magic mirrors.

After discussing and rejecting several venues, La Marmoset and Vénénos settled on Suite 13 at the Hôtel du Libre Échange as suitable for the parley. The establishment normally catered to bourgeois husbands and wives conducting respectable assignations with acknowledged mistresses and lovers.

The meeting of Opera Ghost and Grand Vampire was set, naturally, for midnight.

Business concluded, La Marmoset pulled on the schoolteacher again and slapped Vénénos as if he had made an abominable suggestion. She stalked off, blushing violently. His surprised face was a memory of missed opportunity she would take to her spinster's death bed.

At the Hôtel du Libre Échange, special arrangements would be needed. Monsieur Morillon, the manager, would have to be terrified into removing heart-shaped pillows and explicit Japanese prints, then paid off to hang thick black drapes over the frilled pink pretties festooning the suite.

La Marmoset would have paid a hundred francs to see Erik and the Vampire cosy in a love nest with champagne and oysters, but stifled the thought.

One giggled at masked men at one's peril.

Was she not a woman in a succession of masks? In her experience, all women were given – or *driven* – to masks. As a mere Princess of Detectives, she had learned to wear masks which did not seem to be masks. With a twist of a scarf or a touch of paint, she could be someone new, someone else entirely. A fat schoolgirl, a starving widow and a brazen harlot within the same hour, on the same street. Often, she wore men's clothes to enter places barred to her original sex.

She made a finer man than many born to it, she had been told. Who was she really? She didn't know any more.

That schoolmistress, burned along with her unused railway ticket, was as much a person as the woman who put her on and took her off like a bonnet.

No mask could be worse than the naked face of Mr Calhoun when a rage was on him.

Just once in her adult life had she dropped all her disguises and let a man see her true face. She had given up her independence, her profession, her reputation and her thousand names and faces to become one person... Mrs Calhoun. The man for whom she had made such sacrifice served her so brutally she needed to fetch her abandoned make-up kit to cover the bruises.

Like Erik, she finally had no face. Only masks – masks of paper, masks of paint, masks of skin.

She remembered Mr Calhoun's final face – staring furious eyes and open screaming mouth as the waters closed over him, the anchor tied to his ankles pulling him down into the dark.

Standing by the Seine, she at last became the Woman Who Was No One.

Mrs Calhoun drowned with her husband. La Marmoset's agency was wound up, her ties with the Sûreté and the Deuxième Bureau sundered. The earnings of her successful career were in her husband's name, and she had contrived it so he was officially missing, not dead. Lawyers in America controlled his estate and would have no sympathy for her... Tampa Morel, the name signed to the marriage register, wasn't an identity which would hold up in court, so legal access to her own fortune or her husband's was impossible.

She thought of joining Mr Calhoun eternally, swimming down to cling to his corpse.

If The Woman Who Was No One dies, who would care?

She thought of *L'Inconnue de la Seine*... a case known to all detectives.

Some twenty-five years earlier, a young woman – believed to be not French – was fished out of the river, stuck like a specimen bug on a spar of driftwood. A presumed suicide by drowning. Her cold face smiled like the Mona Lisa, and her wax death mask became the template for replicas sold all over the city. That unnamed face was everywhere, even after all this time: in posters, bas-reliefs, prints sold to tourists and popular masks.

L'Inconnue de la Seine, by virtue of an obscure and pathetic death, became a heroine of France. Even with all the publicity, no one came forward to identify her. La Marmoset thought that highly suspicious. Were *l'Inconnue* her case, she would not have so readily written it up as a suicide.

Having rid herself of Mr Calhoun, she was on the point of becoming the unknown's sister – famous for being no one, for being dead, for losing all which could be lost.

Then, alone, she heard music from beneath the city – an

impassioned solo organ recital, distorted eerily by echoes, broadcast by sewer outlets. Later, she would learn that the piece was 'Don Juan Triumphant', from Erik's perpetually reworked, never-finished opera.

She knew of the Opera Ghost Agency and realised now that there was a place for her on its lists. The next day, she approached the Persian at the Café de la Paix. She wore one of her favourite disguises, though it was in truth a disguise no longer – a black veil and widow's weeds. In introducing herself, she hesitated only when it came to giving her name.

'I am… La Marmoset,' she said. 'Yes, that will do.'

The Persian didn't press her. He had also misplaced any real name he might once have had.

She was first called La Marmoset by men – gendarmes, detectives, criminals, magistrates – who resented her involvement in what they took to be their business. To them, she was an interfering monkey. Nothing but a nuisance in skirts – clingy, chattering, agile and facetious. Each and every one of those men had come to speak the name with respect and even fear.

'You were expected, Madame,' said the Persian. 'It is Erik's pleasure to accept you as an Angel of Music.'

At that time, the Opera Ghost Agency was assembling a new trio.

In Dressing Room 313, La Marmoset was introduced to Sophy Kratides, whom she had once glimpsed from afar…

That had been a memorable morning. Frederick Hohner, condemned wife-murderer, was to be executed in rue de la Roquette, just outside La Grande Roquette Prison. As he climbed the steps to the guillotine, he was felled by a rifle-shot from across the prison yard. With his first conviction secure, the state had not troubled to prosecute Hohner on other charges… leaving seven women, at least, unavenged. La Marmoset reckoned the family of one of his other victims must have decided on a point of honour that he should pay for them too.

On the same principle, La Marmoset – present in the habit

of a nun – made a show of drawing a pistol and firing in the direction of the perch from which the fatal shot had come. The response was a bullet in the dirt at her feet.

It was like one of those duels where the parties have thought better of some silly quarrel and choose to discharge in the air then share breakfast. Both women could have made their shots tell.

Neither Queen of Detectives nor Mistress of Assassins felt a need to take the matter further. The inquest was less a formality than usual. The executioner complained of blown-out brains spattered all over his nice shiny blade. The Sûreté wittered about tracking the killer's client but didn't put in any work on the case.

Justice had been served.

The Persian left the two new Angels alone together, though both assumed Erik was listening.

Sophy did not look like an assassin, which was among the reasons why she was a very good one. She had thick, dark hair and a way of arranging herself side-on to present a slender target. She could turn up an inner light that made her a centre of attraction in any room, and fade it down to become all but invisible. An enviable knack – to let people see but not notice you. La Marmoset usually had to employ the more tiresome, limited method of wearing a dress and hat which matched the wallpaper.

La Marmoset raised her veil to show her unadorned face. Sophy looked at her, from several angles, and nodded.

'Nice,' she said, 'but it isn't you.'

La Marmoset knew what the other woman meant and wasn't offended.

The matter of Mr Calhoun was raised.

'Your husband, you…?' The Greek woman made a twisting gesture with her hands and a *kkkrrkkk* sound at the back of her throat.

Knowing she needed Sophy's trust, La Marmoset gave a single nod.

'Good,' said Sophy. 'Me also. He was no husband, my Harry Latimer, but… you know how such things happen.'

La Marmoset did.

'Your Mr Calhoun – justice was served?'

La Marmoset thought about it.

What had separated her from a policeman or an examining magistrate was that justice and law were beside the point. As a detective, she was interested in truth alone. What was done with truth was up to others. It had not been her decision to prosecute Frederick Hohner only for the crime which could easily be proven against him.

With Mr Calhoun, that was changing. She had tried and convicted and carried out the sentence herself.

'A court might not think it, but… yes. Justice was served.'

'Good. With Kemp and Latimer, also. We are friends now.'

The women embraced.

Both had crossed lines, from victim to avenger, from detective to (she admitted) murderess. Sophy had become more herself – indeed, *only* herself – after being taken for granted by men who presumed on her. They hadn't noticed Sophy in the corner as they argued about arrangements concerning her without consulting her. Even Paul Kratides didn't think to ask his sister whether their money was more important to her than his life. How surprised had Latimer and Kemp been to wake up with knives twisting in their bellies? Did they even realise who was ending their wicked lives?

With less clear-cut right on her side in the matter of Mr Calhoun, La Marmoset had become no one… though she saw her friend, in tiny moments of inaction, envied her fluid identity, her ability to take off one mask and put on another. For Sophy, there was too little joy in justice. The Opera Ghost Agency, which at least required her to do things other than kill people, was drawing her out of the numbed shock she still felt at her brother's murder.

La Marmoset and Sophy had worked together on complicated matters and, at the conclusion of every case, agreed.

Justice was still served.

Sometimes, it was down to Sophy to serve it. La Marmoset had never seen anyone better with a pistol or knife. Or at the tidying-up after.

III

THE PERSIAN KNEW *Les Vampires* would have operatives in disguise on the hotel staff, in the café attached to the Libre Échange, idling in the streets outside, and dressed in leotards painted red to match the roof-tiles on which they lay. La Marmoset, veiled discreetly, sat in the foyer of the hotel, as if awaiting a lover who had foolishly stood her up. No vampire would get past her trained detective's eye. Sophy, dressed as a maid, was on the third-floor landing. The Persian pitied the philanderer who made unwelcome advances. It was an easy mistake to make. Monsieur Morillon insisted female staff wear farcically short skirts and sheer black stockings, to foster the air of amatory adventure. It was a wonder no free-roaming husbands had been stabbed in the two hours Sophy had been on duty.

In the evening before the momentous midnight, the Persian and Vénénos supervised as La Marmoset and Ayda Heidari, a pretty young Peruvian vampire, made minute examination of Suite 13. Two-way mirrors were covered and vents which might carry conversations to listening ears were blocked. It was determined that eavesdropping midgets did not lurk under the *chaise longue*. The suite was clear.

Neither *éminence noire* would wait upon the other. Both were set to arrive at the last – not the first – chime of midnight by the ugly carriage clock in the suite. Erik climbed up from the sewers through the hotel's kitchens and the Grand Vampire slipped down from the rooftop via a skylight and rope ladder.

As the twelfth chime tinkled, both appeared in Suite 13.

Though they should have been used to this, the Persian spilled his Anis and Vénénos bit through his cigarette.

Phantom rose through a trapdoor in the floor Ayda had found under the rug but thought locked. Vampire descended from a false cornice La Marmoset had noticed but deemed it best not to mention. Behind masks, mystery men were bad-humoured about losing face. Those who would serve them learned this swiftly.

Hollow laughter echoed through the suite. Erik and the Grand Vampire were pleased with themselves.

They wore evening dress: the Phantom with a blank white mask, violet gloves and a wide-brimmed black felt fedora; the Vampire with a bandit domino, a shock of white crepe hair and a beaverskin topper. Erik's jet-black opera cloak was lined with scarlet silk. The Vampire's caped overcoat had a serrated batwing collar.

Though Monsieur Morillon provided a full table of delicacies and a selection of beverages, neither principal cared for refreshments. Seeing the Vampire's alarming filed teeth, the Persian remembered why Erik never let anyone see him take food or drink. With his lipless mouth, he must slurp like a dog or pour measures straight down his throat. And – too late! – it also struck him that, considering how advancement was gained in *Les Vampires*, a sensible precaution would be to drink nothing in the company of a Vice-President in Charge of Poison.

Had the Anis been unusually bitter?

'To the point, my friend,' began the Grand Vampire, 'you are aware of the death of Count Camille de Rosillon?'

Erik nodded.

The Count, attaché to the Embassy of the Baltic Principality of Pontevedro, was one of those mildly ornamental fellows who flit between balls, engagements and duels. He was so elaborately useless everyone took him for a spy. Erik, who made it his business to know, was aware of the Count's deepest secret – he was entirely as trivial as he seemed, and not in the employ of any domestic or foreign intelligence agency. De Rosillon knew the latest dances before his rivals and was only too eager to teach them to a pretty young wife or daughter or maid or secretary. It was no surprise he should wind up naked with his throat cut, wrapped in silk sheets and stuffed into the laundry chute of the Hôtel Meurice. What was surprising was that the sheets were unstained. When Dr Dieudonné, the lady coroner, cut open his veins, scarcely a drop of blood remained in his body.

'You know what they are saying about the case?'

Erik chortled, an unnerving sound.

'The pretty little things of the corps de ballet whisper that de Rosillon was killed... *by a vampire*! The body was discovered by trap-setters called in to deal with a sudden invasion of rats from the sewers beneath the hotel, and everyone knows that where the *nosferatu* go there follow great swarms of vermin.'

The Grand Vampire scowled.

'...And can you guess what that fathead of a policeman, Inspector d'Aubert, has concluded?'

'Spell it out for me.'

'This d'Aubert – curse his father and his grandfather and his great-grandfather before him! – makes the ridiculous assumption that we – *Les Vampires* – drank the blood of this de Rosillon fellow. In short, he thinks we are vampires!'

'Some say I'm a ghost.'

'That's not been disproved,' put in Vénénos, unhelpfully.

Erik turned to glare through his mask's eyeholes at the Vice-President in Charge of Poison. Vénénos paled, as if he'd accidentally sampled a drink he had intended for someone else.

'Do not be impertinent,' snapped his chief.

'I see your problem,' Erik conceded. 'You have cultivated a certain... *reputation*. Now it has turned around *to bite you*.'

The Grand Vampire warmed to the subject, spots of colour in his chalk-white cheeks.

'A generation ago, the foremost criminals of France were the Black Coats,' said the Grand Vampire. 'Crude robbers, brigands and extortionists, but well organised, disciplined and with a dramatic flair. A story got around that they were in league with the Devil. Those who even thought about crossing them were struck dead, and so forth. I needn't tell *you* how that trick works. When our society rose in competition with the Black Coats, we needed to be more fearsome, more ruthless, more *supernatural*. So, though we are no more undead than your boulevard *apache* is a Red Indian, we declared ourselves *Les Vampires*. You may remember there was a vampire craze at the theatre, early in the century...'

'I know the opera *Der Vampyr*, by Heinrich Marschner, first given in Leipzig in 1828,' said Erik. 'A mediocre piece, but it had its vogue.'

'I don't go to the opera myself. Big draughty houses and fat women singing words no one can understand... I prefer cabaret.'

The Grand Vampire was fortunate not to find a stake thrust through his heart. Erik let him continue.

'So, we took the name *vampire*. We *encouraged* the belief we were monsters of the night, all-seeing, undefeatable, bloodthirsty. The Black Coats went into decline. Who in this day and age is afraid of their grandfather's moth-eaten greatcoat? Who is *not* afraid of vampires? For twenty years, we have proudly declared ourselves children of the night... We have drunk thickened red wine from gold goblets at black masses, we have slept in coffins, we have shunned daylight. And we have cut throats wholesale and tossed bled-out bodies into the Seine.'

'You have convinced me of your innocence,' said Erik, dryly.

The Grand Vampire showed all his white, sharp shark teeth.

'This Inspector d'Aaubert is in charge of the de Rosillon exsanguination,' he said. 'It is just the sort of case a *flic* who wishes advancement dreams of. A culprit – preferably a whole mob of 'em – will go to the guillotine for this little killing. And the Sûreté has declared war on *Les Vampires*.'

'Inconvenient for you, I imagine.'

'They have little chance of *convicting* any of us...'

'Of course,' Erik allowed, magnanimously.

'...but takings are down, across the board. Raid after raid cuts into business. Houses of vice are empty. Smuggled goods pile uncollected on the docks. Robbery in the street is impossible with all these extra vigilance patrols. The bold gendarmes grow bolder. They run us in, my friend, they run us in...'

The Grand Vampire sounded weary. He was not the first to hold his title. If things didn't go their way, *Les Vampires* were prone to getting rid of chiefs. Vénénos obviously wondered how he'd look in a domino and a beaver hat.

'It's not just the police, Monsieur le Fantôme,' the Grand Vampire continued. 'The rooftops of Paris are ours, as the caverns below the streets are yours. Among the chimneys we have mapped out boulevards and squares, highways and hostelries. For a month now, there has been a trespasser on our patch. Almost nightly is he seen. A creature with great black wings and eyes of fire. Fearsome are his talons and fangs. He squats among the gargoyles of Notre Dame, scanning crowds below for prey. He leaps – or flies – across wide streets, silhouetted against the moon. Or crawls head-down like a lizard, on the frontage of the Louvre. Three nights ago, the attention-seeking nuisance was spotted above the rue de Rivoli, near the Hôtel Meurice. The next morning, de Rosillon was found. D'Aubert insists this amateur is one of us. He forgets – or it suits him to forget – that we of *Les Vampires* are *not* seen.'

Erik nodded. He himself was more often heard than seen.

'It may be that this Black Bat is a meddler rather than a murderer,' continued the Grand Vampire, 'but he exists, and he's mixed up with de Rosillon. Yet the police harass us, rather than look out for this jumped-up rooftop rapscallion.'

'You have my sympathies, Monsieur le Vampire,' said Erik. 'You are in a cleft stick. You can't publicly declare your innocence of this murder because your enterprise depends on people thinking you *might* be capable of crimes like this.'

'You have it exactly.'

'A pretty conundrum indeed.'

'*Les Vampires* should like to engage the Opera Ghost Agency to solve this murder – at your usual rates – and hand the culprit over to justice.'

'Is that all?'

'Of course, we'd do it ourselves,' the Grand Vampire declared, with a dismissive wave as if referring to a chore as simple as coshing a priest or dynamiting a charity hospital, 'but we have principles. We can't assist the police. There would be scandal.'

Erik fell silent and shut his eyes.

The Persian knew he had not fallen asleep. He was thinking.

'No,' he said, at last. 'With regret, we cannot take your case. Simple murders are outside our purview. The Sûreté are surprisingly good at solving them...'

The Persian conceded that this was generally the case, though the French police had their limitations and blindspots. The former Madame Calhoun and the in-all-but-name widow Latimer were walking around unarrested and unguillotined. Even the washerwoman in the counting-house of *Les Vampires* had shoved a postman down a well to prove herself qualified for her position.

'The Sûreté believe they have *already* solved this murder. They believe *I* am the murderer. They will look no further for their culprit.'

'I see their reasoning. Again, my sympathies.'

The Grand Vampire slumped on the sofa and spat out his teeth. His original set had been pulled long ago to accommodate the fangs, but he tired of them. They made his gums bleed.

The meeting at midnight was drawing to an end.

'Little escapes *Les Vampires*,' said the Grand Vampire, slyly, 'under or above the roofs of Paris. When our sentries reported this bat-creature, we knew that inside the Spring-Heeled *Chauve-Souris* was a man. Can you guess who we first thought that man must be?'

Erik said nothing.

'You, my dear Phantom,' said the Grand Vampire, gums glistening red. 'You.'

IV

ERIK HAD DECIDED. So the matter stood.

Sophy Kratides cleaned her guns and kept her knives honed.

Inspector d'Aubert announced he was confident a significant arrest would shortly be made in the de Rosillon murder. No one in Paris held their breath.

Lesser vampires were hauled screeching into the sun and locked up. Some elderly criminals put aside vampire capes and dragged their old black coats from the back of the wardrobe. The Grand Vampire went underground.

Small items in the newspapers reported sightings of a bat-shaped man or a man-sized bat. A vampire scare took fire. Women wore garlic-smeared chokers until lovers complained. Godless roués sported silver crucifix tie-pins and carried hip-flasks of holy water filched from the font in Saint-Sulpice.

Many veiled ladies showed up for de Rosillon's funeral. Afterwards, two fought a duel for the right to declare themselves his widow. Neither were hurt badly. Both soon found patrons to soothe their grief.

The Agency successfully concluded small cases. Unorna exposed 'Sesostris, the Sorceress of Ecbatana', a fraudulent medium who sold bogus maps to the lost treasure of Monte Cristo. La Marmoset solved a puzzling mystery which began with poisoned pet cats and thwarted an attempt on the life of a popular lady novelist who had just made a will in favour of her English butler.

For her part, and off the books, Sophy mercifully crippled a ponce who signed his name on girls with a branding iron. She left the women to dispose of him as they saw fit.

The Agency disapproved of side-ventures, but justice must be served as she saw it… not according to the dictates of a man behind a mirror.

Sophy was in two minds about masterminds.

But she liked La Marmoset – in most of her persons – and warmed to the strange-eyed new girl, Unorna. She was even fond of the Persian.

The world of the opera house was endlessly diverting. Coming and going by the stage door, she was often taken for a singer or a dancer. Like Erik, she was emotionally attached to the company – fiercely critical of missteps, yet partisan as the longest-serving claqueur. Protective of chorus and corps de ballet, she cast an eye over the crowd of young men who gathered at the stage door, cautioning girls against fellows who struck her wrong.

There were always one or two...

The great success of the season was a revival of *Macbeth*. Anatole Garron gave the performance of his career in the title role, and was widely praised and toasted. Erik sent a rare note of approval to Garron, who was suitably humbled. As a rule, the Phantom paid scant attention to baritones – or to male opera singers in general – but, like *le tout-Paris*, he admired the magnificent, murdering thane.

It was adjudged that Garron bettered Ismaël, who had originated the French version of the role some twenty years earlier. Then, the much-awaited piece was a sorry failure. Ismaël lived long enough to fume in silence as his successor took curtain calls. Even Signor Verdi, who would only really be satisfied if he could sing all the parts and conduct the orchestra himself, thought Garron 'quite good – for a Frenchman...'

Wherever Garron went, the cry of 'Macbetto' followed him.

Couturiers put higher prices on tartan. The success set off a fashion for Scottish plaids.

In Dressing Room 313, the Persian read the latest notices. All the newspapers – and some of the newspaper *critics* – who had dismissed *Macbeth* as overblown and tuneless in 1865 now declared it a masterpiece. Throughout the run, the raves poured in.

But the house was not entirely happy.

With receipts up, everyone thought they should be paid more – but the Management always said expenses were up in excess of income.

And there were accidents.

'In England, they say *Macbeth* is unlucky,' observed Unorna.

La Marmoset, who wore a frock coat and trousers, cocked an ear. She was gumming a precise little goatee and moustache to her face.

'In an English theatre, it is not done even to mention the title,' Unorna explained. 'When it *must* be talked of, actors call it "the Scottish play".'

'Pah!' said La Marmoset, experimenting with a new character – a French literary lion with more opinions than published works. 'The superstition of fools and dullards. For Anatole Garron, *Macbeth* has proved lucky.'

'But only at the expense of some other fellow,' said Sophy. 'A *detective* might suspect someone jostled the hand of fate...'

Opportunity came late in Garron's career. Aside from an early role in – strange to relate – Marschner's *Der Vampyr*, he had seldom been given star parts. He was so convincing as a vampire, producers were reluctant to cast him as a normal man, yet Méphistophéles, a plum non-human bass-baritone role, was literally out of his range.

As *Macbeth* went into rehearsal, Giovanni Jones – the company's premier baritone – happened to choke on a stew-bone and lose his voice. Jones's Macbetto costumes were taken in for the less substantial Garron, who surprised everyone with his impassioned performance. All Paris applauded... except Jones, who remembered Garron had insisted he try the *lapin en cocotte* at the little restaurant in Impasse Sandrié. The bitter, laid-up singer muttered that his successor didn't need acting ability to play an ambitious second-rater who'd go to any lengths to get a king out of his way and steal a crown.

'It's the nature of the piece,' said La Marmoset. 'All the witches and prophecies and ghosts and murders. Gloomy associations.

The same with *Faust* and its devils. Bad things always happen when *Faust* is given.'

Sophy noticed the Persian shuddering at that.

'So, when *Macbeth* is playing and a stagehand stubs his toe or a dancer's brother falls over miles from the house or a bit of Birnam Wood catches fire... why, it must be the curse! The hens cluck and cross themselves and spit three times. Yet things are *always* happening, good and bad. They happen for reasons observable to the trained mind. When mishaps mishappen while a *comedy* is on stage, no one says dark forces are at work.'

'There *are* curses,' said Unorna, who was laying out a Tarot deck. 'There are spirits all around.'

'Are there vampires?' asked Sophy.

The Witch of Prague shrugged slowly like a stretching cat. She gave one of her peculiar half-smiles. Her grey eye glistened and her brown eye gleamed.

'I have no reason to believe there *aren't*,' she said.

Why was the Witch really here? Sophy half-thought her less interested in Erik's reputed magic powers than in the tricks which convinced people he was a ghost.

'There are more things in Heaven and Earth, Horatio,' intoned Unorna.

'That's *Hamlet*, not *Macbeth*,' said La Marmoset. 'He is overrated, that Englishman. His comedies – ha! – they are not funny. His tragedies – heh! – they are not sad. And his histories – ho! – they are all lies. He is not fit to fill the inkwell of Pierre Gringoire or cut the quill of François Villon.'

La Marmoset was now completely a made-up character. Her hair was oiled and plastered, with a kiss-curl on her forehead. She even seemed to be balding.

Sophy admired her friend's knack of disguise, but – in quiet moments – worried about it too. When she and Paul were little and pulled faces, their English nanny had an expression that frightened them: 'When the wind changes, you'll be stuck like that!'

What would happen to La Marmoset if the wind changed?

Unorna surveyed her scrying cards and frowned.

She gathered them up quickly, shuffled and laid them out again.

Then she meticulously tidied the pack and kept its secrets to herself.

'We are bored, *Daroga*,' said Sophy. 'Find us something to do.'

'Ah, the Angels are restless,' commented the Persian. 'And, as usual, Erik is occupied elsewhere. I find myself governess to girls who *all* act as if they've only just celebrated their sixth birthdays.'

The Angels laughed, but it was true.

Left to their own devices, they made mischief.

La Marmoset wrote anonymous letters to the newspapers, naming the culprits in open police cases. She could glance at the briefest report of a crime and pick out vital clues that had been missed. This hobby was not popular with the police... or criminals.

Unorna cultivated carnivorous orchids in a specially heated chamber beneath the boiler room. She fed them on rats bought from the house catcher at five centimes a rodent. From these blooms, she distilled potions which stank out the place.

Sophy threw on a shawl, put a bayonet in her reticule, and went about the city until she spotted a woman with a black eye or a thick lip. She would follow the poor soul to the man – husband, father or employer – who had hurt her, then cut off one of his hands and slap him with it.

'Be patient and Erik will provide amusement... perhaps more than you would like.'

As if invoked, the shadow of the Phantom rose behind the mirror...

Sophy suspected he had ways of knowing what others thought, either by Unorna's method of mental telepathy or La Marmoset's method of observing telltale twitches.

The Angels and the Persian all noticed him at the same time.

'Ladies, *Daroga*,' he began.

The voice, a forceful purr, seemed to come from everywhere in the room at once. A trick of acoustics, or ventriloquism. Once, when the women thought themselves really alone, Unorna tried to match the effect – but had to admit defeat.

'Tonight, the final performance of *Macbeth* will be given,' intoned Erik.

Posters were up all over the building with 'Last Night' plastered across them. Scalpers offered tickets at twenty times the listed price. If not otherwise occupied by skirmishes with the police, *Les Vampires* would have counterfeited tickets and sold them at forty times the listed price.

'I shall watch the performance,' continued the Phantom. 'As a special concession, you may join me.'

Box Five was permanently set aside for Erik's use.

'Afterwards, there is to be a masked ball to celebrate the great success.'

At the Paris Opéra, Sophy thought, there would be a masked ball to celebrate a great failure... or commemorate the opening of a ham pie.

'I have approved of the production... of Garron... and we shall bestow upon the ball the honour of our attendance.'

Without the triviality of invitations, of course.

'Costumes will be provided for you all. Tonight is the night of *Macbetto*!'

V

AFTER TWENTY-SEVEN CURTAIN calls, Anatole Garron was borne from the stage on the shoulders of the entire company. Applause thundered for a half-hour after his final bow. The huge, heavy curtains shook. The musicians of the orchestra pit left in their wax earplugs. Stage-hands up in the rigging clung dearly to ropes. Patrons with long memories made sure they weren't sitting directly beneath the great, rattling chandelier. No one wanted to be added to the tally of accidents ascribed to the curse of *Macbeth*.

In Box Five, everyone was in a good mood.

Erik was in a trance, elbows on the plush velvet rest, tears trickling down his mask. Music reached his cold heart if all else failed.

La Marmoset delighted in pointing out clues left by the Macbettos which would have put a trained detective on their scent from the first alarm. Sophy enjoyed anything with murder, especially when the villain was exposed in the end and properly beheaded. Unorna hummed along with the witches, chorusing prophecies and incantations.

The Persian had stayed awake throughout.

He rarely mentioned his indifference to European music. The setting of the play – a French translation of an Italian opera set in an Englishman's idea of Dark Ages Scotland – reminded him of the Mazenderan of his youth. He had first met Erik in that province, in the service of the Khanum. Beside that power-behind-the-throne biddy, Lady Macbetto was a merry milkmaid. The Khanum ruled through the proxy of her feebleminded son not her lackwit husband, and would have scorned Macbetto's tally of a few ordinary dirkings as the fumbles of a mere starter. She took pride in killing with imagination and ingenuity. That was why she had employed a skull-faced foreign freak in the first place – to build palaces of the perverse and mazes of murder, for her own entertainment and that of her favourite daughter-in-law, the giggling, bloodthirsty little Sultana. Nothing he had seen during the Paris Commune was worse than the Red Nights of Mazenderan.

Then, the Persian had been *Daroga*, a humble chief of police – something detectives, criminals and assassins of his current acquaintance tended to forget. He knew all too keenly that a trained detective of the Dunsinane Constabulary might look askance at a witness who claimed to have found the victim's butchered body then impulsively executed the nearest suspects before they could be questioned. He also knew such a solution would be a tricky sell to superior officers when time came to write out an arrest warrant – especially if the person of interest happened to be a newly crowned king. In his experience, absolutist tyrants didn't bother even with transparent cover-ups like smearing blood on the dead patsies. The Khanum wanted her people to know how messily her enemies died. She made no song and dance about regretting her crimes or getting bloodstains off her nightgown.

The after-show ball was held in the great foyer of the Palais Garnier so members of the company – and special guests – could make entrances at the top of the imposing marble staircase then descend at an even pace so all eyes could admire their costumes. All well and good for those who had been in the opera, but guests from outside had to be spirited through the stage doors and the wings up to the first floor so they could appear as if by magic and parade down to the party.

A lone bagpiper – who said he was Scotch, though his hair was dyed red and he spoke with an Albanian accent – stood at the foot of the stairs, setting distant dogs to whining with tuneless skirls. Eventually, Monsieur Rémy, secretary to the Director, paid the piper to stop. The Persian was grateful the functionary got to him with coin before Erik did with a strangling cord.

With a simple tartan eye-mask and matching sash, the Persian mingled with the celebrants. All around were people in costume – Macbettos, Lady Macbettos, witches in sets of three, the odd Hecate (not actually present in the opera), Bancos, Duncanos, chieftains, ladies in waiting, ladies who were fed up and no longer waiting, ghosts of kings despatched and apparitions of kings yet to come.

The Persian counted seven sets of witches... including competing trios of artistes from the Alcazar d'Hiver and Le Chat Noir who were certain to belabour each other's tall hats with prop besoms before chucking-out time.

The most entertainingly ill-behaved *beldames* were tourists from out of town, the consorts – some said wives – of an Eastern

European nobleman. According to the weekly gazetteer of notable visitors, they were the Countesses Dorabella, Clarimonde and Géraldine. Two dark, one fair, all surpassingly beautiful. Their Count was on a boring business trip to London. Determined not be seen dead in that drizzly hole, they occupied an entire floor of Le Grand Hôtel. With a line of credit from the House of de Rothschild Frères, the red-lipped hoydens haunted the high-priced shops of Paris, a city worth the sacking. They reputedly picked up and tossed aside lovers the way other women went through hairpins. A rash of mystery illnesses, nervous collapses and religious conversions afflicted their cast-offs.

There were surely enough unattached – indeed, *suddenly* unattached – politicians, guardsmen, poets and financiers in the house to keep the Countesses busy for a few nights. But if one sighted a likely prospect, they all were interested and fellows were being forever nipped and pinched and dragged into antechambers for brief, debilitating liaisons. The three wore long white shrouds and jewelled headdresses and went barefoot on the marble floor. The Persian wondered why they didn't freeze their toes off. He kept well out of their way.

The decadent Des Esseintes had got his Shakespeare mixed up and come as Cleopatra, attended by bare-chested pageboys painted gold. Louis-Amédée, Marquis de Coulteray, was the most impressive Duncano, blood-boltered from head to foot and licking gory lips. On his arm, got up as Hecate, was Joséphine Balsamo, Countess Cagliostro. The Persian still instinctively put her first on the list of suspects for any and all mysterious crimes committed in Paris. She never apparently aged, which was one of the characteristics of the traditional vampire – though he couldn't imagine her lowering herself to drink anything less effervescent than champagne or putting on bat-wings and hopping from one chimney pot to the next.

Giovanni Jones stalked through the crowd with an oversized cardboard dagger stuck out of his back. In a company where several guests dressed as the proverbial spectre at the feast, the baritone made the extra effort to secure the role for his own.

The Persian recognised a comely Prince Hamlet as Ayda Heidari and patted his pockets to make sure his wallet and watch were still about his person. Then he remembered *Les Vampires* liked to send an obvious thief into a crowd to make people do exactly what he had just done so the pickpocket you *didn't* recognise knew where to strike. Ayda saw his aghast look and came over to say she was off-duty tonight.

'Did you enjoy the opera?' he asked.

'Too much blood,' she said, and was whirled away, pounced on by a duchess of a certain age who mistook her for a young lad – or perhaps didn't much care who was inside the doublet and hose. Opera balls were notoriously licentious.

With a threefold pincer movement, the Countesses trapped the singer Gravelle under a twenty-foot statue of Salome holding a severed head on a plate. As they competed to lick him all over, his bass baritone rose to tenor yelps. One of the Countesses bit his earlobe too enthusiastically. A knot of gawkers obscured the view, which was just as well.

The Persian was surprised to see the bold vampire hunter Inspecteur d'Aaubert holding court by the buffet table, in full dress uniform with plumed hat and sword. A very fair woman in a simple green dress was at his side.

Making it his business to drift closer to the group, the Persian overheard the Inspector expressing confidence in the likeliness of an early arrest in the stone-cold murder at the Hôtel Meurice.

'The nights of *Les Vampires* are numbered.'

'Our old friend must be missed,' suggested a tall gentleman who had a Viennese accent.

'Of course,' said d'Aubert. 'The Count de Rosillon was a fine fellow, very high up in... you know... intelligence.'

The policeman made gestures which suggested but did not outright state that the victim was a dauntless servant of the state murdered for getting too close to exposing a treasonous conspiracy.

'You surprise me, Raoul,' said the tall gentleman. 'The Camille

I remember would be the least likely to be accused of association with... intelligence.'

The Persian took a drink – champagne sacrilegiously diluted with Scotch whisky – and attached himself to the group. The Phantom might have refused the request of the Grand Vampire, but it was a good idea for the Agency to keep up on the latest Parisian crimes.

None of d'Aubert's cronies were suspicious characters – which, experience suggested, was what made them worth watching.

The Viennese wore a smart black cloak. A fanged bat-mask was pushed up into his hair so he could drink. He had a pencil-stroke moustache and arched eyebrows. Beside him was a square-faced, square-shouldered woman in middle-age with iron-grey hair, determined eyes and pince-nez. The Austrian was affable and easily distracted but this lady – whom the Persian took to be Dutch – was grimly intent on pinning the policeman down.

'My learning I have placed at the disposal of the Sûreté,' she said, 'but my letters unanswered go. Impertinent sergeants turn me aside when in person I call on your office. Realise you not how ridiculous is your theory of vampires? Why, a fact accepted by all European science is that... *such things, they cannot be*!'

D'Aubert looked trapped. He must have hoped for a nice evening off at the opera.

The blonde in green rescued the Inspector by talking to the Persian.

'We haven't met,' she said, 'but I know who you are. You are a retired police chief from the East, aren't you?'

The Persian was surprised. Few noticed him as more than a slinking background figure.

This lady was rather dazzling, too. Very sharp smile. Pearly teeth.

'I'm the new coroner,' she said, extending her dainty hand, 'Geneviève Dieudonné.'

The Persian clicked his heels and pressed his moustache to her knuckles. Her fingers were slightly cool.

'A *retired* police chief,' snarled d'Aubert. 'I suppose you've a theory about the de Rosillon murder too. A great many amateurs buzz about this case, like flies on... on substances flies like to buzz on.'

'I only know what I read in the papers, Inspector,' the Persian said. 'I am happily retired and content to leave murders and vampires to active officers.'

'An example it would do some very well to follow,' responded the policeman, looking pointedly at the Dutch woman.

'I am Michel Falke,' announced the Viennese. 'Dr Falke.'

'Another coroner?'

'A lawyer, though I do not practice. I have an interest in crimes of this stripe. Twenty-five years ago, when I was first in Paris, vampire rumours were rife. Doubtless you remember, Raoul? Mysteries were a passion with our little circle at the Sorbonne. Even then, you were a bloodhound.'

Inspecteur d'Aubert was eager for those old rumours to be aired. Or perhaps he didn't care to be reminded of his student enthusiasms.

Beneath his suavity, Falke was taut as a bowstring. His eyes gleamed when he spoke. The Persian wondered if he were another adept of mesmerism.

'There *are* vampires, you know,' Falke continued. 'In my homeland, the Karnsteins preyed for centuries on the peasants around their estate... and the undead stalk Europe still.'

'Nonsense and stuff,' said the older woman. 'Such rot I have heard from my deluded husband these many years long. We have no place for folkish tales in this Century Nineteen.'

'This is Professor Van Helsing,' explained Dr Dieudonné.

'I have heard of—'

'Not *him*,' said the woman. 'You are thinking of my mad husband, the head-of-fatness who sets stock in such things. Abraham is in the news often, for breaking into churchyards and abominably mistreating the dead. I am Professor Madame

Saartje Van Helsing, occupant of the Erasmus Chair of Rational Philosophy at the University of Leiden.'

'The Professor is a debunker,' said Dr Dieudonné. 'She banishes ghosts not with bell, book and candle but with the clear light of logic.'

'Is not *this* house haunted?' asked Falke. 'One hears stories of a Phantom.'

The Persian choked a little on his drink.

Madame Van Helsing took in a deep breath, obviously to deliver a stern lecture on the non-existence of phantoms... when a fanfare sounded. All attention was drawn to the top of the stairs.

Erik made an entrance.

The Persian was astonished. The *Macbeth* craze had reached further than he would have thought possible.

The Phantom wore a kilt, a sporran, a tartan sash and a tam o' shanter with a feather stuck in it. Dirk and claymore were thrust in his belt. Even his tartan socks had little tartan tags on them. His mask was red and trailed blood-coloured ribbons over his mouth.

He was accompanied by three pretty witches. Unorna wore a *papier-mâché* nose and a stuck-on wart to set off her pointy hat. Sophy was green in the face and showed striped stockings. La Marmoset had sculpted her hair up into horns and sported black lipstick and cheeks hollowed by paint.

They were an extraordinary group, but no more than any other present.

As Erik descended the stairs, the crowd's attention was drawn to the scandalous Countesses' latest jape. Having dropped the used-up Gravelle on a divan, they were swarming all over Franz Liszt. Tugging at his long white hair and fumbling with his cassock, they hissed impertinent questions about how a heroic libertine of his reputation could in old age become a monk. The Persian recalled that the composer, now extremely infirm, was an ordained exorcist. Could he get rid of these tantalising temptations with holy water and the sign of the cross? Or would he even want to?

Upstaged, Erik stood in a corner, looking ominous – his usual trick at masked balls.

The Angels scurried over to the Persian and his new acquaintances.

VI

THEY WERE NOT on a case, but minds could not be turned off like gaslights.

La Marmoset was in costume, but not in disguise. No imaginary person buzzed around in her brain. It was rather soothing. Was this how Erik felt with his mask on, in his shadows, untroubled by the need to show a face to other people?

Unorna and Sophy kept quiet, but took in tiny details. They were learning the method from her.

'Now *that's* suspicious activity,' said the Queen of Detectives.

'What is?' asked the Persian.

'Everything…'

She made a gesture which encompassed the whole room.

'Those Romanians…' said Unorna. 'Tchah! We know of them in Prague. *Tsigane*, harlots and thieves!'

Unorna meant the Countesses, who had abandoned an elderly composer to rush at a young army officer. They took turns trying on his helmet and fiddling with his sword-handle, while laughing so shrilly that his gold braid and medals shook.

'They are thoughtless and foolish,' said Sophy. 'They should have a care not to be presumed upon by scoundrels.'

All three women had jewels stuck randomly in their hair and hung off their persons, like ripe red apples hung from Christmas trees. The coffers of their husband must be deep… and he must be a tolerant, careless fellow to let such kittens off the leash. Or else he didn't yet know about his ladies' Paris holiday.

'I believe that's why they are here,' said the Persian. 'They can afford to be presumed upon and so are…'

The Persian introduced Inspector d'Aubert, Dr Dieudonné, Professor Van Helsing and Dr Falke.

'I know La Marmoset of old,' said d'Aubert. 'How are you, Madame?'

The policeman looked sheepish. He probably expected aggressive advice on catching the murderer. From experience, she guessed he had long since exceeded his annual quota of listening politely to important people who would easily solve the case themselves if only they would lower themselves to take such a poorly paid position as policeman.

'I say, Inspecteur, isn't that one of those vampires,' she said.

D'Aubert looked around, just in time to miss Ayda Heidari absconding. She had stolen the champagne glass from out of his hand – just for practice, La Marmoset suspected.

'There are not such things as…' began Madame Van Helsing.

'Professor, in Paris we have another type of vampire,' said Dr Dieudonné. 'A notorious band of criminals. They call themselves *Les Vampires*.'

Madame Van Helsing smiled in thin-lipped triumph.

'My point is made and lined underneath,' she told Falke. 'This is how notions get put about. Brigands claim to be blood-drinking spooks when perfectly ordinary men they are. Your Countess Mircalla Karnstein, for one, was a pathological erotomane with a fixation on young girls.'

'…Who committed crimes over four hundred years.'

'Her descendants inherited her delusion.'

'Camille de Rosillon *was* drained of blood,' said Dr Dieudonné. 'I should know. I looked for it.'

'It is my belief that the Count was murdered in a butcher shop, hung up and bled out into a trough.'

'You can't prove that,' said Falke.

'And you can't prove otherwise,' said the Professor.

Madame Van Helsing was so sensible it might count as a form of madness. La Marmoset wondered how she would react to the sort of magic Erik was capable of. The Phantom could make a long-dead parent whisper a forgotten childhood endearment in her ear trumpet. Would she simply be blind and deaf to things in which she did not believe? Or would her mind crack, sending her off to the nearest asylum?

Falke was diffident and distracted, but only on the surface. He slouched, as if trying to seem shorter than he was, and gave off the air of being puffy and out of shape. When La Marmoset brushed his arm while reaching for champagne, she felt an electric tingle. He had solid muscle. She knew the type. The skin on his knuckles, though expertly made up, was broken. This was a man who got into – and won – fights, not just a fellow who scored points in drawing room arguments and won settlements in petty sessions court.

Dr Dieudonné was too young to have been through medical school – no easy task for a woman, even in this changing century – and had risen to the trusted position of coroner in Paris without having a powerful patron. Someone considerably better connected than an inspecteur de la Sûreté. She was new to her post too. Camille de Rosillon was the first important corpse to show up on her slab. They had only the doctor's word that the Count arrived in her morgue without blood.

If La Marmoset were on a case, she would say she had three fine, plump suspects.

The Countesses let up a shriek of laughter as another hapless man escaped from them. Their kisses left raw, angry marks on his neck. He would have trouble explaining the love-nips to his wife and his mistress.

Six fine suspects, La Marmoset corrected herself.

She mentally added the Marquis de Coulteray, who was waving bloody hands at the Princess Addhema and Countess Cagliostro… then gave up. She had been right earlier. *Everyone* was a suspect, and there were unsolved crimes enough to go round.

A hush spread through the crowd as the chamber orchestra who had supplanted the piper stopped playing. Glasses clinked and conversations dwindled. Even the Countesses stopped laughing and paid attention. A lone jeer came from Giovanni Jones, who got self-conscious as people stared at him and shut up.

Eventually, there was appropriate quiet.

Firmin Richard, Director of the Opéra, stood halfway up the stairs, a full glass in his hand. Beside him, out of make-up and giddy with success, was a broadly grinning Anatole Garron.

'Our old friend is finally living up to his potential, Raoul,' said Falke to Inspecteur d'Aubert. 'Well I remember how Anatole and Jones strove to top each other in the bars and salons around the Sorbonne, duelling not with pistols but Schubert *lieder*. Strange to think that all these years later, the old rivalry persists. One up, the other down...'

D'Aubert was somewhat chilly at Falke's mention of their student days – which, it seems, involved a number of now-prominent people.

La Marmoset scented a mystery there. And added two more suspects to her list.

She must stop this. She should be Queen of Not On Duty tonight.

Yet what Unorna had said about *Macbeth* stuck in her mind. The 'Scottish play' was often connected with strange events.

Crimes had been committed, perhaps.

M. Richard proposed a toast...

'All hail Anatole, Thane of Glamis...'

'Hip hip...' cried the crowd, raising high their glasses.

'All hail Anatole, Thane of Cawdor...'

'Hop hop...'

'All hail Anatole Garron, Vampire Hereafter!'

'Hurrah,' responded the hall before they realised quite what they were hurrahing.

Only Madame Van Helsing didn't drink. Her glass froze on its way to her mouth.

'A *vam*-pire!' she expostulated. 'A *VAM*-pire!'

Inspecteur d'Aubert reached into his tunic and pulled out a crucifix. He then put it back again and continued as if nobody had noticed.

Everybody had.

Dr Dieudonné shrugged and tossed back her drink.

The Countesses whooped and called for more champagne and tossed coins and trinkets at waiters. Their lips got redder as the evening wore on, La Marmoset noticed. Bluestockings tutted at their antics and were seen off with thumb-through-the-fist salutes.

M. Richard continued, explaining what he meant.

La Marmoset looked at Garron, who was quite flushed – or else hadn't scrubbed off all the stage blood.

'With our star ascendant, it has been a matter of some urgency – and heated discussion – in the offices of the Paris Opéra as to how the Great Anatole might follow up the triumph of *Macbeth*. After consideration, and in full consultation with the man himself, we have decided the next production of this house will be an entirely fresh staging of Marschner's *Le Vampire*... and Anatole Garron has agreed to take again the leading role of Lord Ruthven.'

Black banners unfurled from the ceiling to reveal fifty-foot tall long-faced caricatures of Anatole Garron with red eyes and fangs. A thousand black paper bats powered by elastic bands fluttered down onto the heads of the delighted, alarmed, surprised assembly. The Countesses leaped in the air and caught the toys in their little fists and mouths like children playing with snowflakes.

Cleaners sighed. La Marmoset knew they'd be finding the blessed bats in unlikely places for months.

'If I have stirred you as Macbetto,' began Garron, slightly hoarse, 'I shall terrify you as Ruthven. All Paris will learn to tremble in fear at the scratch at the window, the shadow in the corner, the soft breath at the throat... for this is to be the Age of the Vampire!'

Cheers rose – suggesting a greater general enthusiasm for the opera than Erik had shown. What would the Phantom think? Would he be torn between admiration for the singer and concern over his indifferent taste in vehicles?

Still, what else was there for the Great Anatole? He couldn't play Marguerite.

'I say,' drawled Dr Falke, 'not to be cynical, but do you think the Paris Opéra might be – ahem – cashing in on this vampire murder? If so, an argument could be made that it's in rather poor taste. What with poor Camille's killer still on the loose. Irresponsible, even.'

'It'll all have blown over before *Le Vampire* opens,' said Inspecteur d'Aaubert.

Giovanni Jones slunk by, dagger bent out of shape, openly weeping. Des Esseintes, Queen of the Nile, had a comforting, bloody arm draped across the eclipsed baritone's shoulders.

La Marmoset watched them go.

'We know what Garron did to play *Macbeth*,' said Dr Dieudonné. 'What do you think he would do to play *Le Vampire*?'

VII

AT THE END of each evening, the rubbish of the Palais Garnier – champagne bottles, torn programs, scribbled-on scores, broken toy bats – was carried to a yard behind the building. By dawn, a pack of children would have picked through the garbage for saleable or edible scraps. These efficient, meticulous, cunning little creatures could turn a profit from almost anything discarded by the Paris Opéra. Sometimes, little remained to be carted off to the barges which went up and down the river, removing the detritus of the greatest city in the world to foul islands of refuse upwind of fastidious folk who didn't want to know of such places.

The Opéra yard was the sweetest-smelling rubbish tip in

Paris, thanks to the heaps of discarded flowers. Many of the corps de ballet simply returned to florists at quarter-price the nightly bouquets sent by their admirers in the Jockey Club. More sentimental girls let tributes adorn their dressing rooms a few days before tossing them away. The children were careful with the flowers. Single uncrushed blooms were prized. They could be sold on the streets as *boutonnières* – or, if cadet *vampires* were involved, waved in front of the noses of tourists to distract them while tiny hands lifted watches and purses.

On the morning after the *Macbeth* ball, the children discovered a man among the flowers. Nothing more could be stolen from him. He was white as marble, naked, smiling. A deep red crescent was cut across his throat.

The children all recognised the dead man…

Around the corner, Simon Buquet was sharing a smoke with Macquart, the old soldier who kept the stage-door. A rag-picker marched up, tugged Buquet's sleeve and offered to sell him some news. It was, she said, *very important* news. The little perisher's solemn look persuaded him not to cuff her round the ear. He dropped a few coins into her outstretched hand.

'The Great Anatole is dead, m'sieur,' she said. 'Killed by the vampire!'

Knowing the child wouldn't dare make up something like that, Buquet allowed her to lead him to the rubbish yard. Though white as a fish belly, the dead man was who she said he was. Buquet judged that he had bled out, but no blood pooled around him. As one would expect of a vampire's victim. Buquet crossed himself and paid the bearer of bad news again. She ran off with her tribe.

Buquet found a horse blanket to throw over poor Garron.

Officially in charge of a scenery construction gang, Simon Buquet was the house's top bully-boy. A less-refined establishment would call him a chucker-outer or a trouble-stopper. A patron who tossed bottles at an unpopular comedian found an interview with Monsieur Buquet but a brief stop-off en route to an urgent appointment with his dentist. He was kept busy ensuring that the house was relatively free of posh tarts, pickpockets, bogus performers' agents, embittered former employees and the more obvious ticket touts. Vendors of pirated song-sheets, pesterers of ballerinas and troublemakers in the employ of rival houses knew to stay well out of his way. The house was still haunted, but Buquet's crew could do little about that. A wary truce existed between them and the Opera Ghost.

As a young man, Buquet had been chief of La Firme, the rowdiest of claques. His hooligans disrupted many a performance with fireworks, fought running battles with rival factions in the auditorium and the Place de l'Opéra, and were paid handsomely to applaud Carlotta and hiss her rivals. A difference of opinion as to whether the ballet should be given in the first or second act inspired La Firme to such a riot at the premiere of *Tannhäuser* that Wagner permitted no further Paris productions in his lifetime. Curiously, this commended Buquet to the Management, who were glad of the excuse not to deal with the impossibly demanding German. An invitation was extended and, following the example of crook-turned-thieftaker Vidocq, the master of the mob crossed the lines, transferring allegiance from the stalls to the house.

This was far from the first suspicious death Simon Buquet had come across in the course of his duties.

He summoned Macquart to stand guard and prevent the corpse being hauled off to the barges. Then, he roused a call-boy who was asleep on a coil of rope in the wings and entrusted him with a scribbled note he insisted be given only into the hands of Monsieur Richard or Monsieur Moncharmin.

As an afterthought, he allowed that once the note was delivered, the lad should fetch the police.

The sun rose.

The terrible news spread around the house almost at once. Emotions were loudly expressed. Opera folk vented feelings so broadly that, in comparison, an Italian at a wedding seemed like an Englishman playing poker. Shock, at the loss of a colleague. Amazement, at his sudden fall, in the moment of his greatest triumph. Terror, that no one could now think themselves safe from the vampire.

Weeping and wailing came from the ladies' rehearsal room. Garron had been a favourite with the chorus. His precipitate rise to fame had stirred ambitions in passed-over understudies. What roles might they command if certain divas patronised the restaurant where Giovanni Jones ate that fatal stew!

Enquiries arrived by messenger from baritones – asking with some tact if and when auditions were to be held for the suddenly vacated plum role of Lord Ruthven in *Der Vampyr*. Deliveries of black flowers came from the Great Anatole's many admirers. Crowds of women in tartan and black gathered in Place de l'Opéra to mourn.

As under the Hôtel Meurice after the death of Count de Rosillon, a frenzy of rats swarmed in the sewers and tunnels beneath the Opéra. Extra catchers were called in but superstitiously refused to work. Rats in a place visited by a vampire were vicious beyond the norm.

Through the fog of hangover, folks struggled to remember the end of the previous evening's festivities. When had they last seen Anatole Garron? Was he dizzy from the success of Macbetto and giddy at the prospect of Ruthven? Or momentarily sober, a bat-wing shadow falling across his face as an omen of doom. At the ball, had he come to blows with croaking, accusing Giovanni Jones?

Everyone agreed that the baritone had joined d'Aubert and Falke, stout comrades of his student days, in impromptu renditions of the songs of his youth. Those who paid attention thought the Great Anatole might have been interested in toasting an immediate future with the slender, calculating Ayda Heidari?

Some whispered Garron left the ball quietly, following a figure dressed like a tartan cousin of Poe's Red Death up a spiral staircase. Others proclaimed the baritone made his grand exit with the irrepressible Countesses, declaring that he would stand them all the drink they could wish for. He had meant champagne, of course – but had some creature or creatures taken him at his word and greedily drained him of blood?

Monsieur Richard and Monsieur Moncharmin were shaken. As soon as the production was announced, queues formed outside the ticket office. Advance bookings for *Le Vampire* had been taken this morning. Money might have to be refunded...

VIII

THE ANGELS WERE sanguine about the news. The Persian visited Dressing Room 313 and found them idling.

'I told you *the Scottish play* was bad luck,' said Unorna.

The seeress often acted as if each fresh misfortune were foretold to her... though, for some reason, she had omitted to mention the horror in advance of its occurrence.

The Persian had the beginnings of a sore head. He had drunk more than a few of those revolting champagne-and-whisky cocktails.

This business with Garron did not help.

'There's a new Number One suspect,' said La Marmoset, who had talked with the gendarme posted to keep sensation-seekers and souvenir-hunters out of the rubbish yard and was thus *au courant* with the investigation. 'It is but a short hop from Phantom to Vampire. It's almost as if d'Aubert doesn't *want* to solve the case.'

'D'Aubert will have no more luck laying his hands on Erik than he did the Grand Vampire,' said the Persian. 'There was a whole world under Paris even before Erik started building his own cities and labyrinths down there. In my country, he was known as the Trickster or the Trapdoor Lover before ever anyone thought to call him a Phantom. Better men than the

Inspector have tried and failed to find him.'

'Perhaps,' agreed La Marmoset, 'but it is relatively easy to find *you*, Monsieur. I suggest you forego your eleven o'clock table at the Café de la Paix.'

The Persian saw the Queen of Detectives' point.

'Are there such things as *vampires*?' Sophy asked. 'When I was little, my brother frightened me with stories of a *vrykolakas* that lived in our stairwell. That thing gave me nightmares. It was just an old mop, with a ragged head that looked like wild hair, but I made Paul chop it up and burn it. The bad dreams stopped... for a time.'

'My grandmother talked about *djinni* and *ifrits*,' the Persian said. 'I believed only in what I saw or could make or could find out. Now, I know there are strange things all around us... stranger even than men in masks and clockwork brides. But I am certain that Erik is no more a vampire than he is a ghost.'

'Though he does sleep in a coffin,' said Sophy.

'...is seldom seen in daylight,' said Unorna.

'...habitually wears an opera cloak,' said La Marmoset.

'...lives among swarms of sewer rats and other vermin,' said Sophy.

'...does not age,' said Unorna.

'...mesmerises pale young women who grow paler in his company,' said La Marmoset.

'...and his teeth, in a certain gloom, resemble fangs,' admitted the Persian. 'I can see how the police might put these things together.'

At the ball, Dr Falke mentioned a previous Paris vampire scare. Twenty-five years ago – before the Persian or Erik came to the city. The creatures are supposed to live a long time. Had this vampire taken a quarter-century nap and woken up thirsty?

'Yesterday, Garron was so alive, with fine prospects,' said Unorna. 'Now, he is thrown away and used up. He dared to invoke dread powers and this was his reward.'

Had the vampire been at the Opera House last night? That would limit the field to only six or seven thousand suspects –

including waiters and attendants. Looking back, it was hard to think of anyone present – including Anatole Garron – who did *not* act as if they might be a murderer.

'This does not speak well of our professional pride,' said the Persian. 'We were all at the ball, and yet the guest of honour was spirited away and murdered.'

'Feh!' said La Marmoset. 'I am Queen of Detectives, not Queen of Bodyguards.'

She looked at Sophy, who shrugged. The assassin didn't need to say that her field was causing mysterious deaths, not averting them.

'There were vibrations in the aether,' said Unorna, 'but indistinct. What was to happen would not be stopped.'

'Thank you, ladies… that's all most helpful, I *don't* think.'

'Remember,' said La Marmoset, 'it is none of our business… the Director refused the Grand Vampire's commission. These murders are d'Aubert's to solve, which is as good as saying the vampire has a free pass for the season.'

The Persian had no argument.

A horn honked and a *pneumatique* popped up in its tube. This was how Erik kept in touch when he retreated to the deepest part of his labyrinth – the house on the shore of an underground lagoon where he maintained a pipe organ whose tones were not helped by all-pervading damp.

In a sad little hut decorated for a funeral was the coffin Sophy mentioned. There Erik slept, because – according to him – 'One must get used to everything in life, even eternity.' The Persian understood the narrow box also helped relieve rheumatic pain. He was perhaps the only person who remembered that the Phantom of the Opera was a sick man. He was strong and supple, but had too little meat on his bones. His skeletal appearance was due to congenital infirmity. Being Erik *hurt*… not just the soul-pain he poured into 'Don Juan Triumphant', but constant physical aches in his joints, his bones, his muscles. Having not much of a nose, he was susceptible to colds and chills. A doctor would probably advise that he not spend so much time in a basement with an open sewer running through it.

The Persian took the scroll out of the container. The note was curt.

This was a moment without precedent. Erik had reconsidered.

The Persian understood. It wasn't because he was now a suspect… it was because he now took the vampire as a personal affront.

The laundry chute of the Hôtel Meurice was neither here nor there. It was no business of the O.G.A. who used it to dispose of a random wastrel. But to kill the Great Anatole and leave him naked in the shadow of the Paris Opéra – and to stir up a bloodthirsty mischief of rats in the tunnels where the Phantom trod – was an affront which would not be borne. The vampire had dared trespass in Erik's *home*. It might have been a calculated declaration of war.

'Ladies,' announced the Persian, 'we enter a new profession. We are now vampire hunters.'

IX

THE SÛRETÉ HAD offered a substantial reward, raided every low dive in Paris and sent brave patrols up onto the rooftops, but failed to catch the Grand Vampire.

La Marmoset found him within two hours.

Posing as proprietor of a confectionary shop in Place Pigalle, the chief of *Les Vampires* wore a ginger wig and less startling false teeth. Perhaps this was his true vocation and being the Grand Vampire was a chore undertaken through a family obligation. Who *wouldn't* want to pass their days surrounded by bonbons? No wonder he'd lost his original choppers.

The Queen of Detectives approached the counter and presented a sealed envelope. She browsed among jars of gobstoppers and mint sticks.

The Grand Vampire cast an eye over the letter, then nodded once.

The Opera Ghost Agency was now employed by *Les Vampires*.

Trust the Persian to ensure they got paid. After the attack on the opera, Erik might be of a mind to waive any fee and treat this as a personal matter. A former police chief himself, the Persian was more practical. As in the opera, the artist must always be paid. One of the few points on which La Marmoset agreed with Inspecteur d'Aubert was that too many amateurs were crowding into the detective business.

La Marmoset was disguised as a pampered woman of wealth and indulgence. Just in case anyone was watching – though she was pretty sure no one was – she stayed in character by purchasing an expensive box of imported Swiss chocolates. She also bought packets of sugared almonds for Sophy and Unorna, whom she thought of as the dear little daughters of the imaginary lady of leisure. She kept the receipt, which would be presented back to the Grand Vampire when his bill was tallied.

A German governess brought in two exceptionally spoiled lads, who ran around the shop hooting like owls, filching items they stuffed into cheeks or pockets. The ninny fussed with her reticule and looked with adoration at the little pests. The manager smiled tightly. By night, he could have annoying customers garrotted. Here, he was required not to have small children murdered. His smile got tighter. A single drop of sweat ran down his cheek.

La Marmoset left the shop.

Business necessities attended to, she hired a fiacre, instructing the driver to take her to Île de la Cité. Just as Paris must have the greatest opera house, the greatest museum, the greatest university and the greatest cathedral, so it must have the greatest morgue – and here it was, in the shadow of Notre Dame. On the lintel above the main door was an inscription: *Liberté! Égalité! Fraternité!* The building's many tenants were free of life, equal in death and brothers and sisters to clay.

In the Morgue, *les macchabées* – the bodies of the unknown

dead – were frozen by ammonia and displayed on tilted slabs. This was ostensibly so friends and relations could identify the deceased. Too often, grieving or hopeful relatives had to fight through crowds of morbid curiosity-seekers who thought it a jolly game to gawp at the sorry state we all come to.

The Morgue was one of the attractions of Paris. Some nameless corpses attained a post-mortem fame. This was where the wax mask of *L'Inconnue de la Seine* was made by an intern who chanced to notice her strange smile. The first replicas were sold outside the Morgue, to admirers who prized the impaled woman the way devotees admired actresses or singers. A death-mask to put up in a student garret or bourgeois home, alongside a portrait of Carlotta or Sarah Bernhardt.

The Queen of Detectives knew the Morgue well. Once, she had lain for half a night on one of the slabs to trap Bernard Hichcok, an elegant maniac who paid return calls on women he had strangled. Bribing his way in after hours, Hichcok brought flowers and liked to sit and make small-talk before impressing unwelcome kisses upon dead paramours. La Marmoset startled the villain by sitting up and clapping handcuffs on him. She told the wretch she had cleared a spot for his next visit – when, thanks to Madame la Guillotine, he would need a separate slab for his head.

The ghouls were out in force today. A dead celebrity always had the morbidly curious lining up around the building. Those who couldn't afford the price of a ticket to the opera might still catch Anatole Garron's final bow... And the better-off would pay to get to the front of the queue.

Two gendarmes held back the throng.

La Marmoset now wore the face she most often used on official business – essentially her own, with fifteen extra years of lines around her mouth and eyes – and was recognised by the policemen, who admitted her with respectful salutes. Her easy entry made the crowd more resentful.

'You, woman,' shouted a respectable-seeming fellow with a

Vandyke beard, 'what do I have to do to get into this building?'

'You have to die, sir,' she replied.

Leaving the ghoul sputtering, she stepped into the foyer of the Morgue.

It was chilly out, but colder within. The stench of lye and ammonia wasn't pleasant. No amount of refrigeration could entirely suppress decay, so a whiff of rot was in the air too. A small kiosk sold strong pastilles and scented cigarettes, which – from experience – she knew were no use in covering the noxious smells. Her heels clacked on the stone floor and her breath frosted. She wrapped her scarf tighter.

Garron, of course, was no *macchabée*. His identity was known. He was here in his capacity as murder victim. The Count de Rosillon was on ice too – unsolveds could be kept almost indefinitely. It was ten hours to freeze a man solid, including his guts; a woman took a little quicker, prompting misogynist jokes among the staff.

La Marmoset climbed a small staircase to a lecture theatre. Another gendarme stood guard, bayonet fixed.

'Pleasure to have you back on the beat, mademoiselle,' he said, saluting.

'Can't say I've missed this place, Patou.'

'Not my favourite watch either. But it's safer duty than hunting the Black Bat up among the chimney-pots. Inspecteur Legris fell off the Musée de l'Orangerie and broke his leg.'

Patou held the door open for her.

The rank of benches in the theatre were less plush than the tiers of seats at the Opéra, but an eager audience was gathered for Garron's final appearance. Harsh, fizzing electric light showed the scene in unforgiving detail. A prop rather than a performer, the baritone lay naked on a dissecting table, innards exposed by a Y-shaped incision.

Dr Dieudonné bent over the body, hands in his chest cavity as if squeezing the lungs.

La Marmoset remembered, as her toes lost feeling, how the

cold of the Morgue bit. Dr Dieudonné took sensible precautions against the conditions in her workplace. Her long hair was pinned up under a small cap and she wore a plain apron over trousers and stout boots. A few moments watching the coroner at work made La Marmoset revise her opinion. She might still hold her position through patronage, but she deserved the job. She was precise and professional.

Perhaps Dr Dieudonné was older than she looked. After all, just now, La Marmoset looked older than she was.

'...As in the case of de Rosillon, almost all blood is absent from the body.'

Dr Dieudonné pulled her hands out of the corpse and wiped strands of gristly tissue off on a towel.

Sophy and Unorna were in the front row. They had saved a place beside them. As La Marmoset made her way down to her spot, she glanced at the audience. The theatre was crowded with police officials, representatives of the Management of the Paris Opéra (Monsieur Moncharmin, but not Monsieur Richard), reporters and sketch-artists from a range of publications, nosy politicians, well-connected cranks and ghouls (was that veiled connoisseur of horrors really the Countess de Cagliostro?), witnesses like Simon Buquet and Jean Macquart, and an examining magistrate who had already fallen asleep.

Inspecteur d'Aaubert was also on the front row, but on the opposite side of the room. He still wore his dress tunic, with his plumed hat on his lap. The policeman hadn't shaved this morning, and looked in a sorrier state than his old friend on the table.

It did not take a Queen of Detectives to deduce that Raoul d'Aubert was unhappy at the involvement of the O.G.A. He would be unhappier still if told who was paying their bill. Urgent, delicate negotiations had been conducted with his superiors, and the Agency were recognised consultants on the murders. The Sûreté would likely come in for a severe press barracking about the vampire. The promised early arrest in the de Rosillon case hadn't happened and Inspecteur d'Aubert was seen drunkenly singing Schubert with the victim an hour before the second murder.

La Marmoset felt sorry for the luckless flic, but also noticed his furtive, almost sneaky attitude. Little in his prior record suggested the ineptitude d'Aubert had shown on this case, and he was rigidly suppressing a bad case of the shakes. He looked more like a suspect than the investigating officer.

D'Aubert knew both victims. He had been at the Sorbonne twenty-five years ago, a contemporary of de Rosillon and Garron. Perhaps he was deliberately following a false scent in his war on *Les Vampires*? The Grand Vampire was an awfully convenient culprit. He was guilty of so much else it wouldn't even be much of a miscarriage of justice if he got his head lopped off for these murders.

'Dr Dieudonné,' said La Marmoset, raising a hand, 'may I ask a question?'

'If you don't mind it being set down in the record,' said the coroner.

A gnomish secretary was transcribing everything in shorthand.

'Not at all,' said La Marmoset. 'Would you say Anatole Garron met his death in exactly the same way as Camille de Rosillon?'

'I would.'

'It follows that both were killed by the same person?'

'It is most likely. Though the method is sufficiently unusual that it might be a system practised by a group or cult, like the Thuggee stranglings of India.'

'A group or cult like *Les Vampires*?' prompted d'Aubert.

'We're familiar with the handiwork of that society in this building,' said the doctor. 'They aren't usually this imaginative. Generally, their creativity goes into masks and costumes. When it comes to killing, they favour tried and tested methods. Guns, knives, poison, blunt instruments.'

'Were the dead men *bitten*?'

'I see where you're going, Mademoiselle La Marmoset... and you raise an interesting ambiguity. In both cases, the throat was cut with something sharp, like a straight razor or a bayonet. The wound was *sawed*, as if merely inflicting fatal injury weren't enough. In my notes on de Rosillon, I floated the suggestion that this might betoken a need to punish the victim or assuage some sadistic impulse. Those remain tenable theories, but in the case of Garron, I notice something else pertinent to your question…'

Dr Dieudonné indicated the neck wound, which was deep enough to show the bone.

'It strikes me that the severe cutting of the throat might serve to conceal or erase another wound. Perhaps not fatal, but highly telling.'

'A bite?'

'I should say a puncture or punctures. With Garron, there's a discoloration here, at the edge of the wound…'

She tapped with a scalpel. The audience craned to look.

'It's slight, but there's something here. This was definitely not made with the same weapon that slashed the throat. Perhaps – I say *perhaps* – it is due to a bite. There's an inflammation which even suggests venom, as if he were bitten – let's use that word with caution – by a snake or stung by an insect. The lack of blood to test means it'll be difficult to determine if this is the case or not.'

'Mosquitos are the vampires of the insect world, are they not?' ventured Rochefort of *L'Intransigeant*.

'Rare in France in September,' said Dr Dieudonné. 'And I should say I can't rule out the possibility that this wound is entirely unconnected with Monsieur Garron's death. He could have nicked himself shaving or been pricked with a tie-pin the day before he was killed. I will look again at the Count de Rosillon and see if I can find any similar marks.'

The coroner looked at her audience.

'Can I make an appeal – which I know the gentlemen of the Fourth Estate will blithely ignore – that we do not use terms like "vampire" overmuch? These are appalling crimes. Two men have been done to death. Ascribing the murders to monsters out of childhood fables does a disservice to all-too-real victims. It is beyond my duties to dictate the course of the investigation, but I would respectfully warn against wasting time looking for bat-creatures when a cunning, contemptible human murderer is at large.'

Dr Dieudonné was impassioned and rational.

'What about his smile?' asked Grévin of *Le Charivari*, without looking up from his sketch-book.

The dead were usually slack-faced, but Garron was smiling broadly. With no colour in his cheeks and lips, it was a strange, pale smile, but a smile nevertheless. His death mask might set off another craze. Considering his fame, would he become *Le Connu de la Scène*, named and notorious successor to *L'Inconnue de la Seine*?

'I noted a similar expression in the de Rosillon case. An unusual circumstance. I can't think what would account for it.'

'I can,' said a voice from the back of the room...

La Marmoset turned and saw Dr Falke, dressed as if for a promenade, with a mint-striped stock and pearl stickpin. He gestured for attention with a silver-topped cane. The Viennese lawyer had expressed an interest in the de Rosillon case. Now, with another old friend on the slab, he popped up again.

What a helpful fellow, she thought. Helpful fellows always bear watching.

'Would you share your insight, sir?' suggested Dr Dieudonné.

'With pleasure. Vampires have proverbial powers of fascination, do they not? Before they strike, they beguile – like the cobra...'

A reptile known for venomous fangs, La Marmoset remembered.

Most of the room had turned to look at Dr Falke. Pens scratched down notes.

'Could it be that these men were sought out by deadly seductresses? It would account for their state of undress as well as their expression of ultimate bliss. Might the victims not welcome

– even enjoy – the attentions of their murderess? If we must look for a vampire, we should seek out *a female of the species.*'

For the first time, Dr Geneviève Dieudonné was shocked.

One might almost think she was accused of being the guilty night-creature.

X

T HE THEATRES WERE getting smaller, Unorna noticed... as if the walls were closing in. Over the last twenty-four hours, she had gone from the cavernous auditorium of the Paris Opéra to the bijou lecture room in the Morgue.

Anatole Garron starring in his last *Macbeth*... and his own autopsy.

Had she had a premonition of his death?

Honestly, she wasn't sure.

She had known *something* was wrong – but, as La Marmoset liked to point out, something was *always* wrong. Even with Garron dead on a table, opened like a fresh-caught fish, she couldn't be sure the *something wrong* was this. For one thing, her feeling hadn't gone away. Usually, when she scried mischance, the premonition became more insistent as the fated event drew nearer, as if a screw were being tightened or a flame turned up... and a gush of release – almost of *relief* – when the worst was over, like a dish of ice-water tipped down the back of her neck. The cold splash hadn't happened. Something was *still* wrong... which, translated to detective language, meant she was sure the murderer was not yet done.

Prophesying more blood spilled was like saying the sun would come up tomorrow morning. It wasn't clairvoyance – it was a safe bet.

Always sceptical, La Marmoset needled her with specific questions she could only answer vaguely. Until she gave the name and address of the murderer, she was of no proven use to a Queen of Detectives. Sophy was almost superstitiously accepting of her gifts. Occasionally, when she thought she wouldn't be noticed, the woman would touch Unorna's hair or coat for luck. Neither understood what it was like to *be* Unorna, though Erik might have an inkling.

She believed he was born with extra senses to make up for the lack of a face.

The Paris Opéra was a cacophony of sensations. Even empty of all but night-watchmen and rats, the house *sang* to Unorna. Constructed with acoustics in mind, the Palais Garnier contained and amplified everything said, done or felt under its roof. She had to fix on a calm centre and hold firmly not to be overwhelmed. Though she dare not mention them to her living Phantom, she sensed ghostly presences – human and otherwise – in every corner.

Faust, Marguerite and Méphistophélès were as real to audiences as the singers who took the roles. If not more so. After enough performances, the characters grew ghosts which jostled the spirits of the dead. She envisioned spectres of divas who died on stage, blood pouring from their mouths, and sensed the chill shades of actors who quietly dropped in a far corner of the house while the stage-manager hurried to get understudies into costume.

Everywhere in the building, she was aware of a psychic maelstrom: ambitions, heartbreaks, cruelties, and ecstasies. Transcendent talents, vaunted or thwarted. Deluded hacks, crushed and discarded. Great loves and hates, betrayals, ravishments, murders, bitter rivalries, unacknowledged parentage, heroic sacrifice, profound despair, soaring genius and eternal damnation – enacted broadly on the stage, played more intimately in dressing rooms, rehearsal halls and offices. During the Commune, Erik had helped build prison cells and torture chambers in the basements where he now made his home. The ragged dead from those times were silent extras amid the noisier ghosts of the opera.

Inside the house, performers and audience raised a perpetual, invisible riot of emotion. They left much of it behind with dropped programmes and used powder-puffs.

Being a *sensitive* in this environment was like seeing every page of an encyclopaedia at once. Unorna could only pick up a word here or there.

People who didn't exude emotion like leaky gas-jets had something deeply and even dangerously wrong with them. Unorna was wary of those she *couldn't* read: they were either skilled enough at psychic self-defence to keep up their guards or lacked so much in their souls that they might be capable of anything.

One such was Dr Geneviève Dieudonné. Was the coroner an adept of an occult discipline? Or did she just need to be a particular kind of twisted to do her job?

At the end of her summation, Dr Dieudonné discreetly signalled that the examining magistrate should be woken up and told Anatole Garron had been unlawfully done to death – most probably by the unknown person or persons who had served Camille de Rosillon the same way.

'My notes will be turned over to the police, and – on instructions from on high – shared with the detective agency who are consulting on the case. My advice, ladies and gentlemen, is to look for a murderer – not a large South American bat. Thank you and good day.'

As they filed out of the autopsy room, La Marmoset turned to her.

'Could you ask Garron's ghost to name the killer, Miss Witch?'

Unorna didn't respond. The detective would only come back with something bitterly funny.

And nothing was comic about the tattered, yowling spirit trailing out of the corpse's insides. The scraps of the dead man didn't yet realise what had happened. These might never cohere into a true ghost. Despite the claims of bogus mediums, the dead seldom spoke... except to scream.

It was difficult enough to get a useful answer out of a living man most of the time.

Unorna also kept quiet about what a visit to the Morgue was like for her.

Respectable Parisians walked through display rooms, peering with curious jocularity at the laid-out dead – noticing this one's angelic calm and that one's grotesque scrofula; that this girl almost had the blush of life and that fellow must have been in the river so long the fish ate his eyes. She didn't understand how people who didn't have to be here could look at the dead like pictures in an exhibition.

How would they like to know that the dead looked back? Seldom kindly.

From the theatre in the Morgue, they travelled – three in a fiacre – to a yet-smaller venue.

Everyone in Paris was talking about vampires. They had agreed they should make the effort to listen.

'They have vampire stories in Eastern Europe,' said La Marmoset.

'Prague is in *Central* Europe,' said Unorna. 'But, yes, Hungary and Transylvania have the most vampires.'

'I said vampire *stories*.'

'I know you did, Miss 'Tec. Don't leave Sophy out. Greece has even older vampire stories than the Carpathians. Lord Ruthven, in the book, became a vampire in Greece. The opera changes it to Scotland.'

'There again,' said Sophy.

'The opera house has tartan left over from *Macbeth*,' said La Marmoset.

'They may still use it,' Unorna responded. '*Le Vampire* isn't cancelled. When *Macbeth* was announced, Garron was not yet the Great Anatole but just an understudy to Giovanni Jones. If they've started on costumes and sets, they'll not want them wasted.'

'Misfortune means publicity,' said La Marmoset, 'and publicity means ticket sales.'

'The newspapers have already changed headlines from "Will

there still be *Le Vampire* at the opera?" to "Who will be *Le Vampire* at the opera?"' said Sophy.

'That puts me in mind of a riddle,' said La Marmoset. 'All right, here it is... What have we three in common with the Management of the Paris Opéra?'

Unorna and Sophy didn't know.

'We're all looking for a vampire.'

They all laughed.

'Just the one?' said Sophy. 'Witches and Angels come in threes. Vampires might too.'

Unorna, previously, hadn't laughed much. Her fellow Angels might vex on occasion, but she had learned from them that it didn't hurt to smile.

'Hold up, driver,' said La Marmoset. 'This is the place.'

They got out of the carriage on Boulevard de la Chapelle and paid off the driver.

They were outside an institute for retired railwaymen. A poster announced: 'I Do Not Wish to Believe – Fallacies About the Undead Exposed' – a lecture by Professor Madame Saartje Van Helsing, University of Leiden. The illustration was a black bat with a red X superimposed.

'Why are we here again?' Sophy asked La Marmoset.

'The lecturer's husband, the more famous Professor Monsieur Abraham Van Helsing, likes to quote our poet Baudelaire, who said "the finest trick of the devil is to persuade you that he does not exist". It's the epigraph of his book about diseases of the blood and soul.'

'I see,' said Sophy, not seeing at all.

La Marmoset spread her hands and looked at Unorna.

'Sophy,' said Unorna, 'we have a vampire problem, do we not?'

Sophy nodded.

'Who in Paris is trying hardest to persuade us that vampires do *not* exist?'

'Madame Van Helsing.'

'Yes... and why is she determined to prove the non-existence of something most people profess not to believe in anyway?'

Sophy smiled, getting the point. 'A vampire might want us off the scent. That blonde coroner sang the same song earlier.'

Leaving the Morgue, Unorna had noticed Dr Dieudonné in a broad hat and tinted glasses – though the sun was close to setting – in earnest conversation with Inspecteur d'Aubert.

'She merely hummed the tune,' La Marmoset said. 'Professor Madame will make a symphony of it, I believe.'

They went into the hall. A few elderly characters turned to stare – Unorna suspected they were the first women under the age of sixty ever to set foot in the place.

The walls were decorated with photographs of hulking, obsolete locomotives which – according to the whiskery pensioners – were more magnificent than those currently in use. Safety regulations were killing the railways, Unorna overheard. The veteran who expressed this sentiment lacked an arm. The nodding fellow who agreed with him wore an eyepatch and was scalded across half his face. He sucked on a long-stemmed clay pipe.

According to the programme La Marmoset picked up, the hall was used for debates on topics of the day, small social events, amateur theatricals and lectures by distinguished experts in fields of interest. Judging from the sparse turnout, interest in Professor Van Helsing's field was limited.

Autopsies were a bigger draw than debunking lectures.

Besides the retired railwaymen, who probably came to every event held in their hall, there were few patrons. Jacques Rival of *La Vie Française*, an inky youth who had been at the autopsy, was here to fill in a boxed footnote to a larger article on the burgeoning vampire scare which would bear the byline of a more established reporter. The Professor's 'There are no such things' quote would be printed in far smaller type than the screaming 'Can such things be?' headline.

Even in Prague, Unorna had noticed this phenomenon of the popular press – people who believed in nothing professing to believe in anything, for the sake of a *story*. Even before teaching her how to draw a basic pentacle, her tutor Keyork Arabian told her that the first lesson of modern magic was never to talk to the newspapers.

Sophy nudged Unorna and nodded to draw attention to Ayda Heidari, who slipped in quietly and sat next to a gent given away as a police spy by the size of his boots. She was not the sort of vampire Madame Van Helsing professed did not exist. That Ayda was here suggested the Grand Vampire was keeping an eye on the investigation. Bored, she stole the flic's wallet and put it back in a different pocket.

The only real surprise appearance was a tall, wide, soft fellow with a yellow crown of hair and a corset-defeating *avoirdupois* – the baritone Giovanni Jones, hated rival of the late Anatole Garron.

He did not seem to be the type to be interested in vampires... or, rather, to be interested in vampires not being real. Though, now Unorna saw him here, it came back to her that the official biography in the opera's brochures mentioned Jones had an interest in weird and arcane matters dating back to his student days, when he had been torn between studies of music and metaphysics.

Could he have summoned a vampire to dispose of his arch-enemy?

'Want to go into your dance?' prompted La Marmoset.

She hadn't wanted to risk it – for obvious reasons – in a citadel of the unhappy dead like the Morgue. This wasn't an ideal situation, either – but Unorna felt obliged to make the effort.

'It'll look like I've fallen asleep,' she told La Marmoset and Sophy. 'Don't let me fall off my chair and do myself an injury.'

They promised to look out for her.

Unorna sat back and opened her mind to the vibrations in the hall.

She did not intend to enter a full trance, merely to test the aetheric waters.

She rose above herself and looked down.

There were ghosts in the room.

Some chairs were occupied by indistinct forms, tethered here because they lacked the will to go anywhere else. The locomotives in the photographs puffed. All these ghosts seemed made of steam…

The ghost of the railwayman's lost arm was attached to his shoulder, a transparent tube with an inflated glove at the end of it, flapping like a flag in the wind. His friend's face wasn't handsome under his blur of scarring, though. A bright eye shone through his patch. The fellow might be faking it for a pension.

Giovanni Jones was red from head to foot, and dripping. Blood invisible to everyone else – and to himself – seeped from every pore, and pooled around his shoes. The residue of undetected crime. Bat-winged imps buzzed around the singer. If he were stalked by the bloodless shade of Anatole Garron pointing and intoning 'Thou art the man!' Jones could not have looked more guilty.

Unorna knew even the police thought it worthwhile to have a long, hard talk with the man who most loudly expressed the opinion that the Great Anatole ought to be killed on the night he actually was. La Marmoset admitted most murders could be solved by arresting the victim's worst enemy – but cases like that seldom came to the Agency. They were called in when it wasn't so simple. Jones was on friendly terms with Camille de Rosillon, who had died before Garron inherited the kilt of Macbetto. If Jones were the vampire, he must have another motive. Unkind critics often pointed out how poorly cast he was as seducers like Don Giovanni or fighters like William Tell. It was hard to believe the balloon-shaped baritone spent the after-hours crawling up walls or leaping between tall buildings.

He was guilty of *something*, though. Then again, so was everyone.

Before coming to Paris, Unorna gave little thought to crime. Her interest in sin was spiritual rather than legal. Working with the Opera Ghost Agency changed her mind. Her sisters had been hurt, spiritually and physically, by men. Crimes had been committed against them.

They were good at what they did because the memory of pain was a spur. La Marmoset, Angel of Light, had a mania for finding out how a thing had been done and who was to blame. Sophy Kratides, Angel of Vengeance, was set on the righting of wrongs through bloodshed.

What Angel was Unorna?

She thought of herself as the Angel in a Mist. It was not necessary she knew everything... or that she turned the wheel of justice. She was here to help when matters weren't clear, when light could not be shone and vengeance was futile.

Erik called her the Angel of Magic.

Her path was solitary, but at this stage she needed to be with others. She was learning.

She sank back into herself.

The room was slightly less sparsely populated than before, but there were still more empty seats than occupied.

'What have you seen?' Sophy asked.

'Gio Jones, covered in blood,' she whispered.

La Marmoset made a face. 'This is in a dream, right?'

Unorna allowed that it was not literal blood.

La Marmoset shrugged.

'The fellow at the back is wearing an eyepatch over a good eye,' Unorna said.

'I know,' said La Marmoset. 'He's someone in disguise. His scars are crepe.'

'Any ideas?'

La Marmoset inclined her head. 'Ayda's from *Les Vampires*, checking up on us... so he's not one of them, unless he's checking up on her. He's too good at make-up to be a policeman, so he might be another consulting 'tec, out to rook us of our fee. Or he could be someone from the opera company.'

'I think I've seen him before, with more of a face.'

'Or less of one,' said Sophy, oddly.

Under Unorna's influence, she was starting to have *insights*. Or starting to think she was.

A small, bald man took the podium and introduced himself as Henri Paillardin of the Society for Rational Psychical Research.

'I have investigated many a haunting and can report that, invariably, it comes down to something up with the plumbing… or doses of strong spirits of the drinkable rather than the intangible kind. Our proud motto is 'There Is Always an Explanation'. With great pleasure, we welcome the distinguished Professor Madame Van Helsing of Leiden…'

The lecturer made an entrance to polite applause.

She wore a tweed caped overcoat and a matching skirt.

A little ghost boy trotted about five feet after her. Unorna had noticed him at the ball – he was attached to Madame Van Helsing. A dead son, probably. Not an uncommon form of haunting, and relatively benign. In most cases, a vague sense of presence serves to soften the curse of grief.

As the Professor approached the podium, a reedy fellow darted out and thrust an open book at her, also presenting a reservoir pen and beseeching the distinguished visitor for an autograph.

She examined the book, which bore the title *Ziekten van den Bloed en Ziel*.

'I write this not,' she snorted. 'Ordure of a horse, it is.'

'But… but…' gasped the bibliophile, pointing to the name *Professor Van Helsing*, embossed under the title.

'That my husband is.'

The autograph-seeker's face fell and ink squirted out of his pen onto the floor. He wrapped his book back up in brown paper and left the room.

'So it's started well,' said Sophy.

M. Paillardin coughed to cover embarrassment and whipped up more applause, which was grudging this time.

Madame Van Helsing climbed the podium. Her tame ghost sat on the floor, playing with a phantom cup-and-ball toy.

'There are such things not,' said Madame Van Helsing. 'Such things not… as vampires.'

Several hands shot up.

'We'll take questions at the *end* of the session,' said Monsieur Paillardin.

'Such things are, however, as vampire *rumours*. And they do much harm. Some among you may think it amusing to believe, or pretend to believe, in vampires and goblins...'

Madame Van Helsing took the same line on the undead as La Marmoset and Dr Dieudonné. Unorna was not prepared to go so far. She had not met a vampire – that she knew of – but had seen things which would shake a Society for Rational Psychical Research. In Norway, she had certainly met a goblin.

'These madnesses come in fashions. Don Quixote tilted at windmills in the belief that giants they might be... irresponsible pseudo-scientists now put about romances which would inspire a modern-day Quixote to chase after vampires. Corpses animated by demons, who blood drink and in coffins rest by day. Where is there harm, you might ask? Here – here there is harm!'

The Professor rattled the podium, gripping fiercely.

'There is a vampire delusion running among us now,' she continued. 'All Paris knows of the dead men drained of blood.'

'It's a publicity stunt for the Paris Opéra,' shouted someone at the back. 'They're putting on *Le Vampire*...'

'Publicity for *Le Vampire*'s not much good if you haven't got a Lord Ruthven,' said Sophy.

'It should be banned, I say,' said a tiny, angry-looking woman. 'No good will come of it. Think of the children. You tell 'em, Prof. No good.'

'Regrettable is it that vampires parade on stage,' agreed the lecturer. 'Regrettable more is that to the stage they are not confined.'

The little ghost boy nuzzled the Professor's skirts like a kitten. She was insensible to his presence. Unorna wondered at the effort of will it must take to ignore an attendant spirit like this. She was certain the child would be apparent to Madame Van Helsing if only she paid attention.

'What about the Black Bat of the Rooftops?' asked Rival.

'A foolhardy adventurer in silly clothes,' said the Professor.

'The two dead men, drained of blood, grinning like it was Christmas, throats gashed by sharp fangs…'

'Murders plain ordinary.'

Two more people got up and walked out.

'This in Paris has happened before… with tragic outcome. Twenty-five years ago, inspired by a course of lectures given at the Sorbonne by my deluded husband, this city set out to find a vampire who did not exist… Innocents were accused. The mob was set off. There were tragic outcomes.'

A coughing started up in the room. Giovanni Jones seemed to be choking on that bone again.

'The extent full of those horrors have never revealed been. When I began my research into the scare, it was only a horror historical… but now, with the fresh killings, it has become a horror present. We must not again let happen the worst.'

Jones was doubled over now, racking with coughs.

Ayda fetched him water from a jug on a sideboard. He looked up, clutching his stomach. Blood was dripping from his lips.

Unorna started.

'Yes,' said Sophy, 'I see it too. It's real this time.'

Jones brushed aside the jug, which exploded on the floor, and tried to stand.

Madame Van Helsing and Monsieur Paillardin looked at this interruption with annoyance.

Jones got to his feet. The blood was all down his front now.

His eyes were wide with pain, but he was smiling.

'*Sacrebleu!*' gasped the one-armed old railwayman. 'He's a bloody vampire!'

XI

L A MARMOSET AND Unorna warily approached the stricken Giovanni Jones.

Sophy Kratides held back. When there was commotion, someone had to pay attention to everyone else in the room. Commotions were also distractions.

The suspicious one-eyed railwayman assumed a *savate* stance. Grey powder shook out of his hair.

Madame Van Helsing frowned at the interruption.

M. Henri Paillardin of the Society for Rational Psychical Research fainted dead away in terror. He seemed to have run out of rational explanations.

Ayda Heidari had a small pistol in her hand.

Fair enough – Sophy slid a jack-knife out of her sleeve.

Jones flailed, beating away people who might have helped him. His eyes were red as his shirt-front.

The smile was widening, as if fishhooks inside his cheeks were tugging his lips.

He was a big man – well-cushioned but towering, surprisingly powerful. His lungs were capacious enough to produce a voice which filled the auditorium of the Paris Opéra, after all. La Marmoset ducked under his elbow and tried to get a hold on him.

Croaking, he pushed her away.

He would not be told anyone was trying to help. He saw only enemies around him.

'This outrageous is,' declared Madame Van Helsing. 'I must be let finish. Heard must be truth.'

That ship had sailed and sunk, Sophy thought.

Jones blurted up a mist of blood. He roared and charged like a blinded bull elephant, ploughing across the room, knocking chairs and patrons aside. The plainclothes policeman got tangled up in his chair and fumbled for a whistle.

The doors were flung open and Jones staggered onto the street.

La Marmoset gave Sophy the nod. She was best placed to follow.

Pulling on her coat and scarf, Sophy left the railwaymen's institute.

A trail of blood was on the pavement.

She wasn't the only person following the tracks. In the gutter, she saw an eyepatch and a half-mask of crinkled crepe.

The fake railwayman had a head start.

She walked briskly down the street. If she ran, she'd attract attention. Someone would get in the way.

The institute was near the Gare du Nord. Crowds were coming to and from the station even in the middle of the evening. She lost the trail amid so many scything feet and sweeping dress hems... but found it again, only to realise that it petered out.

Was Jones poisoned or possessed?

The frontage of the station was illuminated like a theatre. Carriages were lined up for disembarking passengers.

She found the railwayman's old coat stuffed into a street waste bin.

Crowds passed on all sides. Her quarry had got away.

'That lady's got a knife,' said a small child in a sailor suit, pointing.

'Don't be silly,' said his mother. 'She's much too respectable. Look at her.'

Sophy had jammed her knife up her sleeve.

She had lost Jones and his other pursuer, though. She did not like to lose people – unless it was on her terms.

La Marmoset would probably be able to identify the fake railwayman from his coat. Perhaps he had stained it with a unique blend of tobaccos or had his name written in onion-juice in mirror writing inside a pocket. By the time the Queen of Detectives had made her deductions, it would be too late for some poor soul, though...

She was being unfair, she knew. Not all Great Detectives were alike.

Under the coat, she found the imposter's clay pipe. She noticed the bowl was empty and still white. Picking the thing up, she found it wasn't a real pipe but a disguised blowdart gun. So, Giovanni Jones had been stuck with something poisonous.

At least she had learned – *detected* – something, even if she'd lost the trail.

Something small and furry darted between her feet. And another one. There were squeals and squeaks all around… *rats!* Speeding towards the station, whiskers twitching, cramming into the gutters and grates, as if summoned by a rat-horn inaudible to human ears. The vampire's familiars.

'There are people up there,' said the observant little boy. 'On the front of the station.'

'Ridiculous,' said the mother. 'The nonsense I have to put up with!'

'But, Maman…'

The child was hauled away, wailing at the injustice.

Sophy looked up and saw the sharp-eyed lad was right again.

Surmounting the station were nine commanding statues: eight representing destinations in other countries, the central figure standing in for Paris herself. Below, on the façade, fourteen more modest statues represented less important cities; on a narrow ledge between these minor arcana, under the great clock, people were struggling.

Giovanni Jones… three women in white, agile like acrobats… and a masked man, all in black with a billowing cloak.

The women were the Countesses Dorabella, Clarimonde and Géraldine. Up to no good, Sophy would be bound – though she hadn't expected their high-living would stretch to high-flying.

Were they more familiars of the Black Bat?

Sophy couldn't read the situation.

The struggle was a mess. She couldn't tell whether the Countesses were attacking Jones while fighting off the man in black, or the victims of a combined assault by the vampire singer and his dark master, or were getting between the two strange men, to protect one from the other, or keep them apart for their own ends.

She was the wrong Angel for this. La Marmoset or Unorna would both *know* what they were looking at.

Others in the crowd had happened to look up. Soon, everyone

on the street was staring. Whistles sounded, so the police were on their way too.

'The vampire… the vampire…' went the whisper, which became a cry.

Yes, but which was the vampire?

Gasps of alarm rose as Countess Clarimonde lost her foothold and tumbled backwards… then gasps of wonder, as she seemed to catch on invisible wires and propel herself up to get a firm grip on the neck of the statue representing Rouen. She held on so hard that the crowned head came off. She caught the stone head in one hand and bowled it like a cannon-ball at the man in black. He deflected it with one ribbed cape-wing, and it smashed through a window. Shards of glass pattered down onto the pavement and people backed away.

The other Countesses grasped perches with their toes and clawed at the Black Bat with dagger-nails.

Were these really the frivolous playthings of a Romanian nobleman? They were more like harpies!

Jones dangled, limp as a deflating gas-bag. His braces were hooked on the sword-pommel of the statue representing Lille. He still smiled.

The man in black wore a snarling mask with shiny dark glass over the eyes and flared batwing ears. His chin and mouth were exposed.

All the better to bite you with?

Sophy assumed the Black Bat had worn the railwayman disguise.

His intricate cloak-wing contraption reminded her of a Da Vinci drawing. He wore a tight tunic with double rows of shiny buttons. Odd implements hung from a tool-belt. His boots had springs in the heels and his gauntlets had suction cups in the palms. The outfit should have been unwieldy, but he moved with practised ease, swatting the bothersome women.

The Countesses were barefoot, their shift-like evening dresses hiked up over their white limbs.

They already had admirers below, for their déshabillé... and the possibility that jewels might fall from their tiaras into eager hands.

How had they got up there?

Sophy scanned the front of the station, and saw a ladder...

She ran towards it.

Countess Géraldine got her hands around the throat of the man in black, hissing at him through gleaming teeth. Ungallantly, he punched her in the ribs and she sailed off into space, only to be caught by Countess Dorabella.

This seemed a personal fight.

Sophy had almost got to the ladder when Giovanni Jones's strained braces snapped. The big baritone fell onto a carriage, crushing the wooden roof. The startled horse reared and neighed, and the coachman had to fight to keep the beast from bolting.

Looking up, she saw the Countesses leaping from statue to statue, and the Black Bat silhouetted against the sky. He was on the cornice, next to the great shield-bearing statue of Paris. His cloak-wings spread and he launched upwards, catching the wind like a kite. He flew out of sight.

The Countesses were gone too – through the broken window into the station.

Only Jones was left behind.

Sophy got to the carriage just as the singer rolled out of its wreckage like several sacks of potatoes.

He was still smiling. His throat wasn't cut but pierced – two deep holes gouged into his jugular vein.

'Ho, let me through,' said a woman. 'I'm a doctor.'

'It's not a doctor he needs,' Sophy said.

'He needs the kind of doctor I am,' said Geneviève Dieudonné. 'I'm the coroner, remember?'

Sophy looked at the French woman, who knelt by the body.

She pulled on thin white cotton gloves and touched the neck-holes with the tips of two fingers.

'I thought as much,' she said. 'The murderer was in too much of a hurry to make a mess of the throat this time, so we can see the real fatal wounds.'

'A vampire bite?'

The coroner flashed a sharp smile up at Sophy. 'There's a resemblance to the traditional two little punctures, isn't there? Lord Ruthven and Mircalla Karnstein couldn't have done it more neatly... or obviously. Because they're not so *little*, these punctures. They are, in fact, enormous.'

She easily slid her fingertips into the wounds, then took them out again.

'Imagine having teeth this size,' she said. 'You'd never be able to close your mouth.'

Gendarmes gathered around, accepting the coroner's authority. La Marmoset and Unorna were also here. Drawn to the station by the hullabaloo, they'd witnessed the aerial spectacle.

Dr Dieudonné took hold of Jones's face, feeling the stretched cheek muscles.

'Here's that smile again,' she continued, 'and the lack of lividity which suggests enormous loss of blood.'

'He was poisoned,' said Sophy. 'Shot with a blow-dart.'

'Poisoned and bled out,' said Dr Dieudonné. 'A touch excessive, though it squares with the possibility of venom in the wounds of the other victims.'

'Was the old railwayman a vampire?' asked Unorna. 'Did you see?'

'He flew away,' said Sophy. 'His wings were mechanical.'

'That explains a lot,' said La Marmoset. 'We've been chasing a very ingenious, inventive fellow. But it's stage magic, not sorcery.'

'The Countesses don't use tricks, though,' put in Unorna. 'They could hardly have secretly strung the front of the Gare du Nord with the invisible wires they use in the circus. And those are never *really* invisible.'

'I don't know about the women,' admitted Sophy. 'But the bat-creature of the rooftops is a human man. Madame Van Helsing said his clothes were silly, but she's wrong. They're very clever.'

Dr Dieudonné stood, brushing dust off her knees.

The coroner looked at Sophy, La Marmoset and Unorna, smiling brightly, eyes a-glitter behind dark spectacles.

'You're those Opera Angels, aren't you?'

XII

IN LA MARMOSET'S previous experience, coroners sat in their nice cold morgues and waited for bodies to be delivered before involving themselves in criminal investigations.

Geneviève Dieudonné was a new breed, evidently. She preferred her murder victims fresh-killed, and was interested in things beyond the simple – or, as in this case, not so simple – means of death.

She was unusual in several ways. Most of them suspicious.

Dr Dieudonné kept turning up in *l'affaire du vampire*, like a new-minted silver coin in a purse full of dull brown change. At Garron's autopsy, La Marmoset saw how deft the doctor was. Now, she noticed she was also *quick*.

Standing over the bulky body of Giovanni Jones, the coroner had already made notes, which – with a trace of ghoulish excitement – she was eager to share with the Opera Ghost Agency.

'As I was telling your colleague, the murderer didn't have time to finish with this one. Perhaps now we can see what he's really up to.'

'He?' prompted La Marmoset.

'Murderers are *usually* he...'

Sophy snorted at that.

'Vampires can be women,' said Unorna. 'The Karnstein case...'

'I'm aware of it,' said the coroner, off-handedly. 'If there was such a person as Mircalla Karnstein, she wasn't typical. Your usual vampire is a fatal man. Lord Ruthven, Sir Francis Varney, Arnold Paole, Ezzelin von Klatka...'

Dr Dieudonné seemed as eager as Saartje Van Helsing to dismiss the existence of vampires... unless they were men. In which case, she'd happily hoist the lot of them on poles.

'...rotting dead-alive aristocrats, leeching the blood of peasants. It's easy to see how the tales got started. The myth is a caricature of social injustice, is it not? Vampire stories tell us the rich are literally apart from the rest of humanity. Not really people, but monsters or devils. Predatory parasites. Spreaders of venereal disease. I'm surprised Émile Zola hasn't written a novel about vampires.'

The gendarmes strung ropes to keep back *badauds*, the specific breed of Paris bystander who gather and gawk at any opportunity. Word spread that the vampire had struck again, and this new victim was also a famous opera singer. When people heard *which* famous opera singer, interest faded into disappointment. It would have been so much more titillating and horrifying to see the Great Anatole dead in a gutter than the plump has-been Giovanni Jones. Even in obituaries, he was upstaged.

'I'd like to get Monsieur Jones to the Morgue now,' said Dr Dieudonné. 'With every passing moment, he can tell us less.'

La Marmoset realised what struck her as strange about Dr Dieudonné. The coroner thought like a *detective*.

'Surely, he can't tell us anything any more,' said Sophy.

La Marmoset and Dr Dieudonné looked at her with similar indulgence.

'She means the condition of his corpse gives things away,' said Unorna, 'not that he can literally talk. You know, it's what she's always looking for... clues.'

The police requisitioned a luggage cart from the station. Dr Dieudonné supervised as two brawny gendarmes tried to heft the literal dead weight off the flagstones. Giovanni Jones was not easy to get a grip on.

There was no dignity in death.

At last, the sweating flics wrestled Jones into the cart. His arms and legs flopped over the sides.

A keening moan came from his open mouth.

La Marmoset jumped. Several in the crowd screamed.

'He's not alive,' said Unorna. 'I can tell.'

'Just wind from inside,' said Dr Dieudonné, pressing fingers against his chest to be sure there was no heartbeat. 'Not uncommon, but you never get used to it.'

'You said the throat-cutting might be to hide the real killing wounds,' reminded Sophy, pointing to Jones's neck.

'Yes. Here they are, fresh and unobscured. A breakthrough in the case.'

'Isn't there another possibility? That the vampire drank the blood of the earlier victims, then cut their throats... to *stop them coming back*!'

La Marmoset looked at Jones. Was something stirring inside this hulk?

'One way to become a vampire *is* to be bitten by another vampire,' said Unorna.

'It doesn't work like that,' said Dr Dieudonné. 'Just being bled doesn't pass on the condition. There must be an exchange of blood. Even that doesn't always work.'

'You sound as much an expert as Madame Van Helsing's husband,' observed La Marmoset.

Dr Dieudonné regarded La Marmoset shrewdly. The living snagged her attention less easily than the dead.

She paused for thought. Then smiled.

'In my profession,' she said, 'you learn gruesome things. Facts and fables. Little suitable for polite company. As you can imagine, I don't entertain much.'

'You're not married?'

'No. Odd, that. You're... widowed?'

'Separated.'

'My condolences... or are congratulations in order?'

'We're all better off without Mr Calhoun.'

La Marmoset thought she and Dr Dieudonné had the measure of each other.

'Delightful as this has been, ladies, I must accompany Monsieur Jones to the Morgue. If you run into Raoul d'Aubert, you might tell him about these developments. I'll work through the night and get my report on his desk by morning. I'm a little surprised he's not here already.'

So was La Marmoset.

D'Aubert had known Giovanni Jones... and Camille de Rosillon and Anatole Garron. They were university contemporaries. As was the Austrian lawyer, Dr Falke.

The vampire was fishing in a small pond.

The police carted away the corpse, making slow progress through the terrified, fascinated crowds. Dr Dieudonné scrounged a tarpaulin to throw over the dead man.

The coroner turned and saluted the Angels, then was on her way.

'There's something about that woman,' said Unorna. 'Chilly.'

'I don't know,' said La Marmoset. 'I get the impression that if any of us weren't here, she'd have a job with the Opera Ghost Agency. Whatever it is about her... we all have a touch of it too.'

'From what I saw this evening, I shouldn't be surprised if Erik sacks us and hires the Countesses,' said Sophy.

'I envy them,' said Unorna. 'Where they come from, they don't have to pretend not to be what they are. They're indulged, protected. We're out in the wild.'

'What *are* they?' La Marmoset asked.

'Children,' said Unorna, 'of the night... and what a racket they make!'

La Marmoset hadn't taken the Countesses seriously – but this skirmish with the Black Bat showed them to be formidable. She put them back on her list of suspects.

'So, Detective Majesty, where next?' asked Sophy.

'Police Headquarters, obviously. We need to see Inspecteur d'Aubert.'

Sophy – who didn't like the police – pouted.

'I don't see why,' she said. 'Erik went above his head to get us on the case. We aren't civil servants. We don't need to report to him.'

'We're not reporting to him. We're interviewing him. Three of his classmates are dead... which makes him either the most likely next victim or a prime suspect.'

Sophy couldn't disguise her pleasure at the thought of a dead or arrested police inspector. But La Marmoset thought it best not to take her into a nest of gendarmes, and there was another lead to follow.

'Unorna and I will run over to the Préfecture now. You see if you can find Dr Falke. He's been in and out of this business too, so he's another candidate for either the Morgue or the guillotine. I'm starting to put together a puzzle picture... it seems to go back twenty-five years.'

'To d'Aubert's student comrades?' prompted Unorna.

'Yes, and Madame Van Helsing's Paris vampire scare. We should find out more about that.'

Thanks to the Communards burning down the Préfecture de Police and its archives – a loss criminologists lamented more than the destruction of the Library of Alexandria – it was frustratingly difficult to find accurate details of cases before 1871. Setting aside whatever nonsense appeared in the sensationalist press, La Marmoset usually had to rely on the shaky memories of old thief-takers and older thieves.

'Right ho,' said Sophy. 'Meet you back at the Opéra. Remember to keep looking up. The bat flies!'

She pointed at the sky.

When La Marmoset looked back down again, Sophy was gone. She practised tricks like that. Good girl.

La Marmoset and Unorna took a fiacre back to Île de la Cité. The new Préfecture was on Place Louis Lépine. A former barracks, the building was fortified enough to hold off a concerted attack from the streets. No one was going to burn this one down.

Of course, if the enemies of order were flying these days, they'd have to bar the upper windows and skylights.

Walking into the front hall, La Marmoset was greeted heartily by comrades. Once, she'd seen more of this place than her own home. She'd spent nights in the cells, in disguise as a rowdy tart, worming secrets out of other prisoners, and once even aiding a daring escape. She'd used the shooting range in the basement and the observatory on the roof. She'd had her own office, and established an elaborate identity as her own flirtatious secretary, Mimi Bienville. More young officers asked to step out with imaginary Mimi than her real boss.

Signing in at the front desk ahead of them was Inspecteur Bec. A bald, jolly fellow with a prominent moustache and an even more prominent nose, he was a policeman who'd rather let a bank robber get clean away than work a minute past his allotted shift. When assigned a case, his first impulse was to find another officer to take it off his plate. Amiably perplexed by crimes, he felt no personal enmity for law-breakers and seldom troubled to make an arrest or turn over a dossier to an examining magistrate. Nevertheless, he was frequently decorated and promoted. He cheerfully gave the impression that the police budget was perfectly adequate and crime no very great problem, which made him more congenial to superiors than detectives who had the poor taste to frighten politicians with talk of criminal conspiracies like *Les Vampires*.

'Hullo,' said Bec, spotting La Marmoset. 'I thought you were retired. Have you come to report your husband missing, ha ha ha?'

He must be the last man in Paris not to know that Mr Calhoun actually was missing.

'I did that several months ago, Bec.'

'Oooh – come to check up on us, then? I'm sure we shall run the rascal to ground. We're the Sûreté, you know. Perfect fiends for locating missing persons. I believe we have a whole department for it. Who's your pretty little friend? Is she down a husband too, or just reporting a missing kitty-cat?'

'I'm not married,' said Unorna.

'Don't look at me, Mademoiselle,' chuckled the inspector.

'There's a Madame Bec at home and she has very definite views.'

'Unorna has no cat either,' said La Marmoset, impatient. 'Though she is a witch, and ought to have a familiar.'

'Don't we still have laws against that sort of thing? Sorcery and necromancy. Is she turning herself in?'

La Marmoset wondered why the vampire had spared Inspecteur Bec.

'We're here to see Inspecteur d'Aubert,' she said.

'Funny you should ask after Raoul,' he responded. 'I've been called away from hearth and home to cover his shift because he seems to have gone missing. Very unlike him.'

…And very unlike Bec to volunteer for extra duty.

'Madame Bec is in a bate about it because her parents are visiting. I suppose that makes me a suspect in the disappearance. If you'd met my wife's papa, you'd say I had a huge motive to get Raoul out of the way.'

Unorna's eyes rolled upwards. La Marmoset wondered whether Bec was sending her into a trance. Or was she summoning dark powers to give him hives or curdle his cows' milk?

'You've heard that Giovanni Jones has been murdered?'

'We've had reports from half of Paris about a flying monster and three wicked angels,' said Bec. 'Say, that wouldn't be you lot? The Opera Popsies.'

'No – it's another outfit. Tourists.'

'Rum do. This city gets crazier by the minute.'

'It was always crazy. You just learn to see it more clearly.'

Inspecteur Bec looked at her with a smile.

'I daresay you're right, Madame. You usually were. By the way, you're not the first to come in here asking after Raoul. He's popular with the ladies tonight. Another party is waiting for him to come back.'

Bec nodded sideways and La Marmoset followed his direction.

On a hard bench sat Saartje Van Helsing, glum and determined.

'Can you find us a room, Inspecteur?' La Marmoset asked. 'We'd like to talk with the Professor.'

Bec saluted. He was only too happy to dodge another possible case – especially something as noxious and likely to lead to reprimand and recrimination as *l'affaire du vampire*. He believed in the old gendarme's maxim of only going after the crooks you know you can catch.

'I believe I have just the place for your *tête-à-têtes*. From now on, we shall call it the Ladies' Lounge.'

XIII

IN THE FOYER of the Préfecture de Police was a kiosk selling cigarettes, newspapers and souvenirs. There were similar kiosks in every public building in Paris, from the Opéra to the Morgue. While the beak-nosed bald policeman talked with Madame Van Helsing, La Marmoset went to the kiosk. She returned with a postcard which she gave to Unorna.

'When I prompt you, describe this face,' she said.

Unorna looked at the card. Then La Marmoset took it away.

'Remember, you have great psychic powers.'

'I don't make claims like…'

'Just for this evening, you do.'

Inspecteur Bec escorted Madame Van Helsing past the front desk.

La Marmoset and Unorna followed. They went along a corridor and up some stairs. The policeman showed the Professor through a plain door, then looked back and beckoned La Marmoset.

They were ushered into a windowless room lined with bookshelves and furnished with comfortable chairs and a well-upholstered divan. Books and magazines had long since overflowed the shelves and were piled in stacks where a visitor might trip over them.

Madame Van Helsing was not pleased to see the Angels.

'Raoul d'Aubert I wished to talk with,' she said.

'He's not available at the moment,' said Inspecteur Bec. 'La Marmoset is taking over his duties for the evening. She's our finest lady detective so she will be most suited to handle your delicate matter. Rest assured, she's as dogged as any man... and a sight daintier than our clod-hopping officers. By the way, La Marmoset, whatever happened to that girl who worked for you when you were here... the delightful Mimi?'

'She entered a convent,' said La Marmoset. 'She suffered a general disappointment in Frenchmen.'

'Shame,' mused Bec. 'I'll leave you ladies be now. Shall you be wanting coffee and *petits fours*?'

'We'll rough it, Inspecteur, thank you.'

Bec lingered a moment as they settled in armchairs, then shut the door on them, chuckling to himself.

'What funny is?' asked Madame Van Helsing.

'This room is for the convenience of officers of inspector rank and above who entertain their mistresses in work hours,' said La Marmoset. 'They're usually listed in the visitors' book as "confidential informants".'

'Oh,' said the Professor, disapproving.

La Marmoset shrugged. 'Men,' she said.

An ugly lump of statuary on the coffee table represented plump, naked Leda in the grip of a visibly concupiscent swan. A large, indifferent painting over the mantel depicted the abduction of the Sabine women – or rather, the revels in the Roman camp on the evening after the abduction of the Sabine women. Unorna had seen less scandalous display at the Witches' Sabbath on Walpurgis Night.

'That daub was confiscated on the orders of Chief Magistrate Barrière,' said La Marmoset. 'This is where they keep confiscated obscene materials.'

Unorna had thought Paris less hypocritical in this matter than most cities. Even Keyork Arabian had asked her to get hold of 'French postcards' for his private collection. She could probably lay her hands on specimens from this stock that the old magus would appreciate.

In this room, even the paperweights were pornographic.

'Hah,' said Madame Van Helsing. 'Why here are you? I wish intercourse with Raoul d'Aubert.'

La Marmoset didn't smile, though her lips twitched.

'Would you mind if we talked in German?' La Marmoset asked the Professor. 'My friend is from Bohemia and finds French hard to follow.'

'I have no objections.'

Unorna's French was fine, but it would be a relief not to have to endure the Dutch woman's strangulated syntax. She was bound to speak better German.

La Marmoset had cleverly diverted an argument. Madame Van Helsing was thinking about the language in which this interview would be conducted, not of whether there should be an interview at all.

Unorna looked around the room. Madame Van Helsing's ghost-child sat in a corner, playing cat's cradle. She smiled at the spirit but got no response.

'What is she staring at?' the Professor asked La Marmoset.

'I apologise,' said Unorna. 'It's been a distracting evening. You mustn't mind me.'

La Marmoset pressed on…

'At your lecture, you talked about an earlier vampire scare. You suggested, before the interruption, that your husband was responsible for that panic… and its tragic outcome.'

Madame Van Helsing nodded.

'We believe these current murders are connected with that business. The dead men – Camille de Rosillon, Anatole Garron, Giovanni Jones – were your husband's students, were they not?'

'More than students – his disciples. A blasphemous notion, of course, but Abraham is given to such self-flattery.'

'There were others?'

'In *Le Gang de Schubert*? Yes – Raoul d'Aubert, Michel

Falke, and… the girl. She wasn't a student, of course. Not at the Sorbonne. She joined *Le Gang* to sing the women's parts. They began as a music society. German music, not French.'

That explained the name.

'Your husband lectures in medicine. He specialises in diseases of the blood…'

'*Diseases of the Blood and Soul.* His book. Yes, he teaches medicine, but does not practice… though he is now in England, consulting at an asylum – the best place for him, in my opinion. His friend John Seward, another acolyte, called him to treat a young lady with pernicious anaemia. She has, of course, died… but Abraham is still in London, making trouble for those who loved her. Few would seek out a doctor with such a poor record. All his patients die.'

'His other speciality is the occult.'

Madame Van Helsing looked disgusted.

'I cannot deny it. After the death of our son, he turned away from science… and looked for answers in fairy dust. I'd rather it were absinthe, opium or barmaids. He has sought truth and found only pain. And he hurts others.'

Unorna had assumed the ghost was a dead son. She fancied the boy smiled weakly.

'How does your husband hurt others?'

'He sends them on wild ghost chases. At first, they were humouring him. One of the worst things you can do with the superstitious is indulge the belief but treat it as a joke. It's playful but dangerous. A delusion set in, wilfully embraced by the boys. They were scarcely out of school, you know. They knew nothing of life. They fancied they were hunting dragons and saving maidens. Then they fancied that the maidens *were* dragons. Look around at these books, these prints, these statues – men desire women, but hate us too, in a way. We are not real to them, but fantastic creatures. Mermaids, fairies, witches… and vampires. To think of us as such means not considering how we really are.'

In German, Madame Van Helsing was less ridiculous.

Unorna *was* a witch, but saw what the Professor meant. No man in her life – from the magus Keyork Arabian to her would-be suitor Israel Kafka – treated her as entirely a person. They looked at her queer eyes and saw little difference between her and the pictures in this room.

'How did they get onto vampires?'

Madame Van Helsing shrugged.

'Who knows where boys get their ideas… maybe it was the opera? That piece Anatole played in. The story about Lord Ruthven. Then a disease started in the slums… a rash, a fever and anaemia. Children were most susceptible. Few died, but many sickened. The rash, the stigmata, resembled a vampire bite – two punctures, red because the children would scratch off the bandages, no matter what they were told. I was Abraham's assistant, then. I trained first as a nurse. He studied diseases, but I looked after the diseased. De Rosillon, the worst of the group, played the game first – he said the children must be victims of a vampire. A woman vampire, of course – for who else would prey on children? He said that the monster must be exorcised.'

'How do you exorcise a vampire?' asked La Marmoset.

'This kind of vampire? Soap, better housing and a proper diet will banish the disease in, oh, a hundred years or so. And getting rid of the rats – and, yes, bats – which spread the fever. The kind of vampire my husband believes in? You drive a wooden stake through their hearts.'

'That's right,' said La Marmoset. 'A stake through the heart. That's the detail that snagged in my mind.'

Madame Van Helsing looked suspiciously at the Queen of Detectives.

Unorna sat quietly. She knew the popular understanding was simplified. In some regions, the stake was to pin down the vampire alive so its head could be hacked off. To the east, an iron nail through the eye was favoured.

'My friend, believe it or not, *is* a seeress,' said La Marmoset. 'All through this business, she's been seeing a face. A face I think you know and can put a name to.'

The Professor shut up. She did not want to say any more.

Unorna opened her eyes wider. She saw Madame Van Helsing notice her *heterochromia iridis*.

'Unorna,' prompted La Marmoset. 'Who do you see?'

The ghost child seemed to be listening as intently as his mother.

'A woman... a girl, really,' said Unorna, remembering the postcard. 'Pale, white, like marble or wax. Hair parted in the centre, short and tucked away behind the neck. Eyes shut, as if she were asleep. A square-ish chin, strong. And a smile... that smile, you can't mistake it, closed-lipped like the Mona Lisa, sad and wise and cold... cold like the grave.'

Tears coursed down Madame Van Helsing's cheeks. The ghost was close, hugging Mama round the waist, head resting in her lap. Without thinking, she touched his hair, patted him like a dog. She *knew* he was there, even if she dare not admit it to herself or any other.

'I know that face,' said La Marmoset. 'It's famous. You see it all over the place. *L'Inconnue de la Seine*, the nameless corpse from the river. She was found transfixed on a length of wood... at about the same time as your husband's students were hunting vampires. She's famous for being unknown, unidentified. She must have been foreign, they said at the time, new to Paris...'

'Yes, she was Austrian,' Madame Van Helsing admitted, 'like Michel Falke.'

Unorna had a sense of being on the lip of a precipice.

'I see her here,' she said. 'She wants you to help her.'

'You can give her a name, Professor,' pressed La Marmoset. 'Vampire or not, she haunts this city... and she haunts these boys, now men. She isn't the who, is she? But she is the why. Her name, Saartje, her name...?'

Madame Van Helsing wiped her tears on the heel of her hand.

'Caralin,' she said. 'Caralin Trelmanski.'

XIV

WORKING WITH LA Marmoset, Sophy Kratides was learning to be a detective.

The skills would be an asset in her chosen profession. You can't kill a man if you can't find him first.

She remembered Michel Falke.

He must have been added to the guest list of the opera ball by his old student friend Anatole Garron. To send an invitation, the Management must have a Paris address for him.

She returned to the Opéra. The house was dark tonight out of respect for Garron. Tomorrow, *Così Fan Tutte* would be hauled out and run as a fill-in until *Le Vampire* was ready... or replaced by something less cursed. Monsieur Richard and Monsieur Moncharmin wouldn't want to lose two nights' ticket revenue on the trot, so another way of paying tribute to the luckless Giovanni Jones would have to be found.

The administrative section of the building was deserted. Thanks to La Marmoset's lesson in basic lock-picking, she easily got into Monsieur Rémy's office. The efficient secretary kept a cabinet of address cards. Dr Falke had his place in the F section.

The Viennese wasn't staying at a hotel. He had a private address on Rue des Martyrs.

In Dressing Room 313, Sophy put on a long, burnt orange coat with a concealed inside pocket tailored as a holster for a Colt Thunderer revolver. She also clipped a throwing knife to her garter and found a not-too-dreadful hat to match the coat.

If this was really a vampire hunt, should she find a crucifix?

Raised in the Orthodox faith, Sophy thought Catholic religious objects were frivolous gewgaws. They made them too pretty, as if compensating for spiritual hollowness. Crucifixes represented execution by torture and shouldn't be ornate trinkets. She had a notion that if these charms were to be of any use, you had to believe strongly in them... and she hadn't believed in anything much since God and Sherlock Holmes let her brother die.

If she had to kill a vampire, she'd improvise a stake from a broken chair leg or something. She could readily believe in jagged wood.

She stuck the card she had taken from Monsieur Rémy's files in the corner of a mirror.

'Tell the others where I've gone,' she said.

No answer came. Though, in the dead silence of the empty house, she might have heard a rattle of strained breath. She assumed – a little superstitiously, she admitted – Erik was *always* listening.

'Thank you,' she said, and left.

It was past eleven o'clock, but the streets were still busy. The character of the crowds was changing from gaiety to desperation, convivial merriment to aggressive drunkenness.

Before she'd even hailed a fiacre, a man contrived to stumble against her and put his hand into her coat. He sought a soft bosom but found a hard revolver and was drunkenly puzzled. She broke two of his fingers and left him yelping.

Dr Falke's address turned out to be a private courtyard between two restaurants. The lawyer's Paris address was a three-storey house with shuttered windows. The front door lock was more of a challenge than any at the Opéra. La Marmoset hadn't yet given Sophy the advanced burglary course.

She stood back and looked up at the building.

Something struck her as odd.

There were two main drainpipes. It had rained a little early in the day, and one pipe was trickling water into a grate. The other was dry. She examined the outlet and found it dusty inside. The pipe wasn't connected to a gutter. Feeling the brickwork around the pipe, she found indentations artfully contrived to look like random cracks. They were foot-holds and the pipe was the central column of a disguised ladder.

Taking care, she scaled the building. The ladder was designed for someone with longer limbs – and probably not wearing a dress – but she reached the roof with relative ease.

Now, she was up in the territory of *Les Vampires*.

She took a moment to look at the lights of the city. The hubbub of the streets was muted here, but the wind more cutting.

The roof of Falke's building was unusual, a flat area surrounded by walls of sloping tile. The main feature was a large circular skylight – a swirly star pattern, individual panes between brass spokes.

Creeping across the roof, Sophy looked down into the building.

No lights were on in the room below. She could barely discern shapes.

She found a lever which worked pulleys and chains. The skylight irised open, and a spiral staircase corkscrewed up from below to afford easy access to the house. She took a moment to admire the ingenious design. Like the invisible ladder, this was custom-made.

With the skylight open, she heard sounds from below, deep in the house.

A wheezing, gurgling noise… and someone playing the piano. *Für Elise.*

She crept quietly down the spiral staircase. She drew her Colt and tapped around walls until she found a door.

Beyond was a dimly lit corridor. She paused as her eyes got used to the gloom.

The piano sounded louder and the other noises more disgusting.

She didn't need Unorna's extra senses to know something was more than wrong here.

She turned a corner and came face to mask with the Black Bat of the Rooftops. Its cloak wings were folded and it hung upside-down from a rail. The huge-eyed helmet looked as much like an insect as a bat.

She nearly shot the creature, but realised she was only facing an empty costume and held fire. The wings were soft leather.

There was more than one costume – a whole rack of them.

Including the carnival bat outfit Falke wore to the Opéra ball. If, as seemed certain, Falke was the Black Bat, that masquerade had been an impudent gesture.

On a rack by the costumes were tools – grapples fired by pistol devices, long coils of thin black cord, knives with blades serrated like batwings, things that looked like musical instruments or torture devices, a collapsible sniper rifle she rather envied, fat black smoke-bombs with little batwings, wire nooses.

She saw how the war of the roofs was fought.

Along with the gurgling, she now heard thumping and strangulated screams. This was at least one floor below.

She found stairs and hurried down.

At the end of a corridor, a door was open a crack. Bright light seeped out. The music and the noise came from beyond.

She peeped through.

Across from the door, a man sat at a piano playing Beethoven, coat-tails flopped back over the stool.

Angling herself, she saw to one side of the room. Another man thrashed about in a bathtub, leaking blood. Something like a black octopus was wrapped around his neck, the sac pulsing and fang-spurs penetrating his jugular vein.

She kicked the door wide open and fired into the ceiling.

A sprinkling of plaster fell on the carpet. The pianist stopped and spun round on the stool.

Michel Falke smiled as if she were his welcome guest for a late-evening rendezvous.

The man in the tub was Inspecteur d'Aubert.

The exsanguinating thing wasn't an animal but a contraption. It resembled a set of black bagpipes. Blood sucked out of d'Aubert's veins was discharged through a long rubber tube which fed into the plughole. The policeman was bleeding out into the plumbing. No blood pooled around the victims because it went down the nearest drain. That explained the rats, too. They swarmed beneath the murder sites to feed on the run-off gore in the sewers. As a mere side-effect of these crimes, Paris would have to cope with rats with a taste for human blood.

D'Aubert's face was white and his eyes dull, but he smiled as Jones had done. That calming poison was in him.

The thrashing was just mechanical now.

'Miss Kratides, isn't it?' said Falke. 'I knew one of you would find me. I expected your detective friend. Or one of the Grand Vampire's brood. They don't care for the competition.'

Sophy wasn't the sort of idiot who needed to listen to an explanation.

She shot Falke in the heart.

A loud clang sounded and Falke's starched shirtfront shredded to show battleship plate. Her ears rung. She'd be hearing that for days.

Moving fast, Falke came and took her Colt away. In a trice, he had her knife from her too.

She kicked his shin, but hurt her foot. He wore chainmail long-johns. His evening clothes were cut for a larger man, to allow for armour. A red-eyed black bat was painted on his bullet-dented chest-plate.

He picked her up and plumped her down on a sofa.

She watched as he detached the vampire-machine from d'Aubert, and wrung the last blood from it. The sac churned with a clockwork mechanism which he shut off. She had noticed how cleverly his clothes and gadgets were made. If he ran them up himself, he was one of the geniuses of the age. He kept his inventions for himself rather than share them with the world. Mostly, he used his toys to kill people.

Not that she had any qualms about that as long as the proper people got killed.

'I know about you, Miss Kratides... Sophy, if I may. I have made a study of the shadow-people of Europe. There are more and more of us, haven't you noticed? I think myself lucky *you* were the one who found me... for you are uniquely likely to understand what I have been doing as *Die Fledermaus*. The wretches I bled out cheated justice – they were the murderers and I their executioner! I worked long and hard to punish them as was fit.'

She did know what he meant… but she also knew you didn't have to put on an attention-attracting costume and invent an entirely new means of murder when the world had enough knives and bullets to settle things with less fuss. Falke might be a genius, but he was also mad.

A pity.

'You work for a man in a mask,' he said. 'Why don't you come and work with me? I've accomplished all I set out to do when I began this, many years ago… but I shan't stop. Others are out there, unpunished. *Les Vampires*, for a start. And those respectable men – the politicians, churchmen, newspaper proprietors, soldiers – who have as much blood on their hands as the lowest thieves and ponces. Not just in Paris, but in Vienna, Madrid, London, Rome. So many fat throats and swollen veins, awaiting the vampire's kiss. Think of what we could achieve together. Think of who we could kill!'

She hesitated. Her pistol and knife were on top of the piano.

'Would I get wings?' she asked. 'Like yours?'

She remembered him flapping away from the Countesses, soaring above the Gare du Nord.

'If I am a bat, my dear, you shall be a *bird*,' he said. 'Pamina, daughter of the Queen of the Night.'

Dr Falke was eager, embarrassingly boyish. With the last of his old friends dead – and what had that all been about? – he was a merry widower. Suddenly freed from a marriage long gone cold, he was casting about for unsuitable new adventures with a younger partner. Sophy wondered if he'd actually talked honestly with anyone in the last twenty-five years. Especially a woman.

Somehow, she knew this was about a woman.

She glanced at the open-eyed d'Aubert, legs kinked to fit into the tub, uniform soaked with blood, angry sucker-wounds in his neck, mirthless grin showing his teeth.

Falke saw her dart that look and *knew* she would turn him

down. He was mad, but not foolish.

'A shame,' he said, advancing with his vampire-machine, angling the two spiked tubes at her neck. 'But it'll be over soon. If you don't fight, I think you'll find it relaxing. The first needle delivers a blood-thinning agent which is also a mild, merciful euphoric. It's humane. And I shall play, of course. Beethoven for Raoul. Mozart, I think, in memory of the Pamina you shall never be.'

What was it about music and maniacs? Was this just a Paris thing?

She tried to stand, but he got his foot on her stomach, pinning her to the couch.

She flailed, pushing away the vampire-machine, which was convulsing again. The razor-tip of a tube cut across her palm and blood welled.

Falke was calm, regretful, determined. He was enormously strong – twenty-five years of medicine balls and barbells, she'd be bound.

Whatever happened to Sophy, this would not end here. Erik would not let her death drop. Nor would La Marmoset or Unorna.

She was prepared. Her brother had been tortured for weeks and not yielded. She could endure minutes of agony without giving in to terror.

'What do you call a bat without wings?' she asked.

He seemed briefly intrigued, then shook his head in irritation.

'A rat,' she said. 'Just a rat.'

His face froze, as if she had slapped him. Good. He could still be shamed into anger. When punishment came, he would feel it.

Falke ground his shoe into her stomach and aimed the skewer-tipped tubes at her throat. Sophy was aware of her own rapid heartbeat, the pulse of blood, a pounding in her ears.

Then Falke stopped, stricken. He dropped his infernal contraption into her arms, took his foot off her and staggered back against the piano.

He was seeing a ghost.

Sophy sat up, throwing the vampire-machine away like an awkward cushion, and turned.

A figure stood in the doorway. Demurely dressed, in a style a quarter of a century out of fashion, she was young and pale. Her hair was tied back and parted in the centre. She smiled sadly. Her smile opened to show sharp teeth and her eyes flashed red.

Her appearance affected Dr Falke more than being shot in the chest.

'Caralin,' he said, falling to his knees.

The apparition advanced, gliding across the room.

'But you're dead,' he whimpered. 'I know you're dead. *I* ' *killed you!*'

The woman stopped, standing over Falke.

Sophy saw who it really was.

XV

'We NEED A woman,' said de Rosillon.

'Are you banished from that corner opposite the gates of the flower factory?' asked Raoul. 'Stand there with even a half-full purse when the shift changes and you have your pick of green-fingered lovelies…'

Arsenic dye used in the manufacture of artificial flowers stained the hands. The factory girls were literally poisonous, though Michel Falke knew every student in Paris had availed himself of that corner.

'You think only of low things,' said de Rosillon, exciting jeers from *Le Gang de Schubert*. They knew the young Count all too well. 'I don't mean we need a woman in the general sense of bed-warming… we need one because Uncle Franz wrote many fine pieces with soprano parts. If our repertoire is to expand, we must find a woman who can sing.'

It was true. Falke thought of '*Viel tausend Sterne prangen*', for soprano, alto, tenor, bass and piano. If they were serious, *Le Gang* should find a woman or women.

This was about Gio Jones, though.

The fat young baritone was their only first-rate voice. De Rosillon rankled at the way *Le Gang* must revolve around him. Anatole was a soloist to equal Jones but couldn't match him when they sang together. The star gave the satellite performance shakes.

From the piano, Falke looked askance at the squabbles of the singers. But he thought de Rosillon was right.

It was proposed that they each look out for likely prospects.

'If she's a beauty, so much the better,' said de Rosillon. 'Give the audience something to look at besides your wobbly belly, Gio.'

Jones preferred audiences who shut their eyes and just listened.

In response to de Rosillon's needling, Jones belched. Very loudly, and not at all musically.

A disappointing evening. The much-vaunted song thrushes of Madame Ondine's Academy for Young Ladies were all croakers. Their choir might as well gather around a pond in the moonlight.

Falke returned glumly to the Café Musette de Saint-Flour, informal headquarters of *Le Gang*. The woman hunt, begun as a semi-joke, was bogging down in earnest.

Having made the grand proposal, de Rosillon wasn't going to do anything as radical as stir himself and pitch in. He decided his function in the endeavour was to assess the candidates put forward by the others. Raoul roped in several *chanteuses* who could be heard over shrieking patrons in inns and cabarets. They all fell at the first fence – unable to prop a score the right way up on a stand, let alone read music. Garron was beaten in the street by a schoolteacher after his stuttering approach to a gaggle of convent girls was misinterpreted. And Jones was against the whole idea, of course.

'Michel, you're late,' said Raoul as he arrived.

'No joy at Madame Ondine's,' he said.

'It doesn't matter,' said Raoul. 'We have found our prize…

Hurry in, hurry in, and meet your countrywoman, *la belle* Caralin.'

The others were squeezed into their usual nook, as was a newcomer.

She was an insubstantial girl, especially next to Gio. Later, thinking back, Falke couldn't have described her. Her image in his mind was watery. Everything about her seemed neither one thing nor the other. He couldn't even have said what she was wearing.

But he heard her sing – and that would stay with him for the rest of his life.

Astoundingly, Jones – who had actively not been looking – found Caralin, though Falke never got the details of it straight.

Was she some relation of the family in whose house he was lodging... or another boarder? She was Austrian, as Raoul had said, but from Styria – a savage, forested region remote from his native Vienna. He couldn't place her accent or her station. She was in Paris for her health, but he never knew her to see a doctor. Prone to spells of weakness and lassitude, she rose above her infirmities when singing.

More than once, Falke was asked what was actually wrong with Caralin and had no answer. It was something like consumption, but not consumption itself. When she coughed into her kerchief, there was sometimes pinkish discharge – but no blood. To look at her, you'd not think she had blood in her.

Which was how the story started, he supposed.

Joining *Le Gang de Schubert* was good for Caralin and better for *Le Gang*. She lost her ghostly pallor and seemed less fragile. The fellows competed for her attention, though not exclusively as suitors. Caralin was at times their pet, like a six-year-old, but occasionally acted like their great-grandmother. She needed to be protected from the world. They were in thrall to her, almost in awe of her.

But Falke still couldn't say what her hair colour was.

She wore it parted in the middle, though. And her smile stayed with him.

'I'm going to ask Caralin to move in with me,' said Raoul.

Falke was surprised. He had thought to ask her the same thing.

He wondered if Gio, Anatole and de Rosillon had the same idea.

Looking back on it, Caralin wasn't *with* any of them – and had given no indication that she might be – but gave each the impression they were making slow, steady progress to union beyond the regular congress they had with flower girls… something deeper, more lasting. Spiritual, as well as fleshly.

'I believe she's special, Michel. When she sings, she's like the sirens who tempted Odysseus.'

'What colour are her eyes?' Falke asked his friend.

Raoul was puzzled, almost irritated. 'Why, eye-coloured of course.'

As he struggled to recall the face of a woman he loved, Falke wondered whether Caralin's eyes might not be red.

'Ho, fellows,' said de Rosillon, joining Falke and Raoul in their nook. 'I've a notion to ask Caralin to move in with me. What do you think?'

'I believe she's moved in with Gio,' said Falke, who had no grounds for saying so.

De Rosillon was aghast.

'Gross-Fat Jones! Surely not.'

'He likes ladies to close their eyes when he sings.'

'He'd like them to wear a blindfold when he's bouncing on top of them, I'll be bound,' said Raoul. 'Doesn't mean they will.'

Garron came into the Saint-Flour Musette.

'What's this about Caralin and Gio?' Raoul demanded of him.

Garron shrugged.

'I was thinking of…' he began.

'We did too,' said Falke.

'Oh well. Just a fancy.'

Falke couldn't remember asking Caralin to move in with him.

But she did.

When they were together, she blotted out everything else. She consumed him. He'd been in love before... this was more like brain fever.

He knew his friends hated him.

At one time or another, they all said, 'Do we even need the piano?'

Schubert wrote a great many pieces for *unaccompanied* voice or voices.

Though they were beyond Schubert now. Beyond music.

He still found Caralin hard to describe. When she was with him, he couldn't imagine anything else. When she wasn't – and *where did she go?* – he was too distracted with worry to concentrate.

If he tried to sketch her, he just found himself drawing the Mona Lisa with a thinner face.

The others met in secret to talk about them.

Whenever he arrived late, they fell silent.

The music was never right. They found it harder to select pieces, and quarrelled whenever they attempted a song.

Caralin never took sides.

Even when Falke was arguing for something, she didn't support him. That part of *Le Gang* was none of her concern.

She fell ill and disappeared. For three weeks, Falke haunted infirmaries, convents and hospitals, searching for her. He even visited the Morgue.

He subjected Jones's landlord to a barrage of questions he couldn't answer. The man had no idea who Caralin was. Now, Gio denied there had ever been a connection. He said it was d'Aubert who found her.

Raoul referred him to Anatole.

Anatole thought it was Falke...

'She was your girlfriend, remember? We thought she'd be like one of Raoul's popsies but then that *voice* came out...'

While Caralin was missing, *Le Gang* worked together to find her. That she was gone altogether was worse than that she was with Falke.

On their rounds, they found the hospitals of Paris busy with a mysterious disease that was striking down children, the elderly, the weak. Scratch-marks on throat or chest, like bites; pallor, anaemia, bad dreams, spells of sleeping. Most but not all recovered, and those who died succumbed to other conditions they became too weak to fight off rather than the ailment itself.

Falke was in a panic that Caralin was a victim.

Then she came back, healthy. Healthier than before, it seemed. She almost had roses in her cheeks.

He was too relieved to press her about where she had been and what she had done. Whatever it was, it had been good for her.

The Professor made a dramatic entrance into their lives.

With Caralin away and the mystery illness on their minds, Anatole saw Van Helsing was giving a course of lectures on 'diseases of the blood and soul'. He suggested they sit in. At that time, they were all worried about her health.

When she came back, they were still drawn to the lectures.

Van Helsing had theories about the bites and the loss of blood.

Raoul asked pertinent questions. The Professor theorised that in this matter the search should not be for a disease but a culprit. A creature was behind the outbreak, and – worse! – was a thinking being who knew what they were doing.

The word 'vampire' was mentioned.

The epidemic, suddenly, was over. No more bitten children.

Le Gang did not set off to engage the forces of darkness, but shifted from music to mystery. There was no denying the thrill of it.

Van Helsing presented them with cases – hauntings, manifestations, unusual animal attacks. Raoul took the lead, but the others had useful interests and skills. Falke had a knack for designing and making gadgets. They dispelled their first ghosts without leaving his digs, as he showed how such and such a phenomenon was most likely created by deliberate trickery.

De Rosillon had funds to equip a coach for ghost-hunting expeditions, Anatole a swot's ability to delve in libraries and public records for lost explanations, and Gio made a formidable figure when it came to scaring off pranksters.

Most matters Van Helsing placed before them turned out to be criminal enterprises dressed up with phosphorus paint and hidden doorways. The Black Coats, the best-resourced secret society of the Second Empire, liked to scare people away from their smuggling or coining enterprises with fabulous beasts and frightful spectres. *Le Gang* had many a battle with the Coats, even earning the respect of the official police. Raoul was certain of a place in Vidocq's old office after graduation.

In other – more troubling – cases, smashing a mirror or pulling back a curtain only revealed a deeper mystery.

Van Helsing assured them that there were such things as ghosts and vampires.

Caralin became sickly again. She couldn't sleep and went out late at night, without even bothering to make an excuse.

Falke – hating himself for thinking it – was certain she was with one of the others – any of them, all of them – when not with him.

He quarrelled with Raoul, his closest friend, then begged forgiveness and asked for his help. He was desperate, he said, desperate and desolate.

'About what?' asked Raoul.

He could not answer.

Caralin gave Falke no cause to doubt her, but...

In a graveyard where strange lanterns had been seen, de Rosillon made some foolish remark which prompted Falke to beat him senseless. Raoul, Anatole and Gio stood by and watched, making no move to intervene – as if hoping their friends would kill each other so they could have better chances with Caralin.

When he was exhausted and de Rosillon unconscious, Falke turned to find Caralin gone.

This time, she didn't come back for three months.

* * *

The disease, which Van Helsing insisted was the spoor of a vampire, returned.

Some victims reported nocturnal encounters with a beautiful woman. She lured children off pathways and subjected them to mesmerism. They woke up with torn clothes and deep scratches.

De Rosillon, bumptious again, said that happened to him all the time. Only his wallet was usually missing too.

Children remembered the musical voice of the vampire, but gave varying accounts of her. Small girls thought her old and bent, almost a crone. Budding lads described a wanton, voluptuous hoyden. A few listless, haunted victims recalled a wan maiden, scarcely more than a child herself. All mentioned her *voice* – but couldn't quote anything she had said.

Le Gang set out to catch the vampire.

Van Helsing lectured about famous female vampires… Elisabeth Bathory, the *Lamia* of Ancient Greece, Mircalla Karnstein.

On their nightly expeditions to derelict cemeteries and disreputable parks, *Le Gang* found many suspect women – mostly *demimondes* loitering in dark places. As de Rosillon said, they specialised in bait-and-battery, inveigling customers into the bushes for a quick poke then having a confederate bludgeon the poor clods for their valuables.

Few of them went after children, though.

With Caralin gone, Falke applied himself to the vampire hunt.

On Van Helsing's recommendation, he read Dom Augustin Calmet's two-volume *Traité sur les apparitions des Esprits, et sur les vampires ou les revenants de Hongrie, de Moravie Etc.* (1746). Picking through lore and legend, Falke tried to find hard facts. He sharpened stakes and contrived spring-loading mechanisms for firing them across rooms and through inch-thick boards. He designed a metal collar, with inset silver crosses, as a defence against vampire attack.

Even the others thought he was taking it too seriously.

'It's just some new pox,' Raoul said. 'And de Rosillon's footpad fillies.'

Falke was convinced. There was a vampire in Paris.

'It's Caralin, isn't it?' Raoul said. 'When she's not here, you go mad... not as mad as when she is here, but mad all the same.'

Falke denied it.

Caralin came back, healthy again. She would answer no questions.

Van Helsing said the vampire was still at large.

He believed he had found the monster's address on the map. In the centre of a cluster of red crosses marking attacks was the Hôtel d'Autriche, an abandoned palace. Once the Paris residence of Maria Theresa of Austria, mother of the late queen Marie Antoinette – though it was likely the Hapsburg Empress never set foot in the place. It gained a reputation as uncanny in the rational days of the Revolution. Sans-culotte mobs who set up households in former palaces shunned the Hôtel d'Autriche, supposedly frightened off by the headless ghost of the guillotined queen.

Van Helsing prepared for an expedition to the mansion, to find the grave of the vampire and bar her from it. Before facing the monster, he must fast and pray... though *Le Gang* suspected he also needed to wait for his shrew of a wife to leave the city so he could face evil behind her back.

Raoul proposed they venture to the Hôtel d'Autriche without the Professor.

They would wear Falke's anti-vampire collars. The sly creature they were after preyed only on the weak, the young. She was not expecting men who knew her for what she was.

Caralin was against the proposal. She said abandoned palaces were places to avoid. She coughed a little, stressing the unhealthy air that could be expected.

All other votes went against her.

Even Falke disagreed. Since Caralin's return, he was more convinced than ever that she was deceiving him.

He was sure one – or all! – of the others knew where she had been.

Getting them all to a haunted mansion might help solve the mystery of Caralin. Then, he would take steps.

He must have her free and clear.

At the risk of losing all else.

The Hôtel d'Autriche was in Le Marais, surrounded by high walls and gloomy, marshy gardens. It must have an evil reputation not to be occupied. The district was popular with the landed and wealthy. De Rosillon's people had a *hôtel particulier* around here.

As befit the respectable people who lived in the fine homes, the streets were well-swept and deadly dull. Anyone who passed on foot or – more likely – in a carriage was quiet. They were eerily like ghosts after the raucous, earthy folk Falke knocked about with in the student quarter.

It struck him that, after graduation, they were expected by their families to live in places like this, go to church on Sundays and marry girls who wouldn't rob them honestly like the flower girls and the tarts of the Quartier Latin did. At once, he saw the future as living death.

When he was a lawyer, would there be vampire hunts? Would there be Caralin?

'Spooked, yet?' asked Raoul, heartily.

'Just the night chill,' said Falke.

Raoul handed him a flask of something they probably used at the flower factory to wash off the arsenic.

The spirits burned his throat going down and made his eyes water.

Anatole and Gio found a way in by hefting a rusty gate off its hinges.

Caralin hung back, but Falke put an arm round her.

'He'll protect you from the monster,' said Raoul.

'But who'll protect you from him?' said de Rosillon. The young Count laughed like a devil. He'd been drinking all day.

'Remember, this thing is dangerous,' said Anatole. 'Professor Van Helsing has made that plain.'

'We're *Le Gang de Schubert*,' sang Gio. 'Fearless and bold…'

'There's a difference?' asked Raoul.

Anatole was first into the mansion, climbing through a broken ground-floor window. He waved a lantern around. Falke saw decaying plaster and cracked floor-boards.

They all followed.

De Rosillon proposed they split into three teams to search the upper storeys, the extensive ground floor and the basements.

Somehow, Falke was paired with Raoul to search above.

Gio and Anatole were together on this level, and Caralin wound up consigned below with de Rosillon.

Falke saw de Rosillon was delighted at the outcome, which he had contrived.

Was Caralin in it with him?

The fire burned in his stomach. He took another drink.

The expedition upstairs was thwarted. The main staircase had collapsed. Much of the first-floor landing had fallen into the hallway. Looking up, Falke saw stars and felt spots of rain on his face – so the roof was gone too.

Raoul prised a jagged length of wood from a fallen bannister.

'A natural vampire-impaling device,' he said, handing it to Falke.

Falke wondered if he could thrust it through his friend's ribs. His heart wasn't protected by an iron-and-silver collar.

They waited a few minutes. The mansion was quiet.

'Funny,' said Raoul.

'What is?'

'I can't hear Gio clumping around. Usually, you can tell him a mile off. With all these creaky, rotten boards, I'm surprised he's not crashed through to the cellars.'

Both stood still and listened.

Falke had to agree. It was odd.

'Let's find them and pack it in,' said Raoul. 'This was one of de Rosillon's foolish notions. We should have learned not to listen to him long ago.'

The notion was not so foolish if de Rosillon's desire wasn't to skewer a vampire but be alone with Caralin...

They looked in every room on the ground floor. In what must have been the ballroom, a rigged-up shack suggested gypsies or tramps had tried to squat here. The camp was cobwebbed and abandoned.

Gio and Anatole weren't to be found.

'They must have gone below,' said Falke.

'What ever for?'

'Perhaps they heard something.'

Raoul looked sober and serious.

'Let's find them all and get back to the Saint-Flour Musette for supper. I don't like this place. Not because it's haunted by vampires, but because it's obviously a death trap. Agree you?'

'Agree I,' said Falke.

The cellar door was open, but they heard nothing from beneath them.

Falke called out. No answer.

'There's light,' said Raoul.

Carefully going down uneven stone steps, they found a lantern propped up on the last stair. Falke thought it was Gio's.

The basements were a vaulted space. They smelled of earth and vile things.

Falke noticed Raoul had produced a primed pistol.

'You keep the stake,' he said. 'I'll trust a lead ball.'

'You didn't bring silver.'

'Waste of money, my friend.'

'I hope you won't regret the economy.'

They zigzagged between columns. The basements of the Hôtel d'Autriche extended under the whole house and beyond. Beneath the gardens was a labyrinth or catacomb which had mostly fallen in and was partly flooded.

'Caralin,' called out Falke.

The name came back at him.

'Anyone?' called Raoul.

The same.

Falke was now seriously jittery.

'The vampire can't have got them all,' he said. 'Not with the collars.'

'Vampires worry me less than other creatures of the night,' said Raoul, striding off with lantern in one hand and pistol in the other. 'This is just the sort of lair the Black Coats like. A hand over the mouth and a dagger in the ribs are as deadly as a vampire's kisses – more so, since I'm sure they're real while I have doubts about Van Helsing's sanity.'

Falke gripped the spar of wood.

'What…' said Raoul.

The lantern was dropped and the pistol discharged.

A pool of burning oil spread and Falke was blinded for a moment.

Where was Raoul?

Someone lay on the uneven ground beyond the fire.

Falke went to help him. It wasn't Raoul but de Rosillon, with his collar torn off. He had red scratches in his neck.

Falke's heart clutched with terror.

'Michel… Michel…'

He heard his name called.

'Caralin,' he cried. 'Caralin.'

He walked away from de Rosillon towards the voice, only he wasn't sure where the voice was coming from and got turned around.

He wasn't even sure it was her.

He tripped over an iron grille and felt cold air coming up from it.

A strangulated sound rose too.

Fire from the dropped lamp lit up the basement. Falke saw through the grille.

A fat white face, glistening with drops of blood, was pressed close to the bars. Gio Jones, with a great chunk bitten out of his neck, shaking with pain. His fingers wrapped around the grille like white worms.

'Her,' he said, 'her…'

Then his fingers relaxed and, with a sigh as if all the air in him were escaping at once, he fell down into a deeper darkness. Falke heard a thump as he landed on stone.

He found Anatole a few moments later, sat in a lopsided chair, throat slit like a pig's, a pool of blood in his lap. His eyes were rolled up, showing only the whites. His coat had been ripped off and his shirt torn away, exposing his shoulder and chest. His skin was covered with little rat-like bites that bubbled blood.

He heard a musical laugh behind him… and was struck a blow on the head.

He was woken up by water on his face.

It was raining on him.

Dawnlight was in the catacombs too. He must have been out for hours.

He felt his throat. The collar was gone. He could find no wounds.

Had he been spared?

He got to his feet, unsteady. He found Raoul's improvised stake and used it as a walking stick.

'Michel,' shouted someone.

A man's voice. He was relieved.

'Raoul? Where are you?'

'In the shadows,' he replied. 'I can't come into the light.'

'What? Why?'

'Come here, Michel... here...'

His head throbbed, from the blow and after-effects of drink.

What had happened? De Rosillon, Gio and Anatole were dead. Only he and Raoul had lived through the night.

And Caralin.

Where was she? Where had she been all this time?

'I've found her,' said Raoul, as if reading his mind. 'Down here, where the dark is deepest.'

Falke went to his friend. He saw an outline in the murk. Raoul's face, eyes bright.

A lucifer flared and Raoul lit a candle. He was standing by an open trapdoor.

He indicated that they should go down a level.

Falke followed the candle as it descended. They went down a narrow, sloping passage walled with wet stone blocks. Iron rings were set into the stone at intervals.

The passage fed into a crypt.

All around were coffins in niches or open tombs. Only a few scraps of bone remained inside.

'What happened?' asked Falke.

'She killed them,' said Raoul. 'Killed them and drank their blood.'

'Caralin?'

'Who else?' said Raoul, bitterly. 'Admit it, you knew all along... When she was away, the vampire was active. Her strange pallor, that thing with her voice, the way she gets in your head and turns you around. The place she comes from! Styria – well-known as the hunting ground of Mircalla Karnstein. Her very name...'

'I don't believe it,' said Falke.

Raoul stood over a tomb, holding up a candle.

'You don't,' said Raoul. 'Then look...'

Caralin lay in the tomb, hands folded on her chest, blood on her mouth.

Falke felt fire in his head.

'She killed our friends,' said Raoul, 'but what she did to us is worse... she's *changed* us.'

Candle flames danced in Raoul's eyes. He opened his mouth to show new fangs.

Only one thing was to be done.

Falke speared Caralin through the chest.

She groaned and her eyes popped open... She coughed and a bloody rag came out of her mouth.

As he worked the spar through her, he saw her hands and feet were bound with stout string.

Her eyes were angry, then empty.

Raoul swore, and spat out his fangs.

'Why didn't you stop him, you fool?' shouted de Rosillon, stepping out from behind a screen.

'He was too quick,' said Raoul, aghast.

Anatole dashed in and tried to pull out the stake, which was stuck too tight.

'That's hardly any use,' said de Rosillon.

'What's happened?' said Gio.

Falke saw red paint on his friends' necks, wounds made of flaps of fabric gummed on.

'Michel's killed a vampire,' said de Rosillon.

'Caralin?' said Gio.

'Yes, her. Who else?'

He could not get what Raoul had told him out of his head.

She had changed them, he said. Caralin had made vampires of them.

That – like everything else – was supposed to be a joke, a prank on him. But it felt true. In the catacombs under the Hôtel d'Autriche, he became a monster.

Raoul's fangs were from the joke shop, but the chill in Falke's heart was profound. He could feel his bones rearranging.

Nothing for it but to put her into the Seine, de Rosillon said.

No one else knew her in Paris. She never mentioned any family. She'd be just another unknown woman.

She was smiling as she slipped under the waters.

'I suggest we all leave town for a while,' said Raoul. 'Let things simmer down. It was a ghastly mistake, and we'll have to live with the consequences…'

'I shall sing a mass for poor Caralin,' said Gio. 'Several.'

'This can't come out,' said Anatole. 'We'd be ruined. Michel would have it the worst. Disgrace, prison, the guillotine. We have to help him. It's for his sake.'

'I agree,' said de Rosillon. 'We must help Michel.'

'In time, we can come back,' said Raoul. 'And put this unfortunate incident behind us. A student prank that turned out to be not so funny, eh? It's the time of our lives when such things are *de rigueur*.'

Garron, the best actor and most honest man in *Le Gang*, was sent to tell Van Helsing they had destroyed the vampire. Cringing with shame, he reported that the Professor believed him. He was not sure about Madame Van Helsing, but she would keep quiet to preserve her husband's reputation. It was in nobody's interests that this story got out.

So, the vampire was done away with… and *Le Gang de Schubert* was dissolved.

It would be twenty-five years before Falke came back to Paris… as the monster they had made of him. To avenge Caralin, he would revive the fear of the vampire in the city that ignored her in life but made her a totem – and an icon – in death.

XVI

DR FALKE WAS so terrified by the apparition that Unorna could feel the psychic backwash from outside the room. She went cold with *someone else's* fright.

This house was permeated with fear and rage, and shame and cruelty. It had shouted at her in the courtyard, before La Marmoset picked the front door lock. It was worse inside. How could others *not* feel it? Most people didn't, she knew... it was as if they were deaf or blind from birth and never understood the sense they were missing.

For all its horrors, the house in Rue des Martyrs had no ghost. Not until now...

La Marmoset, the dead-alive image of *L'Inconnue de la Seine*, came as a shock to the man they knew to be the vampire murderer... but Falke had expected her for years. He had even been piqued that the dead woman cared little enough to haunt him. Along with terror was strange joy, a *hope* of some outcome beyond imagining.

Falke had confessed to killing Caralin Trelmanski. He wouldn't be the first murderer to stay in love with his victim. Did he see this revenant – La Marmoset wearing that sad smiling face – as a chance to take back what he had done?

No, it was stranger than that. Falke's story was more of a tangle.

From what Madame Van Helsing said and the scraps of clues La Marmoset put together, Unorna had an idea of what had happened twenty-five years ago to drive the man mad.

Even now, with a corpse in the bathtub and a good friend barely saved from a hideous death, she felt sorry for Falke. He wasn't a true vampire, just a tinkerer with an inescapable mania for revenge. Against his friends, whom he held responsible, but against himself too – for willingly believing what he was led to believe, for acting out of a deep-seated urge to kill the woman he loved. Unorna understood that the black seed was in him all the time. That he thought Caralin a vampire was an excuse, not a motive. The impulse to hurt or kill was there already.

Michel Falke sat on his piano stool, just staring.

La Marmoset glided across the floor – taking tiny steps under her long dress – and reached out. He gripped her wrist and pressed his cheek against her hand.

Unorna stepped into the room.

Sophy was wrapping a torn strip of cloth around her scratched hand. She was otherwise unharmed.

The corpse in the bathtub was Inspecteur d'Aubert.

'What do we do with him?' Unorna asked.

Sophy drew a thumb across her throat.

Unorna wasn't sure she was ready to go that far. Sophy already had the beginning of a retinue of ghosts – smoky, indistinct, unindividuated. Her kills, either spirits or memories. The more ghosts there were, the more likely it was that Sophy would sense them. She wasn't as spirit-blind as La Marmoset or Madame Van Helsing. Eventually, she would feel their unwelcome touch.

There were consequences beyond the legalities. Murder was not good for what was called *karma* in the East. Unorna had qualms about coldly executing this murderer, though he would doubtless go to the guillotine if handed over to the police and courts. She didn't want Sophy or La Marmoset to add to burdens which could become crushing. Killing his friends hadn't made Falke better. He was more a wretch now than before.

'There must be another way,' she said.

La Marmoset stood back from Falke.

He slid off the stool and rat-scurried across the floor, reaching for a peculiar black device: a leather bag with steel-tipped tentacles.

'Don't let him use that,' said Sophy, sharply. 'It's the vampire-machine! It's how he kills them.'

Too late! Falke hugged the thing to himself, and jammed two spikes into his own throat. The bag began churning and writhing. Some device inside was pumping.

A dribble of blood came from a long, trailing tube.

Unorna and La Marmoset tried to wrestle the device off him, but he held on tenaciously.

Even Sophy joined the effort.

Falke coughed, spitting blood. The spikes were fish-hooked deeply into his neck.

They managed to get Falke off the floor and onto a divan.

'There must be a switch,' said La Marmoset.

She tugged at tubes, but the contraption kept working. The floor was slick with blood.

Unorna sensed other presences in the house. Not ghosts, but perhaps not fully living people, either. Shadow-folk… masks.

She heard a susurrus of hissing.

In the doorway stood the Countesses Dorabella, Clarimonde and Géraldine. They wore flimsy, immodest gowns and were barefoot, but it was obvious they were dangerous.

They might file their teeth and sharpen their nails. Or else they grew fangs and claws.

Quick as cats they were, and just as nasty when crossed.

'Stand down, Angels,' said Countess Dorabella. 'We're here for him.'

La Marmoset turned to them. The face of *L'Inconnue* gave them pause.

'It's just a woman, dressed up,' said the Countess Géraldine. 'That detective.'

Sophy had a gun in her hand. The Countesses laughed at that.

'*Les Vampires* hired us too,' said the Countess Dorabella. 'We are neglected by a brute of a husband, and must lower ourselves to paid employment. They set you to catch the murderer and us to hunt the Black Bat of the Rooftops. It turns out our quarries were the same.'

'We found him first,' said the Countess Géraldine.

'We found him best,' said Sophy.

'We will take him from you,' said the Countess Dorabella. 'He is ours.'

'We'd like to see you try,' said La Marmoset.

All three Countesses hissed through bared teeth at that. Unorna saw they were strong, heartless and determined.

And out for blood…

So, she decided to give it to them.

She picked up the gushing outflow tube of the vampire-machine and aimed it like a hose. A jet of blood squirted across the room. She played it across the Countesses' faces. It got in their mouths, their eyes and their hair. It striped across their gowns, which clung stickily to them.

The effect was extraordinary.

The Countesses' eyes seemed to come alight with red flame. Suddenly, they were mad – like kittens doused with burning oil. They shrieked and tore at each other, licking and biting and frothing.

La Marmoset and Sophy hauled the shaking Falke upright. Unorna was able to direct the fountain blood more squarely on the Romanian women.

Savage Carpathian she-wolves would have served each other more mercifully.

The Countess Dorabella had the Countess Clarimonde's eye out; the Countess Géraldine's mouth was clamped around a red weal on the Countess Dorabella's upper arm, teeth worrying the wound; the Countess Clarimonde had her talons out and was shredding the back of the Countess Géraldine's gown.

Falke, incidentally, was a dead weight.

Nothing more could be done for him... or to him.

'There's a way out through the roof,' said Sophy.

They left Falke and the Countesses in their bloody mess and hurried upstairs.

La Marmoset took off her wig and peeled away the face of *L'Inconnue*. For a moment, Unorna saw her real face – unmemorable as it was – but as she walked along the passage she applied paint and freckles to create a new mask. An unfamiliar woman emerged – a secretary or shopgirl.

Sophy lingered a moment by a rack of cloaks, helmets and devices.

'His wings,' she said. 'And other things we could use.'

A noise from below suggested the Countesses might have settled their differences and tired of the stale blood of the dead. They would be coming for a reckoning.

'Angels with wings,' mused La Marmoset.

The Countesses, spattered with blood, were at the end of the passage.

Sophy took a bat-winged ball from a rack, twisted its top, and pitched it. It burst to release clouds of thick, foul smoke. The Countesses choked on it.

Leaving behind the rest of Falke's gear, Unorna, La Marmoset and Sophy made it up through a skylight onto the roof.

The sun was rising. Unorna had an idea this would confine the Countesses – night-birds, or bats or whatever – to the shadows of the house. They could pursue no further. When they recovered from blood delirium, they might or might not want to take up the fight again. She thought it most likely they'd tell themselves it was a draw and leave well enough alone. The Angels would have new stratagems to deal with them if they pressed the matter.

'Is it over?' asked Sophy.

Unorna looked to La Marmoset.

'This is an act curtain,' said the Queen of Detectives. 'But the opera never ends.'

XVII

THE CAFÉ SAINT-FLOUR Musette, once the haunt of *Le Gang de Schubert*, had become better known as the Brasserie des Martyrs, patronised by Baudelaire and Vallès. Now, it was the Divan Japonais, decorated in a supposed Japanese style which strayed all over the Orient. The crockery was Chinese willow-pattern. The waitresses wore hobbling kimonos. Tiny trees grew out of porcelain pots. Paper lanterns hung from the ceiling.

La Marmoset thought it appropriate to have this meeting where she now knew the story began. Dr Falke's house was only a few minutes' walk from his old watering hole. He had never really got beyond his student days.

As befits a Phantom, Erik hadn't deigned to communicate since the conclusion of the case, but the Persian assured the Angels that their patron was pleased with the outcome. He didn't hold the deaths of two baritones against them. The Opéra could always find more baritones.

The Grand Vampire had no cause to complain. He had hired the O.G.A. to stop Inspecteur d'Aubert's campaign against *Les Vampires*. Being dead, he was no longer making a nuisance of himself. Inspecteur Bec, his replacement, was a more live-and-let-live policeman. If *Les Vampires* didn't bother him, he was inclined to leave them alone too. The Sûreté had learned its lesson. It was a devil to make charges stick when witnesses suddenly became scarce and even the sorely aggrieved were unwilling to co-operate in cases against the organisation.

Unorna showed Sophy how to take tea in the Japanese fashion. The young woman was well travelled. In Falke's house, she had impressed La Marmoset. At a point when the methods of detection – the rational vision of the world espoused by Madame Van Helsing – were of limited use, her sensitivities came into their own.

The Countesses had left Paris. Apparently, a terse note signed with the letter D had been delivered to the House of de Rothschild Frères, terminating their line of credit. They packed their long trunks, leaving behind heaps of new clothes in lieu of a settlement of their hotel bill, and took an express train to Transylvania to await punishment when their master came home.

Dr Geneviève Dieudonné arrived late in the afternoon, just as the sun was setting. Ayda Heidari, representing *Les Vampires* in an unofficial capacity, joined the party soon after. All the masterminds – Erik, the Grand Vampire, the brains of the Sûreté – were happy to move on and not think about *l'affaire du vampire*. It was left to the women to put the last pieces of the puzzle together.

'The case is still open,' said Dr Dieudonné. 'With Bec in charge, I doubt there'll be new developments. I performed Raoul's autopsy, and – thanks to your report – can at least put the method of murder on the record. They showed me that mechanical blood-sponge device, but wouldn't let me cut it up to see how it works. It'll end up a curiosity in some museum of horrors.'

'What about Falke's body?' asked La Marmoset.

'That's a bit of an issue, actually,' said Dr Dieudonné. 'It wasn't where you left it. Most of the evidence you described – the mechanical wings, the masks and cloaks – were gone.'

'He was dead,' said Sophy. 'I'm sure.'

'Are you a qualified coroner?'

'No.'

'Then you're not sure. Though you're probably not wrong. You won't be surprised to learn the most popular theory with the sensationalist press is that the Vampire Black Bat of the Rooftops can't be killed.'

'He's not up there anymore,' said Ayda. 'We would know.'

'There was some delay in having the police go over the house,' said Dr Dieudonné. 'Possibly, other official bodies got there first and rooted around in Falke's treasury of inventions. In which case, in a year or two, Moroccan rebels will learn to fear flocks of night-flying Foreign Legionnaires.'

'I knew we should have taken some of his toys,' said Sophy.

'Do you really want a flying Phantom?' asked Ayda.

Sophy shrugged. La Marmoset knew Sophy was taken by the notion of flight. Falke had offered her wings. She would always wonder what she had missed.

Probably, a painful fall to Earth after the fashion of Icarus.

Even if *Die Fledermaus* was still somehow alive, he was finished with Paris. La Marmoset had put together most of the story and understood what had driven him mad – his own culpability as much as his friends' cruel joke.

'What about her?' asked Unorna.

The Witch pointed to the wall where, between snarling Japanese demon masks, hung a bas-relief of *L'Inconnue de la Seine*… unknown no longer, if only within their limited circle.

Caralin Trelmanski.

'Shouldn't we say who she was?' suggested Sophy.

'We know her name,' said La Marmoset. 'But we don't know who she was. Unorna and I don't use the names we were born with.'

'Or the face, in your case,' said Unorna.

'But that doesn't make us unknown. As *L'Inconnue*, she's famous… as Caralin, she'd just be nothing. The victim of a prank.'

'More than one prank,' said Dr Dieudonné. 'I looked for her. At the Morgue, we have had several bodies on ice for decades… she isn't one of them. After her face became famous, she was lost. I hate to think of what kind of admirer would steal her, but such things happen. It may be she was taken away to preserve her from the *badauds*. Falke may have done it, to give her a proper burial or keep her as a memento in a trophy room we've not yet found.'

'Or she could have walked away,' said Ayda. 'And there are such things as… vampires.'

Dr Dieudonné smiled over her tea.

'She had a stake put through her heart,' said La Marmoset. 'Traditionally, that keeps vampires in their place.'

'According to the autopsy report, Falke bungled the impalement,' said Dr Dieudonné. 'He was a law student not a medical student. He shoved his stake through her *lungs*. Nasty way to die, for a human being…'

'If there are vampires, your group should change its name,' La Marmoset said to Ayda. 'You came out best this time, with a Black Bat of the Rooftops for competition. If you were up against a Mircalla Karnstein or a Lord Ruthven, who knows how it would have ended?'

'We were confident of success,' said Ayda.

'Why?' asked La Marmoset.

'Because, for once, *Les Vampires* were watched over by Angels.'

Entr'acte: The Case of Mrs Norton

'IRENE ADLER,' SAID the Persian.

'Irene Norton,' said the woman who had sat at his table. 'I'm a married lady, now.'

'I'd heard. My congratulations.'

'Thanks.'

The Café de la Paix was busy, as ever. It was the hour when he accepted approaches. The Opera Ghost Agency had nothing much on, and the current Angels – Ayda Heidari, Ysabel de Ferre and Hagar Stanley – were idle. That was not good for them – or Paris.

He smiled to see Irene. She was, he admitted, one of his *favourites*.

But she was not expected.

'Was there not an... *understanding* between you and Monsieur Erik?' prompted the Persian. 'You were to confine your activities to other countries?'

'I'm married. I'm through with *activities*.'

'A fine point. Not one I would want to argue with our patron.'

Irene frowned. Her perfect mouth almost pouched into a moue.

She was older, of course. As was he.

Everyone got older – with a few mysterious exceptions, like the Countess de Cagliostro ... and the Phantom of the Opera.

The Persian understood Erik had stolen something from the Khanum which froze him in time.

It wasn't just the tiny traceries around Irene's eyes and the tighter corset. She was different. Her way of speaking was changed.

No longer an American eagle, she was an Englishman's wife. A Norton.

The Persian had followed her career, of course. Erik had him keep track of all the Angels, fallen or flown. Cuttings books were maintained. Irene had triumphed modestly as a singer, and immodestly as an adventuress. He knew of her liaisons with crowned and uncrowned heads, her coups in Europe and the Americas. She had amassed and lost several fortunes.

But all that was apparently done with. The cuttings book could be closed.

The Persian had been surprised to read notice in the London *Times* of her marriage to an English solicitor of no particular distinction.

Geoffrey Norton. No, *Godfrey* Norton.

That was that. *Finis* to Irene Adler.

Irene Adler had been the toast of Europe, *habituée* of courts, palaces and great opera houses. Mrs Godfrey Norton would queen it over a villa in a London suburb. Irene Adler made demands of ambassadors and princes. Irene Norton would approve menus and keep an eye on the servants. Church on Sunday morning, and roast dinner on the table after.

And children. Lots of brats, taking after the father – handsome, but running to fat.

'I am not in town to tread on toes,' she said. 'God – my husband – has taken a position in Paris. With Liddle, Neal & Liddle, the bankers. He doesn't know about the *understanding* and, speaking plainly, wouldn't understand it.'

'The mists part,' said the Persian. 'You announce your presence and wish to petition for leave to stay?'

'Mists be damned, *Daroga*. I wish to petition Erik... as a client.'

The Persian ordered another pot of coffee.

'It's God, of course,' said Irene. 'I'm sure he's keeping something from me. Something secret.'

The Persian lifted an eyebrow.

This Angel had fallen indeed. The Irene Adler he knew would not permit a man to keep secrets from her.

Of course, any man who could get Irene to marry him must be quite a character. The Persian hadn't thought there breathed a man extraordinary enough to pull wool over her eyes, to give her the runaround she had given men in the life she said she was through with.

The English had songs about birds in cages – the sort of sentimental nonsense Erik wouldn't consider music. Surely Irene's eagle wings could not be clipped by something as mundane as marriage?

'Something criminal?' he prompted.

'Something diabolical,' she said. 'It must be. He's so calm. So sure of himself. So sure of *me*.'

'What does he know about...'

'My *past*? Everything.'

'*Everything*?'

'Everything. Well, except... a few things he wouldn't understand. Things he wouldn't believe. You know what I mean.'

'Yes.'

'I heard the Agency chased a vampire a few years ago. That sort of thing.'

Irene lit a cigarette.

'What do you know about *his* past?'

'What is there to know?' she said, puffing. 'He's an English solicitor. He went to a school. He played something called rugby football. He joined a respectable firm. He has several aunts. I've met them. They're authentic.'

'And his present?'

'After that business with the King of Bohemia, I had to quit England. We were newly married. God proposed we extend our French honeymoon and looked for a job here. Liddle, Neal &

Liddle have a Paris branch. They needed someone to handle legal affairs. Boring transactions. Deeds and bonds and the like. God speaks French, by his own lights. So we're here.'

'*Bienvenue à Paris*.'

'Ha ha ha. That's exactly how God speaks French.'

The Persian saw Irene was as close to distraught as she could be. She finished her cigarette as if setting a record and started another. If any other woman – lately married, but a few months beyond the honeymoon – were to sing him this song, he'd assume her husband had taken his first mistress and advise her to pick up a fencing teacher or an unpublished poet.

But no one – not even an English solicitor – would marry Irene Adler and take a mistress.

The woman was one of the original trio. Perhaps the cleverest, most devious operator ever attached to the Agency. Subsequent Angels all pressed him for memories of her. In tight spots, they asked, 'What would Irene Adler do?' Ysabel de Ferre, who didn't care for *anyone*, wanted to grow up to *be* Irene Adler.

Irene had fought Countess de Cagliostro and walked out on the Opera Ghost Agency... outshot all comers in Buffalo Bill's Wild West Show and stolen A.J. Raffles's cufflinks from the shirt he was wearing... matched wits with Professor Moriarty *and* Sherlock Holmes, and got the better of both of them... gone up in a balloon and down in a submarine, and set the fastest time from Berlin to Warsaw in a Benz Motorwagen... been courted by plutocrats and pirates... had crown jewels pressed on her as keepsakes by besotted royals and showed spirit by tossing them into north Italian lakes. She had played many sides against each other and taken trick after trick for her own.

A husband who could deceive her was more than extraordinary.

Godfrey Norton must be scarcely human. No man at all.

'He's done nothing suspicious. Nothing at all. You see what I mean?'

'That's what makes you suspicious.'

'I knew you'd see it. People like us see it. Others don't. Innocent men seem guilty. All the time. Guilty men don't. And even they have tells. I've known enough of all sorts. Fools and villains, dupes and geniuses, innocent and guilty.'

Irene hadn't changed that much. She was not a fluttery wife, jealous of every pretty shopgirl.

She was angry, but cool. Angry with herself for being put in this position, but not so furious she'd make more mistakes.

She would not be driven mad. She would not stay at home and watch the wallpaper fade.

After masterminds and monsters, she would not be bested by a *husband*.

'God never asks about before… about what I was, what I did. When I was an Angel of Music… and afterwards. My exploits and adventures. He knows, in a general way of knowing. But it's as if he's not interested.'

'Not interested in *you*? Is he – perhaps – of the other persuasion? You said he went to an English school. Many take wives to conceal such an inclination.'

'I don't mean *that*. He is interested in the bedroom mazurka, like all men. And his interests are aimed at women – at *me* – not some passing lad. Believe me, I've known enough menfolk to spot a three-dollar bill a mile off.'

'I had to ask.'

'You did.'

Irene found her cigarette case empty. The Persian had only cigars.

'What I mean when I say he's not interested in my past is that *he should be*. He should be *obsessed*… to distraction. Any man would be. I've known them ask so many questions I get bored and make up all sorts of foolishness. Just to get rid of them.'

'Surely, your husband is extraordinary?'

Irene shook her head. 'No. I had my fill of extraordinary. You get tired of it in the end. Don't you?'

The Persian didn't answer.

'I wanted an ordinary man. A fine man, to be sure. But not another damn genius... I love God for what he is. What I thought he was. What he cannot be. I've made a mistake...'

'Which is not like you.'

'No it isn't! Thank you for saying so. I've tricked myself. After tricking everyone else, it was the only thing left. Without meaning to, I've hooked someone so extraordinary I can't see the join of his mask. And he's hooked me, deep. Do you know what it takes to frighten me? To put the honest fear into people like us?'

The Persian thought a moment.

'Yes,' he said. 'I have an idea of what that might be.'

'Will the Agency take my case?'

Could this be a trick? Was Irene setting out to use the Opera Ghost Agency in some way? As an alternative or a preliminary to divorce or mariticide? Were she and this Norton working some scheme against Erik? Against her successor Angels? Against *him*? He did not think so. He had seen her lie often enough to think her sincere now.

'I shall advise it,' he said.

'I'll be here tomorrow.'

'Irene, this is Ayda Heidari,' said the Persian. 'She's a vampire.'

'The rooftop kind, not the bloodsucking bat kind,' said Ayda.

'She was with *Les Vampires*, but is on the side of the Angels for the moment.'

Ayda smiled. The young Peruvian was quick-witted and had good instincts. The O.G.A. were fortunate to have her while she was deciding what to do next. She had acquitted herself well in the Matter of the Aquarium Abductions and the Mystery of Roger Mariette.

'I'm pleased to meet you,' said Irene.

Ayda was in awe of Irene Adler.

'I am Mrs Norton,' Irene said.

'Erik thought it best not to unloose the whole of our present troika on your husband. Not at first. Ayda, if you would…'

Ayda nodded and looked down at her hand like a policeman giving evidence in court. Angels didn't take notes, but Erik taught memory tricks. Ayda liked the invisible notebook device.

'It'll take a few days' watching to be sure of his routine, but yesterday your husband left the offices of Liddle, Neal & Liddle on Rue de la Pompe at five o'clock precisely and walked to the apartment you have on Avenue Victor Hugo. He stopped only…'

'…to buy me flowers. I know.'

'…to buy flowers. I assumed they were for you.'

'God's not a petty cheat, Mademoiselle Heidari. He's cleverer than that.'

'He spent the evening at your apartment. The lights went out at…'

'I know when.'

'Monsieur Erik likes us to be thorough in every detail.'

'I know that too.'

The Persian saw Irene was cool towards Ayda. He suspected she'd like the sharp-witted, fiercely moral, beautiful gypsy Hagar even less and the amoral, determined, imaginative Ysabel least of all. Odd – she had liked Christine and Trilby, *her* Angels. All of Erik's recruits were unique, so she should not feel herself forgotten and replaced. But each of the women would be reminders of what Irene Adler had been.

It hurt to see Irene in distress.

'While you were asleep, your husband got up for a few minutes. He used the water closet. He did nothing else.'

Irene nodded.

'It's not suspicious,' said Ayda. 'He is English. He drank much tea with your evening meal.'

'I've never said God wasn't English.'

Ayda was cowed. She was reluctant to say more.

'Go on, Ayda,' said the Persian. 'What else?'

'Not much. This morning, Mr Norton got up, dressed, shaved, breakfasted, kissed you and went to work. He has the English papers delivered to his office, also *Le Figaro* and *Le Matin*. I believe he is working to improve his French.'

'You *are* a super sleuth.'

'No,' said Ayda, tartly, 'that would be Miss Stanley. I am a spy. I *was* a thief.'

Irene was being snippy.

'I brushed against your husband last night and took his wallet,' said Ayda. 'It contains nothing incriminating, unless you count a portrait photograph of you as *La Belle Hélène* in Warsaw. I gave him back the wallet this morning.'

'He didn't miss it.'

'He wouldn't. I substituted a leather pad of the same size and weight.'

'You're a cunning little vixen.'

'We're all clever, Mrs Norton. The question is whether we're clever enough. Clever enough for you. And clever enough for your husband.'

Irene seized on that.

'You think he's hiding something?'

Ayda nodded. 'Of course.'

'And your *evidence*?'

Irene was almost angry, as if she now wanted to defend the husband she had turned Ayda loose on.

'You,' said Ayda. 'You think he hides things from you, that he has secrets and dark purposes...'

'Yes?'

'...and all I know about you suggests you are usually right. You see what I don't. You're in the room with him, not shinned up a drainpipe outside the window. If you think he's false, that's evidence enough for me.'

Irene blew smoke. She showed her old steel.

'You are darn tooting right, Mademoiselle Heidari. Ayda. I needed to hear someone say it out loud.'

'I recommend that Hagar looks at Liddle, Neal & Liddle. They look respectable enough, but they're bankers and therefore likely to be bigger crooks than the vampires I used to run with. Do you think your husband's secret is to do with his business?'

Irene chewed it over. 'It would be dull if it were. I don't see God as an embezzler or pedlar of crooked stock.'

'Men like him are the best at it, Irene.'

'You are good,' said Irene, directly. Earlier, she had been cold. Now, the Persian saw she meant it.

'I also suggest that Ysabel take a run at him, if you've no objections.'

'She is your… ah, seductress?'

'Ysabel de Ferre, Duchess of Jorsica,' said the Persian. 'Though good luck finding the place on a map.'

'I know her by reputation.'

'She has one of those, all right.'

'So had I.'

'I don't mean Ysabel should throw herself at Mr Norton,' said Ayda. 'Just see if she can *intrigue* him. Is he intriguable?'

'I should think not. I've intrigued him. He'll stay intrigued.'

'Ysabel likes a challenge.'

'You know I once beat Annie Oakley and Frank Butler in a shooting contest? The best shots in the world, or at least in Buffalo Bill's Wild West Show.'

'I had heard that.'

In Dressing Room 313, the Persian read aloud the account in the *Illustrated London News*. He liked to keep Irene's legend alive.

'Shooting isn't my game. Intrigue is. If I can beat the best in something that *isn't* my game, how likely is it that I can be beaten in something which is?'

Irene was even teasing now.

'I didn't mean to suggest…'

Irene laughed. 'I'm not offended. Let your doxy drop handkerchiefs and lift her hem and pop her blouse buttons for all the good it'll do. God stays on my side… of the bed.'

The Persian hoped Irene would not come to regret becoming a client of the Agency.

* * *

After three weeks, the Persian knew more about Godfrey Norton than his own brother did.

The Englishman had done nothing dishonourable in his life.

Given a prime opportunity by Ysabel to do something dishonourable, he made his excuses, put on a bowler hat and left. The Duchess had laid out the possibility for a financial coup as well as an afternoon's dalliance. Godfrey Norton sent a stern cable to the eighty-five-year-old 'Young Mr Liddle' advising the bank not to take on Ysabel de Ferre as a client.

He even told Irene about his brush with an *adventuress*.

Was he a new product of the *Système de M. Coppélius et Sig. Spallanzani*? The patent mechanical husband. Unless the doll-making process was very much improved, it was unlikely. Still, he had Hagar check up on the *fabricants de mannequins*. Both had died years ago. Another token of leaves falling from the calendar. Olympia, the Clockwork Angel, was still on display in Erik's lair. Occasionally, he would wind her up and have her dance. She was even useful to the Agency from time to time.

Irene came to the Café de la Paix for regular reports. The Persian looked forward to the meetings, but was always disappointed. When she wasn't there, he believed in the Irene of old... but when she was sat in front of him, puffing on cigarettes, it was a blow to the heart to see her so fractured.

She was not reassured by the progress of the investigation.

The more innocent Godfrey Norton proved to be, the guiltier he seemed to her.

Ayda, who had been following the man all this time, whispered that their home life was becoming chilly. The Nortons didn't argue, but didn't get on as before either. Mr Norton was puzzled, but patient. On his daily walk home, he stopped frequently at the florist's and the chocolatier to buy gifts. Then, he had a spring in his step, and quivered with what Ayda read as eager anticipation, but disappointment waited at his hearth. Only he was too polite and decent to let it show to Irene.

Even in this state, he wasn't tempted by Ysabel – who was furious enough to want to be off the case entirely.

Ayda reported that she might as well drop the boy's clothes and oversized caps she'd been wearing. Godfrey Norton didn't notice women who weren't his wife. Ayda could wear a can-can dancer's costume and walk three paces behind him for weeks and he wouldn't turn round to see who was rustling feathers.

Hagar went over the books of Liddle, Neal & Liddle – abstracted from their offices as a special favour to the Agency by Ayda's old comrade, Irma Vep of *Les Vampires* – and found not a centime in the wrong column. The gypsy was a genius with figures, and – without setting eyes on handsome, upright Godfrey – cultivated a platonic admiration for the bank's beautiful books, with their infallibly correct tallies and carry-overs. If Hagar Stanley had her way, Godfrey Norton would be put in charge of everything to do with money. When this case was resolved, she would move her personal accounts to the firm of Liddle, Neal & Liddle.

The Angels found nothing to Godfrey Norton's discredit.

Irene frowned. And bought more cigarettes.

The Persian had only one recourse. He sent a telegram to another alumna of the Opera Ghost Agency, now re-established under her own shingle.

'La Marmoset is the greatest detective in Europe,' said the Persian.

'Really?' said Irene, stubbing out a cigarette. 'What can you tell from this ashtray?'

'That you smoke too much,' said La Marmoset.

The woman who had joined the Persian and Irene at his table in the Café de la Paix did not look like anyone he'd ever met before. She had short, dark hair and large, tinted spectacles. She carried an umbrella with a fox-head handle and wore a long red coat.

'Mrs Norton has concerns about her husband,' said the Persian.

'Husbands,' said La Marmoset, biting down on the word.

'Just the one,' said Irene.

'I was referring to the species, not the specimen,' said La Marmoset. 'Little good comes of husbands.'

Evidently, the memory of Mr Calhoun was still fresh.

'You have been beaten?' ventured La Marmoset.

'No,' admitted Irene. 'Not at all.'

'Robbed?'

'Decidedly not.'

'Deceived with other women?'

'I wouldn't need a detective if that were the case.'

La Marmoset smiled. 'No, you would need Sophy Kratides…'

Irene knew the name. 'The assassin? No. I wouldn't *hire out* murder.'

'Nor should you. It's inefficient.'

'I don't want God killed,' said Irene.

'God?'

'Godfrey Norton,' explained the Persian. 'Her husband.'

'You married God? All women think so, then discover the Devil in their home.'

'Are you married?' asked Irene.

'Not at present.'

'But you have been?'

'Yes. I'm sorry to say.'

'Then you'll understand. It's not that God has done anything… has given cause for suspicion… has ever been anything but transparent and kindly and loving. It's that…'

'Yes, I understand perfectly.'

Officially, Mr Calhoun had abandoned his wife and disappeared.

The Persian was unnerved by the way Irene and La Marmoset were together. They stoked each other's fires.

'May I have a cigarette?' asked the detective.

After a month, La Marmoset turned in her report and her resignation.

'I thought there was no such thing as a blameless husband,' she said. 'I was wrong. I have torn up my bill. There is no mystery to solve.'

Irene was near tears.

La Marmoset apologised again and left the café.

The Persian attempted to comfort Irene.

'He is a monster,' she said. 'He must be.'

Nothing would break her conviction.

Even the Persian now saw only freakishness in Godfrey Norton's decency.

It must be a mask.

The Angels, skilled and dispassionate, had drawn a blank. La Marmoset, predisposed to think the worst of husbands, had failed.

'I hesitate to bring it up, but Erik has a suggestion. A last resort, as it were, but still a resort.'

'Anything,' said Irene.

The Persian didn't want to say more, but Erik had spoken.

'If you will consent to be hypnotised…'

Irene was horrified. The Persian knew how she felt about submitting to a mesmerist's will. It was why she had left the Agency.

'Under the fluence, Erik can sort through your memory,' said the Persian. 'He can turn up things you know that you do not know you know. You may have seen a clue others have missed. Ayda, Hagar, Ysabel, La Marmoset. They're talented, but you're closer to Godfrey. Something in the picture of your life together is wrong – a splash of dark where there should be colour. Erik can help you find it. He has done it before, with clients. I have seen a man sketch in detail a face glimpsed and forgotten years before. A woman recall in accurate particular the figures set down in a ledger which lay open on a desk in a room where she was attacked. In both cases, crimes were exposed and criminals brought to justice because of this.'

Irene was still unhappy about the idea.

In her day as an Angel, Erik used his skill to control his protégées – to make dolls of them. If he had set aside such methods, it was at least partially because using hypnotism meant he could not have Irene – or anyone with her spirit – as an agent.

It was only with her departure that the Persian realised Erik *could* change his mind.

Yet, the matter had come up again. Did Erik relish the chance to bring his errant Angel to book, to make her submit to him?

For Irene, the loss of control was terrifying. Perhaps the most terrifying thing she could think of.

But, in the end, she agreed.

The Persian wished that she hadn't.

In Dressing Room 313, Irene sat before the long mirror. It was strange to see her back here.

The Persian turned off the electric light. A plain oval mask appeared in the mirror, lit from below, floating in the murk beyond the glass.

'Irene,' said Erik, the voice coming from everywhere in the room.

'Erik.'

'You are welcomed.'

'Thanks,' she shrugged. 'Big of you to let me back in your country.'

Erik chuckled without warmth.

'You must relax, Irene. You must not resist.'

'Must I not?'

'Your resistance is for show, I know. We are old friends, are we not? You have decided to let me help you. Please do not pretend you are unwilling.'

Irene looked at the Persian.

Should he stop this? Could Erik really help her?

Music began. A piano piece. A phonograph of one of Satie's *Gymnopédies*. The Persian recognised the style of play. Erik had taken to recording himself on wax cylinders. He retained a love for novelties and gadgets.

'Am I feeling sleepy?' asked Irene, mocking. 'Can I see the swinging watch?'

Could a mask frown?

'Just look into the mirror and let the mirror look into you. Listen to the music, to the music between the notes...'

The Persian felt himself lulling away and scratched a thumbnail across his palm. He knew better than to let the Phantom bewitch him.

Irene looked at the mask in the mirror. Her hands fell into her lap. Her eyes did not close.

Irene's face was ghostly in the mirror, superimposed on Erik's mask. Relaxed, she looked younger, more like her old self.

She was 'under'.

'You have cause to suspect your husband of hiding shameful thoughts and deeds from you,' suggested Erik.

'No,' answered Irene. 'Not at all.'

The Persian was surprised. Irene had been so certain.

'Godfrey Norton has done nothing to make you suspicious of him?'

'He has not.'

'He is completely devoted to you and to your marriage?'

'He is.'

'Godfrey Norton loves you?'

'Yes.'

'He is an honest, industrious man, who thinks only of making a home for you, and of the family you will have?'

'Yes.'

'You will have a family? Children?'

No answer.

'You have no reason – *no reason at all* – to doubt Godfrey Norton?'

'No.'

'Have you a reason to doubt yourself?'

No answer.

The Persian was heart-sick. Irene Adler had left their world –

the world of exploits and adventures – for marriage and family. For love and happiness. To be Irene Norton.

And for Irene Adler, that wasn't enough.

She couldn't admit it to herself, and that had driven her to… something like madness. For Irene, mere *ennui* was a nightmare.

The Satie continued.

'Irene,' said Erik, raising his voice.

Irene's hands rose to her face.

'What? What did I say?'

'Irene, you are right,' said the Phantom. 'You must leave at once, leave Godfrey Norton, leave your apartment, leave Paris.'

'Leave God?'

'You know this. You have always known this.'

'Yes.'

Irene was not jittery anymore.

'What is it?' she asked him. 'What did I tell you?'

'Terrible things,' said Erik. 'Unspeakable things.'

She smiled tightly. 'I knew it. It had to be.'

'You have a way out,' said the Persian. 'Money, papers?'

'Of course,' she said, half-smiling. 'I never go into a room without knowing the ways out. Always have an exit prepared. Do you still teach your Angels of Music that, Erik?'

Erik said nothing.

Irene stood. Her posture was different. She was alert again, electric.

'Allah be with you,' he said.

She kissed him on the cheek and left the dressing room.

The Persian turned on the light and made the mask vanish.

'It was the only answer she would hear,' he said to the man behind the mirror. 'You have helped her.'

The phonograph recording finished.

The Persian was alone in Dressing Room 313.

'You are the Persian?' said the Englishman.

'I am *a* Persian.'

The Café de la Paix was busy, as ever. It was the hour when he accepted approaches. 'You are who I have to see to... to hire the Opera Ghost Agency?'

He looked up at the man. He knew him at once.

'It's my wife,' the man said. 'She's missing.'

The petitioner hovered, not wanting to sit at the table until invited.

The Persian was sorry for him. But only one answer was possible.

'I regret that we cannot take your case, Mr Norton.'

Act Three: Guignol

'Slitting a throat ... it's like peaches and cream.'

Oscar Méténier, *Lui!* (1897)

I

I F NOT FOR the masked juggler, one might miss Impasse Chaplet. In such a gaudy district, it would be easy to walk past the ill-lit cul-de-sac, even with footprints stencilled on the pavement. Once, the red trail was enough to lead those 'in the know' to the *Théâtre des Horreurs*. Now, a less exclusive audience required more obvious signposts.

When lone tourists wandered into this *quartier*, basking crocodiles slid off mudbanks to slither after them, smiling with too many teeth. Kate Reed knew better than to stroll along Rue Saint-Vincent after dark, peering through her thick spectacles at grimy signs obscured by layers of pasted-up advertising posters. Holding a Baedeker's Guide open was like asking for directions to the city morgue in schoolgirl French.

She walked briskly, as if she knew exactly where she was going – a habit learned as a crime reporter. Montmartre struck her as less vile than the Monto in Dublin or Whitechapel in London. *Les Apaches* had a swaggering, romantic streak. It was put about that the crooks of Paris tipped *chapeaux* and kissed hands when robbing or assaulting you, seldom stooping to the mean, superfluous twist of the blade or kick in the ribs you could expect from an Irish lout or an English ruffian...

...though, of course, she was here because of a string of

unromantic disappearances and ungallant murders. The 'superfluity of horrors' promised by the playbills was spilling off the stage into the streets. On the map, red 'last seen in the vicinity of' and 'partial remains found' dots clustered suspiciously around Impasse Chaplet. The Sûreté shrugged at a slight rise in unsolved cases, so a local tradesmen's association – which, at a guess, meant an organised criminal enterprise ticked off by poaching on their preserve – placed the matter in the hands of the Opera Ghost Agency.

Looking around for suspicious characters, she was spoiled for choice.

Strumpets and beggars importuned from doorways and windows. Barkers and panderers even stuck their heads out of gutter-grates, talking up attractions below street level. Here were cafés and cabarets, bistros and brothels, poets and painters, cutpurses and courtesans. Drinking, dining, dancing and damnation available in cosy nooks and on the pavement. Competing musicians raised a racket. Vices for all tastes were on offer, and could be had more cheaply if the mademoiselle would only step into this darkened side-street…

Montmartre, 'mountain of the martyr', was named after a murder victim. In 250 AD, Saint Denis, Bishop of Paris, was decapitated by Druids. He picked up his head and climbed the hill, preaching a sermon all the way, converting many heathens before laying down dead. Local churches and shrines sported images of sacred severed heads as if in gruesome competition with the *Théâtre des Horreurs*.

A troupe of nuns sang a psalm, while a superior sister fulminated against sin. As Kate got closer, she saw the nuns' habits were abbreviated to display legs more suited to the can-can than kneeling in penitence. Their order required fishnet stockings and patent leather boots. The sermon was illustrated with lashes from a riding crop – a chastisement eagerly sought by gentlemen for whom the punishment was more delightful than the sin.

A solemn gorilla turned the hand-crank of a barrel organ. A monkey in a sailor suit performed a jerky hornpipe. The ape-man's chest-board proffered an art nouveau invitation to the *Théâtre des Horreurs*.

His partner – face shaved and powdered so that at first you might take it for a human child – wasn't happy. The monkey's arms were folded like a jolly tar's, sewn together at the elbows and wrists. The stitches were fresh. Tiny spots of blood fell. The creature's tail was docked too. It wasn't dancing, but throwing a screaming fit to music.

A busker who so mistreated a dumb animal in London would be frogmarched by an angry crowd to a police station, though he could do worse to a real child and have it taken all in good fun.

She slipped a small blade out of her cuff – she had come prepared for this expedition – and surreptitiously sawed through the string which tethered the monkey to a *colonne Morris*. The creature shot off between the legs of the crowd, ripping its arms free, shedding clothes. The ape-man gave chase, clumsy in his baggy costume, and tripped over a carefully extended parasol.

Kate looked up from the parasol to its owner, who wore a kimono decorated with golden butterflies and a headdress dripping with flowers. Her sister Angel of Music had abetted her intervention. They weren't supposed to acknowledge each other in the field, but exchanged a tiny nod. As ever, Yuki presented a pretty, stone face. Kate would not have suspected softness in the woman, but remembered monkeys were worshipped in Japan.

As Yuki walked on, Kate instinctively looked for her other shadow – and saw Clara frowning disapproval from across the road. The third Angel was strange, even by the standards of the English. Yuki's background was outside Kate's experience or imagining, but she was easier to warm to than Mrs Clara Watson. The beautiful widow might be the worst person in this affair, yet she was also in the employ of an agency devoted – in a manner Kate had yet to determine – to the cause of justice.

Kate and Clara both had red hair. She guessed her colleague

was seldom bothered by lads cat-calling 'carrot-top' or 'match-head' at her. Kate kept her ginger mop short and tidied away under caps and bands. Clara let her luxurious, flaming mane fall loose. Kate had the plague of freckles which often came with her colouring. Clara's skin was milk with rose highlights, flawless as the powder mask Yuki wore on formal occasions. Six inches taller than her sister Angels, Mrs Watson gave the impression of looking down on them from a far greater height.

Still, they were required to perform as a trio. In the circumstances, Kate could put up with the worrying wench. One did not become an Angel of Music unless one had a past... usually an immediate past fraught with scandal, peril and narrow escape. They had all quit countries where they were settled and fetched up in Paris. Clara, an Englishwoman who'd never set foot in England, was long resident in China, but had fallen foul of some mad mandarin *and* the colonial authorities. Her field of interest was prison reform ... not in alleviating the sufferings of unfortunate convicts, but in heightening and aestheticising their torments. Yuki had come from her native Japan, where there was a price on her head. Of her crimes, she merely said she had 'settled some family debts'. Kate was on the wrong side of the financier Henry Wilcox. She had written in the *Pall Mall Gazette* about his penchant for purchasing children as 'maiden tributes of modern Babylon'. He was no longer welcome in his clubs – justice of a sort, though she'd rather he serve a long sentence in a jail designed by Clara Watson. Wilcox's writ-serving lawyers and hired bully-boys made London unhealthy for her this season.

Before quitting London, Kate secured a letter of introduction from the Ruling Cabal of the Diogenes Club to the Director of the Opera Ghost Agency. What the Club was for Britain, the Agency was to France: an institution, itself mysterious, dedicated to mysteries beyond the remit (or abilities) of conventional police and intelligence services. Status as a (temporary) Angel of Music afforded a degree of protection. She was grateful to be in the employ of an individual more terrifying than any colossus of capital. Those who'd happily see impertinent females skinned alive, beheaded by a Lord High Executioner or bankrupted by a libel suit thought twice about crossing Monsieur Erik.

Yuki casually tapped the pavement with her parasol – a fetish object she clung to after nightfall, though a stout British brolly would be more practical in this drizzle-prone city – and drew Kate's attention to the red paint footprints. The gorilla was the first living signpost on the route to the *Théâtre des Horreurs*. The prints – spaced to suggest a wounded, staggering man – led to the juggler, who kept apple-size skulls in the air.

The shill wore a *papier-mâché* mask. She had seen the face often the past few days – on posters, in the illustrated press, on children scampering in the parks, on imitators begging for a sou in the streets.

Guignol.

All Paris, it seemed, talked of the capering mountebank. Mention was made of his padded paunch, his camel's hump, his gross red nose, his too-wide grin, his terrible teeth, his rouged cheeks, his white gloves with long sharp nails bursting the fingertip seams, his red-and-white striped tights, his jerkin embroidered with skulls and snakes and bats, his shock of white hair, his curly-toed boots, his quick mind, his cruel quips, his shrill songs…

Kate understood Guignol to be the French equivalent of Mr Punch. Both were based on Pulcinella, the sly brute of Neapolitan *commedia dell'arte*, changed in translation. This incarnation should not be mistaken for any of his like-named or similar-looking ancestors. This Guignol was new-minted, essentially a fresh creation, a sensation of the day.

The juggler was not the real Guignol – if there even was a 'real' Guignol. He was skilled, though, keeping five skulls in the air.

He stood aside, not dropping a skull, to let Kate into Impasse Chaplet.

The racket of Rue Saint-Vincent dimmed in the cobblestoned alley. She heard dripping water and her own footsteps. What she first took for low-lying mist was smoke, generated by a theatrical device.

At the end of the cul-de-sac was a drab three-storey frontage. It could have been an abandoned warehouse, though gas-jets burned over the ill-fitting doors and firelight flickered inside.

Originally, the building was a convent school. The mob who attacked it in 1791, during the anti-clerical excesses of the Reign of Terror, were sobered to find nuns and pupils freshly dead amid spilled glasses of poison. The headmistress, intent on sparing them the guillotine, had ordered arsenic added to their morning milk. Since then, the address had been a smithy, a coiners' den, a lecture-hall and a sculptor's studio. Doubtless, the management of the *Théâtre des Horreurs* exaggerated, but the site's history was said to be steeped in blood: a duel between rival blacksmiths fought with sledgehammers; a police raid that left many innocents dead; a series of public vivisections ended by the assassination of an unpopular animal anatomist whose lights were drawn out on his own table; and three models strangled by a demented artist's assistant, then preserved in wax for unutterable purposes.

A dozen years ago, the impresario Jacques Hulot bought the place cheaply and converted it into a theatre at great expense. The bill offered clowns, comic songs and actors in purportedly amusing animal costumes. Patrons found it hard to laugh within walls stained with horrors. After a loss-making final performance, Monsieur Hulot slapped on white make-up and hanged himself in the empty auditorium. Cruel wags commented that if he had taken this last pratfall in front of paying customers, the fortunes of his company might have been reversed. The showman's adage is that the public will always turn out for what they want to see – a lesson not lost on the heirs of Monsieur Hulot, who transformed the *Théâtre des Plaisantins* into the *Théâtre des Horreurs*. A space unsuited to laughter would echo with screams.

Kate was not alone in the alley. Yuki had strolled past the juggler, but doubled back as if seized by idle curiosity. She joined a press of patrons who needed no bloody footprints to mark the way. Kate noticed their pale, dry-mouthed, excited air. These must be *habitués*. Clara should be along shortly. Kate let others surge ahead, towards doors which creaked open, apparently of their own accord.

A crone in a booth doled out blue *billets*. Admission to this back-street dive was as costly as a ticket for the Opéra. Freshly painted-over figures on an otherwise faded board indicated the price had risen several times as the craze took fire. Erik, a partisan of the higher arts, might bristle at such impertinent competition. Another reason the Opera Ghost Agency had taken an interest in *l'affaire Guignol*?

Ticket in hand, Kate stepped under a curtain held up by a lithe woman in a black bodystocking and Guignol mask. She joined an oddly solemn procession, down a rickety stairway to an underlit passage. One or two of her fellows – other first-timers, she guessed – made jokes which sounded hollow in this confined space. The smoke-mist pooled over threadbare patches in the carpet. She couldn't distinguish genuine dilapidation from artful effect.

Notices – not well-designed posters, but blunt, official-seeming warnings – were headed ATTENTION: THOSE OF A NERVOUS OR FEMININE DISPOSITION. Kate looked closer. THE MANAGEMENT TAKES NO RESPONSIBILITY FOR MEDICAL CONDITIONS SUSTAINED DURING PERFORMANCES AT THIS THEATRE... INCLUDING BUT NOT LIMITED TO FAINTING, NAUSEA, DISCOLORATION OR LOSS OF HAIR, HYSTERICAL BLINDNESS OR DEAFNESS, LOSS OF BOWEL CONTROL, MIGRAINES, CATALEPTIC FITS, BRAIN FEVER AND/OR DEATH BY SHEER FRIGHT AND SHOCK. Every poster promised NIGHTMARES GUARANTEED.

Two women in nurses' uniforms required that everyone sign (in duplicate) a form absolving the management of 'responsibility for distress, discomfort, or medical condition', etc. Uncertain of the document's legality, Kate folded her copy into her programme. Only after the paperwork was taken care of was the audience admitted into the auditorium.

It was about the size of a provincial lecture-hall or meeting-place. The chairs were wooden and unpadded. No one was paying for comfort. Unlike the grand theatres of London and Paris, this playhouse was not illuminated by electric light. The *Théâtre des Horreurs* was still on the gas. Sculpted saints and angels swarmed around the eaves. A relic of the convent school, the holy company was – after a century of alternating abuse and neglect – broken-winged, noseless, obscenely augmented or crack-faced. The house barely seated 300 patrons, in circle, stalls and curtained boxes.

Kate took her seat in the middle of the stalls, between an elderly fellow who might be a retired clerk and a healthy family of five – a plump burgher, his round wife and three children who were their parents in miniature. After the warnings and waivers, it surprised her that minors were allowed into the performance.

The elderly fellow was obviously highly respectable. He was tutting approval over an editorial in *La Vie Française*, a conservative Catholic publication, which breathed fire on all traitors to France. Treason was defined as saying out loud or in print that Captain Alfred Dreyfus, currently stuck in a shack on *Île du Diable*, was not guilty of espionage. To Kate, the oddest thing about the affair was that everyone seemed to *know* Dreyfus was innocent and that another officer named Esterhazy was the actual traitor. Papers like *La Vie*, published and edited by the powerful Georges Du Roy, still ruled it an insult to France to question even a manifestly wrong-headed decision of a military court. Dreyfus was a Jew, and the line the Anti-Dreyfusards took on the issue was virulently anti-Semitic. A military doctor pledging to a fund established to benefit the family of Captain Henry, who had committed suicide when it came out that he had patriotically forged evidence against Dreyfus, stated a wish that 'vivisection were practised on Jews rather than harmless rabbits'. Dreyfus, his novelist supporter Émile Zola and caricature rabbis were burned in effigy on street corners by the sorts of patriotic moralists who would denounce the *Théâtre des Horreurs* as sickening and degrading. The gentleman reader of *La Vie Française* could evidently summon enthusiasm for both forms of spectacle – unless he had come to lodge a protest against Guignol by throwing acid at the company.

She looked about, discreetly. Yuki was seated in the back row, presumably so her headdress wouldn't obstruct anyone's view of the stage. In England – or, she admitted, Ireland – a Japanese woman in traditional dress would be treated like an escaped wild animal. The French were more tolerant – or less willing to turn away customers. After all, Yuki was plainly not Jewish. Clara had wangled a box. Kate caught the glint of opera-glasses. It was only fair she get the best view: she was the devotee of *contes cruels*.

A small orchestra played sepulchral music. Refreshments included measures of wine served in black goblets marked poison and sweetmeats in the forms of skulls, eyeballs and creepy-crawlies. Kate bought a sugar cane shaped like a cobra and licked its candied snout. She was used to keeping an itemised list of out-of-pocket expenses. She trusted the Persian, Erik's representative above ground, was less of a fussbudget about petty cash than the editors with whom she was used to dealing.

A lifelong theatregoer, Kate had filed notices on the stuffiest patriotic pageants and the liveliest music-hall turns. She'd been at the opening night of Gilbert and Sullivan's hit *The Mikado* – which Yuki professed never to have heard of, though everyone asked her about it – and the closing night of Gilbert's disastrous 'serious drama' *Brantinghame Hall*. She knew Oscar Wilde, though she'd not yet found the heart to seek him out in his exile here in Paris. She'd laughed at the patter of Dan Leno and the songs of Marie Lloyd, stopped her ears to Caruso's high notes and Buffalo Bill's Indian whoops, gasped at the illusions of Maskelyne and fallen asleep during Irving's *Macbeth*. She'd seen a train arrive in puffs of steam and the Devil disappear in clouds of smoke at the *Salon du Cinématographe*. She did not expect to be much impressed by a French spook show.

The nurses took up a station at one side of the stage, joined by a tall man in a white coat. He had a stethoscope around his neck. Kate wondered if this 'doctor' ever had to do more than administer smelling salts or loosen tight collars. The warnings and the medical staff were part of the show, putting the audience on edge before the curtain went up. Not immune, she admitted a certain *frisson*. The smoke-mist was thinner in the auditorium, but her head was fuzzy. Opiates mixed with the glycol might account for 'nightmares guaranteed'.

The music stopped. The house gas-jets hissed out.

In the darkness... a chuckle. A low, slow, rough laugh. It scraped nerves like a torturer's scalpel.

Rushing velvet, as the heavy stage curtains parted. A drum beat began, not in the orchestra pit. With each beat, there was a squelch...

A series of flashes burned across the stage. Limelights flaring. Sulphur wafted into the stalls.

The scene was set: a bare room, whitewashed walls, a table, a boarded-up window.

The beat continued. A drum wasn't being struck.

A middle-aged woman lay face-down. A grotesque imp squatted on her back, pounding her head with a fire-poker. With each blow, her head reddened. Spatters of blood arced across the white wall...

Was this a dummy, or an actress wearing a trick wig?

The imp put his whole weight into his blows, springing up and down, deliberately splashing that wall. Kate even smelled blood – coppery, sharp, foul.

The imp flailed. Blood – or whatever red stain was used – rained on patrons in the first two rows. Kate had wondered why so many kept hats and coats on. A few were shocked, but the *habitués* knew what to expect. They exulted in this shower of gore.

Murder accomplished, the imp tossed away the now-bent poker.

The orchestra played a sinister little playroom march. The imp went into a puppet-like caper, as if twitching on invisible strings. He took a bow. Applause.

Guignol, in all his mad glory. Eyes alive in his stiff mask.

'A disagreement with the *concierge* has been settled,' he squawked.

His harsh fly-buzz voice was produced by the distortion gadget Punch and Judy men called a swazzle. It was rumoured that Guignol, whoever he was behind the mask, had his swazzle surgically installed. When he laughed, it was like Hell clearing its throat.

Already, before the show had really started, Guignol's costume was blood-speckled.

'Welcome, pals, to the *Théâtre des Horreurs*. We've much to show you. We are an educational attraction, after all. For the world is wild and cruel. If you are alarmed, upset or terrified by what you see, tell yourself it is fakery and sham. If you are bored or jaded, tell yourself it's all real. Many have said they would die for a chance to go on the stage – how heartless would we be not to grant such wishes?'

It was only a mask. If its expression seemed to change, it was down to shadows etched into the face by limelight. But the illusion of life was uncanny.

Guignol was the theatre's third mask, rudely pushing between the Tearful Face of Tragedy and the Laughing Face of Comedy.

The Gloating Face of Horror.

Erik, who spoke with musical perfection from behind a dark mirror, was also masked. Could this whole affair be down to a squabble between false faces? The monsters of Paris contesting the title of King of the Masquerade?

Stage-hands carried off the limp, dripping *concierge* – who bent in the middle like a real woman, rather than a dummy.

The list of the disappeared contained several women who

might have been cast as a *concierge*. However, it would take a degree of insanity compounded by sheer cheek for a murderer to commit his crimes before paying witnesses. There must be a trick she wasn't seeing.

Now, Guignol sat on the edge of the stage and chatted with the front row, advising patrons on how to get stains out, admiring hats and throats and eyes. He slowly turned his head, an unnerving effect inside his mask, and looked up at Clara Watson's box, blowing her a kiss. He leaped to his feet, did a little graceful pirouette, and flourished a bloody rag in an elaborate bow.

Was the clown on to the Angels? Kate couldn't see how. He was probably just playing up to whoever had bought the most expensive seats in the house.

'Now, heh heh heh, to the *meat* of the matter... the *red* meat.'

Iron latticework cages lowered from the proscenium, each containing a wretched specimen of humanity. The cages were lined with spikes. Chains rattled, groans sounded, blood dripped.

Guignol set the scene with, 'Once upon a time, in the dungeons of Cadiz...'

Tall figures in black robes and steeple-pointed hoods dragged in a young man, stripped to the waist and glistening, and a fair-haired girl, in a bright white shift...

By now, Kate understood the *Théâtre des Horreurs* well enough. Whenever she saw white on stage it would soon be stained red.

'There was a plot, once,' Guignol continued. 'A wealthy young orphan, a devoted lover, a cruel uncle who held high office, a false accusation, a fortune for the coffers of the church if a confession could be extracted. Scenes dramatised all this. Lots of chitter-chatter. But we have learned it is wasteful of our energies to go into that. Really, what do you care whether an innocent's gold coins be diverted to dry sticks of priests? The preamble is stripped away here, for we understand you want to reach this scene, this *climax*, as soon as possible. And so our piece *begins* with its climax, and then...'

The youth and the girl were clamped into cages and hauled aloft. The girl uttered piteous cries. The youth showed manly defiance. A canvas sheet was unrolled beneath the hanging cages.

Braziers of burning coals were wheeled on stage. A burly, shaven-headed brute in a long apron entered. An eye-patch didn't completely cover the ridged scarring which took up a third of his face. Shouts of 'Morpho *bravo*' rose from all corners of the house. A popular figure, evidently. Morpho grinned to accept applause. He unrolled an oilskin bundle on the table, proudly displaying an array of sharp, hooked, twisted, tapered implements. Picking up Guignol's cast-off poker, he straightened it with a twist – exciting more cries of approval – then thrust it into a handy fire.

'Which to torture first?' Guignol asked the audience. 'Don Bartolome or Fair Isabella?'

'Maim the whore,' shouted someone from the circle. 'Maim all whores!'

'No, open up the lad, the beautiful lad,' responded a refined female voice – not Clara, but someone of similar tastes. 'Let us see his beautiful insides.'

'What the hell, do the both of 'em!'

This audience participation was like a Punch and Judy show, only with adult voices. The caged actors looked uncomfortable and alarmed. No stretch, that. According to the programme, the roles of Isabella and Don Bartolome were taken by performers called Berma and Phroso. Few in the company cared to give their full names.

Morpho took out his now red-hot poker and applied the tip to the callused foot of one of the background victims, who yelped. Claqueurs mocked him with mimicked, exaggerated howls of sympathy pain.

No one on stage in the *Théâtre des Horreurs* could frighten Kate as much as their audience.

'You, Madame,' said Guignol – tiny bright human eyes fixing

on her from deep in his mask – 'of the brick-red hair and thick shiny spectacles… which is your preference?'

Kate froze, and said nothing.

'Bartolome, Isabella, the both… neither?'

She nodded, almost involuntarily.

'A humanitarian, ladies and gentlemen. A rare species in this quarter. Madame… no, *mademoiselle*… you are too tender-hearted to wish tortures cruel on these innocents, yes? Would you care to offer yourself as substitute? Your own pretty flesh for theirs? We have cages to fit all sizes of songbird. Morpho could make of you a fine canary. You would sing so sweetly at the touch of his hot hot iron and sharp sharp blades. Does that not appeal?'

Kate blushed. Her face felt as if it were burning already. The elderly gent beside her breathed heavily. He looked sidewise at her as if she were a Sunday joint fresh from the oven. His pale, long-fingered hands twitched in his lap. Kate wished she could change places so as not to be next to him. She looked to the plump family on her other side – Morpho supporters, to the smallest, roundest child – and was perturbed by their serene happiness.

'So, *mademoiselle*, would you care to join our merry parade?'

Kate shrank, shaking her head. Morpho frowned exaggeratedly, sticking out his lower lip like a thwarted child.

'I thought not,' snapped Guignol. 'There are limits to humanitarianism, even for the best of us.'

Guignol stood between the hanging lovers, hands out as if he were a living scales.

'Confession is required from Isabella, before she can be burned as a witch and her properties seized by the church,' he explained. 'I think the most ingenious means of eliciting such a statement will be… to push in her beloved's eyes with hot sticks!'

Morpho jabbed his poker up into Don Bartolome's cage… twice.

The stink of sizzling flesh stung Kate's nose. The young man's cries set off screams from Isabella and quite a few members of the audience.

Red, smoking holes were burned in the young man's face.

...or *seemed* to be. It *must* be a trick.

Isabella sobbed and collapsed in her cage, then rent her hair and shift in shrill agony. She was too horror-struck to sign a confession – a flaw in the wicked uncle's plan. Though, as Guignol had said, the audience didn't really care.

They were all just here for the horror.

Morpho considered a medium-size set of tongs, then shook his head and selected the largest pincers. Cheers and hoots rose from his partisans.

Kate couldn't look away but didn't want to watch. She took her glasses off, and the spectacle became a merciful blur... but she could still hear what was happening.

Putting her glasses back on, her vision came into focus just as a long string of entrails and organs tumbled out of Don Bartolome's opened belly, then dripped and dribbled and dangled...

Just sausages in sauce, she told herself. The *Théâtre des Horreurs* bought pigs' blood and horses' offal in bulk from the local slaughterhouses.

And so it went on. The scene changed, and other 'plays' were presented. Simple situations which allowed for atrocities. In a gloss on Edgar Allan Poe's 'The System of Dr Tarr and Professor Fether', Morpho returned as a maniac who takes charge of a madhouse and trephines his own head-doctor. Isabella and Don Bartolome were done with, but Berma and Phroso came back with other names to be violated and abused all over again: as harem captives of a cruel Eastern potentate; passengers sharing a lifeboat with hungry sailors, drawing lots as to who would be eaten when the rations ran out; a brother and sister sewn together by gypsies who needed a new star attraction for their failing freak show. Kate fancied that Berma, though luminous in suffering, was a little bored with it all, but handsome, wild-eyed Phroso was eager for each new indignity.

He all but begged for the knife, the flail and the cudgel.

Early in the evening, Morpho did the heavy lifting, but his energies flagged as Guignol became more animated, more active. The maestro personally wrestled a bear, throttled a baby, killed the King of Poland...

Saint Denis interrupted the proceedings, his disembodied head preaching against the immoral spectacle. Guignol snatched the head and booted it into the wings, blowing a spectacular, swazzle-assisted raspberry. What was it about Paris and severed heads? From Saint Denis to Dr Guillotine, the city had decapitation on the brain.

The saint's headless body blundered comically and was hauled off by a music-hall hook. Since the usual neck-yank was out of the question, the hook had to snag him by the midriff.

Kate checked her programme. No interval was promised.

II

KATE GOT HER fill of horrors. The elderly gent in the next seat kept his eyes on the stage, but – under cover of his folded *Vie Française* – let his hand wander to her knee. She touched the back of his hand with the point of her tiny blade, prompting a swift withdrawal. The roué didn't take rejection in bad humour. He licked a blood trickle – a darker shade than the stuff spilled on stage – from the shallow cut. He was lucky not to have been seated next to Yuki. She'd have cut off his hand and dropped it in his lap.

The last act was more like conventional drama than the succession of gory spectacles which made up the bulk of the evening's entertainment. Someone must actually have written it.

Members of the company posed as *statues vives*, on display in a waxworks. Guignol acted as guide, recounting crimes which earned respectable-seeming gentlemen and ladies sobriquets like

Ripper, Razor, Poison Marie, Black Widow or Werewolf. This scene transformed as the figure of murderer and corpse-molester Bertrand Caillet came to life and crept into a graveyard to clutch the throat of a lingering mourner.

In a change of pace, Caillet was played by Phroso, given the chance to slaughter instead of being slaughtered. Memory of the actor's earlier sufferings lingered, making his monster pathetic if not sympathetic. The date was 1871. The arrest and trial of the madman was black farce, carried on during the fall of the Paris Commune. So many committees and sub-committees were in session, debating the aims and achievements of the Commune and its increasingly desperate defence, that no official courtroom could be found. Caillet's case was heard in a disused horse-butcher's shop. Witnesses, lawyers, policemen and victims' relatives were called or dragged to the barricades as the Army of Versailles retook the city. Offstage fusillades rattled those giving testimony. Caillet's confession was interrupted as pitched battle spilled into the makeshift courtroom, leaving the shop floor splashed with human blood. The skirmish done, Caillet resumed a stuttering account of his crimes and compulsions.

Guignol cavorted and chortled through *la Semaine Sanglante*, the bloodiest week in the bloody history of Paris. Caillet's homicidal mania was a trifle amongst greater, more cynical horrors. Most of his 'victims' were dead when he got to them. He strangled two or three, but found the results unsatisfactory. Fresh-killed was too dry for his tastes. To prick his amatory interest, a corpse had to have the sheen of rot. Meanwhile, one hundred hostages, including priests and nuns, were executed on the orders of the Committee of Public Safety. In reprisal, the victorious army murdered thirty thousand – the innocent, the guilty, the uninvolved, anyone who was passing.

To Kate, it seemed every one of the deaths was enacted on the tiny stage. Berma appeared as the Spirit of Liberty, tricolour sash barely wound across half her torso, and was shot down. She danced at half-speed to the drum-rattle of rifle discharges.

Ribbons of thin, scarlet stage blood splashed around. The orchestra played 'La Marseillaise' out of tune. The *prima diva* of horror – who had been earlier tortured, violated, shocked, throttled, mutilated, dismembered, disfigured and degraded – received wild applause for her last death scene of the evening. Even Morpho's claque joined in. Funeral garlands were thrown on the stage. Without breaking character, Berma died under a pile of black and red flowers.

This piece was closer to home than mediaeval dungeons or exotic locales of Guignol's other horror tableaux. 1871 was within the memory of much of this audience. They'd lived through the Commune, lost friends and relatives, suffered wounds. In all likelihood, some of the moneyed, middle-aged folk up in the circle had taken part in the slaughter. A pack of bourgeois women had poked a dead Communard general's brains with their umbrellas, while regular army officers arranged the efficient execution of whole districts.

As the barricades fell, the bickering Committee of Enquiry into the lunacy of Bertrand Caillet remained in session. Proceedings were disrupted by fist-fights, a duel, assassination and the purge. Through an error of transcription, a Monsieur Dupond was thrown before a firing squad convened for a Monsieur Dupont. *Enfin*, the senior judge – who'd absent-mindedly signed the death warrant of the Archbishop of Paris while listening to Caillet's confession – proclaimed *himself* insane in a vain attempt to evade his own executioners. When Guignol took the judge's head, no one was left to rule in the case of the sad, forgotten prisoner. A venal turnkey (Morpho) let Caillet go free.

The dazed maniac was drawn by his lusts to his old stamping grounds. Caillet arrived at Père Lachaise Cemetery as the last of the Commune's National Guard were put against its wall and shot. No one paid the amateur of murder any attention, except a guard dog which bit him as he was rooting in a grave for a sufficiently putrid corpse. The ragged ghoul succumbed to this festering, untreated wound and joined the pile of corpses.

At last, Guignol – who played the guard dog himself – was making a point; albeit while dancing in entrails and tearing the eyes out of dwarves, nuns and a disapproving censor. If Bertrand Caillet was a monster on the strength of his crimes, what was to be said of the politicians and generals who could have a hundred people – a thousand, thirty thousand, a million, ten million! – eradicated at the stroke of a pen? The *tableau vivant* returned, but poisoners, stabbers and stranglers were replaced by politicians, judges, officers, priests and newspaper editors. Their hands were red with stage blood.

The human waxworks went unnamed, but Kate recognised many. The Minister Eugène Mortain, famous for surviving corruption scandals and maintaining a dozen mistresses at the public expense; the examining magistrate Charles Pradier, who vowed to restock *Île du Diable* with journalists who argued the innocence of Dreyfus or the guilt of Esterhazy; General Assolant, recalled from Algeria after a run of harsh police actions and put in charge of the Paris garrison to maintain public order; Père de Kern, confessor to government and society figures, and reputedly the most depraved man in France, though always humble in public; and Georges Du Roy, publisher of *La Vie Française*, *L'Anti-Juif* and the children's story paper *Arizona Jim*.

Solemnly, Guignol passed amongst the wax monsters, awarding each a rosette and ribbon, inducting these worthies into the *Légion d'Horreur*!

Kate hadn't expected the detour into political agitation, if indeed this was that. How was Guignol getting away with it? Newspaper offices were burned to the ground and journalists submitted to the system of Dr Tarr and Professor Fether for less. For an institution eager to make powerful enemies, the *Théâtre des Horreurs* was surprisingly *un*-persecuted.

Even before the attack on the people best placed to have the place shut down, the programme seemed calculated to offend *everyone* – Catholics (especially Jesuits), Protestants (especially Freemasons), Jews (no surprises there), atheists and free-thinkers, conservatives, moderates, radicals, anyone not French enough, anyone not French at all, the medical profession, the police, the law, criminals, cannibals, the military, colonialists, anti-colonialists, the halt and lame, circus folk, animal lovers, people who lived through the Paris Commune, the friends and relatives of people who failed to live through the Paris Commune, women of all classes, drama critics.

In a city where a poetry recital or a symphony concert could set off a riot, this house was tolerated so completely that she sensed an invisible shield of protection. Was the *Théâtre des Horreurs* so profitable it could afford to bribe *everyone*? Including the Paris mob, who were notoriously easier to stir up than buy off.

In parting, Guignol sang a song whose last refrain was – loosely translated – 'If these shadows have offended, you can all go stuff yourselves!'

The curtain came down. Thunderous applause.

'I didn't like it at the end, Papa,' said one of the fat round children. 'When it made my head hurt from thinking.'

The fat round father fondly cuffed the lad around the ear.

'There, that'll take the ache away.'

Guignol poked his head out of the curtain to take a last bow.

After some minutes of capering and farewell, Guignol departed and the house lights came up.

III

THE SHOW LET out after eleven o'clock. Kate kept her head down and made for the *Sortie*.

To escape the theatre, she had to run a gauntlet of minions in Guignol masks hawking souvenirs: Toby jugs with Guignol features; phials of authentic *Théâtre des Horreurs* blood; postcards of the stars in sealed packets so you didn't know what you were getting (how many leering Morphos did a collector have to buy to secure that elusive bare-breasted Berma?); tin swazzles seemingly designed to drive parents to acts of infanticide suitable for dramatising next season; and enamel pins with Guignol faces or bloody pulled-out eyes.

Succumbing, she purchased a profusely illustrated pamphlet featuring photographed scenes, with diagrams showing how effects were done. It might come in handy in the investigation. She was convinced a connection existed between the crimes in the streets and the crimes on the stage. It was as if the real horrors extended the argument of the *Ballade de Bertrand Caillet*. Doubtless, victims didn't care much whether they were killed to make a philosophical point or just plain ordinarily murdered.

Leaving by a side door, she saw a cluster of devotees around the artists' entrance. Some wore amateur horror make-up as if hoping to audition: dangling eyeballs, running sores, vampire fangs. A *mec* in a short-sleeved sailor shirt showed off a raw tattoo of Guignol's grin. Others wore cheap masks and competed – despite their lack of swazzle – to imitate Guignol's voice. A tipsy toff in evening dress struggled with a huge bouquet of black roses. Kate suspected Stage Door Jeannot was an admirer of the much-abused Berma. He looked more like the recipient than the disher-out of consensual floggings.

Back on Rue Saint-Vincent, she clocked Yuki's headdress bobbing in the distance. She paused a moment to consider her options. They were supposed to make their separate ways back to the *pied-à-terre* the Persian had rented for the purposes of the investigation. Kate had memorised a few routes.

Ideally, she'd have liked a stroll by the Seine to clear her head. The *Théâtre des Horreurs* was overwhelming. An evening with the smell of offal, that funny smoke and packed-in patrons would make anyone light-headed, even without the parade of tortures.

She passed gay cafés and cabarets, but horrors had soured her outlook. Her glasses weren't rose-coloured, but blood-smeared. Music and laughter sounded shrill and cruel. Pretty faces seemed cracked and duplicitous.

Guignol peeped from posters. She thought she saw him in the crowd. It wasn't unlikely. Many cardboard masks were sold in Impasse Chaplet.

She took precautions against being followed, as much for practice as genuine caution. In the front door of a restaurant and out through the kitchens – even a glimpse was enough to dissuade her from going back for a meal – and a quick change on the hoof. She reversed her distinctive check jacket to show anonymous green.

She found a table in the corner of a busy courtyard and ordered *anisette*.

No one tried to pick her up, which was obscurely depressing. If she could sit by herself in a French café and not be bothered, she must be a fright indeed.

She was thirty-two. No age at all… though her soonest-married school friends had nearly grown-up daughters and sons. As an unmarried, 'unconventional' woman, she was accustomed to importunage on a daily basis – in England, let alone Paris. Being Kate Reed was like being a coconut in a shy. Every other chap thought it worth a throw. If the shot went wide, no harm done, old girl. The 'respectable' gents were bad enough – the husbands of her school friends, or even their fathers – but the men who made her skin crawl were the firebrand stalwarts of causes she supported – Irish home rule or women's suffrage – who felt she owed them a tumble because they said the right things on platforms. From now on, she would recommend that these pouncing comrades take a run at Clara Watson, connoisseur of exquisite tortures.

An accordion played. The performer was the image of a music hall Frenchman, down to the beret and waxed moustache – though he'd left his string of onions at home. He was wringing out the 'Valse des Rayons' from Offenbach's *Le Papillon*. Space in the courtyard was cleared for a couple to enact the famous *apache* dance. A slouch-hatted, stripy-shirted rough slung his long-legged partner about in a simulation of violent love-making, in time to repetitive, sinuous music. The *fille* alternately resisted the crude advances of her *garçon* and abased herself in front of him. Throughout, a lit cigarette dangled from the corner of the man's mouth. He puffed smoke rings between cruel kisses. Even dances in Montmartre involved punches, slaps, knees to the groin and neck-breaking holds. The girl pulled a stiletto from her garter, but the *mec* snatched it away and tossed it at a wall. It embedded in a poster of Guignol.

Kate sipped her *anisette*, which stung her nose and eyes as well as her tongue. It was but a step from this anise-flavoured, watered cordial to absinthe. Which led, popularly, to syphilis, consumption and death.

The dancers finished, and were clapped. They collected coins. Kate gave the girl a sou and hoped the bruises under her powder were from overenthusiastic rehearsal.

The point of Guignol's Caillet play was that horror was unconfined. Not limited to one madman, not on one small stage. It was all about, all-pervasive, in the statues of Saint Denis toting his raggedly severed head and the ritualised domestic abuse of the *apache* dance. The Reign of Terror and the Commune were done, but Guignol's Chevalier de la Légion d'Horreur were ensconced in positions of power. Georges Du Roy could throw honest ministers to *les loups* but maintain Eugène Mortain in office. Riots erupted whenever the Dreyfus case was argued. War with Germany was inevitable one week, then alliance with Germany against Great Britain was equally inevitable the week after. Père de Kern was appointed Inspector of Orphanages. Horrible whispers spread about his night-time surprise visits to his little charges, though even Zola didn't dare accuse him in print. A military coup which would have installed General Assolant as a new Napoléon had recently collapsed at the last minute. Kate liked to think herself a reasonable person, but she was working for a faceless creature who supposedly dropped a chandelier on an opera audience because he didn't like the casting of Marguerite in *Faust*.

Was it all in fun?

The horrors were certainly not confined to Paris. The British Mr Punch, Guignol's cousin, knocked his Judy about as much as any *apache* panderer did his tart… and killed policemen, judges and crocodiles. In the East End, Kate spent too much time with women nursing black eyes after trying to stop their old men blowing the rent money going on beer to find Punch and Judy shows very amusing. At least, the *apachette* fought back.

She looked about the courtyard. People were having a good time, even if their pockets were being picked. Despite the horrors, life went on, mostly merrily. Dance done, the performers were drinking together, the girl flirting with her partner and the musician. Kate's jangled nerves calmed, and she tried to shrug it all off.

The stiletto had been reclaimed from the wall. A tear-like triangular divot showed brick under Guignol's eye.

Kate thought about the eyes of Guignol, the living eyes in the *papier-mâché* face. She thought she'd know those eyes again. But would she, really? Guignol was in disguise when he took his mask *off*. He might be anyone.

The programme and pamphlet were no help. There were notes about Berma, Phroso, Morpho (a veteran disfigured by Riffs, apparently) and others. Even Dr Orloff, the resident physician, had a write-up. Guignol's biography was of the *character* not the performer. Guignol was himself, not who he had been… Jean-François Someone or Félix-Frédéric Whoever. Under Berma's photograph was a paragraph about her early life and career. She'd played in other companies, rising from Cleopatra's asp-delivering handmaiden to Juliet and Desdemona, before her engagement at the *Théâtre des Horreurs*. Under Guignol's picture was a list of crimes. Credited as writer and producer of the show as well as its proprietary spirit, he had sprung from nowhere to take over the remains of the late Monsieur Hulot's company.

The craze burned throughout Paris, exciting much commentary. W.B. Yeats, Gustav von Aschenbach and Odilon Redon hailed Guignol as a genius, though Kate would have laid money they wouldn't have him round for dinner. Paul Verlaine and André Gide lampooned Guignol as a fraud, though the inconsistent Gide also said he loved the imp like a brother. Léo Taxil had boosted the Mad Mountebank of the *Théâtre des Horreurs* in his periodical *La France Chrétienne Anti-Maçonnique*, then claimed to have *invented* Guignol... only to discover his creation had 'escaped into the wild'.

She was no wiser about the masked man.

Thinking about Guignol made her jittery. It was too easy to imagine that face – *those eyes* – looking at her from a dark corner or between a press of people. Kate still felt he, or someone wearing his face, was nearby... and could lay a hand on her at any moment.

Was that why she wasn't being preyed on? A greater predator had marked her as his own.

She poured the last of the water into the last of the *anisette* and drank up. Then she left, hurrying towards the rendezvous of the Angels.

Was she being followed still? Had she ever?

It was as if Guignol were waiting wherever she turned. In the limelight, up on a stage, his atrocities were often absurd. In spite of herself, she had laughed. In the dark, a step or two off the main street, the clown would not seem funny.

Kate felt a chill up one arm. She looked down and saw the sleeve of her jacket – and the sleeve of her blouse – had three long slits, as if claws of supreme sharpness had brushed her when she was distracted, cleaving cloth but not skin.

She heard the laughter of Guignol, but could not be sure it was in her head.

IV

MADAME MANDELIP'S *HÔPITAL des Poupées* was in Place Frollo, a triangular 'square' even further off Rue Saint-Vincent than Impasse Chaplet. The small shop was seldom open for business and got little passing traffic. The front window was crowded with dusty dolls. All the fixed smiles and glass eyes reminded Kate of her childhood playroom. She'd been afraid of the old-fashioned, slightly battered dolls her aunts kindly passed on. The effect of the frontage was deliberate – to ward off the curious. If there ever had been such a person as Madame Mandelip, she was long gone.

Kate was last home to the safe house. She rapped on the door, to the rhythm of the first line of 'La Donna è Mobile' from *Rigoletto*. She could never repress a smirk at the childish trimmings favoured by the overgrown boys of the Diogenes Club and the Opera Ghost Agency. Secret knocks, passwords, invisible ink and codes, not to mention false moustaches and – inevitably – masks. The blade up her sleeve reminded her she wasn't immune to the appeal of deadly play-acting.

The Persian let her in. He was Erik's cat's paw. Few took his master for more than a myth, but the Persian was familiar around the Opéra and the city, trusted to collate reports from the songbirds, often an intermediary or bill-collector. One theory was that he was a ventriloquist, and the mask behind the dressing room mirror simply an articulated puppet. Kate knew that wasn't true, but saw how the notion could get about.

Olive-skinned and unostentatious, the Persian was sometimes addressed as *Daroga*. That wasn't his name but a title – police chief. Erik and he had served the Mazanderan Court many years ago, though they were no longer welcome there. Far-fetched rumours of their doings in Persia had reached the Diogenes Club. Reputedly, Erik fled the Court with a potion of longevity stolen from the Khanum, the Shah's mother. That would explain how the Director of the Opera Ghost Agency seemed not to get older over the decades. Another fine wheeze for not seeming to age would be to wear a mask and seldom even show that in public.

Clara and Yuki took tea.

'So, ladies,' Kate asked, 'what did we think of the play?'

Clara Watson grimaced. 'I was bored... except for the eye-gouged dwarf. He was adorable.'

Yuki shook her head, rattling tiny bells set among her flowers. 'I did not understand much. There was no honour, just wasted effort. And to cut off a head... it is not so easy as they make out. Even with a sharp sword. The head does not come off like a doll's, at the merest love tap.'

Kate didn't want to know how Yuki came to have an expert's knowledge of decapitation. No, she corrected herself mentally, she *did* want to know. She wanted to know *everything*, even if uncomfortable and upsetting. That made her a good reporter and qualified her as an Angel of Music. Still, Yuki's history – a tale of blood and fire suitable for the *Théâtre des Horreurs* – was not her present concern.

She poured herself a cup of tea, and added milk and sugar – which made her a barbarian to everyone else in the room, except perhaps the dolls.

'Can't say I found the performance dull, myself,' Kate admitted. 'Though it did get a teensy wee bit monotonous after the fourth or fifth disembowelling. It was, in its own ghastly fashion, entertaining. Guignol, horrid though he is, has that *quality*. Whoever he might be, he's a star. At least in his own house. Grotesque, but a star. As for everything else... well, no one goes to the *Théâtre des Horreurs* for the stirring drama, the lavish sets, the witty scripts or even the acting – though, under the circumstances that's more convincing than is comfortable. The place says what it is in the name, and it's peddling a very old act. Gladiatorial combat to the death and public executions were entertainments once...'

'Only in Europe have those arts become lost,' said Clara. 'In China...'

Kate had heard quite enough from the English woman about the delightful pastimes of China.

The Persian intervened before the Angels fell to squabbling. He had his notebook open and a pencil in his hand.

'Miss Reed, Mrs Watson... in your expert opinion, did any real crimes take place on the stage tonight?'

'Only against art,' said Kate.

The Persian was pensive. Kate reckoned the management of the *Théâtre des Horreurs* actively encouraged rumours connecting the Montmartre disappearances with their show of horrors. Everyone in the performing arts knew the expression 'dying to please the public'.

'It is not Max Valentin's Canary Cage illusion,' said Clara.

Kate didn't know what she meant.

'Maximilian the Great is a stage magician,' Clara explained. 'A very inferior one. Most of his act is old tricks, borrowed or stolen and performed indifferently. He had one illusion, though, that puzzled his rivals. Magicians are competitive and take pride in seeing through sleights of hand or mechanical devices. Prizes were offered to anyone who could duplicate Maximilian's illusion. None could manage it. Max holds up a square-sided cage, in which a dear little canary sings, then folds the cage flat. Off comes the top. Down go the sides. Poof! The canary is gone. And yet the birdie sings again. Each night, from a different place – the back of the stalls, the cleavage of a female assistant, the pocket of a patron on the front row. Each night, a disappearance and an appearance.'

'I think I can guess the trick,' said Kate. 'Canaries are cheap, right?'

'Yes, that is it. In the end, the escape artist Janus Stark saw through it. The springs that collapse the cage are unusually powerful. Each night, a canary is crushed – killed in an instant. And another canary takes its place, only to have its moment in the cage at the next performance. Once word got out, Maximilian's bookings dried up. Europeans profess to be foolishly sentimental. For my part, I believe many canaries would choose a moment of public transcendence – singing and dying – over living on unheard. Before this evening, I entertained the notion – indeed, I hoped it was the case – that the *Théâtre des Horreurs* was offering a chance to make such an ascension. That would have been, in an oriental manner, magnificent. Reality, as so often, is a disappointment.'

Kate knew Mrs Clara Watson was no canary. She was too busy being absolutely cuckoo.

The Persian pressed his point. 'So, no harm is done in the performance?'

'Everything we saw was faked,' said Clara. 'Oh, animals died to supply meat for the trickery... but no human blood was spilled. Human blood has a particular tang, and a look that can't be mistaken. What we saw was conjuring – dollops of red paint slapped onto the face while the audience is distracted by Guignol's patter, thin strips of flesh-toned gauze pasted over fake wounds and torn off to let the stage blood show... and a great deal of shouting and straining.'

For a while, Kate had also tried to distance herself from Guignol's show by looking for the joins, trying to see how the illusions were accomplished. But the performance bombarded the audience with so many horrors it was impossible not to surrender, to cease caring about fakery and reality and just to react to what was there before you. She would remember Guignol, the Life of Bertrand Caillet and the *Légion d'Horreur*.

'I did wonder about the *concierge* whose head got bashed in at the beginning,' Kate said. 'She matches some descriptions on the list of the missing.'

'She came back as the dog-faced woman in the freak show segment,' said Clara.

That was one of the giveaways. Guignol's company was quite small. Parts were doubled, tripled, quadrupled and more. If Don Bartolome and Isabella were really murdered before the audience's very eyes, how did Phroso and Berma return as so many other doomed characters? A wild-eyed matron billed as Malita played the *concierge*, the dog-faced woman and the mourner attacked by Caillet. Actors were not as interchangeable as canaries.

'But *someone* is snatching people in the vicinity of Impasse Chaplet,' said the Persian. 'Witnesses attest this Guignol is almost always about when the crimes take place.'

'Guignol is a mask,' Kate said. 'Anyone can wear a mask. Especially in Paris. This city has more masks than Venice during carnival.'

'It's true,' said Clara. 'Guignol masks are everywhere.'

The English woman took a cardboard mask from her reticule and held it up in front of her face.

'They sell these at the theatre,' she squawked, trying to imitate Guignol's voice. 'For two francs.'

'It might be that the real Guignol is not only innocent, but the true culprit or culprits are trying to throw suspicion on him,' said Kate. 'Any place as successful as the *Théâtre des Horreurs* must have enemies. Attendance at Le Chat Noir and La Gaîté Montparnasse is down. One way to scare off audiences is to put it about that they're likely to be killed if they go near the Guignol show...'

'You don't understand people, Katie?' said Clara. 'Since the murders began, ticket sales at the *Théâtre des Horreurs* have soared. I'd argue that the *only* thing that makes paint spilled on that stage interesting is the association with blood spilled on the streets.'

'You're getting your personal proclivities mixed up with general principle, Clara. People are not all like you.'

'Oh yes they are, dear. Most just don't like to admit it.'

Kate looked at Yuki, who kept quiet for most of their discussions.

'You know what *she's* done,' Clara said. 'Yuki's more like me than I am myself. I've mostly watched. She's *acted*... That parasol of hers has put men in their graves.'

The Japanese woman sipped tea, without comment.

'You're the freak here, Katie.'

Kate blushed again. She held her cup tight.

'There now, see,' said Clara, sweetly. 'Wouldn't you like to slap my face silly? Perhaps take that spoon to my eyes? Break that cup and grind that china into my neck?'

The English woman simpered, as if she'd won an argument. Kate knew a lost cause – after all, she was Irish. She recognised a distraction too.

Yuki finished her tea and contemplated a pair of *apache* dolls, which she manipulated while humming. Daintier than the couple Kate had seen perform at the café, but still… in this affair, even children's playthings had slit-skirts and knives in their garters. Clara would say that was just honesty.

Lord, perhaps Clara was right? She was the freak, and *Guignol* was normal.

Nobody important – or even noticeable – had been killed yet, so there was no general outcry. The victims were drudges, drunks, old whores, foreigners and idiots. Corpses found in the river, the sewers or piles of garbage were rotten, and got at by rats, birds or fish. That parts were missing was expected. That victims were tortured before death was impossible to confirm. The police had other priorities.

'I don't understand the lack of press coverage,' said Kate.

The Persian and Clara shrugged.

'In London, a story like this would catch fire. It's not just the murders, but their proximity to the *Théâtre des Horreurs*. That would be a gift to a British editor. Think of it: an opportunity to take a lofty stand against the decline of public morals exemplified by the appalling spectacle of Guignol's show, while at the same time having an excuse to describe in lurid detail the atrocities on and off stage, with illustrations of Berma in torn clothes being prettily abused. It'd run for weeks, *months*. There'd be protests outside the theatre, questions in the House, bans on advertising, petitions for increased censorship. Of course, in London, the Lord Chamberlain would never allow anything like the *Théâtre des Horreurs*.'

'Now who's the cynic, Katie?'

'Paris can't be that much more blasé, Clara. Montmartre may

be *toujours gai*, but France has no shortage of bluestockings, hypocrites and moralists.'

'What are you suggesting, Miss Reed?' asked the Persian.

'A fix is in. I know how it works in Dublin and London. I doubt Paris is different. Newspaper proprietors are in competition with each other but belong to the same clubs. If they agree a story should be buried, it sort of goes away. No matter what reporters think or feel. Sit in the Cheshire Cheese in Fleet Street and any scribbler will give you a long list of startling stories he's had spiked. The owners horse-trade, of course. You don't cover my brother's arrest at a boy-brothel in Bayswater and I'll drop the investigation of the fraudulent stock company which lists you among the directors. We'll not mention the peaceful natives your old regiment massacred in the Hindu Kush... providing you spike the exposé of the gambling ring which paid my school's old boys' cricket side to drop easy catches three times in a row. A discussion between gentlemen. It's in the interests of gentlemen, which is to say the powerful, that things stay this way. I've read the French papers since I got here, and – though the battles between Dreyfusard and Anti-Dreyfusard factions are more bitter than any London press feud – I sense the same system running smoothly. If the "Guignol Murders" isn't a story – and that's the headline it'd get in Britain – then it's in the interests of well-placed individuals that it not be.'

The Persian looked at her closely. He had been quietly sceptical of her value to the Agency. The more usual Angel of Music, Kate understood, had Yuki's experience with head-severing or Clara's taste for blood. The rolls included adventuresses, amazons, girl wonders, savages and divas of diverse deviltry. She must seem an ink-stained step down from such formidable women.

But she had just demonstrated why Erik took her on.

'Do you have any theories as to who these "well-placed individuals" might be?'

'Funny you should ask... and funnier no one else has thought to, eh? As I said, I've been looking at the Paris press. I can't believe there's *really* a serious publication called *The Anti-Jew*, by the way. I've read society pages and the sensation papers, the heavy journals and the frothy dailies, the *échos* and the classifieds. The *Théâtre des Horreurs* gets surprisingly good press... it's an amusement, looked down on but talked about. A sight of Paris, like the Folies Bergère or that hideous ironwork erection on Champ de Mars. It gets poor notices from drama critics, of course – with some enthusiastic, if demented exceptions. I expect the management courts bad reviews. Who'd want to attend an *inoffensive* Theatre of Horrors? The matters that interest us – the murders – are never mentioned on the same pages as Guignol's gaggery. The connection which is so obvious to us, and to the people who have engaged the Agency, is ignored by the press and, as a consequence of what I referred to as "a fix", also by the police. Everyone knows of the crimes around the theatre, but it's down to us to look into them... that in itself tells you how well-placed our phantom – excuse me, our *other* phantom – might be.'

'Not just a newspaper proprietor, then?'

'No. We are looking at someone with political connections. Probably, this being as priest-ridden a country as my own, the Catholic Church too. Oh, and "pull" in the army. I imagine you can name someone who fits that bill.'

'She means Georges Du Roy...' said Clara.

Kate shrugged, not confirming or denying.

'...and his circle,' continued Clara. 'Mortain, Assolant, Pradier, de Kern?'

Prosper-Georges Du Roy de Cantel, once humble Georges Duroy, had risen from the ranks. This was literally the case – he had soldiered in the Franco-Prussian War, the action against the Commune and Algeria. Mustered out, he worked as a reporter, then became editor and – through advantageous marriage – proprietor of *La Vie Française*, an upper-middle class newspaper. He added publications to his empire, including the vicious *L'Antijuif*. Everyone made the effort to forget his late father-in-law, from whom he inherited *La Vie*, was one of the Jewish financiers now cast as Satan in the Modern Testament of France. Kate had some respect for the earlier part of his career, when he was a fiery exponent of causes as well as a ferociously ambitious social climber. He had campaigned righteously against Panama Canal feather-bedding and unconscionably in support of the Dreyfus conviction, bringing down several governments. Moving from publishing into politics, he represented Averoigne in the Chamber of Deputies – though he had more influence through his papers than speeches made in the National Assembly. Presidents took suggestions from him as orders. Founder of one of several competing Anti-Semitic Societies, his editorials suggested he saw Jews under the bed… or behind every imaginable ill besetting the Third Republic. When it deigned to cover 'the Montmartre Disappearances' at all, *La Vie* pointed the finger at mad rabbis.

The Persian was unreadable. Did he think even Erik might hesitate to act against Du Roy?

'You'd like it to be him, wouldn't you, Katie,' said Clara. 'A proper villain for the melodrama. You were driven out of England because you crossed someone like Georges Du Roy. How much more satisfying to bring him down than to find out the killer is… well, Bertrand Caillet? A broken wretch, as powerless and low-born as his victims.'

'Caillet?' said the Persian. 'The ghoul? I don't see…'

'He was in the play, *Daroga*. One of the *horreurs*. Guignol threw him out as an example… a small monster in a world run by huge ones.'

The Persian looked at Kate. 'You're basing your theory *on a play?*'

'She was prompted by the play itself,' Clara admitted. 'At the end, Guignol brought on Du Roy and his gang and represented them as the Legion of Horror. The priest in the next box, who muttered "whore" with wet lips whenever Berma was tortured, went bright red at this outrage. I admit I was surprised. It was out of place. The notion of the *Légion d'Horreur* is quite funny.'

'The rest of the performance was random nastiness,' Kate

said. 'But this was pointed. Almost an editorial.'

'Yes… disappointing. I thought Guignol was supposed to be a Pan-like unfettered spirit, not some mere bomb-throwing anarchist.'

'You're missing the point, Clara. It's not the offence that's interesting and suspicious – it's the quiet.'

'The quiet?'

'Why hasn't Guignol been called out? If Du Roy is no longer up to a duel himself, plenty of his faction is.'

'There is no honour in French duelling,' said Yuki. 'Pistols – *tchah*!'

'For some reason, Guignol is protected. He has a license to insult the people you would think would most be capable of shutting him up.'

'She sees Freemasons behind it all… or Jesuits,' said Clara. 'She's as bad as Du Roy and his Jews.'

That stung, but she pressed on.

'I suspect that if we find out why the *Chevaliers de la Légion d'Horreur* tolerate the *Théâtre des Horreurs* we'll learn what's behind the murders. If it's as big as it seems, I'll tell you from experience no one will thank us for bringing it to light… if we're even allowed to.'

The Persian smiled, very slightly – a rare thing for him.

'Miss Reed, you misunderstand. Our Agency has not been commissioned to expose these murders, *but to end them.*'

V

A N ITEM OF business remained.

Kate showed the slashes in her sleeve.

'You've been careless,' said Clara.

'In that case, so have you.'

Kate pointed, and Clara twisted her neck. Parallel cuts in her bodice opened like wounds, just above her hip.

Clara whistled. 'I didn't even feel a breeze.'

Yuki found the neat slashes in her kimono, like vents in her sleeve.

'Only something sharp could do this without us noticing,' the Japanese woman said. 'Very fine blades. A skilled hand.'

She took three teaspoons and slipped them between her fingers, then made a fist. The spoons were spatulate claws. She scratched the air, to demonstrate.

Kate supposed Yuki could do more damage with spoons than the average *apache* with stilettos.

She remembered the sharp-nailed fingers of Guignol, three little daggers poking through ruptured gloves.

'I saw... I think I saw Guignol,' said Kate.

'A man in a mask,' said Clara. 'He could have been anyone.'

'I saw him too,' said Yuki. 'The real Guignol. The one from the theatre. Different costume, different *mask*... but the same eyes.'

The Persian did not show concern.

'I think we can take it that we've been warned,' said Kate. 'All of us are alive only because Guignol let us live.'

Yuki put the spoons down. Despite the counted coup, she still fancied her chances in a parasol-against-claws duel.

Well, maybe...

Clara was annoyed. She didn't have as many dresses with her as she'd like. Expelled from China with only a few negotiable jewels, she couldn't pay European couture prices. She'd asked for a dressmakers' allowance on top of her salary. The Persian countered that any clothing needs would be met by the costume department. As a result of long-standing agreements, many resources of the Opéra were at the disposal of Erik. Kate thought it'd be funny if Clara were to swan about dressed as Emilia di Liverpool or Maria Stuarda. For her own part, she'd fish out her travelling sewing kit and make invisible repairs.

The English woman examined the rents in her dress, touching her own unmarked skin, feeling her unbroken ribs. She was white as porcelain all over. Did she bathe in arsenic or bleach?

'This was not a warning,' said Yuki. 'Snakes do not give warnings. They simply strike. This is an invitation.'

'To a tea-dance?' sneered Clara.

Kate remembered the dance she'd seen at the café. The *apache* flinging his girl around, beating her up to music.

The girl got her slaps and slices in, though – and that's how the man liked it.

'Couldn't we just cut off the clown's head?' asked Clara, wearily. 'And burn down his bloody playhouse. That would solve the Guignol problem. No theatre, no theatre murders.'

'Easy to say, hard to do,' said Kate. 'Too many Guignol masks around. It'd be a risky call picking which head to chop.'

'Chop them all. Pile up the heads.'

'You should be in show business, Clara. I know exactly the company for you.'

Childishly, Clara poked out the scarlet tip of her tongue and pulled a Gorgon-face. Kate couldn't help laughing.

The Persian again defused the exchange of unpleasantries.

'Angels, please. This is not a school-room. Seemliness is required. This latest development is a cause for concern. Monsieur Erik will take any action against his Agents very hard. There would be... counter-actions.'

'So we can be the first casualties in a war of the masks?'

'Miss Reed, the Opera Ghost Agency will not allow that to happen.'

Yuki was fascinated by the tears in her sleeve. 'A personage who can do this will be difficult to stop.'

VI

KATE SPENT THE next few days trying to determine if any connection existed between Guignol and the Georges Du Roy circle.

Representing herself (not untruthfully) as an interested foreign journalist, she paid calls on distant associates among the Paris press. She spent dusty hours in newspaper archives and government records offices. If nothing else, her French was improving. She had promised to send reports to the *Gazette* on anything that might interest English readers. Without telling the Persian, she had drafted an article on the Guignol craze, with a description of her evening at the *Théâtre des Horreurs*. It was supposed in London that entertainments in Paris were *spicier* than home-grown fare. Newspapers were duty-bound to describe in detail the frightful, salacious attractions the British public was spared.

She left her *carte de visite* at the dreary Hôtel d'Alsace, Oscar Wilde's digs. The *concierge* said the poet was too poorly to receive even a fellow exile. Back on Rue des Beaux Arts, she could identify his room from a twitching curtain. Kate missed the Oscar of old. His passion for gossip might have opened up the mystery like a paper flower. Wilde was out of prison but in Paris; Zola was in London to avoid prison. The lesson was that upstart genius should be put firmly in its place.

It wasn't lost on her that Wilde and Henry Wilcox were guilty of essentially the same crime. Wilde was formally sentenced to hard labour and informally to humiliating exile, yet no one even tried to prosecute Wilcox. Consorting with rent-boys – even she, a partisan, said Oscar was a fool in his choice of bed-mates – got an Irishman chased out of England. Consorting with their figurative (and sometimes actual) younger sisters didn't prevent Wilcox from driving an Irish woman out of the country. Any excuse to be rid of the mouthy micks, she supposed.

Kate fancied she occasionally saw Guignol out of the corner of her eye. At Madame Mandelip's, Clara reluctantly admitted to the same impression. Could they both be followed by the same clown? Or were masks handed out to minions? Yuki said she was no longer being tailed. Was Guignol warier of the Japanese Angel than the others?

Something *was* going on between Guignol and the *Légion d'Horreur*, but it was identifiable only by ellipses. That Du Roy and the others took no measures to suppress the *Théâtre des Horreurs* after the accusing tableau was singular. An unanswered public rebuke was extraordinary in a city where offhand remarks provoked duels, vitriol-douches and near-revolution. In Paris, poets started more café brawls than stevedores. Rival high-fashion couturiers slashed each other with scissors in the 8th Arrondissement. An unknown patriot shot Fernand Labori, Zola's defence lawyer, in the back. Marquis d'Amblezy-Sérac, the minister charged with enforcing laws against duelling, fought – and won! – a duel in answer to a challenge from Aristide Forestier, a magistrate who insisted that the right of every Frenchman to try to stick a sword into or put a bullet through any other Frenchman with whom he disagreed was an unwritten yet enforceable clause of the Code Napoléon.

Did Guignol have something on Du Roy which kept him safe? A Lumière cinematograph of the French patriot sharing a bubble bath with Captain Dreyfus, Lily Langtry and the Kaiser? A suppressed family tree which proved the avowed anti-Semite was secretly a Jew? Or was Guignol the creature of the *Légion d'Horreur*, afforded token license because of appalling services rendered? The murders were part of it, but not – she was sure – the whole story.

As she asked her questions and looked through files, Kate was aware of a parallel investigation. Clara Watson was moving through shadier circles on a like quest, securing entry to the murkier dives of Paris to wring information from wretches and débauchées. Pursuing her own predilections, the English widow attended bare-knuckles bouts held among racks of skulls in the catacombs. She picked up whispered horrors from opium dens, salons of vice, black masses and condemned cells. She collected gossip from the Guild of Procurers, *Les Vampires* and a branch of the Suicide Club. Clara's underworld voyages often crossed paths with Kate's more respectable lines of enquiry. That suggested they were both getting warmer. Still, answers were elusive.

Other stories circulated, which Kate felt were connected. Henriette and Louise, two orphan sisters, were missing in Montmartre. Friends said they were running away to join a circus. No circus admitted to taking them in. Their pale little faces, idealised in illustrations, epitomised the disappeared. Even the Sûreté took an interest, but an array of famous criminologists – Alphonse Bertillon, Frédéric Larsan, Inspecteur Juve – failed to find the lost girls. After an afternoon at the Bureau of Missing Persons, Kate knew less appealing people vanished by the dozen in the *quartier* without exciting public interest.

At the *Hôpital des Poupées*, Yuki took over the window and arranged a display of *kokeshi*. Kate found the limbless wooden dolls disturbing, like human-headed fence-posts. Meanwhile, the Persian awaited regular reports from Kate and Clara.

After a week, the Angels were again in conference in the doll salon.

There was a little blood on Clara's coat. She told them not to worry – it wasn't hers. The English widow wasn't leery of sailing into dangerous waters. Clara might be mad, but she was intelligent and – in her own way – cautious. She even did good detective work.

The Persian asked Kate for a report on the *Légion d'Horreur*.

'Georges Du Roy and the others go back a long way,' Kate said. 'The real Bertrand Caillet was tried twenty years before the Commune. On stage at the *Théâtre des Horreurs*, he is arrested in 1871, during its last days. The play shifts the murderer's story forward in time to contrast his crimes with the greater carnage of *la Semaine Sanglante*. It's as if Guignol is telling us where to look.'

'You see the hand of Guignol everywhere,' said Clara.

'Don't you?'

The widow shrugged. 'Perhaps.'

'Whatever the point of the show might be – and I've no reason to believe it isn't primarily the obvious one, to shock and appal and titillate – the *Légion d'Horreur* were all in Paris at the time of the Commune. I can't prove it yet, but I believe this was when our five respectable fellows first met.

'Assolant and Du Roy were soldiers with the army of Versailles, young officers commanding *un escadron de mort*. They weren't in the fighting, they carried out executions. It's hard to credit now, but Mortain and Pradier were Communards. They began in politics as radicals, followers of Blanqui and social justice. As the Commune fell apart, they changed their spots. Père de Kern was a hostage, one of the few to survive. De Kern brought the others together, serving as intermediary. Mortain and Pradier betrayed comrades to the Squadron of Death and got free passes from Assolant and Du Roy. In the aftermath of Bloody Week, Mortain and Pradier were listed as spies for Versailles. It was claimed they only *posed as* Communards. Anyone who could say different was put against a wall. Assolant was promoted, but Du Roy did a spell in Algeria before leaving the army to begin his ascent as a man of letters and then in politics.

'The five have been allies for nearly forty years. They look out for each other. If financial scandal threatens to engulf Mortain, a stern editorial in *La Vie Française* insists on his innocence. A chorister who accused de Kern of vile practices finds himself up before Judge Pradier on dubious charges and transported to the penal colony of New Caledonia. When Assolant is implicated in an attempted coup, Du Roy nominates him for further honours and accolades. In 1871, they were enemies. Now, they are closer than brothers.'

'Interesting, Miss Reed,' said the Persian. 'But I am reminded of Mrs Watson's objection of a few nights ago... that you would *like* these people to be guilty. You despise men of their class and position. It would suit your prejudices if they were outright monsters.'

Kate tried to take this into account. Investigating Henry Wilcox, she had at every turn questioned her own instincts. Erring on the side of wariness, she hadn't put anything in print until she had two or more reliable sources. Unsubstantiated rumours were set aside, no matter how credible she found them. Here, she used the same method … all but ignoring a wealth of second- or third-hand stories, sticking to verifiable facts, even if evidence suggested records had been altered or destroyed. She was satisfied she had enough to indict Du Roy and his cronies on a raft of charges going back decades – though she wouldn't have trusted the French (or British) courts to deliver a just verdict. What she couldn't do was make a firm link between the *Légion d'Horreur* and the Montmartre murders.

The Persian looked to Clara, whose expression was hard to read.

'I have decided to withdraw my objection,' said Clara.

Kate noted the odd, legalistic turn of phrase.

'On what grounds?' asked the Persian.

'I now believe Katie is right. These are the guilty men.'

'You have proof?'

'Of course not. These are not men who leave proof. It's all feelings and intuition. You employ only women, and this is what you must expect…'

Kate wanted to slap Clara for that, even if she was a convert to the cause.

'In quarters where people aren't easy to scare, the names of these men give pause,' explained Clara. 'There are creatures out there in the dark, people you might call *monsters*, who are more terrified of Georges Du Roy than of… well, than of the Phantom of the Opera. They can't be worried about a harshly worded article in *La Vie Française* or an inconvenient ruling in the Assembly. The others have evil reputations too.

'Dr Johannes, the Satanist, says Père de Kern is the worst man in Paris. He doesn't mean it in the inverted sense that a devout diabolist should abjure a moral churchman. Johannes means it literally. The Worst Man in Paris. Monsters aren't born – they are made. The orphanages supervised by de Kern are factories for making them – cruelty, privation and hypocrisy applied systematically to warp young minds and bodies. De Kern has raised *generations* of them, an army of freaks. I would admire the enterprise, but for its utter lack of aesthetic qualities.

'Assolant is a butcher, of course, and a blunderer. He killed more Frenchmen than Germans even before he was given the pull-string of his own personal guillotine in Bloody Week. Mortain and Pradier are make-weights. They have survived this long because Du Roy shields them. According to their cast-off mistresses, Mortain follows the leanings of the Marquis de Sade – a sure sign of the poseur among true practitioners of the Art of Torture – while Pradier is inclined to the pitiful vice of Sacher-Masoch.

'They are the guilty men. Everyone I have raised this matter with says so. Then they cannot say what it is they are guilty of. Or will not, despite… *methods of extreme persuasion*.'

When she said 'methods of extreme persuasion', Clara shuddered with what Kate took to be delight. She was no poseur in her preferred art.

Kate's *frisson* was of another character.

'Could any of the *Légion be* Guignol?' she asked. 'I mean, we've all assumed that the nimble masked performer is a younger man. There are drugs and potions. A Du Roy or a de Kern could quaff something to turn them into an agile imp for a few hours. Long enough to get through the show.'

'But the curtain comes down on a condemnation of these men?' objected Clara.

'Does it? Or is that tableau a *boast*?'

Clara thought for a moment.

'Or the snook cocked against the *Légion d'Horreur* might be a feint,' suggested Kate. 'Like the taunts of Hyde against Jekyll.'

'Unlikely,' said Clara. 'These people have enough enemies without becoming their own dark shadows.'

'That's true,' said the Persian.

Kate admitted it. 'Guignol could be someone from their history – a survivor of Bloody Week, tipped alive into a corpse-pit by the Squadron of Death, crawling out with a mania for revenge. A subordinate thrown to the wolves to take the blame for crimes they got away with, back in town after years of fever and abuse in a far-off mangrove swamp or desert stockade. Or one of your army of freaks, Clara, shaped by harsh treatment into a broken *übermensch*. But if that's the case, why not kill them? Ridicule seems feeble revenge.'

'A Frenchman would rather be assassinated than made to look silly,' said Clara. 'The French, they are a funny race, they fight with their feet... they make love with their face.'

'I've heard that before, more crudely put.'

'I was trying to spare your delicate Dublin sensitivities.'

'There are rhymes about the English too, in Dublin. Oh, and everywhere else they've run up their flag and marched about.'

'So we are no nearer a provable truth,' said the Persian, interceding again.

Since their last verbal fencing match, Kate realised – rather alarmingly – that Clara Watson *liked* her. She wouldn't have thought the scarlet widow capable of such a feeling, and it was little comfort. One story put around about Clara was that in Benares she made arrangements to have her best friend infected with leprosy. As Angels of Music, Kate and Clara had to sing in the same register. They had taken to a banter each found amusing which outsiders mistook for hostility. It was a little like flirting.

'Our Daughter of Erin might be in a mist,' said Clara, 'but this Child of Boadicea has yet to admit defeat...'

It wasn't hard to imagine Clara in a carriage with head-lopping swords attached to its wheels. In China, she had probably had such an unlikely conveyance manufactured to order. She could easily persuade a tame warlord to line the road with peasants just to try it out.

'Just say what you know, you sick witch,' snapped Kate.

'Why, Katie, such a tone! You've gone quite red in the face. I would be concerned for your health...'

'It is time to tell,' said Yuki, quietly.

Clara stopped simpering and put a card on the table. A white oblong marked with a red ring.

'What is that?' asked the Persian.

'An invitation,' said Clara. 'Presented at the *Théâtre des Horreurs* after midnight on a certain night of the month, this secures entry to an unadvertised additional performance. The *cercle rouge* guest list is select. You can't buy your way onto it. Not with money, at least. The names we've been discussing – some of them, at least – *may* be regulars, though whether as performers or audience I haven't been able to tell. That's ink, not blood, on the card. But it took blood to get it. The Grand Vampire, who you'd think beyond being shocked, told me he didn't want ever to see the *après-minuit* again, but that I would most likely enjoy the show. Make of *that* what you will.'

The Grand Vampire was the chief of *Les Vampires*, Paris's most daring criminal organisation. His position was so dangerous and hotly contested that the mask stayed the same but the man behind it changed regularly. The Opera Ghost Agency and *Les Vampires* had a wary truce. Some years before, a previous Grand Vampire had engaged the Angels of Music on a confidential matter, which the Agency had brought to a satisfactory conclusion.

Kate picked up the card. The circle was stamped into the thick paper and the red was some sort of gilt. Not easy to forge, though the design and printing department of the Opéra would have their methods.

'How long do we have to wait?'

'Only until tomorrow,' said Clara. 'I hope your delicate stomach is up to it.'

She flipped back through her notebooks.

'Yes, Katie,' said Clara, 'the disappearances tend to be in the week leading up to each month's *après-minuit*… and the bodies are often found during the few days *after* the special performance.'

They all looked at each other.

'For myself, I shall spend tomorrow shopping for a new hat,' said Clara. 'It doesn't do to attend a theatre twice in the same outfit. Also, I understand that *chapeaux* with veils – if not full masks – are customary for *cercle rouge* audiences.'

'You buy a hat,' said Katie. 'I'll get a revolver.'

'Very sensible. No dramatic critic should be without one. A lead corset might also be a wise investment.'

VII

KATE HAD NOT been joking. She needed a gun.

Yuki could walk into a lion's den – taking those tiny steps because she was hobbled by her traditional dress – with nothing but her parasol and come out with a large rug. Clara's stylishly tailored topcoat had neat pockets in the lining, filled with a range of cutting, slicing, throwing, sawing and gouging implements. Kate was the least dangerous of the Agency's current roster. The little apple-peeling knife she'd been keeping up her sleeve would be little use against Guignol and the whole *Légion d'Horreur*.

The Persian gave her a chit to present to Monsieur Quelou, Chief Armourer of the Paris Opéra. He had his own subterranean domain, with sandbags against the walls and the smell of gunpowder in the air. Besides the swords, spears and axes required by Wagner's warriors and Valkyries, the House maintained enough functional rifles, pistols and small cannon to defend the building against the Mob... which Kate suspected was most likely the plan. It didn't take a Gatling gun to execute Tosca's boyfriend and few productions in the classic repertoire required field artillery, but Quelou kept those too. Erik had lived through the Siege and the Commune. He also had cause to be wary of angry, torch-bearing crowds. There was little about the building and its protocols he hadn't had a skeletal hand in designing.

Quelou first offered her a pair of pearl-handled custom pistols, suitable for Annie Oakley – scarcely a subject for musical drama, Kate thought. The guns felt light to her, more for show than showdown. After consideration, she settled for a plain, battered 'British Bull Dog' Webley. She knew the model – issued first to the Royal Irish Constabulary – and it fit nicely into her reticule. The gun gave her bag enough weight to use as a club if she wasn't in a position to haul out the iron and fire it.

The armourer gave her a lecture on the gun's use. She put on ear-baffles and fired at a straw target with a photograph pinned to it. It was an autographed picture of Emma Calvé, reigning diva of the Opéra Comique – the Paris Opéra's great rival. Kate put a bullet in La Calvé's throat. Her eye was good and the gun was sighted properly.

Before she left, Quelou cautioned her, 'Mademoiselle, take care... don't feel *invincible*.'

She thought she took that on board. Within a quarter of an hour, his words haunted her.

Outside, in the Place de Opéra, she relaxed slightly. After so much time spent in Montmartre, it was a relief to be in a more civilised district, without *apaches* in every alley. Looking up at the imposing façade of the Palais Garnier, she even had a comforting sense that Erik was nearby, watching over his Angels. Strange that such a creature should be her patron, but she was used to strangeness.

She sat at a pavement café table and drank bitter coffee while nibbling a crescent-shaped pastry. Pretty girls – from the company's chorus and corps de ballet – chirruped and chattered all around. Likely fellows tried to talk with them, getting mostly short shrift.

She opened a copy of *L'Intransigeant*, a virulently anti-Dreyfusard paper left at her table. She scanned for items of interest, catching on paragraphs and translating them in her head – she was a long way from fluency, but could now read complicated passages with something like ease. She found a piece by Henri Rochefort, a supporter of Du Roy, about the civilian judges who ruled that Dreyfus was allowed to appeal against his military conviction. 'They should have their eyelids cut off by a duly trained torturer,' wrote Rochefort, 'and large spiders of the most poisonous variety placed on their eyes to gnaw away at the pupils and crystalline lenses until there is nothing left in the cavities now devoid of sight. Then, all the hideous blind men would be brought to a pillory erected before the Palais de Justice in which the crime was committed and a sign would be placed on their chests: "This is how France punishes traitors who try to sell her to the enemy!"' With public discourse on this level, the stage blood and trilling screams of the *Théâtre des Horreurs* were almost quaint.

The girls at the next table laughed at something.

Kate folded *L'Intransigeant*, resolved to put it in a public waste-paper bin and spare other idlers its venom.

What was all the amusement about?

A familiar barrel-organ ground.

It was the ape-suited street performer of Rue Saint-Vincent, *l'homme-affiche* of the *Théâtre des Horreurs*. He had recaptured his abused partner or procured a replacement. Did the animals come from the same disgusting business which supplied Maximilian the Great with canaries?

The monkey's get-up had changed. Now, it wore a miniature Guignol mask and costume.

'Dance, Sultan, dance,' said Petit Guignol. The shaggy gorilla shook his legs.

The mountebank must be a ventriloquist too, and particularly skilled. The shrill little voice, so like Guignol's swazzle, not only seemed to issue from the mask, but wasn't muffled by the stiff, snarling false face of the gorilla.

She couldn't bring herself to shout bravo, though. She remembered the sewn-together arms.

'Eh, Sultan, what have we here... the pretty ladies of the Opéra...'

Mass giggling.

'And a... well, a not-so-pretty lady, *associated with* the Opéra.'

The monkey jumped up on her table and snatched the last of her croissant, shredding it with little fingers. It couldn't eat through the mask.

Furious, pained eyes stared out from Guignol's face. She

recalled the real Guignol's wild gaze.

The gorilla shambled closer to her table.

Her hand went to her reticule. No... this was someone she'd done mischief to getting their own back. That didn't mean she could shoot him. Quelou would warn her to save her shots for when they counted.

She tried to smile at the beast, who was disinclined to show gratitude to his former liberator. She imagined Sultan had punished him for his bolt for freedom.

Her face burned. She was blushing again.

The chorus girls laughed with good humour. Malign chuckles came out of the puppet-faced monkey. That *must* be Sultan throwing his voice.

Suddenly, Petit Guignol tugged at her hair and pulled her out of her seat.

'Dance with me, Brick-top, dance,' shrilled the voice.

Applause. She nearly stumbled, but stayed upright, whirled round and round by the trained beast.

The music stopped, but the dance went on. Petit Guignol passed her to Sultan, who gripped her with powerful, hairy-gloved hands. She was face to mask with the mock gorilla. Another set of eyes glared at her, burnt-cork make-up on the lids to blend with the black mask – mirthless, purposeful.

Sultan waltzed with her, further away from her table.

She saw a waiter holding up her surprisingly heavy reticule, miming 'Eh, mademoiselle, you have left your bag...'

So much for being armed.

She struggled now, but the capering thug in the stiff-furred, reeking gorilla suit had a firm grip and deft feet. She was borne away, across the Place de l'Opéra. Petit Guignol dropped to all fours, assuming the role of a monkey rather than a little man, and scampered after them.

'*Au secours, au secours!*' shrilled a voice – *an imitation of hers!* – that earned more laughter. 'I am borne away by this base creature! Who will come to the aid of a poor, defenceless woman stolen by a dreadful beast of the jungles?'

The café patrons clapped, assuming this the finish of an act. Some threw coins, which were collected by a rough who also picked up the abandoned organ. Sultan had not come for her alone. But he had come for her.

This was – she realised – an abduction.

She was turned round and around. She was being waltzed towards a black carriage, its door open. Where a family crest or an official seal might be displayed was a simple red circle.

'What hideous lusts will this naughty creature slake upon my helpless form! What depraved desires does he ache to fulfil!'

She tried to compete with the fake cries of distress but couldn't get breath to shout.

'I must admit, though, that it is quite exciting!' continued the high-pitched voice. 'One comes to Paris for experiences… and this promises to be a very great… *experience*. Oh, if he wasn't so handsome… if I weren't so homely! I shall elope with Monsieur Sultan! We shall pledge our primitive troth and experience natural love in the trees!'

The knife edged out of her sleeve, but Sultan knew all about that. He squeezed her wrist painfully. The implement fell to the ground and was kicked away.

Finally, close to the carriage, the ape let go of one of her hands. She tensed, prepared to administer a kick to the groin.

The huge, rubber-palmed hand pressed something sweet-smelling over her face… and she went into the darkness of a swoon.

VIII

KATE WOKE UP in the dark, with a fuzzy headache. She knew she'd been chloroformed, but not how long she'd been unconscious.

She was slumped in an upholstered chair. She had a sense

she was underground. A weight dragged at her ankle. She was shackled to the chair-leg. The chair was fixed to the floor. Her hands were free, but she was too weak to lift them.

The room was cold and slightly damp. She smelled mothballs. She realised she'd been stripped. She wore some sort of shift or nightdress.

Was this the lair of Sultan the Gorilla-Man?

Someone turned up a gas-lamp. Kate saw herself in a large mirror. Her hair was a mess, her skin was unhealthy white and her freckles stood out like pinpricks of blood. Her nightie was immodest, but surprisingly good quality. She had at least been abducted by a better class of ape.

Over her shoulder, she saw her captor, hairy hand up to the gas-jet. His gorilla head was off, but he wore a skin-tight black hood with holes for his eyes and mouth.

'She's awake,' called Sultan.

A row of chairs faced the mirror, as in an expensive dentist's office or a hairdresser's. On the walls were theatre posters and photographs of famous actors. Stuck to and around the mirror were pictures: faces with hideous deformities, gouged eyes, flattened noses or terrible scars. If real, they were models for make-up artists trying to achieve shocking effects. If fake, they were records of previous triumphs to be recreated. On a shelf under the mirror were pots of powder and paint and trays of glass eyes. Faceless wooden heads supported a variety of wigs, including a scabby bald cap and Bertrand Caillet's wolfish shock of hair. Racks of costumes hung nearby, explaining the mothballs.

She was backstage at the *Théâtre des Horreurs*.

Sultan walked over to her, not bothering with the rolling ape-gait, and took hold of her chin. He examined her face.

She would have spat but her mouth was dry.

As if reading her mind, he poured water from a jug into a glass and raised it to her lips, tipping liquid gently into her mouth.

She should have squirted it in his face. Instead, she said, 'Thank you.'

Others entered the dressing room. She recognised Morpho. His scars weren't stuck on. Dr Orloff, the theatre physician, and Malita, the versatile actress. And someone else.

'I told you it cost blood to get a Red Circle invitation,' said Clara Watson. 'I never said it would be mine.'

Kate choked on her water. She rattled her leg-chain.

'Temper, temper,' said the English woman.

So Clara was a Fallen Angel? A turncoat. Kate should have guessed as much. The scarlet widow was too twisted to stay the course. Why hadn't Erik expected this?

Kate made an impractical anatomical suggestion.

'You know, in China, I saw a slave girl actually do that,' said Clara, smiling sweetly.

Dr Orloff stuck the cold end of his stethoscope against her chest. Kate supposed her heart rate was up.

Orloff professionally pinched her bare arms. She winced.

'Good reflexes,' he commented. 'Open wide.'

He touched her under the jaw-hinge and sprung her mouth open, then peered in.

'And good teeth. A pleasure to see good teeth. So many ladies neglect dental care. They just think that if they smile with their lips closed no one will notice the gaps and the green fur.'

'We should keep her scalp,' said Malita. 'We don't get enough red hair… for the wigs.'

That wasn't encouraging.

'Why am I here?' she demanded.

'Katie, you are to be a shining star of the stage,' said Clara. 'The toast of the *après-minuit* of the *Théâtre des Horreurs* – now, what's the expression? – For One Night Only.'

If – no, *when* – she got out of this, she'd even things. A connoisseur of torture, was she? Well, Clara Watson hadn't gone to school in Ireland…

Clara bent down to kiss close to Kate's ears.

'*Courage*,' she whispered. 'And trust. Angels always.'

Then, with a fluttery wave, she left the room.

'See you in the cheap seats,' Kate shouted after her.

'Break a leg,' Clara responded. 'At least.'

Had she misunderstood Clara? If this was a stratagem to discover the secrets of the Red Circle, it would have been nice if she'd been in on it. Or was the Fallen Angel torturing her with the hope of a rescue that would never come?

Malita approached, with a pair of brushes. She began to groom Kate, putting her hair up in a way she hadn't tried before.

Objectively, Kate quite liked the effect.

Under the circumstances, she couldn't bring herself to thank her dresser.

IX

APRÈS-MINUIT DIDN'T MEAN the curtain went up at the tolling of the twelve o'clock bell. While Kate was unconscious, Guignol's company gave a regular evening show. Then, the audience and most of the company left the building and preparations for the Red Circle performance began.

Malita powdered over her freckles (which took several pots) and gave her red, red lips and rouge cheek-blushes. With a pencil that drew blood, the crone added a final touch – a beauty spot by her nose.

Kate was unshackled and wrestled into a cheap tart costume: low-cut bodice, gypsy skirt, beret, tattered red shawl, patent leather boots. Now, Kate thought she looked ridiculous. If she were a doll, she would sit unbought in Madame Mandelip's window.

Malita dragged her – it was hard to walk in the thick-soled, high-heeled boots – out of the dressing room. She was taken along a corridor, up through the wings and onto the stage. The heavy curtain was down. A stock backdrop showed sylvan fields and marble statuary. A stained oilskin was laid over the boards. Stage-hands stood ready with buckets and mops.

Sultan had his head back on but his hairy gloves off. His hands were blacked with coal and he held a hunting rifle.

Want to see something really frightening? A gorilla with a gun.

Other oddly dressed and made-up people were gathered.

A young man in white tie and tails was protesting to a hard-faced Morpho. Kate recognised the Stage Door Jeannot she'd spotted on her first visit to the theatre. His bunch of black flowers was wilting. She gathered he'd slipped backstage in the hope of paying tribute to *la belle* Berma. Others – more obvious wretches – were sober enough to be terrified. A *beldame*, dressed as a duchess but smelling like a down-and-out washerwoman. Two thin children, got up in animal costumes – Henriette and Louise, the orphans who'd run away to join the circus. A noseless, one-armed soldier in uniform proudly announced that he was making his third appearance in an *après-minuit*. Kate guessed such return performances were rare.

Dr Orloff supervised the co-opted, addled or desperate cast.

'Feel free to scream at the top of your lungs,' he said. 'It's a small house, but it takes a lot to fill the auditorium. Our patrons like a good scream. Remember to stay in the limelight. No point bleeding in the dark, is there? You want your moment. If you must beg and plead for mercy, address yourselves to the audience. Our orchestra are blindfolded and callous. Your fellow performers are professionals and will stick to the script.'

'There's a *chance* for mercy?' asked a young woman in an Aztec headdress.

'Of course not,' said the doctor. 'But the begging, whining and tearing of hair amuses some of the Red Circle. It irritates others, who just want to get on with the procedures. But many are happy to delay their pleasure. Who knows, maybe largesse will be extended to your loved ones if you plead prettily enough. You are here to honour a family obligation, are you not, Nini?'

The sacrificial princess nodded.

'Follow your instincts. I'm sure you'll triumph. And Papa will be saved from disgrace.'

It hadn't occurred to Kate that anyone would *deliberately* give themselves over to Guignol. Evidently, everything could be bought. This business got more horrible the more she found out.

The *beldame* sank to her knees, dress pooling around her, and began keening and drooling. Morpho hauled her upright and slapped her silent. Malita stepped in with a cloth and some powder to repair her make-up.

Sultan slung his rifle on his back and climbed a rope into the flyspace above the stage. He was as agile as a natural-born ape.

Could she escape by following him up there? Not in these blasted boots.

Looking up, she saw Sultan crouch on a gangway amid ropes and pulleys. He trained his rifle on the stage and bared his teeth – the big fake choppers in his articulated mask – at her in a grin. An ape-man of many talents – ventriloquist, abductor of women, acrobat, sharp shooter...

So long as Sultan was at his post, there was no point in making a dash for freedom.

Rallying the performers to rebel was not much of a possibility. She couldn't know how many were essentially volunteers, like the Old Soldier and Nini. Most of the obviously co-opted, like Stage Door Jeannot and the Duchess, were in no state to be of any use to her or themselves. The orphans, a fish and a cat, were undernourished.

At this juncture, the best she could hope for was to die knowing the answers.

She put up her hand, as if at a press conference.

'Miss, ah, Reed, isn't it?' Orloff acknowledged. 'How can I help you?'

'Skipping past the obvious business of me not wanting to be in the show, can I at least ask what it's all about?'

'I don't understand. What is *what* all about?'

'This. The *après-minuit*, the Red Circle... Your patrons – who

I'll bet I could name, by the way – what do they get out of this?'

Dr Orloff looked puzzled. Had no one ever asked before?

'I believe I can enlighten our guest,' said someone from behind her – in a slightly reedy voice.

She turned and saw Georges Du Roy.

The journalist and politician was dressed as if for the opera, from top hat to spats. Jewels sparkled on his fingers and his stickpin. Famously handsome, he had wooed his way through the salons to winkle tit-bits for the gossip column that was the making of him. He had softened in middle-age but retained his smooth skin and watery bright eyes. His moustache was dyed and waxed.

She would have walked past him on the street without noticing – yet, he was the true monster in this case. His pink, plump face was his mask.

With him was Guignol, on a leash and all fours like a hunting dog.

'I confess it,' he said. 'My comrades and I, the brothers of the Red Circle, are addicts. Connoisseurs, certainly. Fastidious, perhaps. Choosy, naturally. But addicts. We want what we want. We must have it. *Must*. If we can no longer participate, we must watch. It is the great secret delight of all mankind, you know.'

'Murder?'

'You could call it that… but it's so commonplace a term. Murder is brute stuff. One man shoots or stabs another, in a quarrel or for no reason. Even duels, assassinations, factory accidents… they are over too quickly, not savoured, not *enjoyed*.'

'This is about Bloody Week?'

Du Roy looked wistful. 'Yes, of course. Some of us had an inkling before then. During the siege of Paris, when the elephants in the zoo were slaughtered for food. Or at school or on the battlefield. We trembled, on the verge of self-understanding. We pursued other gratifications, so much less piquant than those we really needed. It was that glorious shining week, those few precious days, when we truly learned what it was that we must have. It was our revelation. Excess, my dear. Excess! A banquet of killing! An orgy of blood-letting. Murder upon murder! Massacre upon massacre! A refinement of the art!'

Kate saw why Clara Watson had sold her for a Red Circle pass.

'You're just... mad. Rich, and mad. The worst combination.'

Du Roy smiled, showing little rows of sparkling teeth. 'Everyone's a critic.'

'Are you satisfied, Mademoiselle *Pomme de Terre*?' asked Orloff. 'You've been privileged above any other in being granted an interview with our impresario. An *exclusive*.'

'I doubt that. What he says sounds rehearsed. I think he's said it all before. He's as bored with it as I was.'

Orloff signalled. Malita slapped Kate.

Kate made fists, then remembered the gorilla with the high-powered rifle.

Du Roy tipped his hat to the performers and retreated, hauling Guignol away. The presiding spirit of the *Théâtre des Horreurs* was surprisingly quiet. Du Roy handed the leash to Morpho, who grinned and tugged viciously. As the collar went tight, a wheezing came from deep in Guignol's throat – air forced through his swazzle.

So, the monster's position was usurped.

This wasn't Guignol's show any more. This was for the Red Circle.

X

D R ORLOFF ARRANGED the cast against the backdrop, as if it were an execution wall. Kate half-expected a blindfold, then realised that would be a mercy. The Red Circle were not disposed to mercy.

Morpho, Malita and Orloff remained onstage. Morpho was stripped to the waist, showing off his battle scars. Malita and Orloff put on butcher's aprons and white coats. The props bench in the wings was piled with hammers, tongs, knives, sickles, gouges, bludgeons and other, unidentifiable instruments of mistreatment. Bottles of poison and acid were also available. A short, round-faced, bald-headed fellow with a permanent smile stood by the table, ready to hand over implements when needed. Very professional.

Kate thought of making a grab for the acid, but knew she'd be cut down. She had no doubt the man in the gorilla suit was an expert marksman. Dying too quickly would spoil the show but she'd still be dead.

The curtains parted and the limelights flared.

Beyond the shimmer, she could make out shapes.

A procession advanced down the aisle, and climbed up a carpeted set of steps to the stage, traversing the invisible barrier between the audience and the drama.

Du Roy escorted a veiled lady in a scarlet hooded cape.

Kate trusted the Red Circle were satisfied with their newest member. She hoped Clara would get bored in a year or two and poison the lot of them. By then, she'd have had opportunity to seduce an intern at the School of Tropical Medicine and secure some new, hideously virulent bacillus for the job. Du Roy wouldn't look so smug with weeping boils erupting all over his face.

The others trooped behind the King and Queen of Horror.

General Assolant was in full uniform, chest sagging with a glittery weight of medals and honours. In this private realm of fantasy, Père de Kern had promoted himself to cardinal. His red robes would have been too grand for Richelieu. His train trailed like a bride's, and was carried by imps – naked children painted red all over and staggering as they began to suffocate. Charles Pradier wore judicial robes and magistrate's hat, adopting the British convention of the black silk handkerchief draped over the top to signify passage of a death sentence. Eugène Mortain sported a tricolour sash over court clothes and had a drunken doxy with him. The fair-haired wench tittered and clucked, marring the solemnity of the occasion. Would she end up taking part in the performance? Blondes were as easy to replace as Maximilian's little yellow birds.

The audience wore red domino masks, for convention rather than disguise.

Attendants in red livery set out chairs on the stage, close to the action. Individual trays for snacks and drinks were bolted to the chair-arms. There was even a folded-up programme placed on each cushion.

Kate would have liked a look at the running order. With pathetic orphan sisters and an Aztec princess in the line-up, she doubted she'd get top billing. The best she could hope for was to be snuffed quickly at the end of Act One. Her corpse would be dragged off for dumping in the sewers while the audience enjoyed an intermission and exchanged opinions about her death scene.

A small group of musicians – blindfolded, as promised – struck up a selection from *Carmen*.

The audience took their seats.

Mortain's mistress evidently had no idea what she was about to see – she was laughing shrilly and flirting with everyone. The others were intent, quiet, perspiring, eager. Du Roy had a habit of licking his lips like a fat lizard. Assolant gripped the hilt of his sword as if he'd like to draw his weapon and hack randomly at the people in front of him – which, she supposed, he might well do. Watching wouldn't be enough for these people. De Kern had his imps kneel down before him to form a footstool. Pradier counted out little pills from a box and swallowed them, washed down with a swallow from a silver flask.

The surprise was Guignol's role.

The masked man was still on a leash, still held by Morpho. Where once he had been master of the stage, now he was a stooge.

Kate saw blood on Guignol's costume, seeping through. The mask was battered, the nose pushed in, as if he'd taken a bad beating.

Even this close to her death, she was trying to understand.

Was Guignol an unwilling participant in the *après-minuit*?

She saw his eyes were shut, as if he didn't want to look.

Morpho tied Guignol's leash to a post, and kicked him.

The show had started ...

XI

THE OLD SOLDIER was the opening act.

The orchestra played a march as he saluted the audience with his remaining arm – the left. He sat on a stool and, with practised ease, worked off his left boot with his right foot. With rather more difficulty, he peeled off his sock one-handed and tried to roll up his trouser-leg, which kept snagging on his knee and rolling down again.

Mortain's blonde roared with laughter. De Kern swivelled his head almost entirely around, like a snake or an owl, and stared her into silence. She needed a swift pull from the flask after that. The priest's head turned back and he gave a 'pray continue' gesture with his free hand. The other was tucked under his robe and horribly busy.

Malita came to the Old Soldier's rescue with a jack-knife and slit his britches for him, from the ankle-cuff to well above the knee. The cloth parted and flapped aside. For such an obvious invalid, the soldier had a healthy-looking leg.

'*Vive la France*,' he said. '*Vive la République*.'

The orchestra played 'La Marseillaise', with some deliberate, comic wrong notes.

Dr Orloff gave the Old Soldier a saw and he got to work.

He fought valiantly against the urge to scream and only whimpered as he performed the auto-amputation. He chewed his long moustache. He had once been right-handed, Kate realised. His left-hand strokes were awkward. The saw kept slipping in its red groove. Nevertheless, he hit bone and parted cartilage before passing out.

Mortain's mistress stuck her fist in her mouth. Mortain took her neck like a kitten's and forced her to keep watching.

The Old Soldier fell off the stool. Sundered veins pulsed and spurted. Kate saw a flash of yellowish bone and clumps of gristle.

Morpho stepped in, with an executioner's axe raised.

'No,' insisted Du Roy. 'He must be awake.'

Dr Orloff applied a tourniquet to stem the flow of blood, then used smelling salts to wake the Old Soldier.

'I am sorry,' he said, through tears of pain. 'I have had... a momentary lapse.'

Morpho brought the axe down. The angle was awkward and the cut not clean.

The Old Soldier screamed. And apologised again.

Dr Orloff positioned the sundered knee over the stool, which made a decent chopping block. Morpho finished the job and tore away the leg, which he then tossed at Guignol, who flinched as he was kicked in the face by a disembodied foot.

The doctor tightened the tourniquet.

It was touch and go for a moment, but the bleeding was stopped and Orloff worked fast with hot irons and needle and thread.

The audience, bored by this, gossiped. The musicians played a cake-walk.

Blood pooled on the oilskin, creeping closer to Kate's toes. Her fellow performers were either in shock or insane.

His life saved, the Old Soldier was carried away... perhaps considering a fourth appearance, though for the life of her Kate couldn't imagine how he'd come up with a new turn.

The Red Circle weren't that impressed.

Stage Door Jeannot, sober at last, tried to make a run for freedom. He slipped in the blood. A crack sounded and a rifle bullet smashed his skull. Instantly dead, he somersaulted in the air and landed in a messy heap of tangled limbs.

There was weak applause at his impromptu performance.

Malita bit her cheek in disappointment. Kate supposed she'd expected to have the fellow to herself in a later, scheduled act.

She smelled gunpowder. A cartridge-case pinged on the stage.

Guignol struggled with his collar, trying to pull free. Mortain's doxy was shocked silent. De Kern moaned with pleasure. Assolant furiously muttered, 'Can't abide a coward – should be shot, the lot of 'em!' Du Roy looked bored – he had said murder wasn't enough for him anymore.

Someone had died in front of her. Kate was beyond fury and terror.

XII

DR ORLOFF WAS less expert than Guignol as a master of ceremonies. He hemmed and lectured, playing for time while the next act was setting up.

Stage Door Jeannot threw him off his script.

The corpse had to be removed and a pool of blood mopped, then the wet patch scattered with sand.

Orloff fussed as all this happened in front of the audience.

Du Roy glared at him. Kate supposed artistes who fell out of favour with the Red Circle got to make one last spectacular exit.

Malita pulled her out of the line of waiting performers. One of the orphans clung to Kate's skirt. Malita was about to slap the little girl. Kate deflected the blow with her arm and told the child everything would be all right. Her tongue went like leather as she lied. Malita led her to the props table.

The prop-master held up a stiletto and stabbed it into the meat of his hand. The blunt-tipped blade slid into the handle. He gave the trick knife to her. Would it be any use? Malita impatiently showed her how to holster it in the top of her boot.

'In the spirit of Montmartre, we present the famous *apache* dance,' announced Orloff. 'Performed by our own celebrated Morpho and a special guest... Miss Katharine Reed of Dublin.'

So this was why she was dressed as a French streetwalker.

The orchestra began the 'Valse des Rayons'.

Malita dragged her onto the stage. Morpho was waiting. The one-eyed ox now wore a tight, striped shirt and a red neck-scarf. A cigarette was stuck in the corner of his sneer. Red and yellow war paint striped his cheeks, as if he had Apache and *apache* mixed up.

She'd seen this act the other night – the mock-fight of rough dance, as the ponce slings his tart around, miming slaps and kicks, with kisses between the blows. For the benefit of the Red Circle, she guessed the fight wouldn't be mock and the slaps and kicks wouldn't be pulled. The idea of being kissed by Morpho wasn't too appealing either.

No wonder they hadn't given her a knife that would stick in anything.

Morpho adopted an odd pose, like a matador – fists at his sides, up on his toes, bottom tucked in, chest puffed out, looking at her sideways with his single eye. There was a touch of vanity in his plumped-up self-regard. Only now, with Guignol tied up, was Morpho a real star.

'Dance, girl,' whispered Malita in her ears. 'If you disappoint, they'll go after your family.'

Malita shoved Kate at Morpho.

She slammed against his chest and he grabbed her hair, which hurt enough to get her attention.

The herky-jerky music continued, with pauses Offenbach hadn't written, as she was rattled around the stage. She struggled, but Morpho was strong and had done this before. He let her go and slapped her face hard, snapping her head around – a few more like that, and her neck would break.

She aimed a kick at his shin. Make use of the damned boots!

Deftly, he got out of her way and she fell over. Sliding on the still-wet oilskin, she got a sandpapery burn on her bare thigh. He jammed a boot in her ribs and she rolled over, trying to ignore the burst of pain.

At this rate, her debut would be over in no time at all.

Morpho took her arms and hauled her up again, lifting her

off her feet and over his head, then wheeling her around in the air. She was dizzy. Flashes went off in her eyes.

Up in the flies, she saw Sultan the Gorilla, rifle-barrel moving as he kept his bead drawn on her...

...and, above him, a black shape, descending silently on the ape sniper. A dangling loop of cord hooked around Sultan's throat. The Punjab lasso!

She had only a glimpse, but it was enough. She had not been abandoned. A Phantom watched over her...

...though she couldn't help wishing Erik had got his act together a little earlier.

Now, she had to get through this *pas de deux* without being killed.

Morpho held her by an arm and an ankle and spun like a top. Her hair came loose and flapped like a flag in the wind. A panorama rushed past, faster and faster.

The Red Circle. The orchestra. The prop table. The stagehands. Guignol, chained. The black chasm of the auditorium. The painted pastoral scene, streaked with blood. The waiting victims.

She tried to look up.

Morpho let go and she slid across the stage, scraping her side raw, ripping her costume. Her shawl came loose and she skidded to a stop.

A breathing moment.

Above on a wildly swinging gangway, unnoticed by everyone else, a slender, cloaked, white-masked figure exchanged *savate* kicks with Sultan the Gorilla. Erik had entered the field.

Morpho mockingly beckoned to Kate.

At this point in the dance, the *apache* girl usually crawled on hands and knees back to her pimp to take more medicine. The little fool would try to stick him with her garter-knife but he'd bend her wrist back contemptuously until she dropped it.

Kate pulled the toy stiletto from her boot-top. It had an edge but no point. Could she jam its spring?

No time.

Malita kicked her rump and propelled her towards Morpho.

Mortain laughed and applauded. A particular aficionado of this act, it seemed. His blonde was watching again, almost lulled.

If she tried to stab Morpho in the chest, the blade would do no harm.

Determined not to die on her knees, she stood and countered his come-hither gesture with one of her own, summoning him to a fight.

He brought out his own knife. A blade sprang from its handle. Not a prop.

She flicked a glance upwards. Erik's lasso was tight around the gorilla's neck. She didn't dare look too long, for fear of drawing attention to the show above the stage.

Morpho puffed smoke and danced towards her.

She slashed at his face, catching his cheek with the knife-edge. Used to scythe rather than stab, the blade didn't retract. She barely scratched him, but a runnel of blood dripped from his face. He gulped and swallowed his dog-end. Coughing and choking, he thumped his own chest.

Now, she got a good strong kick to his shins.

More applause.

'I love it when they fight back,' said Mortain, loosening his sash. '*Encore, encore!*'

Morpho, unhappy with the way this was going, came at her like a wrestler, arms out. If he caught her now, he'd break her spine over his knee.

Sultan's rifle fell from above and slammed butt-first into Morpho's head. His skull audibly cracked and his one eye went red then dull. He collapsed like a sack of bricks. The gun discharged as it hit the floor. Malita yelped, shot in the ankle. The ditchwater Duchess grabbed her by the hair and hauled her into the wings. Her screams grew higher in pitch.

At this point, the orphans – very sensibly – ran off. Slipping between stagehands' legs, they zigzagged to avoid capture.

Henriette and Louise barrelled through the blindfolded orchestra. The musicians made a racket as they missed their places, then stopped playing and tumbled into each other. In the kerfuffle, the children disappeared backstage.

Kate wished them luck and hoped they'd make a better choice for their next circus.

Now, *everyone* looked up. Kate smelled paraffin.

M. Erik had returned to his shadows.

Sultan was lowered slowly, in lurches, on a rope looped around his ankle. He twisted in the air, human hands stuck out of hampering hairy arms. He shook his head, as if trying to get his mask off. He yowled, throwing his voice – his cries seemed to come from all over the auditorium. Drops of liquid spattered on the oilcloth. The gorilla was soaked in paraffin.

'What is this?' cried Pradier.

'It's Poe,' squawked Guignol. 'The tale of "Hop-Frog"!'

Once, Erik had appeared at a masked ball as Edgar Allan Poe's Red Death. Like Guignol, who'd written Dr Tarr and Professor Fether into his show, the Director of the Opera Ghost Agency was an admirer of the gloomy, sickly American poet. Kate preferred Walt Whitman, herself.

She remembered the story of 'Hop-Frog'. The abused jester tricks the cruel king and his toadying courtiers into disguising themselves as orangutans with flammable pitch and flax, and then touches a torch to them.

A ribbon of flame ran down the rope and caught the fur of the paraffin-sodden gorilla man. With a *whump*, Sultan was enveloped in fire. Burning fur stank. A screech sounded, and was cut off as the ape-man sucked fire into his lungs. He kicked and struggled, swinging like a pendulum…

…then the rope burned through. Sultan fell, cracking boards. The props-master had the presence of mind to throw a bucket of water on the dead man. The fire hissed out. Smoke and steam rose. Pradier, an idiot, chittered in delight, taking this for part of the show.

Du Roy stood. He appeared calm, yet a vein throbbed in his forehead.

He looked around for the phantom who had wrecked the performance, then turned – suspicion pricked – to the veiled woman at his side. Kate wasn't the only person who'd forgotten not to trust Clara Watson.

Du Roy drew a small pistol from inside his jacket. A ladies' model. He jammed it up under the scarlet widow's chin and ripped off her veil.

The Master of the Red Circle beheld a face he didn't know.

Yuki shrugged out of the hooded cloak. She wore her kimono. She even carried her parasol.

'Surprise,' gloated Guignol.

The select audience shrank away from Yuki. Gripped by a premonition.

'Find the lady,' said Guignol.

Mortain's doxy pulled off her stiff yellow wig and shook out red hair.

So, Yuki was Clara and Clara was the blonde.

Only Kate was who she said she was – even in this *apache* outfit.

'Whoever you are,' said Du Roy, 'you'll die now...'

Du Roy stood back and straightened his arm, steadying his gun. The barrel was an inch from Yuki's nose.

Faster than the eye could register, Yuki unsheathed a sword from her parasol and made a forceful, yet elegant, pass.

Du Roy looked at a red line around his wrist. His brows knit as he tried to pull the trigger. Wires were cut and the impulse from his brain couldn't reach his fingers. Puzzled, airily irritated, he didn't yet feel the pain.

His hand slid off his wrist and thumped on the floor, letting go of the gun.

Blood gouted like a fountain, which Yuki side-stepped.

'Musicians,' said Guignol, sharply. 'Selection Thirteen, *andante*.'

The ensemble took heed, adjusted their blindfolds and

assumed their playing positions, instruments ready.

They launched into Guignol's idea of an appropriate tune. 'Three Little Maids from School' by Gilbert and Sullivan, from *The Mikado*.

Yuki set about her precise, bloody work – more surgery than butchery.

Among the Red Circle, she lashed out. She held her sword hilt up and struck down, adopting a series of poses, face impassive, ignoring the gouts of gore. She was not hobbled by her dress which, Kate only now realised, was slit to the waist to allow for ease of movement. Her habitual tiny Japanese steps were misdirection.

Screams. Intestines uncoiled. Limbs and heads flew.

The Red Circle got their fill of horrors now.

Three little maids from school are we,
Pert as a schoolgirl well can be,
Filled to the brim with girlish glee,
Three little maids from school!

Père de Kern tried to flee, but his imps gripped his train and he was tugged back onto the killing floor. Yuki laid open his spine. He bucked like a cut-open caterpillar.

Everything is a source of fun...

Mortain lost his innards. Pradier lost his head.

Nobody's safe for we care for none!

Assolant stood up and slid his face onto Yuki's sword-edge. His domino mask fell apart. He detached his skull from the blade, hand pressed over the spurting slice.

Life is a joke that's just begun!

Kate picked up Sultan's rifle. She worked the bolt, ejected the spent cartridge, chambered another. She covered the stagehands.

Morpho and Malita were dead.

Dr Orloff watched, open-mouthed, as his patrons fell.

Three little maids from school! Three little maids from school!

Yuki didn't waste effort. She maimed and killed as she would compose a *haiku* – in seconds, with strictly limited moves.

The orchestra finished the tune.

Yuki sheathed her blade and opened the parasol. She gave a tiny, formal curtsey.

Only now did Kate remember to be terrified.

But not incapacitated. She took a bucket of water from a stagehand and scrubbed the backs of de Kern's imps, scraping enough paint so the children wouldn't die of clogged pores. Whoever they were, she trusted they'd be grateful.

Assolant and Du Roy were still alive.

'Katie dear,' said Clara, sweetly. 'Would you free our client?'

Catching on at once, Kate helped Guignol get loose. He got the enforced straightness out of his bones and kinked up properly.

'That's the way to do it,' he swazzled.

So, Guignol had been coerced into letting the Red Circle take over his theatre. He had taken steps to break their hold over his company.

'You're finished, Hulot,' spat Du Roy.

Guignol mimed a shrug.

Another mystery solved – the secret identity of Guignol. He was Jacques Hulot, once hailed as the funniest man in France, then believed a suicide. Reborn as the maestro of horrors.

'Comedy didn't pay,' he explained to Kate. 'The mob wanted gore, and gore *encore*... So I got a new act. I told truths, showed the world the way it was.'

He capered over to Du Roy.

'But the mob are less bloodthirsty than you, you pathetic wretch. My horrors are a mirror – they do not represent the world as I wish it to be. They are a caution, not a blueprint. Only a few mistake it for one. And few of them have the want of feeling that would admit them to your circle. It takes refinement to be so dreadful. Are you satisfied now? Have you finally had your fill of blood, you monster of France?'

Du Roy let go of his seeping wrist and died.

So there were no heirs of Monsieur Hulot. Guignol, the management of the theatre, was Hulot himself, transformed

... and the *Théâtre des Horreurs* was the risen spectre of the *Théâtre des Plaisantins*.

Amid all the carnage, the clown couldn't help himself. Guignol was still funny.

The tableau at the end of his show, the waxworks of the *Légion d'Horreur*, was a specific charge, accusing the Brothers of the Red Circle. Another living signpost, marking the way for the Angels of Music. These are the guilty men, these are *your* guilty men. Come and stop them, for I – Guignol – am in their power and cannot. Kate had looked for hidden meaning, when it was obvious enough to be understood in the rear stalls.

General Assolant still stood, half his face red. His famous battles were fought and finished well before he arrived at the bloody field to supervise the executions. Now, he'd have real scars to go with his medals.

The officer who despised cowards was trembling.

'Don't be alarmed, General,' said Clara. 'You must remain alive, to tell any others... any of the Red Circle not present, any who might share its inclinations. Your run is over. The show is closed by the order of... Messieurs Guignol and Erik. You understand? Your marching orders are given. Now get out of this place before my dainty friend changes her mind and plays parasol games again.'

Assolant didn't need to be told twice. He scarpered, the sword he hadn't thought to draw rattling at his side.

Kate took a moment and put all her weight into slapping Clara.

The English widow licked a bead of blood from her lip and shrugged.

'You couldn't be told, Katie. You're a good journalist, but no actress.'

'Why didn't you stop the show before it began?' she asked, as much of Yuki as Clara. 'Before anyone was hurt.'

'Your friend Sultan had to be removed,' said Clara. 'A tricky situation.'

Kate saw the sense, but still burned. Stage Door Jeannot had paid for Erik's tardiness.

Nini, the Aztec princess, came forward. She'd taken off her headdress.

'My father's letters?'

'Will be returned to you,' said Guignol, kissing her hand.

Satisfied, Nini left the stage.

Guignol looked at the smiling props-master, the nervous stagehands and the now-sighted orchestra.

'I know you were suborned to this by Orloff. You are on probation, but you keep your jobs... except you, Rollo. You enjoyed this too much. Go find other employment and take your knives with you.'

Rollo shrugged, gathered up a selection of implements and departed.

'Orloff,' said Guignol, drawing out the name, 'you are a mockery of a man, barely a human creature. We have a vacancy for you. You'll find your gorilla suit in the costumes closet. It'll be sewn on. The mask will be fixed to your face with glue, permanently. And you'll gibber amusingly, play the star role when we stage "Murders in the Rue Morgue" and submit entirely to my will... or else you'll share the fate of your predecessor Sultan. Do you understand me?'

Orloff, white with terror, sank to his knees, surrounded by parts of his patrons. They were now literally a Red Circle.

'Now, I want this stage washed and this mess cleared,' ordered Guignol. 'Tomorrow night, and every night, we have a show to put on. The *Théâtre des Horreurs* does not go dark!'

XIII

THE ANGELS SAT with the Persian in the Café de la Paix. Yuki ate ice cream and Clara drank China tea.

Kate was still irritated.

The job was done – the Red Circle sundered, the Montmartre murders stopped – and the client satisfied.

She had thought she understood why Clara betrayed her, but it turned out that the Englishwoman had shammed her way into the Red Circle. Now, Kate was bewildered again. It had made so much sense for Clara Watson to defect. She was a self-declared connoisseur of torture. Whatever was wrong with Du Roy was wrong with her too – perhaps far more so. Erik had taken her on precisely because of this defect.

'What was it, Clara?' she asked. 'Why were you so set against them?'

'The *Légion d'Horreur* were bourgeois hypocrites – salivating in secret, rather than proudly taking their pleasures in the open. Besides, I wanted to see a true artist perform... and I have. I shall treasure the memory.'

'Guignol?'

'Oh, he's adorable... but no. Not Guignol.'

Clara raised her teacup to Yuki, who dipped her head modestly.

'Grace. Elegance. Minimalism. Mutilation. Execution. Perfect.'

Kate would never understand. For her, horrors were just horrors.

She looked up at the frontage of the Opera House and fancied a gargoyle was up there, watching over them.

She'd never understand him either. As a reporter, as a detective, she needed only to know the facts; only as Kate Reed did she want to know more.

The Persian laid a dossier of press cuttings on the table.

'Now, *les filles*, another matter has come to the attention of the Agency. Kate, you will be interested. In the Louvre, guards have been assaulted. It is rumoured that treasures have disappeared. Some talk of a curse upon the building. A strange figure has been seen, drifting through the halls by night, cloaked and silent, wearing the headdress and golden death-mask of a pharaoh...'

ACT FOUR: THE MARK OF KANE

'Mr Carter, if the headline is big enough, it makes the news big enough.'

Herman J. Mankiewicz and Orson Welles,
Citizen Kane (1941)

I

A TICKET HAD BEEN delivered by *pneumatique*. The Special Performance would commence, unusually, at half past ten in the morning.

He entered his box via the trapdoor. Plush upholstery matched the velvet curtains, soft and rich in the electric lamplight. A phonograph apparatus stood on a trolley. A programme lay on his chair. It was an unfamiliar design – not from the Paris Opéra, but a theatre in Chicago.

The half-hour chimed. He cranked the phonograph and raised the needle-arm to the revolving cylinder. After a few seconds' hiss, an anonymous voice issued from the bell.

'Good morning, Monsieur Erik...'

He opened the programme as indicated by a tasselled bookmark. A full-page rotogravure portrait showed a plump, smiling, expensively dressed patron.

'The man you are looking at is Charles Foster Kane, the American millionaire and press magnate. Kane believes his financial and political interests, and those of the United States of America, would be served by war among the Great Powers of Europe. Presently, he is summering at Royale-les-Eaux, a spa town north of Dieppe where he has substantial holdings, ostensibly to acquire works of ancient and modern art for his private collection. In truth, Kane has convened a gathering of powerful, like-minded or simply malign individuals and plans to found a cartel dedicated to bringing about a catastrophic conflict.'

Kane had small, piggy eyes; a ridiculous nose, perhaps artificial; fat, complacent cheeks; and an impertinent double-flick of a moustache.

'Your commission, should you be inclined to accept it, is to ensure this offensive organisation does not come into being and that Charles Kane is dissuaded from further meddling in the affairs of sovereign nations other than his own. As before, should you or any of your angelic associates be apprehended or eliminated, the Minister will profess never to have heard of such fantastical individuals. Long live France. This cylinder will perish within a matter of moments...'

A bar of magnesium fizzed blindingly inside the works of the phonograph. Box Five smelled like a burning wax museum. The cylinder resolved into molten residue.

The Special Performance was at an end.

II

THE YOUNG WIDOW Gilberte Lachaille, following the Persian's instructions, carefully made her way through the labyrinth beneath the Opéra. She avoided the rat-traps, and negotiated several ingenious devices set to inconvenience mammals somewhat larger than the average sewer rat. Out of respect for poor Gaston, she wore a black dress. She left off the veil because it was dark enough under the streets of Paris. Gilberte did not care to vanish entirely into the shadows – though, it occurred to her, disappearance might be the whole purpose of the invitation from Monsieur Erik.

In the absence of the fortune her late husband's lawyers were withholding, she must find means of making a way in the world.

Her hard-earned respectable name counted for little, though it was scarcely her fault – no matter what the Sûreté might imply – that her bridegroom proved incapable of surviving his own honeymoon. Without consulting her, the foolish soul had elected to fortify himself with a philtre to put 'lead in his pencil'. He had misjudged the dosage, to everyone's inconvenience – not least his own. For a reputed man of the world, Gaston turned out to be something of a stiff, in all senses of the term. Aunt Alicia said dead husbands were generally the best of the breed, but also conceded that society was liable to be leery of Gilberte for now. In Grandmama's day, you had to bury at least two husbands in mysterious circumstances before being categorised as a 'black widow'. In this impatient, young, electrified century, a single hasty funeral sufficed.

A skiff waited at the shore of the underground lake. She lifted her skirts and stepped in. No sooner was she settled than the boat began to glide soundlessly across the still surface. It was on a pulley, like a fairground ride.

Gilberte had heard whispers of the masked creature – Monsieur Erik, the Phantom – who kept a lair beneath the Opéra and retained the services of hard-to-place young women in a discreet agency which had been in operation for some years. Many and varied adventuresses had worked for the Phantom. The Angels might be fleeting but Erik's primary lieutenant was always the Persian. This fellow was known to *le tout Paris*. Some believed him the true master of the Opera Ghost Agency.

The Persian stood on the jetty to which the skiff was pulled. Erik's assistant wore a heavy coat with a good astrakhan collar, and a fez. Gold dotted his person – rings, stickpin, shirt-studs, cufflinks, spectacles-chain, fez tassels, watch and fob, two prominent teeth. Courteously, the Persian extended a hand and helped Gilberte ashore. She thanked him, modestly.

He pressed his palm to a stone. A wall parted to give access to a large, comfortably appointed room. Gas-lamps burned, susurrating like serpents. Gilberte stepped in and cast an eye over fine old furniture, assessing values to the sou. These were the quarters of a well-off gentleman. The subterranean chamber was naturally bereft of windows and thus oppressive for her taste.

A portion of the room was curtained off by a thick but translucent hanging. A man sat in the antechamber beyond, lit from behind as if in a silhouette theatre. Her eyes went naturally to this figure, whom she took at once for the fabled Phantom. She did not immediately take notice of the two other women in the room.

'Madame Lachaille,' said the man beyond the veil, 'thank you for joining us this evening.'

It was a deep, mellifluous voice, precise and perfect. Through Mama, the contralto Andrée Alvar, she knew many singers. She recognised a musical quality in this voice. An odd catch suggested the speaker was compensating for a defect of the palate. Erik took care with certain consonants. Gilberte recalled the stories of the face some claimed to have glimpsed, and repressed a shudder.

She curtseyed as she had been taught – not submissively, but confidently. Grandmama would be proud. And Aunt Alicia. And Mama.

'Gilberte, you will be working with these women. Mrs Elizabeth Eynsford Hill…'

Mrs Eynsford Hill was impeccably – if too simply – dressed, and as blankly beautiful as a couturier's mannequin. The woman shook Gilberte's hand, firmly. She had a steel grip in her good green kidskin glove.

'It is a perfect pleasure to make your acquaintance, Madame Lachaille,' said Mrs Eynsford Hill, in English. 'I foresee we shall become fast friends.'

Her diction was classroom perfect, with a musical lilt as if she were hitting notes rather than uttering words.

Gilberte responded, also in English, 'That is my hope also.'

The woman paused, and repeated, 'That is my hope also,' parrot-fashion. It took Gilberte a moment to realise she had been perfectly imitated. Not just vocally; Mrs Eynsford Hill's expression had been Gilberte's, down to the trick of lowering the eyes while missing nothing.

'I beg your pardon. For such insolence.'

Now Mrs Eynsford Hill was 'doing' Erik. She spoke in masculine French, as if from beyond the curtain. As the Phantom, the Englishwoman pulled back her chin and sucked in her cheeks to create a deeper voice. Even those odd consonants were there.

'Elizabeth is showing off,' said Erik. 'It is one of her tells. Having discovered the extent of her talents, she needs an audience. Like many of my Angels, she has a theatrical inclination.'

'You are a widow, I perceive,' said Mrs Eynsford Hill, in what Gilberte now took for her own – if not her *original* – voice. 'I myself, sadly, am not.'

'My condolences.'

The other Angel cooed for attention.

'This is Riolama,' said Erik.

If the Englishwoman was so ordinary she seemed strange for the absence or concealment of lively qualities, this creature was a picture-book fairy come to life.

Riolama might have been taken for a child, though her large, active eyes were adult. Well under five feet tall, she wore a shimmering white-grey shift of fabric Gilberte could not identify (spider silk?), had a wild but untangled fall of dark hair and did without shoes. Her feet were not dirty.

The girl sprang from a tall stool and bent close to Gilberte, flitting like an inquisitive monkey or a bird. She was making up her mind, apparently. After a few seconds, she pecked a kiss at Gilberte's cheek and darted away, back to her perch, pleased.

'Rima likes you,' said Mrs Eynsford Hill. 'She's from Guyana, where the *guano* comes from. Or Venezuela, where various violent volcanoes are venerated. The territory is under dispute.'

The bird-girl tucked her head under her arm, then smiled. Gilberte felt a chill – it was her own once-upon-a-time smile, which Grandmama had schooled her out of. For their own good, girls do not show teeth. In this company, evidently, teeth were acceptable. Indeed, perhaps mandatory.

If whispers were true, the lipless Erik had no choice but to smile and smile. Beyond the curtain, behind the mask, was – she had heard – a skull with yellow eyes. The Phantom could take first prize in a grinning contest with the mediaeval clown Gwynplaine and the Bohemian Baron Sardonicus.

Gilberte was struck that the Englishwoman and the exotic girl both resembled her. Might she be reunited with unknown sisters? Her father, rarely mentioned by the female relatives who raised her, could conceivably have sojourned in London or Caracas.

She had an inkling Mrs Eynsford Hill was not as high-born as her too-correct accent would suggest. In Gilberte's experience, the upper classes were as slovenly as the lower orders in their speech – only their vocal tics and mispronunciations tended to be called mannerisms rather than mistakes. Like Gilberte, the Englishwoman had been taught how to speak to impress others rather than express herself.

'Ladies,' said Erik, 'if we might proceed. It is best we talk English. It is not, of course, a musical language, but it is in this instance the tongue of our enemy.'

Gilberte had high marks in English.

Curtains parted to reveal a screen. The Persian worked a cinematograph projector and images came to life.

The mode was more Lumière than Méliès – snatches of actuality caught by the camera, rather than a staged artifice. A fat man in a straw hat grinned next to a half-crated statue twice his size, like a big game hunter proud of his latest bag and eager to gloat among his clubmen.

'This is Charles Foster Kane,' said Erik. 'He is an American.'

'All too plainly,' commented Mrs Eynsford Hill.

In another scene, Kane – in a shiny silk hat and a fur coat that looked like a whole bear – stood outside the ruins of a castle in Spain. Workmen carried away and crated up huge stone blocks.

'Mr Kane has an acquisitive nature,' continued Erik, 'and a limitless source of wealth. A gold-mine in Colorado.'

Now, the man was in evening dress, squeezed between girls wearing little more than feathers. Gilberte recognised the upstairs rooms at Maxim's. Several of her contemporaries could recount adventures at this locale.

Kane posed with a group of sharp-eyed, ferociously moustached men outside the offices of a newspaper.

'Shortly before the turn of the century,' said Erik, 'a correspondent of the *New York Inquirer* cabled Kane, claiming he could write prose poems about the scenery in Cuba but "there was no war". Kane responded: "You provide the prose poems, I'll provide the war."'

Kane watched troops in Boy Scout uniforms board a ship. Then, he was laughing with Theodore Roosevelt on a podium draped with flags. They made a matched pair of ferocious little boys.

'Mr Kane did indeed provide the Spanish-American War. In this new century, his tactics have moderated. At least, he spurred his own country to fight over Cuba. Now he intends to foment an Anglo-French War.'

Gilberte exchanged looks with Mrs Eynsford Hill.

'Why would he wish such a thing?' Gilberte asked.

'Mr Kane is a patriot,' said Erik. 'With Europe in flames, America would become the pre-eminent world power. The upstart nation, scarcely more than a century old, would dictate its whims from Nanking to Nantes. A continental war would, not incidentally, sell a great many newspapers.'

On the screen, the American was at a zoo alongside a pinch-faced lady Gilberte took for Mrs Kane. He pointed out a cockatoo, which was dragged by a keeper – silently screaming and flapping – from a branch. It was shoved into a canary cage and presented to the magnate.

'Bad man,' said Riolama. 'Mean to bird.'

Gilberte was surprised the girl could speak.

The cinematograph presentation concluded.

* * *

III

I N THE LAST century, Royale-les-Eaux had enjoyed a vogue as a watering place for the wealthy and listless. Mama had sung a season at the Petit Opéra, attached to the Grand Hôtel and the Casino. The burglar Théophraste Lupin had lifted jewels and broken hearts among the ladies who flocked from Paris and further afield to summer balls, concerts and gaming tourneys. Their excuse was the local springs, reputedly a tonic for intimate diseases. In 1890, the waters ran dry and nothing could be done to make them flow again. The Société des Bains de Mers de Royale, who governed far more than the baths, suffered a decline reversed only by the miracle of a Yankee deliverer.

Charles Foster Kane had lighted upon the town and made it his European compound. What could not be bought was leased. A motion was before the Société to change the resort's name to Europa-Xanadu, to further the connection with the magnate's Florida fiefdom. Royale-les-Eaux was an outpost of Kane's empire, an American colony in the old world. Having relocated castles from Spain, Hungary and Scotland to serve as guest-houses, he was filling the halls with works of art purchased or looted from the great collections of the continent. A reserve was stocked with wild boar (a hardy local breed crossed with Australian razorback) suitable for stalking, shooting, scoffing and stuffing. An army of cronies, hangers-on and minions easily filled the place. However, showing the democratic impulse of his peculiar country, Kane decreed his private realm be open to the general public.

As soon as the Angels alighted from the train at the Gare de Royale-les-Eaux, it became apparent that apparent madness was founded on solid business practice. Scrubbed and smiling youths of both sexes, with a stylised 'K' on their tunic breasts, besieged new arrivals. They offered to carry baggage (for fifty centimes), sell post-cards (for fifty centimes), provide ginger beer or gelati (for fifty centimes), serve as guides to the town (for fifty centimes an hour), secure seats at 'exclusive' high-stakes gaming tables (for fifty centimes!), or effect introduction to suitable temporary companions (for considerably more than fifty centimes). It was impossible to take three steps in this town without spending money, as if every franc in every pocket were magnetically drawn to the millionaire's already-overflowing coffers.

Such a shame the fellow was inconveniently married. No, that was beyond consideration. Money was beside the point. One did not marry an American, any more than an orangutan. There were standards.

The Persian had wisely left all gold accoutrements behind save his teeth (and kept his mouth firmly shut to hide them). He swept licensed, uniformed pick-pockets out of their way and located an elderly railway porter. The fellow wore the K-brand, but had plainly been at his post long before the new regime descended. The Persian extended a handsome bribe to make sure their trunks arrived inviolate at the Grand Hôtel. He whispered something terrifying in the porter's ear – presumably invoking their phantom patron – to persuade the man it would be best to follow instructions to the letter.

Outside the station, the tiny town was a Babel. Purple-liveried cowboys cracked whips and held up signs to direct crowds this way and that. Royale-les-Eaux was a combination of Wild West 'wide open town', Tartar war camp and storybook enchanted kingdom. Bath-houses and hotels had sprouted towers and castellations, some of stone and some merely wooden stage flats, to become every possible variety of gaming-hall, bordello or museum of curiosities. A bandstand in the Venetian style stood outside the concourse. An orchestra in harlequin costumes played while dancing girls hopped around behind a singer in a striped jacket and jaunty hat. Over and over, they performed the town's new anthem, alternately in French ('C'est Monsieur Kane') and English ('Oh, Mister Kane').

When the song came round for the third time, Elizabeth said, 'I will find out who wrote that tune, and have Rima drop him in a South American river for the piranhas to devour. Then I shall have his polished bones set in a xylophone which I will sell to a ragtime band.'

Every fourth or fifth building was a peculiar type of café, surmounted by a wrought-iron K inside a circle – the Mark of Kane. Here, patrons queued for thin meat patties and salad leftovers served inside limp circles of bread, along with deep-fried potato peelings unworthy of the name *pommes frites*. This fare was handed over in boxes made of folded newspaper (*New York Inquirer* overruns, Gilberte supposed). No plates or cutlery were involved. Customers fetched their own food and found their own tables, if they could – so waiters need not apply for employment. Cheap trinkets were given as prizes to those who gobbled their Fatty Feast within the shortest time. It would take a diamond pendant to make Gilberte *start* a Burgher Kane meal, let alone finish it.

She dreaded to imagine what went on in the kitchens. Rumour was that the cowboys herded animals into giant mechanical pens where many whirling blades rendered them – bones, skin, hooves, eyes, bowel contents and all – into a thick liquid which was splashed onto grills to create the circular patties. The Burgher Kane slogan was 'over twenty-two thousand sold'. Such cafés were supposedly popular in New York, Chicago and San Francisco. From Royale-les-Eaux, Kane intended to expand across Europe. A conquering army could do no more harm.

With dignity, Elizabeth walked down the street, flanked by Gilberte and Riolama. The Englishwoman ignored everyone who tried to importune her, Gilberte kept an eye out for potential assassins, and the bird girl was nervous in this crowded, cacophonous jungle. Impertinent comments were addressed to the ladies by idlers. The Persian saw to it that every insult was punished with a withering glance or, if appropriate, a cuff.

Gilberte herself had to thump a masher with her parasol before they reached the Grand Hôtel.

IV

THE LOBBY WAS dominated by a twice life-size painting – a poor copy of Hals' 'The Laughing Cavalier' with Kane's face replacing the original sitter's. The curlicued K was everywhere, on doorknobs and antimacassars and wood-panels and the carpet. Gilberte wondered whether the American insisted employees have his mark tattooed on their shoulders like slaves or branded into their thighs like cattle.

At the front desk, Elizabeth announced herself as 'Miss Kathleen Ruston', an English lady whose charitable foundation provided improving literature for bereft children in uncivilised quarters of the world. The little flutter Elizabeth allowed into her voice suggested Miss Ruston found Royale-les-Eaux backward enough to be in need of a tract or two.

A sharp-eyed female receptionist saw through the imposture at once. The real Miss Ruston was detained in Huddersfield by a mystery ailment not unconnected with doctored gin. From her reticule, Elizabeth produced a lacquered oblong, embossed with a gold K – a 1,000 francs board from the Casino. A gilt design on the reverse, resembling an octopus, distinguished it from the ordinary run. The receptionist noted this, and signalled for a superior – a sleek-haired, hollow-eyed young man with a sharp-pointed false beard.

'I am Haghi,' he said. He might have been German or Arab or any nationality. 'Mr Kane trusts you will enjoy your stay, and extends the invitation to join his other "special guests" in the private salon this evening. *Okee geluk, dama.*'

'*Dankzegging, mens,*' Elizabeth responded, sotto voce.

Their host had arranged that Miss Ruston be indisposed,

so her identity could be usurped by a Dutch lady who bore a passing resemblance to the philanthropist but was quite a different character. Edda Van Heemstra – dancer, courtesan, thief, blackmailer and trafficker in government secrets – was not a person to be entrusted with a charitable foundation. Her notion of 'improving literature' ran to illustrated editions of *Memoirs of a Woman of Pleasure* or *My Nine Nights in a Harem*. Detained during a stopover in Paris, Mevrouw Van Heemstra currently enjoyed the hospitality of locked apartments in the sub-basement of the Opéra. Erik provided choice wines from his private cellar and an extensive collection of phonograph recordings for her entertainment.

On only a few moments' acquaintance, Elizabeth had Edda off perfectly, though her Dutch vocabulary was limited to pages of common words and phrases torn from a *Baedeker's Guide to the Netherlands*. Gilberte admired the performance. Elizabeth was successfully impersonating a Dutch harlot imperfectly posing as an English prude. No wonder she scarcely remembered who she really was.

Among Kane's special guests, Edda was high in the magnate's councils. She had been entrusted with procuring documents central to his plans.

The register was presented. Elizabeth signed with a flourish. Forging signatures was another of her talents. Gilberte was beginning to feel Grandmama and Aunt Alicia had neglected vital aspects of her education.

'Eddie, you are a sight for sore eyes,' brayed a loud, American voice.

Gilberte tensed. This would be a real test. Someone who knew Edda Van Heemstra.

Assembling a dazzling coquette's smile, Elizabeth turned to greet the man who had addressed her. Gilberte saw in her companion's eyes that she had no idea who the fellow was.

Well dressed but for a shapeless slouch hat which put his face permanently in shadow, the American thrust out a paw, as if expecting 'Eddie' to shake it like a man. His hand was several sizes too large for his body, thickly furred, with diamond-shaped horny nails. A malformation of the tendons made the fingers curve claw-like, as if he were perpetually clutching an invisible throat.

The hand was his tell. While Elizabeth was practising her Dutch, Gilberte had gone through a flip-book memorising faces, aliases and histories. Erik had excellent, up-to-date intelligence: Haghi, the deferential hotelier, was – without the goatee – also Nemo the Clown, an expert hypnotist, basket-weaver and revolver shot. Gilberte was a fast learner, too. It was her duty of the day to steer Elizabeth through a crowd of 'known associates'.

'This must be the famous Perry Bennett,' Gilberte announced, extending her own languid, gloved hand to the clutcher. 'Edd, you must introduce me.'

Elizabeth's eyes focused. She followed Gilberte's lead.

'Mr Bennett, my companion represents an organisation which must be well known to you, though its name is not spoken even in this company. May I present Mademoiselle Irma Vep of Montmartre.'

'I am especially familiar with the *rooftops* of that district,' Gilberte claimed.

She was also appropriating an alias, but a shadowier one. Irma Vep was perpetually high in the councils of *Les Vampires*. She was a thief, or perhaps several thieves, or perhaps just a cast-aside bodystocking and mask anyone might pick up and put on. Irma sometimes represented herself as Pia Verm, Vi Marpe, Miep Vrå, Mira Pev, Vera Mip, Marie Pv, Eva Prim, Virma Ep or Ma Viper. Gilberte thought the game silly and jokingly suggested she call herself Anna Gram instead.

However, the man with the clutching hand was impressed.

Relations between the Opera Ghost Agency and *Les Vampires* were relatively cordial. Gilberte was borrowing the Irma Vep name with permission.

Riolama peeked out from behind Elizabeth. She wore a sailor suit and had been persuaded to don oversized workman's boots painted pink. She looked no older than twelve.

'This is Rima, an auxiliary member of the, ah...'

Gilberte crooked her forefingers and put them in front of her eye-teeth while opening her eyes wide – the universal underworld sign for *Les Vampires*.

Bennett looked at the waif as if she were an ice cream sundae with a cherry on top. Gilberte knew instantly that he was one of *those* – once a girl turned thirteen, she was of no interest to him. American rogues in his line often wheedled to be appointed as guardians to underage heiresses and were torn by contradictory impulses. Should they rope in a defrocked clergyman and force the girl into marriage at dead of night, or set the fuse to the dynamite and strand her in an abandoned mine?

'What a gathering of like souls!' Bennett announced, in a high-pitched voice which didn't quite match his sinister looks. 'I was on the boat train from London with Madame Sara, Sir Dunston Gryne and Simon Carne. Imagine: the Sorceress of the Strand, the Azrael of Anarchy and the Prince of Swindlers in one place! Dr Materialismus is here, and Abijah K. Jones, the Devil Bug. If only the crowds out on the promenade knew who was among them? What a cut-up that would be! I daresay many would expire from sheer fright to think their sleeves had been brushed by the likes of Baron Maupertuis or Dr Quartz or Wizard Whateley! Professor Fate and Sir Cuthbert Ware-Armitage have been delayed, because their motor-cars collided on the road from Dieppe and they are conducting a duel. But the Assassination Bureau, Ltd. has opened a stall disguised as a gypsy fortune-teller's, and is advertising cut-rate offers.'

The hand remained stuck out stiffly, quivering with Bennett's excitement to be in such company. Gilberte judged him a minor villain – he was like several women in Aunt Lucia's circle who were overly eager to list invitations they had received from prominent people and always worked 'as I was saying to such-and-such-a-person-far-more-distinguished-than-you' into their chatter.

Bennett was also slightly deluded about the company, which

was marginally less distinguished than the American believed. The current Grand Vampire deemed Kane an upstart amateur and had happily turned his invitation over to the Opera Ghost Agency. Since Professor Moriarty went over the waterfall, there was an unofficial contest for the title of worst villain of the age. The Lord of Strange Deaths, from China, and Dr Mabuse, from Germany, were leading candidates. Some would argue for Dr Nikola or the Countess Cagliostro. None of them were here. This was a Great Gathering of Second-Raters.

Beneath his hat brim, Bennett's eyes wandered sideways to see if anyone more famous had come into the lobby. Finally, he fixed on someone.

'You must excuse me,' said Bennett, bowing slightly. 'I see Raymond Owen – a countryman of mine, with similar interests. We must confer on matters of mutual concern. Tethering to railroad tracks has proved a more unreliable method of solving a problem than those of our stripe might wish.'

He hopped off, with a gait that suggested his left leg must suffer from the condition affecting his right arm.

Gilberte looked at Elizabeth and Riolama.

They had passed their first test, and were accepted by at least one of this wicked company.

Haghi struck a bell, summoning a minion to escort the ladies to their suite.

V

'IN XANADU DID Kubla Khan a sacred pleasure-dome decree...'
The words were written in incandescent bulbs over the doors of the Casino.

Gilberte had learned Coleridge off by heart in her English class. It was supposed to be a *stately* pleasure-dome.

The foyer was lined with peculiar contraptions. Patrons fed

them with coins, yanked a crank-handle, and peered through a window as wheels whirred, then ground to a halt displaying miniature playing cards. If the centime-stuffer was fortunate enough to get a winning hand, the machine spat out tokens redeemable only at the bar in the Casino. The machines made a horrid, grinding, clanking sound. Their devotees had an impatient, haggard look she found quite disturbing.

'In America, they automate everything,' she mused.

'Not *everything*,' said Elizabeth. 'There will always be a place for the human touch.'

Interspersed with the gaming machines were Mutoscopes, which worked on a similar principle. Coins unlocked a mechanism, and working the handle ran a strip of pictures past a peep-hole. *The Dance of the Nile. The Execution of Marie Antoinette. Madame at her Bath. Facing the Firing Squad. A Maiden Surprised by a Satyr.* Gentlemen cranked vigorously, and peered at the tiny, flickering action. Live women could stroll past *au naturel* without distracting these addicts from their chemically graven images.

As Irma Vep and Edda Van Heemstra, Gilberte and Elizabeth wore black and white evening dresses with matching domino masks.

Riolama was back in the suite, taking one of her bird-naps.

In the main salon of the Casino, fortunes were won and lost the old-fashioned way at baccarat or roulette tables. A hall the size of a railway station was lit by a multi-faceted globe, which was studded with electric bulbs and mirrors. This interior sun revolved slowly, wavering lights over tiers of gambling concourses, probably to the fury of people trying to concentrate on their cards or the wheel. Gilberte trusted the sphere was fixed more securely to the ceiling than the famous chandelier at the Paris Opéra.

They passed through the busy hall to the inner sanctum. A brass-bound door, emblazoned with the most elaborate K yet, was guarded by a big-browed, jut-jawed giant in evening dress.

He was covered in the flip-book. Edda was supposed to know him from a previous exploit.

'Voltaire,' Gilberte whispered to Elizabeth. 'Strong-arm man for hire. You shot him in the head in New Orleans. He's had metal teeth put in since then.'

'*Daa-hling*,' said Elizabeth, very loudly, 'you've done something marvellous with your mouth.'

Voltaire grinned, showing sharpened steel.

'Most ferocious,' Elizabeth commented. 'And this, of course, is, ah, Irma Vep ...'

Elizabeth presented their special board, and the giant – who obviously thought less of being shot in the head than many folks of Gilberte's acquaintance – opened the door to the private salon.

It was theatrically gloomy. Kane had stripped hangings, murals, frescoes and candle-sconces from an abandoned Transylvanian castle and reassembled the décor in this conference room.

A huge oak table, suitable for a Viking feast, already accommodated many masked or veiled men and women. A Neolithic altar, grooved and stained by centuries of ritual murder, was set at the head of the table, like a lectern.

Elizabeth and Gilberte took the seats allotted to Edda and Irma. Masks nodded at them. Some of the veiled ladies wore enormously feathered hats. A few villains laid daggers, pistols or exotic devices on their place-settings.

An oversized hairy hand waved at them from the end of the table. Bennett must be pleased to be included in the inner circle. They were near the top of the table. Elizabeth had a corner seat, across from a leonine fellow in a *papier-mâché* Guignol mask. To Gilberte's left was a ramrod-straight, severe young woman sewn into a tight-fitting gown composed of metallic plates. She wore a metal mask studded with rivets.

A middle-aged, white-haired fellow with arthritic hands stood by the altar. Henry F. Potter, a banker, was associated with Kane in usury and union-busting throughout the American Mid-West. He had a reputation for dispossessing widows – which, since her bereavement, Gilberte took exception to. In vaudeville parlance, Potter was the 'warm-up' act.

'Friends,' coughed Potter, 'now we are all present, I suggest we take off our masks. There should be no need for disguise in this company.'

To emphasise the point, the banker slipped off a bandit domino which was useless for concealing his identity. She had thought he was just wearing thick spectacles.

Up and down the table, veils were lifted, hats removed and masks slipped off.

Most of the names Bennett had dropped were present: Madame Sara, Dunston Gryme, Dr Quartz, Simon Carne, Baron Maupertuis. Gilberte recognised others from the flip-book: William Boltyn, an American patron of science who claimed to be wealthier even than Kane, along with his pet engineer Hattison; Gurn, promising mercenary and murderer; General Guy Sternwood, hero of the Spanish-American War according to the Kane papers but 'the Blundering Butcher of Las Guasimas' in every other record of the conflict; sleek young Senator Joseph Harrison Paine, the tycoon's bought-and-paid-for voice in Washington; and Julian Karswell, the English diabolist.

Kane's company took in vastly disparate political interests. The woman in the metal dress was Natasha Natasaevna di Murska, sworn enemy of kings and capital. Her father, the mysterious Natas, was mastermind of an international organisation called (unsubtly) The Terrorists. Natasha glared fierce hatred at the plutocrats, robber barons and aristocrats who formed the greater part of Kane's company. Gilberte trusted the Princess of the Revolution hadn't been allowed to bring any of the bombs she famously liked to throw at oppressors of the people into this room.

The fellow opposite Elizabeth took off his Guignol guise to reveal a second mask underneath – a tight-fitting, rough-stitched leather hood with slashes to show his teeth and eyes. He was the Face, whose page in the Agency's flip-book of notable fiends, mercenaries and masterminds was mostly blank. His true features were seen less frequently even than the baleful skull of Monsieur Erik. He put it about that he was so transcendently handsome that normal life was impossible – women and men, equally besotted, would abase themselves in his path wherever he went. Gilberte had heard some good stories in her time, but that one took the madeleine.

Potter rapped the altar with knobby knuckles.

Voltaire wound up a phonograph and that dratted 'Oh, Mr Kane' tune sounded out, played as pompous fanfare. The already dim room-lights lowered and bright spots flared on the altar. Charles Foster Kane himself appeared, arms outstretched, in a dazzling white suit, grinning like an imbecile, enjoying himself immensely. He swept off his straw hat and waved it. He was at once a politician, a pastor, a song-and-dance man and chairman of the board. Gilberte wondered if they were supposed to applaud.

A glance up and down the table showed most of the company were also sceptical. But they stayed. Kane clearly had a species of magnetism. Money, ignorance and energy were a potent combination and – if what she had seen at Royale-les-Eaux was anything to go on – might soon surge around the world.

'Hiya, fellers – and, especially, feller-esses,' said Kane. 'Welcome to the Inner Circle of the Most High Order of Xanadu. I just made that up, you know. Most of you folks are used to secret societies and such, stretching back hundreds of years. I reckoned it'd be a comfort to have a new one to sign up to. I'll have X buttons made up...'

Gilberte suspected there'd be a K on the pommel of the X.

'We've a whole pile of doings to get through today, so I'll try – against my natural instincts – to be brief. I'm a newspaperman, so I ought to know not to waste words gussying up the message with flowery language. We want a war, right?'

A few mumbles, and a little bark of excitement from General Sternwood.

Kane made an exaggerated show of disappointment.

'Come on, Inner Circle, I know you can do better than that! We want a war, *right?*'

'*Right,*' shouted all the Americans at the table, in enthusiastic unison.

'I suppose so,' conceded the English Carne.

'It is inevitable,' decreed the Hungarian Natasha.

'*Ma foi,* maybe,' shrugged the Belgian Maupertuis.

'That's more like it,' said Kane. 'I knew you had it in you. Whoo, this is a tough room. Do you like the room, by the way? The late Count had cobwebs and bats and rats – I even found a dead armadillo behind a sideboard – but I've spruced the old rags and stones up. Anyway, to the point, this war... I know you all take the *New York Inquirer*, so I'll hurry through the setup. Last year, we ran a serial in thirty-two breathless instalments, thrilling our readers with "The European War of the Future". It was a lulu! Wore out three writers. I had them run around interviewing experts in politics, munitions, naval warfare, airships, finance and all manner of things you wouldn't even think of – like military cuisine and fashions in uniform boots, ladies – then doled out their findings in an exciting, rapidly paced tale. We presented the serial as if they were reports from an actual, live war. Nations fell under the savage lance, dashing cavalrymen charged at each other like total lunatics, nuns were violated by heathen grenadiers – always a popular line – and the crowned heads of half-a-dozen countries wound up rolling together in a wicker basket...'

Natasha Natasaevna di Murska allowed herself half a smile at the thought.

'I don't know why we didn't think of it before! We found readers cared more about this made-up war than real ones in Africa and South America. We had better illustrations and more heart-rending quotes. And white people being massacred. Naturally, the boys and girls in the drug-stores and on the street-cars are clamouring for a sequel. What, I hear you ask, could be bigger and better and more popular than an invented European

War of the Future? That's right, *mes amis* and *amigos*… a real-life, actual European War of Right Now. Which is what we are going to deliver.'

General Sternwood – who, of course, wouldn't have to *fight* in this war – applauded. Perry Bennett flapped his normal hand against his clutching one.

'I'm just a sawdust-on-the-floor kind of fellow who misses the spittoon as often as he gets a bull's eye,' continued Kane, 'but I've learned the value of buying the best help there is on the market. I did that with my serial, and I'm doing that with my war. So, I'd like those of you who have already contributed to Plan Thunderbolt to stand up, introduce yourselves and shoot us the low-down on how we're going to pull it off. In case you were worried, I *will* be back later – talking about something I know you'll all be much more interested in than strategic details – *the money*. So long, now.'

Kane sat down, and the spotlights – hung from a rail in the ceiling – wandered around the room. A small, monkey-like fellow up in the rigging pulled levers and ropes to get the effect. 'Evil' Emeric Belasco, a young man with an especially vile reputation. He had two pages in the flip-book, just listing the *variety* of his crimes.

The light came to rest on Elizabeth.

Gilberte found it hard to breathe, but her companion was perfectly prepared.

She stood up and announced her alias. 'You know my record,' she said, offhandedly. 'The Lavender Hill Gold Caper. The Larrabee Inheritance Swindle. The Tiffany Early Morning Diamond Snatch. The Charles Bonnet Art Forgeries.'

Heads nodded. Among murmurs of admiration were a few mutters. Some of these folk only now discovered Edda Van Heemstra had bested them in previous dealings. The Rembrandt in Boltyn's collection had been scarcely dry when sold to him – dashed off by the talented Bonnet, one of Edda's several 'fathers'.

Elizabeth let the grumbles die, and got to business. 'Through the strategic seductions of two junior clerks and one senior forward-planner in the British Ministry of War, I have obtained these documents.'

She laid a folder on the table.

'These are photographic copies, of course. But excellent.'

The folder was passed to Madame Sara, the designated specialist in forgery of government papers. She also did teeth, Gilberte understood. That would explain why the suspiciously golden-haired Italian-Indian adventuress set up shop in London's Strand. The English were notorious for their teeth. The Madame paged through the documents.

'I have the authentic seals,' Elizabeth continued. 'And the proper ribbons. The British are, as we know, obsessed with ribbons.'

Madame Sara nodded, satisfied.

'Thank you, Edda,' said Kane. 'You're a living doll.' Elizabeth sat down. 'Now,' continued Kane, 'our expert on the big game of politics, Senator Paine, will explain the *significance* of these purloined papers.'

The light fell on the prematurely white-haired American dignitary. He was sitting next to the Sorceress of the Strand.

'In all nations, Ministries of War sit around during periods of prolonged peace, irritably finding projects to justify their existence,' began the windy Paine, as if addressing his Senate. 'Great Britain, possessed of an Empire, rarely has periods of prolonged peace...'

Gurn grunted. He had begun his murdering in the South African conflict.

'However, when the British Ministry of War has a spare moment, their armchair generals like nothing more than the drawing-up of *contingency plans*, which is to say imagining what wonderful new wars might be embarked upon. For reasons few can explain, it costs as much to compile a folder such as the one we have here as it does to make a battleship. Thus are military budgets rubber-stamped cheerfully by parliaments and despots alike. Sometimes, as with the Boer War, a conflict might be a long time coming. Plans can be framed well before the outbreak of hostilities. But, there are also nasty surprises. Sudden diplomatic rows get out of hand. An unkind word about an ambassador's wife's hat and the Balkans goes up in flames. From Cleopatra's nose to Jenkins' ear, wars have sprung up from trifles. So, ministries play games of "let's pretend" and *plan* what they would do under certain *contingencies. Let's pretend…* resurgent Viking hordes ravage Scotland! Which regiments would be mobilised, what lines of transport must be kept open, where would artillery be deployed?'

Paine tapped the folder.

'This *contingency plan* is founded upon the "let's pretend" supposition that France makes a sudden, aggressive move against the British in Egypt, to wrest control of the Suez Canal. Furthermore, the French Navy occupies the Channel Islands while building up the fleet – an armada, if you will – in *la Manche*. An army is landed on the South Coast of England. Jean-François strikes towards London and King and Parliament. Of course, France has no such intent, so far as we or the British Ministry of War know. Germany, Russia, Portugal, Switzerland, Japan, Pago-Pago, the planet Mars and the Lost City of Kôr have no thought of waging war on the British Empire – but plans exist to be put in action in the event of attacks by all of them.'

General Sternwood lifted a corner of the folder, took a look at a paragraph, and spat. 'Limey crocks couldn't defend a whorehouse from a flock of sheep – look at how they intend to fortify Andover! And no general in his right mind would set counter-invasion troops ashore on the beaches of goddamn Normandy. They'd be cut to pieces! No, Cherbourg – that's your Frog weak spot!'

The General caught himself ranting and shut up. Paine gave him a stern look.

'If my colleague, Mr… ah… Mr the Face… would take over.'

Paine sat down, and the spotlight fell on the Face.

'Senator, thank you,' said the masked man, who had a rich,

persuasive, unaccented voice. Beneath the leather he might be Quasimodo with the measles, but he was as beautifully spoken as any of the well-mannered gentlemen Grandmama warned Gilberte to be wary of. 'The importance of the papers Miss Van Heemstra has obtained lies not in details, General Sternwood, but in their shape and form. Much of the text can carry over into the documents Madame Sara will prepare. It is a simple matter of editing, of slanting the material, so that a *contingency* plan of defence will be transformed into a *definite* plan of attack. When the folder is passed to the French Ministry of War, it will be stained with the blood of many agents. The British will have made, or seem to have made, desperate attempts to get these plans back. Concurrently, strategic explosions will stir up activity in Portsmouth. An astute observer will believe His Majesty's Armed Forces are hurriedly preparing an invasion. Furthermore, barracks in the South of England will receive shipments of pamphlets to be issued to private soldiers...'

The Face laid a specimen on the table, which was passed around. Stamped as a British Armed Services publication, it was an English–French phrase-book. Flicking through, Gilberte found such useful sentiments as 'We are delighted to accept your surrender, Mayor', 'How long ago did your officers flee in terror, Private?' and 'Kindly tell your daughter not to put garlic in the breakfast we have requisitioned.' She could imagine the outrage in the French press when – inevitably – a copy fell into their hands.

'When the British war plans are delivered to the French government,' said the Face, white spittle flecking the corners of his mouth-slit, 'they will be convinced the Coldstream Guards are on the point of marching up the Champs-Élysées. They must believe they have no time for diplomacy, and mobilise at once against perfidious Albion.'

'Then,' said Natasha, taking over the narrative, 'bombs shall fall from the skies. Our air-destroyer *Ariel*, presently moored on the Scots isle of Drumcraig, will strike against targets in England

and France, chosen for sentimental or patriotic associations. The White Cliffs of Dover. The square in Rouen where the English burned Joan of Arc. Where the *Ariel* does not reach, we Terrorists shall employ agents willing to sacrifice themselves for the cause. Waterloo Station shall be blown up! The vineyards of Champagne shall burn! There must be war!'

Gilberte thought Natasha might be unhappy in love. The armoured insurrectionist fairly squirmed with delight at the thought of carnage on a global scale as other girls her age warmed at the prospect of an extravagant new hat with ostrich feathers or a small but exquisitely stylish diamond pendant.

'Now,' said Kane, reclaiming the spotlight, pausing a moment so that Evil Emeric could fix him in the intersection of two beams, 'the small matter of the big bucks. Those of you who are professionals do not come cheap, and those of you who are zealots are in need of operating costs. Miss di Murska, I know to the last gear and strut how much gelt it takes to launch an air-destroyer. Well, I am not complaining. I'm here to buy a war. My friend Mr Boltyn has thrown in with me, so we can afford all the toys we want. His associate Mr Hattison is an inventin' fool. Thanks to his ingenuity with electrical wires and levers and trickinesses well beyond my brain-pan, each of you will leave this casino a winner, to the tune of better than a half-million dollars.'

Irma Vep herself couldn't have thrilled as much at the sound of that as Gilberte did.

'Personally, I'd like nothing better than to hand the money over in sacks right here in this room… but there are official bodies to be placated. My accountants have to fill in their forms and justify all my expenditures. I'm known for spending freely, but even I can't just say I've bought a job-lot of statues and paintings and hope not to answer any more questions. So, you will legitimately win your war chests. I have leased the baccarat, chemin-de-fer and roulette tables from the Bath Water Society. For this season, I am the bank. Tomorrow night, you will collectively break me.

You may find this shocking, but every game of chance in this town is rigged. Our good friend Mr Hattison has made sure of that. Anyone in the gaming business knows you can't run the racket without letting some mug win large from time to time, to keep the rest of the suckers playing. Tomorrow night, my friends, you can't lose. Oh, it won't be obvious – there'll be reversals, early losses to build up the pot, to keep other players in the game. But, at the end of the evening, you'll walk off with your pockets full of chips.'

Around the table were happy faces. Even the Face's leather mask seemed to smirk. Only Natasha kept frowning.

'I've laid out bait enough to attract all the high-rollers and big operators in the so-called "professional gambler" line,' said Kane, 'and it's my hope the pack will sense blood in the water and bet against you. That smug bastard Johnny Barlowe is here, and you know what he's like, with his "independent air" and his "mass of money, linen, silk and starch". The Man Who Broke the Bank at Monte Carlo, hah! I'm happy to give you good money for services rendered, but I'll be additionally tickled puce if you take what you can from parasites like Barlowe. Not to mention Gaylord Ravenal, Basher Moran and half a dozen other gussied-up sharks in frilly shirts. Take their rolls as well as mine, and go with my blessing. A superfluity of Fatty Feasts, Meaty Morsels and Vril Grills are about to be express-delivered from the Burgher Kane in the lobby, so anyone who cares to join me in dining heartily is welcome to get their faces in the trough.'

Like almost everyone in Kane's company who wasn't American, Gilberte and Elizabeth professed to have dined earlier. They withdrew and tactfully had to detach themselves from Natasha – by telling her an especially oppressive archduke was playing whist in a private room with a bloated factory-owner, a corrupt cardinal and a brutal chieftain of Cossacks. The Queen of Terror trotted off to investigate, regretting she had not worn a bandolier of dynamite sticks to offset her metal-plate dress.

'That girl needs more fun in her life,' Gilberte observed.

It was as Erik had guessed. The casino was the pump of Kane's machine.

Tomorrow night, however things panned out, would be exciting.

VI

IN THEIR SUITE at the Grand Hôtel, the Persian unrolled architectural plans. Riolama was at his shoulder, big eyes taking in details. She was a quick study. The bird girl still didn't talk much. Gilberte couldn't imagine her upbringing, but she had a lively mind.

When he leased the bank, Kane made many alterations. He had openly put in gaming machines, Mutoscopes and a Burgher Kane, stamping his K everywhere. The secret purpose of the work was to turn the Casino into a giant machine. A transparent overlay, initialled by Engineer Hattison, showed electrical wires threading through the building like nerves. The globe of lights in the main salon was hollow, like a diving bell. Using telescopic devices, a small person concealed within could have close-up views of every gaming table in the hall. A panel of switches and levers could dictate each spin of a wheel or turn of the cards. The croupiers were literally hooked up; special garters threaded wires through their shoe-soles to make contact with metal plates – the K motifs in the carpets. The Eye-Ball could apply tiny shocks in coded patterns, conveying instructions to the men on the floor.

Decks of cards, printed and sealed on the premises, arrived at the chemin-de-fer table or the baccarat shoe pre-shuffled to suit the house, backs marked in an ink which showed when viewed through a red lens the controller could slot into the telescopes.

'How did Monsieur Erik obtain these plans?' Gilberte asked. 'I'm surprised Kane is careless with such things.'

The Persian tapped his long nose. 'It's one thing to *pay* for such a system, but another to design it, and quite another again to build it. Few firms are capable of executing such a commission. The fellow who said he didn't care what it cost to have a cathedral-size pipe organ dismantled and reassembled in a cavern under Paris has more goodwill with those specialists than a Yankee vulgarian who quibbled about every franc spent on installing his wonderful cheating machine. Among other accomplishments, Erik is the greatest secret architect of the age. Who do you think the workmen who built Kane's Europa-Xanadu look to for regular employment? We had these plans from the draughtsmen even before Kane did.'

Riolama held up one of the flimsies, looking at it several ways, and made little cooing noises.

'Monsieur Kane is no believer in games of chance,' Gilberte observed.

'Americans always brag about how much they love to gamble,' said the Persian. 'What they mean is that they love to *win*. Kane doesn't even think of this as cheating. He is simply unwilling to play any game where he doesn't make up the rules. He takes undue pride in his own cleverness...'

'The vain in Kane is mainly in the brain,' mused Elizabeth.

'I think she's got it,' said the Persian. 'By Georges, she's got it. The vain in Kane *is* mainly in the brain, and the bane of Kane is plainly to our gain. So have you seen it?'

Gilberte snapped her fingers.

'Gigi, you've seen it!'

Kane, swelling inside his waistcoat from too many Fatty Feasts, could not personally run his machine. He had paid for a marvellous toy, but someone else blew the whistle and rang the bell.

'He takes one enormous risk,' she said. 'He must trust whoever sits inside his Eye-Ball.'

'Just so,' said the Persian, pulling out another plan. 'But Kane takes precautions. In the average casino, the heaviest security arrangements – the biggest guards and the thickest doors – are for the vault where the money is kept. In Royale-les-Eaux, the most inaccessible room is directly above the main hall. Kane keeps his newest acquisitions there, paintings and statues and trinkets. The gallery is also the only point of access to the Eye-Ball. The sky-light is electrified. The windows have shutters, sharpened like guillotine blades, which slice down if something – say, a burglar's limb – is thrust through. Monsieur Voltaire personally ensures no one even gets up the stairs to the main door, which is also electrified. The American cracksman Jimmy Valentine cased the gallery last month, and decided not to bother. Even the authentic Irma Vep couldn't get in easily.'

Gilberte shrugged. Irma could take care of her own reputation.

'It is fortunate for us that birds may fly where bats cannot,' said the Persian.

Riolama chirruped.

'In myth,' said Elizabeth, 'the sculptor Pygmalion brought Galatea to life. We must now reverse the process, for only a statue can get into that room.'

VII

HER FALSE MOUSTACHE itched. She had to remember not to scratch, for fear of losing her disguise.

Elizabeth transformed herself without stuck-on whiskers. Even knowing the travesty, Gilberte could not recognise the young sculptor as Mrs Eynsford Hill. She walked, talked, sweated and smoked like a man.

Voltaire had seen Gilberte and Elizabeth as Edda Van Heemstra and Irma Vep less than a day before. Now, the giant met Jacob Epstein and his apprentice, Priam Vé. No flicker of suspicion sparked in his eyes.

The Persian had hired some roughs to deliver the crate. Voltaire dismissed them and called on the casino's staff – liveried apes with scraped knuckles from dealing with ungracious, complaining losers – to carry the big box upstairs to the gallery.

When they could not exert sufficient lift, the major-domo added his own muscle. Voltaire bent double and the apes hefted the crate onto his shoulders. Mr Epstein insisted he accompany the giant and his burden every step of the way.

Manoeuvring the crate up the wide marble staircase was tricky. Gilberte trusted Riolama knew how to keep quiet, and that the bird girl wouldn't suffer injury through awkward man-handling. Voltaire's collar burst as he strained. The apes assisted, keeping the crate from tipping off his back.

The Persian had hoped Kane would be occupied elsewhere on this busy day, but he was in his gallery with Boltyn, Hattison and the capering Emeric Belasco. The mystery of who sat inside the Eye-Ball was solved. Evil Emeric was the likeliest prospect in Kane's Most High Order. Last evening, he had shown how nimbly he could work such contraptions from on high.

Voltaire, sweat pouring from his prehistoric brow, set down the crate.

'What's this?' asked Kane. 'I said we weren't to be bothered.'

'"Bothered"?' responded 'Epstein', blood rising. '"*Bothered*"! A mistake has been made. No philistine is worthy of owning Epstein's *Rima*. You shall not even set eyes on her loveliness. Kane, your cheque will be returned, uncashed. You, Giant-Man, lift up the crate and take it away from this place.'

Voltaire's fists opened and closed as if he were crushing melons. The casino apes looked helplessly at each other.

'Hold on, hold on,' said Kane, trying to mollify the temperamental artist. 'Did I say I didn't want your *Rima*? I have people who advise me on what to buy. They suggest I back you, Mr Epstein. You will apparently appreciate.'

Elizabeth puffed out, but still glowed with wounded pride.

'I am a sculptor of genius, sir. Not a racehorse or a bond issue. I am not to be backed or invested in. My work has nothing to do with money... which is why it costs so much.'

Kane tried to think that through.

'If we could go over the wiring specifications again,' interrupted

Hattison, who looked as if he hadn't had a full night's sleep in months. 'Everything must be checked and tested...'

Kane, not caring to be nagged, ignored the engineer. He considered the large wooden box.

'Open 'er up,' he decreed. 'Let's have a look at your *Rima*.'

'Very well,' said Elizabeth. 'Great care must be taken.'

She tapped at spots on the crate, indicating where nails should be pulled. The apes got to work with crowbars.

The crate fell apart. A quantity of straw came away.

The bird girl was on a heavy plinth, crouching inside a large nest. Her face turned upwards, features exaggerated, eyes blind. Twig-legged birds perched on her hands and shoulders. Metal waves of hair fell down her back.

Riolama was inside a carapace of metal-painted plaster over chicken wire. She seemed to be cast from bronze.

Voltaire looked at the statue as if falling in love at first sight.

'She's naked,' observed Boltyn. 'What would your mother think, Charlie?'

Kane didn't know what to make of the sculpture, but was vain enough to want not to appear foolish in front of his friend.

'How much did you cough up for this hooer?' asked Boltyn. 'I'll wager there are real girls who'd cost a lot less.'

Elizabeth shot a withering glance at the millionaire.

'It is very *modern*,' said Hattison, trying to toady equally to both his masters. They ignored him.

'I think she's fine,' said Kane, warming to his decision. 'Yes, I see what Mr Epstein means to say in this piece. Look at the strength in these limbs. The muscles of a wrestler...'

The statue's legs and arms were thick, to accommodate the slender body within. Gilberte didn't know who Erik had got to run up this Epstein – probably one of the scenery-makers at the Opéra. It would look better from the back of the dress circle.

Evil Emeric approached the statue, dragging stiff, withered legs. He ran his tongue over his teeth. The stunted cripple had strong arms and a vicious, street-fighter's reputation. Gilberte hoped Riolama was up to the task of taking – and replacing – the little incubus.

'She's a pip, Mr Epstein,' said Kane. 'Leave her where she is. And keep the cheque. Now, we've got a business meeting, so we'll have to cut this short. Have some chips. Enjoy yourself in the casino. Who knows, you might be a big winner...'

Kane pulled a handful of casino boards from his pockets and gave them to Gilberte and Elizabeth.

Gilberte took a last look at Riolama and followed Elizabeth out.

In the foyer, Natasha Natasaevna di Murska was at a window, handing over bundles of large denomination notes in several currencies in exchange for stacks of boards she needed two minions to carry. The Princess of the Revolution was buying into the evening's play on a large scale.

Had Kane foreseen his comrades in the Most High Order would – given the golden opportunity – try to take him for *much* more money than they needed to carry out their parts in Plan Thunderbolt? If so, the millionaire had a less sure grasp of human nature than Erik.

The Terrorists were not the only faction raiding their treasury to buy into the 'sure thing'. Perry Bennett and Raymond Owen passed by, heaving large suitcases she guessed were filled with dollars siphoned from orphans' trust funds.

Madame Sara and Dr Quartz queued for boards, in matching society-fools-on-a-spree disguises. They seemed to have clicked last night, which contradicted gossip about the Madame's amorous proclivities among her own sex. It could be that the pair merely had a great deal in common, specifically shared interests in human vivisection and unusual medical procedures.

Outside the Casino, among the crowds drawn to bright lights, they breathed again. Elizabeth dropped Jacob Epstein. She shook out the hair that had been pinned up under her hat and was her own blank self.

The next moves were down to the bird girl.

A well-dressed, vacant-looking Englishman – half-eaten Vril Grill in one hand and sticky sauce on his chin – bumped into Gilberte. He gabbled an apology and then clapped eyes on Elizabeth.

'Eliza,' he gasped, astounded.

'Stone the bloody crows!' Elizabeth responded, in an unfamiliar voice.

For the first time, Gilberte saw a real expression on Elizabeth's face. Something close to terror, with an overlay of exasperation.

'Madame Lachaille,' she said, recovering her usual poise, 'permit me to present my husband, Freddy Eynsford Hill.'

'Pleased to meet you, eh what, Madame. Did you know you had face-fluff stuck on your lip? Playin' charades, I suppose. Anythin' to pass the time. Rum do, this. I was just wonderin' where the old ball and chain had got to, and up she pops, large as life and twice as bouncy. Eh what, indeed! Don't suppose you fillies'd like to take a spin round the old gamblin' establishment? I've got a feelin' in me nose that this is my lucky night.'

Freddy was plainly an idiot. Handsome, well-mannered, mildly amusing – but an idiot nevertheless. From the cradle, Gilberte had been warned against falling in love with – let alone marrying – such a sorry specimen. Referring to his wife, Freddy had used the English colloquialism 'ball and chain', but she was the one shackled to a frightful encumbrance. Gilberte wondered how Elizabeth had got stuck with such a blithering disaster. Then again, her own marriage hadn't turned out as well as expected.

Freddy made a move to kiss his wife in a proprietary manner. She applied her fingertips to his neck and the dull light in his eyes went out.

Now, Elizabeth was supporting a deadweight.

'I saw a Tibetan mystic do that once. I don't know how it works, but Erik does. Freddy will be asleep for an hour or so. Help me dump him somewhere he won't get robbed or hurt.'

Gilberte took an arm. They carried Freddy through the crowds.

'Lost the family fortune following a seven with a queen,'

explained Elizabeth to anyone who paid attention. 'Paralysed by shock, poor fellow.'

There were tuts of sympathy.

VIII

RIMA CARRIED HER clock within her breast. Inside her rigid cocoon, she counted her heartbeats.

The gentle, arrhythmic drumming – and the other pulses of her body – were like the small, living sounds of the jungle. In her mind, all was green and warm and wet and dangerous.

She had no concept of regret, and so did not miss her native land. Bad things had happened there. Fire, death, pain. Others thought her dead. She knew not whether they were wrong. She might be a ghost. The cruel people had always called her spirit, demon, daughter of the Didi.

How she came here, to these new jungles, did not matter.

She thought of what she must do now, not what was gone.

Rima would do anything for Erik. If she were a ghost, he was Lord of Ghost-Kind. The others were the same, though they might not know it. Eliza and Gigi, from different jungles, were Rima's heart-sisters. Mirror-selves, summoned up from still, reflecting pools.

When the Phantom played music for Rima, it was like a thunderstorm, a waterfall, a thousand birds singing in joy and terror. It was worth the crossing of a great ocean, wider than any bird could fly, to hear him play. The cruel people made thin songs, with flutes like twigs. Erik poured music through pipes tall as trees.

Twenty-five thousand heartbeats. Enough time had passed.

She stopped counting and opened her eyes. Through slits in the mask-piece she saw the room. A crowd of other statues. Paintings piled against the walls.

She flexed thin, strong shoulders and arms, straining against her second skin of wire, plaster and paint. Seams split, the shell sundered. She hatched like a chick. Her arms broke free. She pulled the plates over her chest and face apart. Wriggling out of the statue, she found the room empty of people.

Careful to make no noise, she stepped off her plinth. Her former shell was exploded and hollow.

Rima, free after confinement, danced, rejoicing as feeling returned to her limbs. She wore only her shift and a leather belt. In its pouches were tools. She had been instructed in the use of some items by the Persian. Other implements she was skilled with of old.

A thick carpet was folded away from a closed metal hatch. A heavy padlock sealed it shut. This too held a volunteer prisoner. She set to work with lock-picks. Her fingers were deft. Soon, the padlock was sprung and set to one side. Silently, she lifted the trapdoor.

She found what she expected. A thin perpendicular shaft like the inside of a hollow tree, with rungs set in its side. Twenty feet down, another hatch. Beyond that, the Bad Little Man.

Rima had experience with his kind. Cruel people, who set cunning snares that broke necks. Birds knew to fly away when they were near.

She twisted her hair out of her face and tied it in a knot, then crawled into the hole. She made her way downwards, rung by rung, gripping fast with supple toes. If needs be, she could hang by her feet. About halfway down, she heard noise. Voices, the clatter of many small objects, distorted music. She had passed through the floor, and was in a branch dangling into the great room. At the end of it was the Bad Little Man's nest.

Stout chains hung taut around her, taking the nest's weight. Thick, rubber-coated vines carried the magic lightning.

Rima eased through the narrowing space.

Her face hung over the second hatch, which had a glass window.

She saw the top of the Bad Little Man's head. His thinning black hair was oiled, but white stripes of his scalp showed through. His face was pressed to one of many sets of eyepieces. His hairy hands rested on an array of keys, stops, wheels and levers. The contraption was as intricate as the Phantom's pipe organ.

Hooking her feet on a rung, she took a bundle from her belt, and laid it quietly by the hatch.

The Bad Little Man pulled his face away from the eyepieces. He crooked an ear like a cat, but did not look up.

Rima's breath misted the pane inches above his head.

The Bad Little Man twisted on his chair, and pulled himself to another set of eyepieces. His chair was on wheels which fit to rails within his nest. He could turn like an owl and see in any direction.

Rima unrolled her bundle, which contained a cigarette holder. She fitted it into her mouth and got a grip with her teeth. The holder was stoppered with a tiny cork. The sliver inside rattled slightly.

This time, the Bad Little Man definitely heard her.

Rima reached for the hatch-handle and aimed her holder.

The Bad Little Man looked up. His face was young but withered, eyes black like caves.

She hauled open the hatch.

The Bad Little Man reached for a magazine pistol, but could not lift it in time.

With her thumb, Rima flipped the cork stopper. She spat out a quick breath.

The dart stuck into the Bad Little Man's neck.

Angry eyes fixed on her, but he could not move. Rima knew he was awake in his skull, but his body would not respond. The dart was tipped in venom derived from the poison frog. She had brought a supply from the jungle.

She reached down and twisted the pistol out of his nerveless grip. The gun dropped to the bottom of the nest, clattering into a chamber-pot.

The Bad Little Man's eyes glowed with hatred. His locked teeth ground.

Now came the most difficult stretch. She had to extract the Bad Little Man from his nest and take his place on the wheeled seat. There was scarcely room for one person in this space, let alone two.

Rima hauled the Bad Little Man up by his shoulders. They were closer in the shaft than seeds in a pod. She wriggled, a new-born cuckoo tipping a heavy egg out of a nest or an ant juggling a weight many times its own with its legs. She forced the Bad Little Man's body up as hers inched down. When he was completely above her and out of his nest, he was still a weight. She lifted him into the shaft, crooking his withered legs over a rung. She took off her belt and used it to tie him there, a fly left in a spider's web for a later snack.

The Bad Little Man was strong-willed. He fought the frog-venom, face crimson, spittle on his lips. Inside, he roared with fury. But he was helpless. If he built another nest, it would be less pregnable. With traps for unwary ghost-girls, cuckoos or daughters of Didi.

Rima left him be and settled in his seat. She rolled it this way and that, enjoying the smooth motion. It was a comfortable nest, just her size.

She flexed her fingers and touched the keys. Now, with this building as an organ, she would play her own music.

She looked through a set of eyepieces. A distant view suddenly leaped up at her, close and vivid. She had used binoculars, and knew how they worked. She was seeing down into the big room below.

The Bad Fat Man stood by a long green table. Every other gentleman in the room wore black, but he shone in white.

'Ladies and gentlemen,' he said, 'place your bets…'

Piles of tokens were assembled on a baize grid. The Bad Fat Man elbowed aside a thin croupier. He would personally start off the evening's play. He bent over a miniature carousel. Rima knew this was a roulette wheel. The Bad Fat Man set the wheel spinning. An ivory ball jumped on the whirring carousel like an insect on fire.

Pinned to the giant keyboard in the nest was a chart. It listed numbers, odds, hands of cards and precise times. Beside the chart was a large white-faced clock. As the wheel spun in the casino below, the second hand shuddered.

Rima checked the numbers and times against those she had learned. She imagined her own chart laid over this one. She would play a different tune.

The roulette wheel slowed. The insect tired, close to death.

Rima's hand darted out over a particular key, hovered for a few ticks, then pressed down.

The ball stopped in a compartment within the wheel.

'*Trente rouge*,' said the croupier. 'Thirteen red. *La maison gagne*. The house wins…'

IX

'THE HOUSE WINS…'

Gilberte had never seen a man more unhappy with a streak of good luck than Charles Foster Kane. Only Elizabeth – and perhaps a few croupiers – shared her insight. The casino staff continued to obey orders from the Eye-Ball, though.

Everyone else in the know remembered his plan – 'early losses to build up the pot'. The pot was swollen, and growing. A lake of money pooled in the counting cellars beneath the main salon.

Many of the Most High Order favoured the roulette wheel. Dr Quartz, Madame Sara and Baron Maupertuis had laid fortunes on the baize, and seen their chips swept away. Several initiates had gone to the foyer when their initial outlay was seemingly – indeed, actually – squandered, and returned with freshly purchased boards.

'The house wins again,' said the chief croupier. Chips clattered in a chute, disappearing below. Monies poured down a plughole.

Natasha, Sir Dunston and Senator Paine, preferring baccarat, sat together. An expressionless, wired-up dealer spun cards from the shoe. Gilberte understood that, in addition to the Terrorists' funds, Natasha was gambling with the Face's money. He could hardly be expected to show his, ahem, *mask* in such company, but would not want to miss out on the evening's profit.

Carne, Gurn and General Sternwood played five-card stud with Potter – who was gloatingly raking in chips he was supposed to lose later.

In an antechamber, Perry Bennett was bent over a hazard table, rattling dice. His peculiar hand was adapted to *crapauds-*shooting, but the bones were not falling his way. His friend Owen was betting heavily on the losing run coming to an end, playing the Martingale System – which, under the circumstances, was a sure way to wind up broke.

All around, takers were being took.

Elizabeth, calm again after the Freddy incident, steered Gilberte around the room. They were themselves this evening – Edda Van Heemstra and Irma Vep were mysteriously detained. At the moment, none of their co-conspirators minded the absences – more in the pot for everyone else. Later, when smoke cleared, their no-show act would be remembered. By then, the real Edda would be loose and likely in trouble. As for Irma, Gilberte assumed she'd dance away from blame as she had slipped out of every other trap set for her.

The influx of big money was, as Kane had said, 'blood in the water'.

The salon stank with a hubbub of greed, fear, excitement and desperation. Usually, a casino came alive when a lucky or ingenious soul began to beat the house. Tonight was contrary. Gamblers rarely considered or cared about streaks if the house benefited. After all, odds were always with the house. But, tonight, a record might be set – the biggest single haul in a casino in an evening's play.

Next year, revues and songs would commemorate 'The Bank Who Broke the Men at Royale-les-Eaux'.

Elizabeth and Gilberte repaired to a side bar, to drink champagne and take the edge off all the excitement. This was where the professional gamblers, who knew by instinct that something was more amiss than usual, had retreated. Colonel Sebastian Moran, of London and India, and Bret Maverick, of Natchez and New Orleans, debated the presently standing record for a house win, and whether it was about to fall. The inveterate gaming fiends also remembered a macabre record for the number of casino-related suicides in a single night. The cynical Moran was willing to bet the death toll set at Mother Gin Sling's in Shanghai on Chinese New Year's in '98 would be exceeded by dawn. The more optimistic Maverick considered taking the wager. Both were probably thinking of ways to put a 'fix' in.

Maverick caught Gilberte looking at them and raised a glass to her. She turned away from his alarmingly appealing smile, and thought of cool green beds of money.

Engineer Hattison, inventor of the cheating machine, was also at the bar, nursing ginger ale and radiating smugness. He also overheard Maverick and Moran, and offered stakes against the professional gamblers, claiming that at the end of the evening the house would be the *loser*, rattling off spurious mathematical piffle to justify his position. Gilberte saw Hattison was making a novice mistake by offering an apparent sucker bet. A more experienced confidence man set out bait and let the mark raise the notion of a wager. The Colonel withdrew from the conversation and returned to play. If there was a setup, he was determined to get in on the game and snare a portion of the free money he now believed was on offer. Maverick, however, had an acute sense of the way things were going and mildly took the engineer's bet. Somehow, the Western gambler tumbled that a fix was *supposed* to be in but was actually off. Hattison threw a sheaf of his patents in to bulk up his meagre cash roll.

Elizabeth and Gilberte finished their drinks and returned to the salon.

Kane, on his podium with the small orchestra, was perspiring badly, and trying to catch Boltyn's attention. His fellow millionaire wasn't supposed to be in this phase of the game, but couldn't resist trying to get one up. He sat by Natasha, matching the Queen of Terror's bets and often laying a meaty hand over her delicate fingers in a manner which might well earn him a cut throat before the end of the night. Unless the girl was one of those queer ducks who rattle about revolution all day but secretly wish to spend the night being grossly pleasured by a bloated plutocrat on silk sheets.

Gilberte looked up at the Eye-Ball. She tapped Elizabeth's shoulder.

Faint cracks appeared in the plaster, damaging a 14th-century cathedral ceiling Kane had stuck up to add class to his gaming hell. Fine dust sifted through the cracks. The Eye-Ball's moorings were precisely calibrated. Adding even Riolama's meagre weight was a stress not calculated for in Hattison's plans.

Lights on the globe flashed on and off.

Gilberte whistled silently in admiration. Riolama had mastered the system and was playing it like a virtuoso.

All around the room were cries of exasperation, complaint, despair.

Some of the Most High Order grew irritable, feeling they had fed the pot a little too much. It was time for the great Kane's munificence to be made manifest. Others simply ached for their money back, and their promised money on top of it.

Kane could not make a scene without it becoming generally known that this whole casino was a giant trick. But he knew, even before Bret Maverick, that his crooked path had twisted against him. Finally, he slipped from the podium and waddled with an unaccustomed hurry towards the foyer. The staircase which led to the secure gallery above the Eye-Ball was still guarded. Voltaire stood at his position, suitably resolute, invisibly well-armed. Ironically, Riolama could not have got upstairs without his strength.

Casually, Gilberte and Elizabeth followed the magnate.

In the foyer, just as Kane was about to call out to Voltaire, they caught up with him and, with practised ease, took an arm apiece.

'Oh, Mr Kane...' said Elizabeth, musically.

'Ladies,' he said, not recognising them but not too far gone in panic to miss their appeal, 'ordinarily, I'd be happy to escort you, but...'

'We shan't take refusal kindly,' purred Gilberte. 'This is a special occasion, and we claim you as our prize.'

'We could dance all night,' said Elizabeth, tugging on one arm.

'Or drink champagne as if it had just been invented,' said Gilberte, tugging on the other.

Kane tried to break free, but – for all his meat and money – was not a strong man.

In the salon, general fury erupted at another huge loss. The chutes to the counting cellar were choked with boards like clogged-up drains. As usual in such situations, a stink was rising. Kane turned to look, but Gilberte and Elizabeth insisted on his attention, patting his damp cheeks, smoothing his sticky moustache. If pricked with one of Riolama's darts, he would not be more deftly immobilised.

Bennett and Owen, black-faced and broke, stalked out of the salon, towards the main doors.

'Gentlemen... friends,' cried out Kane as they passed by.

Bennett gave Kane the evil eye and made a vulgar gesture with his malformed hand. Owen drew his thumb across his throat in an equally eloquent sign.

'Don't mind them,' purred Elizabeth. 'They're bankrupt. They haven't got two pennies to hire a cosh-boy, let alone funds enough to have you killed.'

Kane really saw Gilberte and Elizabeth for the first time.

'Do I know you?' he asked.

A commotion exploded in the salon, and spread through the building.

William Boltyn was on the floor, clothes torn, expertly pinned by the dainty boot-heel of Natasha Natasaevna. She cursed him as every variety of capitalist exploiter and blood-sucking oppressor of the people. She took a croupier's gathering-stick and knouted the millionaire as if he were a Russian peasant and she a Cossack. His face was striped with red weals. So, he wouldn't be conquering the Princess of the Revolution in his suite this evening. Others of the Most High Order were with her, getting in kicks and blows. Their pockets were empty, Gilberte supposed. Dr Quartz had actually pulled out his trouser pockets in a caricature of pennilessness. He had gambled away his custom-made surgical instruments.

'The house wins,' announced another croupier, blandly.

A shot rang out and the man was down, wounded in the shoulder. Two hefty guards threw themselves on General Sternwood, who had brought his revolver. Voltaire left his post to see what the trouble was.

Kane was pliable now. It was important he see what was happening, so they steered him back into the salon.

It was pandemonium!

Boards flew like shrapnel on a battlefield. Patrons smashed the furniture. Voltaire and the apes went into action, endeavouring to suppress rowdy behaviour. Madame Sara tried to splash a bottle of vitriol into a croupier's face, and was instantly trussed and thrown onto a table. Acid burned the baize. The Inner Circle of the Most High Order of Xanadu, assuming treachery on the part of their Grand Master, took to quarrelling with each other, flinging accusations and daggers. They had no common cause before Kane gathered them. Old rivalries and enmities bubbled up like marsh gas. Simon Carne and Sir Dunston Greene fenced with swords, leaping from tier to tier. They fetched up on the podium, cutting through the orchestra. Musicians fled diplomatically, grasping their more valuable instruments. Maupertuis brutally kicked Henry F. Potter, as if determined to put the pleading banker into a wheelchair.

Then, all the croupiers started screaming.

This had the effect of stopping fights and destructive

rampages. All the staff were rooted to the carpets, juddering and fizzing, hair standing on end and smoking. Cards spewed from sleeves. Trouser-cuffs caught fire. Crackles of lightning ringed the croupiers' bodies. Riolama had cranked up the electrical devices to their highest setting and thrown all the switches at once. There was a peculiar, tart, burned smell. This extraordinary phenomenon lasted only a few seconds, then shut off – along with all the electric lights.

Maverick strolled out of the side bar, with a fistful of Hattison's paper. He tipped his black hat at the ladies, and his appalled host, and calmly walked out of the building. Back in the bar, Hattison had abjured ginger ale and was thirstily swigging whisky from a bottle.

The hall was dim, but infernal – lit only by a few fires. Yelping staff patted at burning patches of their evening attire. With dreadful curses, they helped each other tear wires out of their shoes.

'Gigi, cover your ears,' said Elizabeth. 'This is not language you should learn.'

Kane was limp now, mumbling about 'roses' buds'.

There was a great rending sound, as if Plan Thunderbolt were torn in half by the Gods, and the Eye-Ball detached from the ceiling. Wires and chains tore through plaster as the globe crashed fifty feet to the floor. It smashed, throwing broken glass all around.

It was a miracle no one had been underneath it.

Gilberte's heart clutched, but Riolama wasn't in the wreckage. Looking up, she saw the bird-girl dangling from a cluster of wires stuck out of the ceiling. With the agility of a born acrobat, she swung from chandelier to chandelier, then found a column she could climb down as if it were a tree-trunk.

Gilberte and Elizabeth abandoned Kane to his ruin, and made a cradle of their hands. Riolama leaped into their grip. They helped her out of the salon, deftly moving through panicking, rioting, complaining crowds.

Heaps of boards were scattered across the floor. Colonel

Moran, on his knees, filled his pockets. Most folks were too afraid the building would collapse to bother with scavenging.

They tried to leave the building in an orderly fashion, along with many less cool heads who were fighting and clawing to get out into the relative safety of the street.

Voltaire stood by the main doors, waiting for them, teeth shining like the family silver. Kane must have summoned him with a silent whistle.

'My good man,' began Elizabeth, 'if you would be so kind as to step aside. This poor girl has had a trying evening and is on the point of fainting...'

The giant's eyes glittered, like his gnashers. He was sceptical.

'*Move your bloomin' arse*!' shouted Elizabeth, in her original voice.

Dishevelled folks streamed past Voltaire, but he stood firm, arms extended.

Now was the time for one of the stratagems they had practised, under the tutelage of the Persian, in the gymnasium beneath the Opéra. It was Gilberte's call.

'Hi Lily Hi Lily Hi Lo!' she trilled.

Riolama flew as if on wires, taking 'Hi Lily' and jamming her toughened heels into Voltaire's metal grin. Elizabeth, the other 'Hi Lily', took a discarded parasol and jabbed its point into the giant's midriff. Gilberte, performing 'Hi Lo', fell to the floor like the dying swan, braced herself against marble, and swept stiff legs against his stout ankles.

Voltaire shuddered but didn't fall.

The Angels recoiled and landed on points, adopting poses of aggression and flirtation. Elizabeth twirled the parasol for distraction. Gilberte opened and closed invisible fans, trying to ignore the pain in her shins. Riolama's arms rose in a crane stance and she stood on one leg.

Even the fleeing guests knew enough to clear a circle.

'Hi Lily Hi Lily Hi Lo' was brute force. For all their delicacy, the trio could fell a tree with it. But Voltaire still stood.

After the Persian had tutored them black and blue, they had suffered under an even more exacting master. To become an Angel of Music, one had to pass muster with Monsieur Erik. Gilberte hadn't believed her throat could hurt so much, or that such sounds could be torn out of her.

Now, they would put their lessons into practice.

Elizabeth began to tap out a tempo with her parasol.

Gilberte found a discarded croupier's scoop. Riolama, alarmingly, picked up a bloody sword.

They tapped in synchronised time. Voltaire's eyes swivelled between them.

The repertoire for three female voices was limited. 'Three Little Maids From School' was too trivial, though perhaps effective in a back-alley brawl. Bizet's 'Les Tringles des Sistres Tintaient' was too coarse, and they all thought Carmen a stupid slut. So, it must be Mendelssohn. 'Lift Thine Eyes To The Mountains'. The 'Angels' Trio' from *Elijah*.

Elizabeth, the most naturally skilled, took the lead. Gilberte had counterpoint, and Riolama – whose high notes turned to bird screeches – fluttered around. Song came from their hearts and lungs. Sound rolled from their larynxes in waves. If Voltaire could hear a dog-whistle, this would hurt.

All around, folks were struck by the beauty, then pricked by the pain. Crystal shattered, and another chandelier fell.

They focused the song on the giant in their way.

Blood trickled from his ears, his nose, his eyes. But he was transfixed.

Riolama took the lead from Elizabeth, and improvised – cockatoo sounds, bird-calls from her jungles. Voltaire felt it in his steel teeth, and clutched his mouth as the sharpened false choppers vibrated.

Gilberte became the dominant voice, and ended the song.

The giant fell to his knees, eyes and mouth red.

Without taking a bow, the trio slipped round him into the street.

A few stunned patrons tried to applaud, then thought better of lingering. More chandeliers would fall tonight.

In song, the Angels of Music had conquered.

Europa-Xanadu was in ruins. A mob was tearing down the façades of every Burgher Kane in sight. Fellows with sledge-hammers smashed gaming machines. Liberated cattle charged down the street, trailing bruised cowboys by their lassos. A circle of small boys filled up a lost ten-gallon hat with piddle. The bandstand was seized. An impromptu barber-shop quartet sang 'Go Home, Yankees' to the tune of 'Good Night, Ladies'.

The European War of the Future was finished before it was begun. The false plans would not be drawn up and passed on, the Terrorists' air-destroyer would not strike, the armies would not march. The Most High Order of Xanadu was set against itself. Some of the most dangerous, vindictive and resourceful people in the world believed Charles Foster Kane had set out to fleece them. The magnate would be lucky to get out of France with his skin. He would have to fortify his Florida fastness against the creatures sure to be set against him by those who felt he owed debts no gold mine could service.

The Persian was waiting with a black motor-carriage and chauffeur.

The three women got into the vehicle. The Persian had champagne on ice for Gilberte and Elizabeth, and chocolate-covered insects for Riolama – her favourite delicacy.

Envelopes were handed to them. In Gilberte's was a notice of a bank account opened in her name in Switzerland, and a generous initial deposit.

'Against a rainy day,' Elizabeth explained.

Their commission concluded, expression drained from the Englishwoman's face – as if she were Galatea turned back into a statue, waiting for someone to vivify her again.

Then, briefly, she was animated as she gasped, 'Freddy!'

Mr Eynsford Hill was tied to a lamppost. Children painted as wild Indians danced around this totem, giving out war-whoops.

'I suppose he'll be all right,' Elizabeth said as they drove by. 'Fickle fortune frequently favours the foolish.'

Riolama happily crunched her chocolate bugs.

Elizabeth needed a strong teacher of music and diction to set her course, while Riolama was happy in an eternal present surrounded by winged friends. Gilberte recognised them both as her sisters.

They took the road from Royale-les-Eaux, leaving Kane's colossal schemes behind in irreparable shambles. Gilberte knew they would be in Paris by sunrise, to sleep away the day and emerge fresh the next evening – ready again to take flight.

X

TWO DAYS LATER, a telegram was delivered to Box Five. A simple acknowledgement of success, and the continued gratitude of his country. And, though they knew it not, the other Great Powers of Europe.

There would be no war this year.

More importantly, a dire threat was lifted. A certain American tycoon was no longer in any position to make good on his plan to buy the Paris Opéra outright and ship the building stone by stone to Chicago.

Beneath his mask, Erik really smiled.

ACT V: DELUGE

'Can the heart of Paris die like this in one night? It did seem dead. I have never seen a more complete image of death than was presented on that Friday night by this once impossibly crowded station... Would whole pieces of Paris collapse? Would all Paris crumble in bit by bit? Perhaps the whole of Paris really was doomed; perhaps it really was to be the end of Paris, which means the end of the world for Parisians.'

Laurence Jerrold, 'Paris After the Flood', *Contemporary Review* (1910)

I

MORNING SNOW TURNED to afternoon rain. Père Lachaise Cemetery was soaked. Streams ran between graves. Kate Reed kept to the paths and still found herself wading through gritty mud. Petals washed from wreaths stuck to her boots. She had to keep taking off and wiping her spectacles.

The weather in France was making headlines around the world. When she told her English friends where she was going, they advised she wrap up warm and carry an umbrella. To them, a heavy downpour meant damp basements, trickles into the servants' quarters and mould behind the Welsh dresser. Not the rising of the Seine and the fall of civilisation.

London rain was sly and malicious. A drumming on church slates during a long, dull sermon. You nodded off in wet clothes and caught a chill. Nothing a mustard bath wouldn't see to. Paris rain was outright evil. It wanted to murder you.

Only Charles Beauregard warned her of the extent of the chaos in Paris. He sat on the Ruling Cabal of the Diogenes Club and made it his business to know how things really stood, especially when they were worse than anyone could imagine.

Monumental stone soldiers – a Zouave, a grenadier, a skirmisher and an artilleryman – decorated the support columns of Pont de l'Alma. Parisians measured floods by the Zouave.

When water ran over his boots, embankment paths were out of bounds. Time to shift the wine from cellar to attic. When it reached his waist, the river became unnavigable. Time to get to work on an ark.

The Zouave was now up to his neck.

As if that were not sufficiently ominous, this was the week of the daylight comet. Some called the baleful shooting star Wormwood. Halley's Comet, more famous but less bright, would soon tear through the sky. At this rate, Kate expected alarums and excursions... pestilence and plague... wars and rumours of war.

The fourth horseman was already here.

At her age, every death seemed a sign of the end of all things.

The international telegram read 'The Persian is dead – Erik'.

At first, she thought the most terrifying aspect of the sad news was that the Director of the Opera Ghost Agency had walked into a post office himself. Obviously, the Persian could no longer perform such ordinary, above-the-streets tasks for him. Then she realised he would have had an Angel send notices to the alumnae.

Kate felt obliged to pay respects in person. Charles knew better than to argue against her trip. She even declined his offer to accompany her. When she needed a useful position outside Great Britain, the Diogenes Club recommended her to the Opera Ghost Agency – but Paris was her own adventure and she didn't need anyone to hold doors open or protect her from *Les Apaches*.

She could not attend the funeral. In accordance with his religion, the Persian was buried within a day of his death. She imagined Erik playing a violin in the rain while three women she didn't know dropped flowers on a wrapped body, laid on its side, head towards Mecca.

A week on, Angels gathered at the grave. With umbrellas.

'If you came to find out his real name, you'll be disappointed,' said an American with a red-eyed raven pinned to her black hat. 'No headstone.'

Mohammedans frowned on ostentatious funerary displays.

Amid elaborate tombs and memorials, the Moslem section of Père Lachaise was austere.

The women had brought simple wreaths or posies.

She added her own tribute. Purple carnations.

'Irene Adler,' said the woman with the bird-hat. 'Last of the first...'

'Kate Reed,' she replied. 'Somewhere in the middle.'

They shook gloved hands.

Two other women were present. Kate got the impression Irene had taken charge. The American had one of those voices which could fill an auditorium with song but – if let loose – empty it of an audience. Sympathetic critics used to call her 'forceful'. The less rapt said 'strident'.

'This is Mrs Elizabeth Eynsford Hill,' said Irene, indicating a slim English lady.

'Pleased to make your acquaintance, I'm sure,' said the woman. She spoke clearly, almost singing. Her bell-like vowels would appeal to Erik, a connoisseur of the human voice, more than Irene's 'Noo Joisey'.

'I am Unorna,' said the strawberry-blonde with mismatched eyes.

'The Witch of Prague,' said Irene.

'Magician,' corrected Kate, politely. 'I've heard of you.'

The Secret Files of the Diogenes Club had a dossier on Unorna. Her standing in European occult circles was high. On the eve of the new century, she reputedly bested Margaret Trelawny, the Witch Queen of Kensington, in a duel of magic. Aleister Crowley, by a long chalk the club's least reliable informant, alleged that after three nights of bargaining, the demon Bifrons – an Earl of Hell – signed a contract with Unorna only to find he had sold his soul to *her*... whereupon she made a gift of it to the Pope, to dispose of as he saw fit. Unorna had a reputation as exorcist, visionary, healer and seeress. If the Hapsburgs listened to her the way the Romanoffs listened to Rasputin, the imperial family might have been spared one suicide pact, several assassinations and an infestation of elemental spirits in the imperial villa at Bad Ischl. Early in her career, Unorna had been an Angel of Music.

'Prague is in Bohemia,' said Irene. 'Not my favourite vacation spot.'

The files ran to *several* dossiers on Irene Adler, which the Ruling Cabal restricted to serious researchers because otherwise some valued members – all men – would have had them out of the cabinets all the time to look at the pictures. Irene was notorious on all the continents except Antarctica, which she'd not visited yet. If penguins could be scandalised, she would be up for the job.

'Kate Reed,' said Irene. 'You're the clever one.'

'Irene Adler,' said Kate. 'You're the slippery one.'

Irene laughed behind a half-veil.

She had returned to the stage – as an actress, not a singer – to tour South America, one-upping Sarah Bernhardt by playing not just Hamlet but also Macbeth, Othello, Romeo and Prince Hal. Every time she appeared in a capital city, national treasures went missing and revolutions broke out. Last year, she made a rare return to her home state to work in Fort Lee, motion picture capital of the United States. For the IMP company, she starred in a series of cinematographs recreating the scandals of her youth in such detail that boards of censorship convened in every territory to suppress them. More detailed still were versions of these flickers in the private collections of plutocrats who each thought they had the only prints.

Irene cut a glamorous figure, but had to work at it with powder, stays and artificial hair colour. The adventuress suffered the indignity of having lived so much in public she could not easily lie about her age. She was fifty-two – five years older than Kate. The willowy Unorna seemed younger than she could possibly be... while the straight-backed, tightly buttoned Mrs Eynsford Hill was youngest of the group but conducted herself like an elderly dowager. There must be a reason for that.

These women had been with the Opera Ghost Agency at

different times, in different trios. Before and after Kate.

Her fellow Angels had returned to the Orient – Clara Watson to China, to pursue her disquieting hobbies and enthusiasms, and Lady Yuki to Japan, to strike more names off her list. It would be months before they heard the news about the Persian, if they ever did.

Irene called herself 'last of the first' – which wasn't quite true. Trilby O'Ferrall, the artists' model, had died young… but Countess de Chagny, the former Christine Daaé, was still alive. She had many children and grandchildren to show for her advantageous marriage. Her gouty husband was above ground too, though the Count made a show of withdrawing from public life in fury at the exoneration of Captain Dreyfus. De Chagny probably forbade his wife from mourning the Persian.

Even with umbrellas, they were all getting wet.

No one wanted to leave first.

Kate had only spent six pell-mell months with the Opera Ghost Agency, tackling Guignol and the *Légion d'Horreur*, Belphégor and the Louvre mummies, the Cruel Pleasures of the Duc de Blangis, and other cases. Some Angels served longer. Sophy Kratides, La Marmoset, Ayda Ferguson, Mun Zhi Fan, Christina Light, Hagar Stanley, Ailsa Auchmuty, Riolama. Others were in and out of the Agency inside a week. Some had glittering or alarming solo careers. Others were mysterious even to the dossier-compiling know-it-alls of the Diogenes Club. Grunya Constantine, Ysabel de Ferre, Elsie Venner, Adelita Muñoz, Marie-Madeleine de Broutignol, Edith Rabatjoie, Hannah Caulder, Gilberte Lachaille, Lois Cayley.

Angels came and went as often as performers on a variety bill, but the Persian was the constant. He sat in the Café de la Paix in the mornings, available to *le tout Paris*, and the world revolved around his table. Anyone could approach with a problem, which he would faithfully pass on to Monsieur Erik for consideration. He was the only man whose judgement the director of the Opera Ghost Agency respected. In Mazandaran, as chief of police, he was ordered by the Shah to dispose of Erik, a proverbial man who knew too much, but saved his life instead. That act of mercy bound them together.

It would have been easy for any of Erik's enemies to walk into the café and shoot the Persian in the head or poison his coffee, but he took no special precautions. Even those who wanted the Phantom dead saw the Persian as protected – an institution of the city, a necessity for the conduct of business. The practical stage manager who implemented the plans of the remote director. Welcome everywhere in Paris, though he could not return to his homeland. Irreplaceable.

The Persian had everything but a name. Just as Erik had everything but a face.

He had faithfully corresponded with Kate, long after her spell with the Agency. He passed on scraps of information useful to her as a reporter or in the investigations she carried out for the Diogenes Club. Many of those nuggets came from Erik. The Phantom contrived to know everything that transpired in the criminal and occult underworlds of a dozen nations, though he seldom ventured far from his home on the shore of the artificial lagoon under the Palais Garnier.

Which, she only now realised, must be flooding.

If water was around the Zouave's neck, it would also top the pipes of the Phantom's organ.

Erik, a master architect, must have designed his lair with the possibility of flood in mind. However, even he couldn't have predicted this season's rains and the rising of the Seine and its tributaries. First, to the southeast, the towns of Lorroy and Troyes were all but swept away. Then, swollen rivers combined into a rushing torrent which threatened the city. Icebergs formed overnight and dashed into jagged chunks against bridge supports. These shot through the water like missiles – smashing boats, breaking legs. Sewers overflowed. Liquid filth tainted food supplies and fouled the air. The Métro was closed, its tunnels turned to underground aqueducts. The Eiffel Tower, which Kate still thought hideous, rose from a shallow lake.

She hoped the Phantom had a dry bolthole somewhere.

Kate looked down at the Persian's grave. The rain was battering the floral tributes. Newly turned earth was becoming swamp. Something showed in the mud.

For a queasy moment, Kate thought the body was floating to the surface.

'What is that?' she asked.

Mrs Eynsford Hill handed Unorna her umbrella and knelt carefully by the grave. Unorna held up two brollies to shelter the English woman. With gloved hands, Mrs Eynsford Hill pulled something out of the ground.

Oilskin wrappings peeled away from an object the size of a shoebox.

'I believe it is a music box,' said the English woman. 'How enchanting.'

It was an ornate cabinet. Painted panels depicted clowns and harlequins.

A key turned...

The box began to tinkle, imitating a pianoforte.

'Now, what is that little tune?' asked Mrs Eynsford Hill.

Kate recognised the opening melody of the second movement of Haydn's Symphony No 94 in G Major. The notes instantly brought back a childhood mnemonic. She had made many stubby-fingered assaults on a solo piano arrangement of the piece...

Papa Haydn's dead and gone... but his mem'ry lingers on...

Irene was alarmed.

'Toss it away, now!' she shouted.

When his mood was one of bliss...

Without question, Mrs Eynsford Hill drew back her arm like a shot-putter and lobbed the box across the cemetery. She had a powerful throw.

He wrote jolly tunes like this...

A long pause as the box turned over and over in the air.

BANG!

The box exploded like a big firework. Flaming fragments rained onto graves, hissing as they were extinguished in puddles.

A stinging stench of sulphur caught in Kate's nostrils. Her eyes watered. Her ears rang.

'What was that frightful racket?' Mrs Eynsford Hill asked, as if someone had dropped a tray of tea things.

'A surprise?' suggested Irene, bitterly.

'Haydn's Surprise Symphony,' said Unorna.

Kate hadn't expected to come under fire at a memorial.

'I used to hurt my nails slamming down that loud chord,' she said. 'My governess despaired of me. I don't have a wide enough reach.'

Had it been a particularly ill-judged joke? Or a serious assassination attempt?

'That charge would have taken your hands off,' Irene said to Mrs Eynsford Hill. 'Maybe your face.'

'Who would do such a thing?' the English woman asked. 'Explosives in a cemetery are in exceptionally poor taste.'

'You could make a list,' said Irene. 'We all have enemies, I daresay. As Angels of Music and on our own account. And our successor Angels will have added plenty of fresh names... which we can ask them about.'

'We can?' asked Kate.

Irene tried to use her umbrella as a pointer, but it turned inside out. She tossed the broken thing away. Rain splashed off her winged headdress. The veil stuck to her strong, handsome face.

Kate looked where Irene pointed.

Three women had appeared in the graveyard, lurking in long green waterproof hooded cloaks – as if waiting for Macbeth, Perseus... or a fourth for bridge.

Angels, of course. The current trio.

The dossiers were slim so far, but Kate knew their names.

Alraune, Olympia, Thi Minh.

II

'IT IS A pleasure to meet you,' Olympia said to her. 'I hope we shall be the best of friends.'

Irene Adler winced as the Angel took her hand.

The vault was warm and dry – and pleasantly lacking in exploding booby traps. Alraune ten Brincken, the weird German girl, had a key to the tomb, which bore the family name of de Boscherville. The whisper was that the creature who'd grow up to be Erik was born in Saint-Martin-de-Boscherville, a town near Rouen. No one was interred here, yet.

The stone cubbyhouse was furnished like a windowless parlour. A hospitality table with liquor and glasses. A phonograph on a stand. A framed poster of Christine Daaé as Marguerite. Other pictures of young women. Irene was surprised Erik had got hold of *that* photograph of her. Masks and cloaks hung from a rail. A wall-mounted mirror, duplicate of the one-way glass in Dressing Room 313, was trying not to look like a secret door. The Opera Ghost Agency maintained nests like this all over the city. Hideouts and observation posts.

'It is a pleasure to meet you,' Olympia said to Kate Reed. 'I hope we shall be the best of friends.'

'Watch out,' Irene warned. 'Her shake's like getting caught in a wine-press.'

Too late. Kate's fingers were crushed too.

Irene could usually ignore the twinges in her knuckles. Not now. All her pains demanded attention. Even – no, *especially* – the ones doctors said she imagined. Like nails through her eyes.

After that close brush with the music box bomb, she was sensitive.

'It is a pleasure to meet you,' Olympia said to Unorna. 'I hope we shall be the best of friends.'

Unorna held her hand up palm out like a Red Indian and said,

'Blessed be.' When she was called a wise woman, it wasn't just a polite way of saying witch.

'It is a pleasure to meet you,' said Elizabeth Eynsford Hill, mimicking Olympia's pure soprano. 'I hope we shall be the best of friends.'

Irene knew about the English woman's strange education. Another victim of thoughtless mastermindery.

Olympia would not be put off. She didn't even gabble her words to get it over with.

'It is a pleasure to meet you,' she said to Elizabeth. 'I hope we shall be the best of friends.'

'She's a doll,' said Irene.

'Really, Miss Adler, you are addicted to Americanisms,' said Kate.

'I *am* American,' she said. 'And it's not slang. She really is a doll.'

Kate caught on and looked closely at the dancer.

Irene recognised the model. She was hardly likely to forget the Marriage Club, even after all these years. The face was the same, though the hair was different – bobbed, like a boy's. The slim figure was bulked out by what might have been armour plate under the dress.

'Coppélius and Spallanzani,' she observed.

'Their design,' said Alraune, 'repaired and improved by a new firm, Gaillard and Quentin. To Erik's specifications. He once constructed automata himself, for a Sultan in Constantinople.'

Since Irene's day, the Phantom had apparently become chattier, sharing yarns of his past with Angels. Or else Alraune came to the Agency well-informed.

The German girl was a sly one. And she didn't stand up straight.

Kate touched Olympia's face. The doll didn't mind.

'That's not porcelain,' she said. 'Is it rubber or silk over sponge?' She took her hand away, shuddering. 'She's *warm*. How can that be?'

'Fire in her heart,' said Alraune.

'Not a figure of speech, either,' said Irene. 'I reckon she runs on acid batteries. No need to wind her up every day.'

The art of simulacra had come on by leaps and bounds since Coppélius and Spallanzani worked for Countess de Cagliostro. Their to-order brides were squatting monkeys with cymbals compared with Olympia. The new living doll had many more points of articulation. She breathed like a real girl. Her unblinking eyes sparkled, moist with a fluid – transparent oil? – which might be taken for tears. That whirring and ticking which gave away the old contraptions was muted. Irene made a mental note to pick up a few hundred dollars' worth of shares in Gaillard and Quentin. If electric servants or soldiers caught on like Ford automobiles, fortunes would be made.

'Do such things have souls, I wonder?' said Unorna. 'Or are they tin homunculi – summoned from the void for use and dispelled afterwards.'

'Souls – pah!' said Alraune.

Irene sensed something uncanny in the German too. Alraune was flesh and blood all right – if fashionably bony. But something was missing.

Angels all had something extra. But most had something missing too.

Thi Minh, the little Annamite tumbler, was mute. Once, Erik would no more take on a bird without song than a dancer without legs... but Irene supposed things changed. The girl from Indochina was eloquent with face and hands. She should have been in motion pictures. She looked a perfect little French miss: tiny rouge-free face, chic plain white dress, fashionably boyish bobbed hair. Irene could envision her tied to railroad tracks by a wicked guardian or abducted by sinister cultists – though, even if producers in Fort Lee were hacks, she had to admit the real world turned out to be just as full of scenarios of peril, escape, pursuit and treachery. Thi Minh wouldn't be here if she couldn't undo a knot or evade a cult.

These new Angels weren't like Irene's generation. Trilby and Christine. They were too *thin*. Underdressed, even with rain-cloaks. And unpainted. They didn't look *healthy* at all.

Kate was closer to her idea of an Angel. Though the word made her shudder, they were both Victorians. Dry old sticks who outlived scandals to become respectable. Even Irene's disgraces were quaint now. Pictures that might once have toppled thrones were on postcards.

Elizabeth was more like the new girls. Trim and unflappable, subsisting on air instead of food. She was sort of a wind-up doll, too. Like poor, dear Trilby, she'd made the mistake of *taking lessons*.

Unorna was something different – hard to place.

Irene was glad the witch was on their side.

Alraune poured generous measures of sherry (for Elizabeth) and brandy (for the rest of them). Only Olympia didn't drink. Preferring her own rye whiskey, Irene poured a measure from her flask into the little silver cup which screwed over the stopper.

'I always like a nip after I've almost been blown to smithereens,' Irene said. 'Bottoms up, ladies.'

She took a burning swallow.

'The bomb was to maim, not kill,' said Alraune. 'A coffin full of dynamite would have been more effective.'

'A lovely thought,' said Irene. 'Most people just leave flowers.'

'It was a message,' said Unorna. 'We have been warned off.'

'I heard it loud and clear,' said Irene. 'A telegram would have done just as well.'

'Anyone who thinks a bomb will warn us off doesn't know us very well,' said Kate.

'Doesn't know *you* very well, perhaps,' said Irene. 'They've completely got the measure of me.'

'You don't mean that,' said the little Irish woman. 'The Irene Adler I've heard about wouldn't be scared off by such low tactics.'

'The Irene Adler you've heard about got older and creakier and would like to lie on a divan eating Swiss chocolates with a cold compress on her forehead. She's had quite enough derring-do for one lifetime, thank you very much.'

Kate smiled indulgently. She didn't take Irene's protests seriously.

Irene had cause to rue that Irene Adler Kate had heard about. The Irene Adler foolish men dreamed up and made fools of themselves over. Irene only really got in trouble when she got herself confused with that imaginary Irene Adler.

'How did the Persian die?' Kate asked the others.

'He was gravely ill,' said Alraune. 'He had been for some time.'

'That's not an answer.'

'No,' admitted the German girl.

Irene couldn't help but stare at Alraune's waist-length tangle of hair. It was thick and somehow twiggy, with beads braided in. Along with her huge eyes, the wild mane made her look alarming.

'Was there an autopsy?' asked Unorna. 'Is Dr Dieudonné still coroner?'

'I don't know that name,' said Alraune. 'But... no, there was no autopsy, no police investigation. Just a death certificate. A sick man dies. If not of his sickness, then what does it matter? The rains fall. The river rises. Doctors are busy. The morgue is full. Many have lost their livelihoods in the floods. Many have lost their lives. Not all by drowning. When a body is found floating with its head bashed in... it's best to write it up as if he fell in the water and bumped on floating wreckage. Otherwise, the Prefect of Police would have to take men off shoring up barricades and erecting dry walkways to investigate. For a murderer, the flood might be a blessing... like a curtain to hide behind.'

'So you reckon he was iced?' said Irene.

Alraune shrugged bony shoulders and bit her sensual lower lip. She was not a come-right-out-and-say-it kind of a girl.

'I was in Paris when this happened,' said Eynsford Hill. 'I saw the body before it was washed and wrapped. The Persian had chronic bronchitis.'

'He *was* a cougher,' said Irene.

'It is nothing, my Angels,' said the English woman in the

Persian's voice. 'Just a little tickle in the throat.'

'Those cigarettes he smoked,' said Kate. 'Turkish tar.'

'There was blood around his mouth,' continued Elizabeth, in her own – if not her original – voice.

'Which you'd expect,' said Kate.

'And in his eyes.'

Thi Minh gripped her throat as if invisible hands were throttling her.

'I've seen enough men hanged to know about the blood in the eyes,' said Irene. 'So the Persian was choked?'

Elizabeth, who talked about the death of a friend as if she were considering a menu for afternoon tea, nodded.

'He was carefully strangled,' she went on. 'With a rope or a wire, there's a ligature mark. A red weal. Something broader, like a scarf or a pillow, spreads the pressure. The throat is crushed, but not bruised. But there is no way to stop blood vessels in the eyes bursting.'

Irene had a pang. What a terrible, quiet way to go. Not just killed, but tidied away.

'It was murder, then,' said Kate.

'We cannot prove it,' said Alraune. 'But we know it.'

Irene had not seen the Persian since the business with God. After quitting Paris a second time, she suppressed any stray thought of the Persian or his friend behind the mirror. Now, that stung more than she liked. She'd left many people – mostly, but not exclusively, men – behind on her route from where she started to wherever she was going. It was best not to dwell too much on how they might feel about her departures… whether they remembered her as *the* woman or *that* woman. Mentally, she'd wrapped the Persian and Erik up together in a bundle and decided she could do without the pair of them. A shabby thing, she realised too late. She should have spared time to look out for a friend.

She glanced towards that mirror. It would be almost a window if the light were turned down in the vault. Now, only darkness showed beyond the gaps in the silvering.

She remembered a mask. And yellow eyes.

Irene lumped Erik in with other masterminds she'd run across – Bloody James Moriarty, Blessed Sherlock Holmes and the Lord of Strange Deaths. Not to mention bright sparks like Antonio Nikola, Dagobert Trostler, Dr Mabuse, Augustus Van Dusen and the Face. More and more of the bastards were around these days. On both sides of the fence, and straddling the middle. Genius inventors, master crooks, great detectives, overmen, big fish. Her world was getting crowded with them. They formed secret societies, syndicates, leagues, cabals. They fought their own wars and made their own alliances. She had always skipped from shadow to shadow, a small creature trying to avoid being noticed, squashed or eaten. Colossi were banishing the shadows and spoiling the game. Since her girlhood, masterminds had been getting smarter… and worse.

She'd thought Svengali, the mesmerist who first tinkered with poor Trilby's head, a bad 'un. Between the fluences of Svengali and Erik, Trilby got so discombobulated she eventually couldn't keep on breathing without someone telling her to… and just *stopped*, like an unwound watch. At least Svengali was nakedly honest about what he wanted. A step up from poverty and obscurity. Hot meals and a comfortable bed.

Henry Higgins, the dilettante who raised Elizabeth Eynsford Hill from the gutter, wasn't poor, obscure or hungry. He made a freak of a flower-seller – in essence, Olympia with a pulse – to settle a silly argument. Higgins didn't even fancy the girl and settled an idiot on her for a husband.

Irene had known some bad women. Jo Balsamo, for a start… but also Lady Brentwyche, Altar Keane and Sjena De'Ath. None of those skirts scrambled folks' brains just to show off how clever they were. Except maybe Countess de Cagliostro, who was scarcely human.

'The Persian… *dead*,' said Unorna. 'It's *wrong*.'

'It was him without question,' said Alraune.

'I don't mean to dispute that,' continued the witch. 'He *is* dead, I know that. But he should not be. The pattern is broken by his removal from this plain. He was an important individual. One does not just kill such a man and expect no consequences. The larger world must take notice.'

Irene thought of the Persian. And how he had spent his life.

A thing she had noticed about masterminds is that they liked to keep a toady about to reflect their light back at them. Stooges to egg them on, puff them up and calm them down. A nicer – or, at least, more down-to-earth – guy handily smoothed things over if the great man went too far. Often, these boobies were required to write up their patrons the way Boswell did Johnson – to make calculating machines seem human, admirable or interesting. Sometimes, second bananas were with the firm to get prime movers through the door. Hearty, unassuming ass-kissers like Dr Watson, Basher Moran or Colonel Pickering were welcome in places which wouldn't stand for skull-faced killjoys who corrected your grammar and terrified the maids. Number Two Men rode coattails like Christmas sleighs but brought more to the teams than they got credit for.

Erik, let it not be forgotten, would be dead in an unmarked desert grave if it weren't for the Persian. Sidekicks also got literally kicked when an overman needed a man to be over. Irene remembered Cochenille, the ill-made doll... but also sorry specimens like the Gecko, the pock-marked fiddler who trotted after Svengali like a mongrel who's grown to love the slapping hand, and Bunny Manders, the nance who fagged for that bounder A.J. Raffles at Eton and never grew out of it.

Just as minions deserved more credit, they should also earn more blame. Without them, masterminds couldn't get away with as much.

Maybe the Persian ought to have been held to account for the Phantom... but Irene was old and smart enough to know things were never as simple inside the house as they looked when peeped at through the curtains.

She remembered her own marriage. Had she been the mastermind and God her minion? That made her cringe. Godfrey Norton was someone else she tried not to think of.

'What about... him?' Kate asked, nodding at the mirror. 'What's the Phantom had to say for himself?'

Thi Minh capered expressively.

'M. Erik is... indisposed,' said Alraune.

'What does that mean?' asked Irene.

'They've heard nothing from him,' said Elizabeth. 'And the way below is impassable.'

'Impossible?' asked Kate.

'Impassable,' restated Elizabeth.

'I knew that,' said Kate. 'It's just you're the only person I've ever met who could make "impossible" and "impassable" sound like different words.'

'This is no time for making light.'

'No,' said Kate. 'I'm sorry.'

'We opened the mirror at the opera house yesterday and sent Olympia down,' said Elizabeth.

'It is a pleasure to meet you,' said Olympia, to no one new.

'She doesn't need to breathe,' said the English woman. 'And she's waterproof.'

That made her sound like Erik's ideal girlfriend. It was a wonder he hadn't replaced all the Angels with battery-powered ballerinas.

'She swam through flooded tunnels to the underground lagoon,' continued Elizabeth. 'The little house on the lagoon is swept away. She found Erik's coffin floating, like an abandoned punt. But he was nowhere to be seen.'

'I hope we shall be the best of friends,' said Olympia.

Was Irene imagining it or did the doll sound sad now?

'The *pneumatique* is out of order,' said Elizabeth. 'As are telephone, tickertape and telegraph. All lines of communication with Erik are broken.'

'I'd know if he were dead,' said Unorna. 'And he isn't.'

Irene recalled that Erik was an expert with breathing tubes.

A strong swimmer, he could scythe through dark waters while wearing full evening dress, using his cloak like the fins of a manta ray.

'At the very least, he is busy,' said Alraune. 'Like all Paris.'

'How stands the Agency?' asked Kate.

'Suspended due to flooding,' said Alraune. 'Like all Paris.'

As the only serving Angel who could hold a conversation, the German girl was in a pickle. Irene had a notion Alraune was used to being alone – or at least lonely. A chilly creature, she was attractive yet off-putting. Foster daughter of another mastermind, Professor ten Brincken. Rumours about them circulated in Germany. None pleasant.

Alraune was an alchemical name. It was German for mandrake, the weed popularly believed to grow under gallows, sprouting from the last ejaculate of hanged men. Distillate from the root had the power to cloud men's minds. Irene suspected Alraune's distinct musk had the same property.

Unorna said mandrake was bad luck. She sounded like a fairground gypsy with a grudge, but Irene knew enough to take her seriously. When Irene was in Bohemia, Prince Willy von Ormstein – cause of so much of her trouble, though she admitted she'd gone along with it – officiated at a reception for the Witch of Prague. Unorna had supposedly just saved the city from goblins or golems or somesuch. The witch had buried *her* mastermind, the dwarf sorcerer Keyork Arabian. She was a rare truly free woman.

'It is up to us to pool our talents and identify the murderer,' said Kate.

'Oh, we know who the *murderer* is,' said Alraune. 'That's easy. It's Fantômas, the anarchist.'

Kate's eyes widened.

Thi Minh held fingers in front of her face like an eye-mask and crouched down, looking around warily. She made a bomb of a fist and let it explode, puffing out her fingers and waving them around.

Fantômas was another headline-grabber... always stealing jewels from uncrackable safes or assassinating people said to be impossible to get to. He might be a mastermind. He was certainly a master of disguise, one of those fellows who might be anyone or no one. But he was unusual – a freak among freaks. Even his peers disliked him. Unlike, say, Raffles or *Les Vampires*, he was more interested in making trouble than money. And, unlike the Lord of Strange Deaths – whose declared aim was to end European influence in the Middle- and Far East – he had no real political purpose. Just chaos and carnage. An exploding music box among floral tributes was just his style. He was Jack the Ripper on an industrial scale. Instead of merely slicing a few throats, he took a razor to cities, nations, continents. Irene hadn't been as scared of Professor Moriarty as she was of Fantômas. It would take more than being pushed over a waterfall to finish him off.

'Isn't Fantômas an *imitator* of Erik?' said Kate. 'He wears evening clothes and a mask. He strikes from the shadows and issues press releases, just like Erik's black-edged notes. Even the *name* sounds like Phantom.'

'Once an imitation has been perfected, it makes sense to smash the original,' said Elizabeth. 'So there is only one.'

'It is a pleasure to meet you,' said Olympia. 'I hope we shall be the best of friends.'

The doll sounded distressed. Or was she the same every time, like a wax cylinder? One heard her differently, depending on mood or context.

'I understand that this Fantômas used to go by the absurd name of Gurn,' said Elizabeth. 'He may well have been born with it. I can conceive of no reason anyone who didn't have to would call themselves Gurn. When I was an Angel, the Agency had a *contretemps* or two with him. He came off poorly, which might be a spur to his present mission against us. Then, he was little more than a common ruffian. Before he put on a mask and took up all this nihilist nonsense.'

Irene had heard of an incident at Royale-les-Eaux. Half the villains of the world blamed the other half for what happened in the casino there, but she'd discerned the dainty beating of Angels' wings. Gurn had lost his first stolen fortune in that debacle – which was enough to put the Agency in his sights.

'How do you *know* Fantômas killed the Persian?' asked Kate.

'He has issued threats,' said Alraune. 'Sent letters to the Opera House... put notices in the papers... painted his mark up all over the city. He accuses Erik of being a creature of the 19th century, who deserves to be swept away with the debris of the old world. Fantômas is a spectre of the New Age. No opera... just Phantom. He wants to see civilisation burn and dance in the ruins.'

'Or flood,' said Irene. 'And splash about.'

'He has strangled before,' said Elizabeth. 'You recall the case of Lord Beltham. Fantômas is a master of the night-time noose.'

'So is Erik,' said Irene. 'Remember the Punjab lasso?'

The Phantom learned rope tricks from the Thuggee in India, during his youthful grand tour. Most people look at the Taj Mahal, visit art galleries, have unwise love affairs and send home cheerful postcards. Wherever he visited, Erik picked up ingenious murder methods.

'You're not suggesting Erik killed his only friend?' said Kate.

'His only *male* friend,' corrected Irene. 'And no... this is another player of the great game issuing a challenge, knocking over a pawn so as to get his attention. Using Erik's trademark as a taunt. I am only surprised Fantômas didn't get the Persian under a chandelier and drop it on him.'

Kate looked disgusted.

'This isn't how I think,' said Irene. 'It's how *they* do. Masterminds.'

Unorna nodded her agreement. She understood the shadow worlds, perhaps more than any other Angel.

'Erik used to make explosive devices like that music box too,' said the witch.

'So far as this Fantômas is concerned, we're not even on the board,' Irene continued. 'Or else he'd have fitted us for red rope chokers. He thought Erik wouldn't care enough if he only downed an Angel… so he killed a man. They're fighting a duel.'

'And we're supposed to do what?' said Kate. 'Hold coats?'

'Wait meekly – put in our place by that firework in the Persian's grave – and sign up with whoever wins,' suggested Irene. 'And Fantômas says *Erik* is the 19th-century man.'

Red highlights burned on the Irish woman's cheeks. Irene had known she would feel the sting at the oversight. Kate Reed, of all women, was offended at *not* being picked to be a murder victim.

Irene was angry too. She hadn't expected that.

'This will not pass,' said Kate. 'The Persian meant as much to us – more, I daresay! – as to Erik. Would any of us have stayed with the Agency for more than five minutes if we just had to take orders from behind that mirror? Despite what the world says, we did what we did for the Persian – not the Phantom! With Sophy Kratides retired and Lady Yuki in Japan, we lack our Angel of Vengeance and Angel of the Sword… but Erik called me the Angel of Truth.'

'He called me the Angel of Larceny,' said Irene, smirking.

'Angel of Ill Fortune,' said Alraune.

'He called us all Angels of Something,' said Kate. 'Here's my Truth – we won't sit this out. Erik might be clinging to flotsam, for all we know… or washed down river and stuck in a midden. Unable to take his part in this duel that has cost us so dearly. So we shall find this Fantômas gobshite and bring him to book.'

'It is a pleasure to meet you,' said Olympia, with steely determination. 'I hope we shall be the best of friends.'

'What she said, sister,' said Irene.

'*That's* the Irene Adler I was expecting,' said Kate.

Irene had the feeling she'd been rooked. But she was angry and inspired too.

* * *

III

T HE MÉTRO WAS *fermé*. Parisians were leerier of travelling underground than Londoners. It might be partially Erik's fault. There was no risk of running into a Phantom on the Tube – though the Lord (and the Diogenes Club) knew horrors enough squirmed under London. Black swine in the sewers of Hampstead. Sawney Beane in brick caves below Russell Square. Paris had more prosaic doubts about its still-novel Métro. A fire on a recently opened line had trapped and killed eighty travellers. Gloomy commentators talked of 'the Nécro' and swore to stick to omnibuses. They weren't running either, of course. Kate supposed folk like that had to stay home, hoping the waters receded before their larders emptied.

If time and a working international wire could be found, she should cable *The Clarion* to offer news and notes. All the other British dailies had correspondents here, snug on the upper floors of good hotels, firing off stories overheard in bars. Rescued animals were always popular. Papers which usually ran editorials calling for war against the degenerate French set up appeals, exhorting the generous public to donate used clothes to Parisians whose wardrobes were underwater. Kate thought a mountain of odd socks and worn-out mufflers would be little appreciated. It would take more than forty days of rain to make the average French citizen wear something unfashionable, let alone something British. If the baskets of clothes ever arrived, they would end up stuffed into holes to plug leaks.

The rain stopped for the moment, but vicious cold winds still blew. Dangerous-looking, improvised plank-and-trestle walkways called *passerelles* stretched across flooded streets. Determined souls grimly tottered on these like high-wire walkers with umbrellas and bulky coats. Lampposts tilted at strange angles, lights out.

The Angels made their way from Père Lachaise in fiacres. When horses baulked at flooded streets, they had to get out and consider other transport options. The master of a small boat offered to row them along a canal-like stretch of Boulevard Montmartre for an extortionate fare.

With each disaster, opportunists sprung up to make a fast franc. Or pursue other ends.

Had their anarchist enemy waited for this moment – while *le tout Paris* was waterlogged and distracted – to strike? Kate wouldn't have put it past him to dynamite riverbanks and stop up sewers to make the flood worse. But even Fantômas couldn't summon the rain.

At the crossroads of Boulevard Montmartre, Boulevard Haussmann, Rue Drouot, Rue de Richelieu and Boulevard des Italiens, a makeshift dam barred the way. Made of carts, broken furniture, barrels and an inside-out grand piano, it resembled the barricades the Paris mob put up in times of insurrection. A miserable gendarme sat on a lopsided rocking chair atop the pile, as if manning a position – but the personnel stopping boats and interrogating passersby were civilians. Well-dressed in blazers and student caps. Generally well-spoken, if irritatingly cheerful.

Jules, their pop-eyed boatman, grumbled and gnawed his beard. Kate wondered if he'd be done for price-gouging. Profiteers were hated more than looters. A centime on the price of a loaf of bread was cause for lynching.

The dam didn't completely block the way. A narrow gap was left for vessels to pass through once they'd been looked over.

'Welcome to Suez,' Kate said.

Two young men with hooks on poles pulled the boat towards an improvised quay.

'What treasure have we here, Max?' said one. 'A cargo of fair rewards for our hard-working lads?'

'Indeed, Oscar, indeed,' responded Max. His straw hat was probably not suitable for the weather. 'A most welcome relief.'

Kate recognised the badges on their breast-pockets. Max

and Oscar were Camelots du Roi. The fellowship of rowdy conservative students was affiliated to *L'Action Française*, a well-connected, wealthy faction of Catholics, anti-Semites and Bourbon restorationists. Before this week, the Camelots were best known for affray masquerading as patriotism. To defend the honour of Joan of Arc, they disrupted the lectures of a Sorbonne professor who dared suggest a girl who heard voices was more deranged than saintly. During the flood, the Camelots had sobered up and volunteered to help police, fire brigades and army. Usually intent on overthrowing the Republic with flung beer bottles and obscene songs, the students had won over a sceptical public by tirelessly rescuing old ladies from sinking tenements (except Jewish old ladies, who could drown like cats) and delivering food to convents and orphanages. That said, Kate wondered what right they had to set up a road-block and quiz people about their business.

Besides their student insignia, they wore green armbands.

'Seven lovelies in a boat,' said Oscar. 'A rich prize, to be sure.'

He consulted a leather-bound book, as if looking up rules of conduct for this situation.

'Where are you going this fine afternoon?' asked Max.

'The opera house,' said Kate.

'Alas – there is no performance tonight,' said Oscar.

'We are aware of that, my good man,' said Mrs Eynsford Hill.

Thi Minh made a sad, determined face.

'You're not French,' said Max.

'I'll say we're not,' said Irene. 'I am American... my friends are Irish, English, German, Annamite and Bohemian. Olympia was made in France, I suppose.'

'Olympia?' asked Max, craning his head. 'Which delight is she?'

The Angels parted to let the Camelots see the doll. Her end of the boat sat lower in the water. Her works weighed more than human insides.

'It is a pleasure to meet you,' said Olympia. 'I hope we shall be the best of friends.'

Max and Oscar laughed. If old enough to grow proper moustaches, they'd have twirled them like stage roués. Oscar snuck a peek at his book.

'It's a pleasure to meet *you*,' said Max.

Olympia was blankly pretty. Kate remembered her crushing grip.

'I've an idea, Max *mon brave*,' said Oscar, snapping his book shut.

'An idea, Oscar! Do tell.'

'I believe this boatman guilty of foul offences against the city… to whit, the crimes of *looting* and *hoarding*. He has carried off these young ladies and now keeps them to himself. Do you call that social behaviour?'

'Indeed not, Oscar, indeed not. His name should be taken down. Lists must be kept of the enemies of France, foreign and domestic.'

Kate had little patience with silly young men in any country – and the glint of delight in bullying brought her colour up.

'I propose we tithe the fellow, Max. We should relieve him of *two* of his ill-gotten girls… the fair flower of France, of course, and… the sausage-eater with the lovely hair.'

Alraune shrugged. Kate suspected that if she *were* handed over as tribute, Max and Oscar would be floating face-down within the hour. That sort of thing happened often around the Angel of Ill Fortune.

Irene looked piqued – at being passed over.

Jules lowered his head and kept quiet to avoid a dunking. Kate began to feel protective of the boatman. He might be a profiteer, but he was *their* profiteer. And he only wanted money.

These Camelots du Roi were unreformed rotters, it seems. How disappointing.

There was something else. Oscar and his mysterious book, for a start. Max kept darting glances over his shoulder, as if a superior – *not* the gendarme on the dam – were monitoring him and harsh punishments were dished out for bungling.

Most of the Angels could have trounced Max and Oscar by

themselves – but a fight would escalate. Plenty more Camelots were around. At best, a skirmish with posh vigilantes would be a waste of time. At worst, the Agency's real enemy would have another opening to strike.

But they were held up.

Oscar, marginally in charge, relaxed his grip on his leather book. A bookmark fell out and fluttered down into the boat.

Kate picked it up and was shocked. It was a photograph of her – taken recently, outside a London restaurant. She hadn't known she was posing.

'I wish that hadn't happened,' said Oscar.

He put away his book and produced a revolver. Max was surprised by the appearance of the gun.

'These are the Angels,' Oscar told him.

Max didn't understand. Kate, with a lurch in her stomach, did.

'Excuse me, gentlemen,' said Unorna.

'Ho, who spoke up?' asked Oscar, waving the revolver.

'The blonde,' said Max, cheerfully. 'Perhaps we chose unwisely. What do you say we tithe this rascal three out of seven?'

'Forget that,' snapped Oscar. 'We'll need them all.'

'We aren't the Angels you seek,' said Unorna, low and even.

There was a pause. Kate fancied she heard a humming sound. Unorna made a small, precise gesture which drew the eye in.

'These aren't the Angels we seek,' said Max, waving them on.

'You should let us pass freely,' said Unorna.

'We should let them pass freely,' said Oscar, pocketing his gun.

Kate felt Unorna in her mind too. She radiated persuasiveness.

'You should mend your manners,' said Mrs Eynsford Hill.

'We should mend our manners,' said Max, slightly puzzled.

Jules – asking no questions – used his oar to shove off. The boat slipped through the narrow gap in the dam. There wasn't room to row so Jules used the oar like a punt pole. The gendarme ignored them.

Alraune whispered in Unorna's ear. The witch laughed.

'It looks like a pleasant evening for a swim, gentlemen,' Unorna shouted back. 'You should take a refreshing dip.'

Oscar and Max immediately began unbuttoning their blazers. Thi Minh applauded and whooped silently.

'It looks like a pleasant evening, Max,' said Oscar.

'...for a swim, Oscar,' said Max.

Jules had rowed into Boulevard des Italiens before splashes and yelps sounded out. The water was freezing and filthy. And shallow enough that divers risked bashing their brains out on submerged cobbles.

'That was a low trick,' said Irene, smiling.

'Yes,' admitted Unorna.

'Well done,' said the American.

Kate thought it down to Alraune, who pouted in self-satisfaction. The German was a bit of a snake.

'They had my picture,' said Kate. 'Probably all of our pictures. We are wanted women. The Camelots du Roi *and* Fantômas are against us. Monarchists and an anarchist. How does that make sense?'

'We are peace-makers,' said Alraune, bitterly. 'Deadly enemies set quarrels aside to come after us. Erik should be flattered. He has united France.'

'There has to be more than that,' said Kate.

'She's right,' said Irene. 'A proper explosive device at the Persian's grave or a Maxim gun on that dam would have scotched us wholesale. Orders are to bring us in, not bump us off.'

Thi Minh signed that she wouldn't be taken alive.

The boat ran aground. The Angels climbed out and waded to a dry spot. Kate would have been happier to have feet on solid ground if it were a little *more* solid. The pavement was springy, as if a layer of squishy mud lay beneath the hard surface.

Jules rowed off swiftly, in search of a less troublesome fare.

Place de l'Opéra was in a sorry state.

As Oscar said, the Palais Garnier was dark. The Opéra had soldiered on for a few days, keeping *La Cenerentola* on stage despite failing power and dwindling audiences. For one performance, prima donna Margarita da Cordova had to take the leading role of Angelina *and* fill in as a wicked stepsister when a mezzo-soprano was delayed by a capsizing barge. After that, the Management announced that the week's thin proceeds would go to flood victims and shut up shop.

The house was commandeered by the authorities. As National Academy of Music, it was notionally a government building. Kate trusted it wouldn't become a prison, as during the Commune. Soldiers with rifles stood guard where commissionaires usually welcomed audiences. Stagehands had packed sandbags around the foundations. Men in sou'westers patrolled the roof, shivering in the shadows of the statues of Apollo, Pegasus and the Sphinx.

A chasm had opened up on one side of the square, allowing water into the half-built, now-abandoned Métro Station. The police roped off the site, but curiosity-seekers were drawn to peer into the muddy pit. Charles had shared reports of mysterious frog-men who had become active during the disaster. They raided sunken basements and bank vaults, then escaped through flooded tunnels. The current Grand Vampire denied responsibility. This was a gang with a new gimmick, not a sub-aqua branch of *Les Vampires*. Perhaps followers of Fantômas or some new flamboyant criminal genius. Every bubble or eddy was taken for a sign of the frogs.

In dramatic twilight, the streak of the comet was visible.

A uniformed, death-faced man on horseback – with an extra helping of gilt braid on his peaked cap and epaulettes – trotted into the square at the head of a column of bedraggled soldiers. They wore drab greatcoats and muddy wading boots. Their shouldered rifles had bayonets fixed. A sputtering open-top staff automobile brought up the rear, overstuffed with junior officers and Paris officials. They argued over soggy maps.

'I don't believe it!' said Kate. 'Assolant!'

Irene looked at her, amused by her outburst.

'General Assolant,' Kate explained. 'I'd know that scratched face anywhere. Last of the *Légion d'Horreur*.'

Unorna made the Devil's horns sign and Thi Minh nodded agreement.

'The General is in charge of the relief operation,' said Mrs Eynsford Hill. 'He is strict about looting and brigandage.'

'He shouldn't be in charge of a pastry kitchen,' said Kate.

Paris bitterly remembered the occupation which followed the fall of the Commune. Having held out against Prussians, the populace were served worse by their own troops. Assolant got his start executing civilians in that action. The Dreyfus Case hadn't added lustre to the army's reputation either. Generally, Parisians preferred to cope with floods by the long-established practice of *Système D* – what the English called 'muddling through' or 'winging it'. This season's deluge was so devastating the government had to call out the troops. Like the Camelots, the army had done much to earn public goodwill through heroic actions against the elements and looters... but if Assolant was in command, that would change.

Besides being lucky to come out of *l'affaire Guignol* with only his face mangled, the man was proud, pompous, cruel and inept. From following British Empire news, Kate knew that assigning such an officer to any outpost was lighting fuses on the next mutiny, native uprising and independence movement.

The old legionnaire's scars were a white tangle over one side of his face. Kate remembered when Lady Yuki did that to him. She could still hear the slicing, the fine edge of the sword scraping bones and parting flesh.

'It's a wonder *he* doesn't wear a mask,' said Irene.

The Angels kept back under the awning of a shuttered souvenir shop. It was best to avoid attracting attention. Kate didn't know if Unorna could convince a whole troop of armed soldiers to take a refreshing dip.

'The General's politics are extreme,' said Kate. 'He's one of those guillotine-the-lot-of-them merchants, which is a laugh when you know what his ghastly friends and he got up to at the *Théâtre des Horreurs*. Our wet, sorry friends Oscar and Max are in a club which has been connected with several conspiracies to dismiss the Assemblée National and put someone like Assolant in charge until they can scrounge up a king or queen to run the country.'

'If they even mean to restore that monarchy they go on and on about,' said Irene. 'My guess is they'd settle for a military dictatorship which keeps extending the "State of Emergency" and stays in power until they've finished robbing the treasury blind. I toured South America, and I can tell you it wouldn't take much to turn France into Guatemala with croissants.'

Thi Minh pointed a gun-finger at the mounted General.

'I bet Assolant gave out our pictures and ordered we be detained,' said Kate. 'He's waited a long time to pay the Agency back for his face.'

He couldn't do it alone. Only a sophisticated intelligence-gathering operation could get hold of photographs like the one of her. So, General Assolant – Creature of Fantômas? *Nouvelle Légion d'Horreur?*

Several small boys cheered the little parade. Assolant glared at a gendarme struggling with a poster he was trying to pin up on a board outside the opera house. A warning against drinking polluted water. The policeman let the poster sail into a big puddle and attempted a salute, but tipped over and sat down in water instead. The small boys cheered the pratfall more enthusiastically than the soldiers. Assolant was not amused. Neither was the gendarme.

The staff car's engine groaned and the inhabitants argued more loudly. The vehicle stalled in a puddle which came up over the running boards. Water seeped in around the feet of officers and officials. The soldiers were torn between stopping to help and following their leader. General Assolant rode on, sword clattering on his thigh, cold eyes scanning the horizon for the enemy. Fortunately, he did not look the Angels' way.

'The authorities won't be any use then?' said Irene. 'If they're with him.'

'Assolant is one of the worst men in France,' said Kate. 'I'm sorry he's prospered. He'd happily accuse us of looting, then have us put against a wall and shot. Without the formality of a trial, of course.'

'So noted,' said Irene. 'We knew we were on our own.'

IV

THEY REACHED THE famous terrace of the Café de la Paix by *passerelle*. The boards dipped alarmingly between trestles. Swinging between awnings and lampposts, Thi Minh was the only Angel to keep her shoes dry. Kate thought the Annamite girl a tiny bit of a show-off.

Where the idle were accustomed to gossip, drink and observe the comings and goings of Place de l'Opéra, stagnant water lay six inches deep. The furled and sheathed table umbrellas were another sign of Apocalypse. A malign Poseidon had emptied a giant bucket of cold water over *la vie Parisienne*.

The *maître d'hôtel* waited at his post just inside the café.

'Mesdames,' he said, with an insincere shrug. 'We are not open for customers. Our kitchens are tainted with floating filth. We have shut down. You cannot come in.'

'We're not here for coffee and cake, Gustave,' said Irene. 'Our visit is possibly a matter of national importance. Now, let us pass.'

Kate saw that the *maître d'* was not impressed by high-handedness.

Once, Irene could command a table at any restaurant or a box at any theatre. Even in establishments booked up or sold out six months in advance. A snap of the fingers, a flurry of attendants, a quiet ejection of paid-off nobodies and prime spots were made available for *la bella signorina* and her guests. Bills would be torn up just for the privilege of having Irene Adler as a patron.

No longer.

It was worse than time moving on and Gustave not remembering a famous name from the last century. The *maître d'* knew exactly who Irene had been… but she was no longer on the List. That unwritten document every doorman, shop manager, hotelier, bell-boy, fiacre driver and functionary in the city knew by heart. The people who had to be accommodated.

The List Irene no longer ornamented. The List Kate had never been on.

'You must leave,' said Gustave.

So… another man barred the Angels' way. The last fellows to try that were nursing nasty colds.

'Gustave, we are a memorial party,' explained Alraune, swanning through the ranks.

She attracted an attendant who relieved her of her rain-cloak. Alraune glanced over her shoulder to admire her reflection in a handy full-length mirror. Her tight-fitting yellowish silk dress was cut low front and back. Her large diamond earrings matched a pendant around her throat. She twisted, as if trying to consider the small of her back. Her hair swung, the knobbles of her spine showed, her shoulder blades shifted. The point of the exercise was to get everyone looking.

Alraune was unwilling to stand up straight. Her walk was a matter of organised swaying and her posture was like a supple tree bending to the wind. She would not have passed muster in the corps de ballet. And her low, throaty voice was more smoky cabaret than grand opera. But, like many an Angel before her, she was a performer. She had danced and recited poetry. As an active Angel, Alraune ought to lead this troupe. So far, she had deferred to her elders – Kate, Irene, Unorna – only whispering telling suggestions when she saw fit. Which was quite often.

Now, Alraune was centre stage. Not caring about lists, she was immune to them.

She would not be turned away. Gustave was overwhelmed.

The German was a strange duck. The Angel of Ill Fortune.

She had a hard, ruthless glitter. Her peculiarly strong – if not unpleasant – scent evoked Wagnerian forests and earth spirits. Erik's recruits were, of necessity, seldom nice girls. Clara Watson and Lady Yuki were, in many ways, terrifying. But Kate had *understood* them. Alraune was a 20th-century Angel, like the speaking machine Mrs Eynsford Hill and the agile Thi Minh. She didn't doubt they were up to the job, but couldn't get the measure of them – how they dressed, how they conducted themselves, what they wanted, who they were.

She shuddered to remember how her aunts used to tut at little Katie's silly notions. Now she'd turned into one of them. The old Reeds.

Where did the Ill Fortune come in? For enemies of the Opera Ghost Agency, Kate trusted.

'Ah, you are the *Angels*,' said the *maître d'*. 'I was told you would come.'

Kate didn't ask by whom.

'It is a pleasure to meet you,' said Olympia. 'I hope we shall be the best of friends.'

Gustave looked sideways at the doll. People heard or imagined things in her voice. Sometimes, what they wanted to hear. Sometimes, what they very much did not.

The *maître d'* stood aside to let Alraune pass. The others followed her. Irene didn't crow at Gustave. It must be hard tack for her to be reduced to bobbing along in someone else's wake.

Kate looked at the Persian's spot, heartsick that he wasn't there.

The proprietors had draped black cloth over the table and put a rope around it. A touching tribute to a loyal, long-serving customer. Of course, the café was forced by flood to close mere hours after making the gesture.

The carpet had squelchy spots. The café smelled of damp and less pleasant things. As Gustave said, filth was a problem. Many Paris basements had drain-stoppers like large bath-plugs. When these were removed, rainwater was supposed to gurgle into the sewers. So unusually high was this flood that concierges who pulled up the stoppers were surprised by geysers of fouler water from below.

The café was lit only by stubs of candles. Gas pressure was inconstant and the electricity had given out. The City of Light was guttering.

At a far table, stranded waiters and waitresses played cards. They were quite tipsy – as, Kate realised, was the impeccable Gustave.

He noticed her noticing.

'All we have that's drinkable is champagne,' he explained. 'If this goes on, we shall have to bathe in it.'

Irene paused. Kate knew the American was considering champagne... then thinking better of it. This was not an Irish wake.

The Angels sat at the Persian's table – all around it, as if at a séance.

Unorna's department.

Kate was no great believer in spiritualism, but the world turned out to be weirder than anyone let on when she was a girl. Another revelation she could thank Charles for. She'd willingly followed him off the well-lit path where rational explanations could always be found into the deep, dark woods where the boggarts lived. Working with Charles at the Diogenes Club and the Angels of Music had knocked doctrinaire scepticism out of her, but she wasn't credulous. Ninety-nine ghosts out of a hundred were disinherited cousins wearing bed sheets or the wind whistling through knotholes. And most mediums were despicable charlatans preying on the grief-stricken.

The Bohemian Angel wasn't a medium.

When Irene had called her a witch, Kate said Unorna was a magician.

That was a polite term – it could mean demon-summoning wizardry or pick-a-card sleight of hand. Kate didn't expect Unorna to produce doves from a top hat. Nevertheless, the queer-eyed, russet-tinged blonde had a flair for the dramatic. No question but that she knew some tricks.

Gustave brought candles to the table, then left them alone.

'The Persian wasn't killed here,' said Alraune. 'He was in his rooms.'

'No, but he *lived* here,' replied Unorna. 'More than anywhere else. This is where he was known. This is where he is remembered. It is the best place.'

From her reticule, she produced a familiar astrakhan cap. She put it on the table.

'Are you going to summon the Persian from Mohammedan paradise and grill him about his murder?' asked Irene.

Unorna shook her head. 'It's not about personalities, it's about patterns. Traces in the aether, disturbances on the astral plane. Violent events disrupt the courses of fate. Time takes the wrong paths. I will open myself, become part of the pattern. And I shall see what is to be seen. Please don't be alarmed at anything I do or say.'

Kate looked around the table. Thi Minh intently studied Unorna. Mrs Eynsford Hill perfectly folded a stray napkin and made a pyramid of it in her place setting. Alraune's large eyes grew larger. Olympia was at rest, head on one side like a sleeping dove. Irene resisted an itch to peep under the table, half-suspecting hidden pedals and trumpets squeezed between knees.

Should they all hold hands? Evidently not.

Unorna put her fingers to her temples and brushed her hair away from her face.

She gazed upwards, mouth slightly open. A fiery third eye opened in her smooth forehead.

'*Blimey O'Reilly,*' exclaimed Mrs Eynsford Hill in purest Bow Bells cockney.

'She said *don't* be alarmed,' said Irene, drolly.

Kate saw the third eye was an illusion – a metal disc which caught the candlelight.

Unorna murmured in a language Kate didn't recognise. Nothing European.

'What's that again?' said Irene. 'The deeds to the mine are in an old tin box buried at the north corner of the south field?'

'Hush,' said Kate. 'Give her a chance.'

'I've seen this act before,' said Irene. 'In the travelling shows. Professor Marvel gabbles the ooga-booga and relays messages from his Indian spirit guide, Princess Rain-in-My-Face.'

'That's a remote copy of a copy,' said Alraune. 'Fakery, based on this truth.'

Alraune respected Unorna. They had a connection. Alchemy, perhaps. Even in this group of unusual women, they were weird sisters.

Unorna gave no sign of being offended by – or even having heard – the debate. Her eyes rolled up. Candle flames reflected in the exposed whites. The disc shone as if it were all-seeing.

'Atlantis rises,' said Unorna, in a clear voice. 'Antinea is coming.'

Her mouth gaped open and gallons of green water burst out, drenching the tablecloth.

Some splashed into Kate's lap. It was shockingly cold.

Thi Minh leaped from her chair, knocking it over, and caught Unorna, who was limp as if boneless. Her eyes were open. The disc fell off and rolled away.

She was breathing, but would not wake up.

V

THE ODIOUS GUSTAVE sent people over to help. Merry waiters elbowed Irene aside, eager to lay hands on the unconscious younger woman. After comical toing and froing, Unorna was hefted onto a dry *chaise longue*. Thi Minh, revealing fresh talents, became a perfect nurse. She fussed – turning tablecloths into sheets, tucking up the patient.

Despite Unorna telling them not to be, Irene was alarmed. She was sure the witch hadn't expected to cough up a fishpond and fall into a coma. Something had been done to her. It seemed a risk of 'opening up' spiritually was all sorts of trouble blowing in through unlocked doors.

'Atlantis rises. Antinea is coming.'

That had to mean *something*.

'Atlantis, I've heard of,' said Irene. 'Lost continent... sunken civilisation... hard to find on the map... talked up by Plato, Bacon and Thomas More. But *Antinea* is a new one on me. Any ideas?'

She looked to her fellow Angels.

'Could she have been trying to say *Fantômas*?' Kate asked.

'Antinea... Fantômas,' said Elizabeth, in Unorna's voice. 'Fantômas... Antinea. Hmmn, they both have *ant* in. Otherwise, the words are distinct. She would not be likely to think one and say the other.'

'*I* have heard of Antinea,' intoned Alraune. 'Eternal Queen of Atlantis.'

Irene wasn't surprised at Alraune's arcane erudition. The German girl had a whiff of witchiness herself. She didn't seem the book-learning type, though.

'Atlantis rises,' said Elizabeth, still in Unorna's voice. 'Antinea is coming.'

'Can you parrot *everything* you hear?' Irene asked.

She could see uses for such a talent – not all moral.

'After a few hours, it flies out of my head,' the English woman admitted.

Elizabeth shrugged in a cracked simulation of modesty. She could imitate perfectly, but was on rocky ground if improvising. Thanks to the Henry Higgins treatment, the poor sap was unconvincing as herself.

Another mastermind worth kicking in the pants.

'Some things you'd only need in your head for a few hours,' Irene mused. 'Account numbers... combinations to safes... pages of address books...'

'...why we're here and how much trouble we're in,' said Kate.

Irene had let herself get distracted. It happened more and more. She'd be in the middle of practical, tiresome chores like plucking her eyebrows or hooking up her stays, when a thought would trundle along like a carriage drawn by black horses, with a handsome stranger inside and a mysterious coat of arms on the doors. She'd climb in and race off for hours, dreaming wildly impractical schemes for the sort of things she really didn't do any more. Usually, her reveries involved men who were – in the real world – long since dead or confined to bath-chairs. Then, she'd snap out of it and find the tea gone cold or the bath overflowing.

Trust Kate to jostle her out of it.

Irene stood over Unorna, and considered the weird woman's unlined face.

Had Fantômas got to the Witch of Prague?

Of the Angels present, Unorna was – Irene reluctantly admitted – the most formidable. All could do things, but she could *know* things. Knocking her off the board was a smart move.

Especially if the rest of them did the headless chicken dance.

'I don't understand what she said,' said Kate. 'Atlantis isn't known for rising, but for *sinking*. There might be a poetic parallel with flooded Paris, I suppose. Unorna definitely said "Atlantis rises".'

'Atlantis is important in Gnostic teachings,' said Alraune.

With Unorna taken poorly, the German girl became their resident mystic.

'Atlantean rites are still practised. By those who would raise the ancient city and sink the modern world. Fantômas wishes ruination on everything.'

'He isn't a wizard,' said Kate. 'Anarchists use dynamite, surely? Much more reliable than black magic.'

'And why Antinea?' put in Irene.

'There is a *Lady* Fantômas, or so she calls herself,' said Elizabeth. 'Maudie Beltham. I see her at Ascot. Fantômas throttled her dull husband for her and she's hung gratefully on his arm ever since. She even dresses like him – in the tailcoat, stiff shirt, top hat and black mask. Maudie might want to be Queen of his Kingdom of Ruins.'

'Notice how many of these death-to-all-rulers anarchists take titles like "Lord" and "Queen"?' said Irene. 'Jumped-up little sulks, the lot of 'em. Give me an honest crook any day. Snatches your poke but doesn't lecture you about it.'

'How are we to find Fantômas?' asked Alraune.

Kate laid a hand on Unorna's brow.

'I think he'll find *us*... if, indeed, he's who we're playing tag with. Someone is a clever clogs, all right. Killing the Persian brought us together. From across Europe. Perhaps that was the plan all along. Not to get him but to get to us. Now we're all in the same bowl. Anyone who could strike down the Witch of Prague can do the same to any of us.'

Irene had a queasy feeling Kate Reed was on to something.

She'd been right. The Irish journalist was the clever one.

She hoped Kate had been right too. Irene would have to be slippery indeed to get out of this hale and whole.

'Always think cheerful thoughts, Katie,' she said.

'Forewarned is... well, often useless, I admit. However, we're scarcely the damsels of lore. We don't get captured, kidnapped or killed so some knight errant can ride off on a quest with a personal grudge against the dragon.'

'Knight errants,' spat Irene. 'Never my favourite toy soldiers.'

Thi Minh made a face and claws like a fire-breathing dragon.

A rattle came at the door. Gustave puffed up, ready to tell more lesser folks that the Café de la Paix wasn't open to them.

A blow was administered. The *maître d'* staggered against a cake trolley.

Why hadn't Irene tried that?

A stiff-backed old man in uniform barged into the café.

Kate's friend, General Asshole. No, he couldn't really be called that.

'*Assolant*,' said Kate, making it sound even ruder.

The soldier shifted the wet flap of his cape over one shoulder. He held a revolver.

'This establishment is under martial law,' he declared.

Kate had been an Angel when the General had his run-in

with the Opera Ghost Agency. Irene knew that story. Having knocked around high and low places all her life, she shouldn't still be surprised by the depravity of well-connected people... but what she'd heard about the *après-minuits* at the *Théâtre des Horreurs* disgusted even her. In the years since the fall of the *Légion d'Horreur*, fresh generations of demented exquisites had sprung up. Those who fancied themselves fashionably decadent got hot and bothered imagining the fabled horrors the Angels had put a stop to. In their fevered minds, the *après-minuits* were magnificent rather than squalid, daring rather than cowardly. Some heartless entrepreneur would eventually revive the tradition and need to be shut down all over again. It would be motion pictures of murders now or wireless broadcasts from executions.

Like an ageing rake who bores nephews by insisting the can-can girls of the gay nineties were more alluring than these shameless jazz trollops, Assolant was still around to whine that the old horrors were more horrible, more artistic, more titillating. Yes, and the songs of yesteryear were better than the discordant jungle trash which passed for music in this sad century. Even madmen get old and nostalgic.

Gustave tried to get up but slipped on an éclair and fell again.

Men marched into the café. Not the regular soldiers Assolant had led earlier.

This mob weren't like any soldiers Irene had ever seen. It took a few seconds to realise they were really men, and not some strange species of fish-reptile-insect demon. They wore tight black shiny rubber suits and face-masks with bulbous eye-windows. Tubes from scaly packs on their backs fed into their helmets. Their boot-toes flattened out into flippers. Even their gauntlets had webbing between the fingers.

Irene remembered the stories of thieving frog-men operating during the flood. They left finny footprints.

Was this the army of Atlantis? How had Assolant got a commission in that?

The frog-men occupied the café. Gustave scuttled away like

a kicked crab. Drunken waiters cowered at these apparitions.

Some string was being played out.

Had they jumped too soon on Alraune's identification of their nemesis? Fantômas wasn't a *Chevalier de la Légion d'Horreur*. Quite the reverse. The anarchist considered rich hypocrites fair game and had spent much of his career imaginatively slaughtering them. He was heir of the tradition of the capering satirist Guignol and, as Kate had said, an imitator of the Phantom of the Opera. So far as Irene knew, bizarre respect existed between the masked men. This wouldn't be the first time crimes committed by respectable men were pinned on convenient outsiders. Further from civilisation even than plague-ridden *Île du Diable*, where Dreyfus had languished, was *Île des Monstres*, where France transported criminals deemed less than human. The ones they couldn't guillotine because they weren't sure beheading would work on them. That was where they'd send Fantômas, if they ever caught him… and Erik, if they fished him out of his sewer alive. Maybe *Île des Monstres* had women's cells suitable for Angels with clipped wings.

A fix was definitely in. Assolant was supposed to be in charge of measures against looting – but here he was leading the arch-looters. It must be some ghastly put-up job. A snake was swallowing its own tail and choking on it.

The General strolled over to the Angels, spurs clinking. He was, as Irene might have guessed, not a tall man. Though an infantry officer, he liked to be on a horse as often as possible – so he could look down on people. Civilians, women, Jews and other lesser breeds. The cold eye in the mutilated half of his face rolled as he noticed Unorna.

Assolant gestured with his revolver.

'There are strict edicts against looting,' he said. 'Posted all over the city.'

The raiders – four of them, all tall and made taller by fin-topped helmets – crossed the café to back up the General. They moved deliberately, as if unused to being out of the water. Their packs were portable breathing apparatus, like that used by miners or firemen. Their masks rattled with exhalation. One frog-man bumped into a table, and made a show of knocking it over as if he'd meant to, battering it away with a powerful swipe. Like most masks, their headgear limited peripheral vision. Something worth remembering.

Their side-arms were bulky compressed air pistols with arrowhead darts stuck out of the barrels. Spearguns. Axes and knives hung from toolbelts. One frog-man carried a staff tipped with three sharp prongs. Neptune's trident.

Close up, Irene was relieved that their eyes were plain men's – though they seemed to bulge, magnified by the glass goggles.

'You women are subject to immediate arrest,' said Assolant.

A tiny flicker of his good eye as he passed Kate gave him away. He knew who she was. He had expected to find her here.

With regards to other Angels, he was doing a job – carrying out someone's orders. With Kate, it was personal. She had been there when the *Légion d'Horreur* was smashed. If he couldn't ventilate the Japanese Angel who'd ruined his face, he'd take it out on her Irish friend.

'These, I suppose, are policemen?' said Kate.

Assolant hissed at her. The mug with the trident angled it at Kate's stomach as if waiting for an order to charge.

The General looked at the other women.

Olympia stepped forward and said, 'It is a pleasure to meet you.'

Assolant backhanded the doll's face.

He hurt himself, of course. He should have hit her with his pistol.

'I hope we shall be the best of friends,' she said.

Assolant's white tangle of scars slowly reddened. He sweated cold fury.

Irene was tense. She saw Elizabeth palm a fork from a place setting.

Good girl. Given the choice, a table fork was better than a

cake knife against an importuning gentleman. More likely to pierce than break. Though those frog-hides looked too thick for a simple stab.

'What have you done to this woman?' asked the General, meaning Unorna.

'She has been overcome with the vapours,' said Elizabeth. 'We are endeavouring to give aid and succour.'

'Are you now?'

'If you could alert the medical corps, we'd appreciate it,' said Kate.

Assolant picked up a spoon with his left hand and looked at it.

For a moment, Irene was worried he'd stab Kate's with it.

He breathed on the spoon and polished it on his sleeve.

'Is this silver?' he asked, handing it to Kate.

She looked at it and said, 'I don't think so…'

Suddenly ramrod-stiff, the General aimed his pistol at Kate's face.

'You stole that spoon!' he said, enraged. 'I saw it! You are a dirty looter! You are all dirty looters!'

As one, the frogmen took a step forward. They squeaked and left ducky footprints, but weren't at all comical. The trident hovered near the small of Kate's back.

Assolant thumb-cocked his revolver. He rested the barrel against a lens of Kate's glasses.

'It is within my rights to have you executed.'

VI

'IF YOU SHOOT me, I daresay you'll receive a strongly worded telegram from the British Ambassador.'

Assolant's grim mouth didn't twitch, but he stopped pointing a gun at her eye.

'You are to come with me,' he said. 'All you... *women*. You are looters and profiteers.'

Kate hadn't forgotten the private pleasures of General Assolant and his cronies in *le cercle rouge*. And he hadn't forgotten she *knew* about him.

He hadn't even the smidgen of decency to be ashamed of what he was – a cowardly, blundering sadist. But he did fear what might befall him if his true character were known to the world. He ached to ascend to a position of untouchability, so he might again murder who he fancied with impunity. He'd once had a taste of that power, and quivered with a dried-out drunk's thirst for the long-abjured bottle.

'What about her?' asked Irene, nodding at Unorna. 'She needs a doctor.'

'I will judge what this foreigner needs,' said Assolant. 'You are to carry her.'

It fell to Olympia to pick up the sleeping Angel. The automaton came in handy for the heavy lifting.

Gustave held the door open. Kate thanked the *maître d'* for his courtesy.

Outside, it was night – and snowing, though slush quickly melted to swell the pools around Place de l'Opéra. A few fires burned in buckets and braziers, but the street lamps weren't lit. The blackout was even more of an affront than the rising river. It was as if Paris had been turned off.

She heard shouts, cries, shots, screams and crashes. Kate recognised the racket. She had been in wars like this before. Small bands fighting street to street, not whole armies meeting on an open battlefield. Pundits envisioned a coming conflict, where the great powers would roll out the wonderful, mechanised weapons – colossal dreadnoughts, submersible destroyers, bomb-dropping airships, heavy guns mounted on automobiles, clouds of poison smoke – they were itching to test on real, bleeding people.

This could be an overture to that grand opera.

The guards by the roped-off chasm were joined by frog-soldiers. They had swept up from below and established a beach-head.

'You will come to the opera house,' said Assolant.

'Will we now?' said Irene.

Assolant shot at a dead cat floating past. The poor thing exploded with a plop of fur and guts.

The report was just a crack, lost in the open air and night-sounds.

What with everything else, no one came to investigate. Chances are they'd only have saluted the senior officer and let him carry on with whatever he was doing. Had General Assolant gone over to the other side, or was there only one side with two faces?

Thi Minh was first on the *passerelle*. Kate followed, as indicated by a trident prod. Frog-men waded at either side of the plank, aiming spear-shooting contraptions at the Angels.

They had been taken prisoner. If Assolant had permission to execute them, he would have done it already.

The General had been a small fish in the *Légion d'Horreur*, a minnow next to sharks like Georges Du Roy or Père de Kern. This action couldn't be Assolant's idea – and he certainly wasn't taking orders from Louis Lépine, Prefect of Police, or Justin de Selves, Prefect of the Seine. The army only grudgingly recognised civil authority at the best of times.

Someone was above Assolant.

Not Fantômas. Kate no longer believed the anarchist had killed the Persian.

A subtler hand was behind this. One of those masterminds Irene went on about. Or just a brute with money and influence.

Frog-men were stationed outside the opera house.

Now she'd seen their diving gear up close, Kate knew they weren't just freshwater pirates. It took money and resources to equip them.

Regular troops in shabby uniforms did scut-work like shoring up sandbag barriers. Smartly dressed Camelots du Roi strutted like beardless field marshals, not doing a hand's turn but giving the impression they were high up in the chain of command. Kate hoped Oscar and Max were on the sick list. They'd relish revenge for their dip in the freezing waters.

The co-operating forces – frog-men, soldiers, Camelots – were identifiable by bright green armbands. Kate had noticed Max and Oscar wearing them earlier. The General had one too. On the band was a curlicue motif. A crown of seashells surmounted the letter A.

For Assolet?

Anarchy?

Army?

Antichrist?

L'Action Française?

Irene nudged Kate and pointed at a banner hung above the entrance of the Palais Garnier. That same green A, but huge – and professionally woven, which indicated planning.

Système A hadn't sprung up overnight.

'A for Antinea,' Irene suggested.

'...or Atlantis,' Kate countered.

'Something fishy, at any rate,' said Irene.

Kate was too weary to groan.

A frog-man shook his speargun in a 'shut up, you' gesture, and Kate and Irene got a move on. A signal rocket went up from another quarter of the city. Soldiers and frog-men turned to take note.

A couple of Camelots gallantly helped Thi Minh off the *passerelle*, though the acrobat scarcely needed assistance. She seemed unconcerned at any probable peril. As an active Angel, it was a point of pride to show no fear. Kate wasn't sure she could hold fast to the principle. She was retired from the Opera Ghost Agency. Then again, the Diogenes Club didn't have a tradition of panicking and pleading in tight spots – and she was still on their register.

Unsteady on her feet and with a face frozen from windblown snow, Kate was grateful for helping hands. She thanked a curly-moustached Camelot. He smiled as if this were all a student lark.

All the Angels made it to the opera house without a dunking.

Unorna, as a witch, would presumably float. With the rest of them, things would go less happily.

When Assolant stepped down from the *passerelle*, the Camelots snapped off salutes.

Only now did it strike Kate as suspicious that so many sprouts of the upper crust had easy access to boats and barges. They had been waiting for rain.

Under the Third Republic, militarist and monarchist conspiracies abounded. Some faction or other was always on the point of staging a *coup d'état*. Rogue Jesuits incensed by the separation of Church and State. Stubborn Montagnards awaiting the second coming of Robespierre. Lunatic anti-Dreyfusards who marched on the Presidential Palace at the head of imaginary columns of troops. If the Angels of the day – Christina Light, Marahuna, Marie O'Malley – hadn't prevented the release of a plague bacillus among the crowds gathered for the opening of the Exposition Universelle, France might have fallen under the dictatorship of the Brass Bonaparte.

Was this another attempted coup? She could see how it would work.

The National Assembly had carried on debating until the last lights went out, then adjourned. Président Fallières was floating about inspecting flood damage and pledging assistance to wet, ungrateful people. If he chanced to fall in the river and drown, a case could be made for instituting martial law. Then, it would be up to the army – which is to say, General Assolant – to decide how long the state of emergency would last.

Just now, she'd be grateful to find Fantômas, the Grand Vampire or the Clutching Hand behind it. Some villain who could be unmasked and brought to book. The Angels couldn't deal with a mass movement. She wasn't even sure they'd have the right to.

Given the general hullaballoo all over the city, the coup had already begun. This could be Year One of *L'Âge d'A*.

They were ushered into the grand foyer of the Palais Garnier. A thousand candles burned, but the small flames did little to cast light around the vast space. Frog-men, Camelots, clerks and scurvy-looking types in fisherman's wading britches – all sporting the green A – milled around purposefully. Women among them wore sparkly togas and headdresses which set off their armbands. Kate guessed many outfits were filched from the costume department. She was sure she'd seen some of the dresses in *Aida* and *La Juive*.

The opera house made a decent headquarters, Kate supposed. But the Louvre offered better pickings for looters and was far less dangerous. Last she heard, the museum was only haunted by an Egyptian mummy. Invading the house Erik took for his domain was a riskier proposition. The Phantom of the Opera knew this huge building better than anyone. Flood or no, he'd hide here indefinitely… and pick off insolent trespassers one by one.

Assolant must realise this. Such an affront would draw out Erik. There would be consequences, casualties, a reckoning.

Great schemes were in motion. But so were petty ones.

In the middle of the foyer, a large-scale map of Paris was unrolled on the floor like a carpet. Candelabra were dotted across it, dripping wax and casting light. Clerks with brooms moved blocks of wood as messages were brought in. Kate recognised an operations room when she saw one. Men in tailcoats crawled over the map of the city with pencils, shading in streets and squares.

Frog-men saw her taking an interest and got in the way.

Mrs Eynsford Hill artfully tripped, fell against a frog-man, apologised, and slipped again, hands scrabbling on his rubbery chest. She did a perfect impersonation of a complete twit, but managed to get a good look at the map.

Kate knew a quick glance was enough. With her trick memory, Mrs Eynsford Hill would know the disposition of the enemy forces – at least until the picture faded in a few hours' time. Irene was using her noggin. She'd taken stock of the Angels' individual talents and saw how they could be applied. It was cold and premature to think of such things, but if Erik needed to replace the Persian he should consider Irene Adler. If only so she could relish the daily squirm from Gustave as he showed her to what was now her table in the Café de la Paix. She'd run up a huge champagne tab and expect it to be written off every month.

Alraune had Olympia make Unorna comfortable on an upholstered divan. The witch was still sleeping. The German girl's glittering eyes took everything in too.

What application might there be for *her* talents?

General Assolant talked with a small, tubby, balding fellow in a long leather coat. Kate had seen him before. The General directed the pig-eyed little man's attention to the Angels. He grinned, crookedly. His bad teeth gave him away.

She remembered exactly who he was.

Smiling, the fellow opened his coat... like a degenerate exposing his tiny male organ to a Salvation Army band. The lining of the garment was outfitted with rows of narrow pockets – each sheathing a knife of a different length, width or shape.

Rollo the Knife-Thrower, dismissed from the *Théâtre des Horreurs* for enthusiastic collaboration with *le cercle rouge*. An artist with blades, he had somehow avoided the one in the guillotine. Assolant had kept up an association with the little torturer. Kate wasn't surprised.

There was a commotion. Soldiers and frog-men rattled into action. Shouts went up. Lanterns waved. A blinding, fizzing purple flare soared, illuminating the illustrated ceiling. A volley of shots – rifles, pistols and spearguns – were discharged. The target was a panel above the Grand Staircase. Isidore Pils' *Minerva Fighting Brutality Watched by the Gods of Olympus* would need repair. Something had moved up there... or someone had imagined something moving up there.

The flare fell to the marble floor and had to be stamped out. Kate blinked until the after-images went away.

Assolant's scarred side was the colour of blood.

'I saw… it,' whimpered a soldier. 'Like a giant bird with a human skull for a head.'

'A ghost,' said another.

'*The* ghost,' insisted a third.

'Just a shadow,' said a rifleman, annoyed that he'd joined the panic.

A frog-man said something indistinct through his breathing apparatus.

'It's just a shadow when you look at it face-on,' said Irene, very loudly. 'But when it's behind you – *then* it's him. The Phantom of the Opera. He can kill with a mere touch. Stop your heart with a whistle. See into your soul with those yellow poached-egg eyes and murder all those you love. If they were half a world away, he would still smite them dead… because he is a demon from Hell. A demon you've enraged by coming here. He loves only this building and music. And you've profaned his temple!'

Irene gathered an audience. It was as if the men *wanted* to be terrified.

Thi Minh used her rain-cloak like the Phantom's cape and gave the troops a bare-teeth rictus, bugged out her eyes and laughed silently. Swiftly, she shinned up a column, hung upside-down with her hair dangling like a rope for a moment, and twisted around to slide out of sight… a perfect disappearing act.

The girl popped up again, and impishly put her hands around one soldier's throat, butterfly-kissing his nose… then tipped another's cap over his eyes with a deft move and ducked under a swiping rifle-butt.

She gestured with long fingers.

'Watch out,' said Irene. 'There's a Phantom about!'

The little group of soldiers quaked like frightened children.

'Ignore these foreign woman,' insisted Assolant, brusquely. 'They are a danger to morale.'

'Flatterer,' said Irene, winking.

Her spook stories would be repeated. Armies were more addicted to gossip and bogey tales than a ladies' sewing circle.

Greater, more fabulous tales of the Phantom's supernatural powers would spread. It wasn't as if anyone needed the fear put into them. They already saw Erik in every corner. They'd be shooting at each other soon.

Who knows? Maybe he had been up there.

He must be somewhere in the house.

An electric crackle and an acrid smell startled Kate. She turned to see an elderly man, with a shock of white hair, marching across the foyer with a high-stepping, grasshopper gait. This extraordinary character was strapped into a black carapace-like corset which extended to leather and wire leg- and arm-braces and spiked shoulder-pieces. His belt hung heavy with holstered implements Kate couldn't name. Like the frog-men, he wore a back-humping pack – but his wasn't for breathing. Sparks fell wherever he walked and gears ground in the joints of his braces. Some sort of electric battery served as motive power. She thought he needed his machinery to walk. He had wing-like leather folds under his arms.

'That's Falke,' said Irene. 'The Black Bat.'

Kate knew his story. A case from Unorna's watch, when she'd been an Angel alongside the detective La Marmoset and the assassin Sophy Kratides. *L'affaire du vampire.*

Falke wore an A armband, though he had a batwing insignia on his chest.

'He's *old*,' said Kate.

'Not *that* old,' said Irene.

'Not just old, but broken.'

'He's compensating well, I'd say. I wonder if those electric britches come in ladies' sizes.'

Sometimes, Kate wondered whether Irene wouldn't be happier on the other side.

Then, she asked herself if there really were sides.

'La Marmoset, a cleverer Angel even than you, broke Falke... and he came back,' said Irene. 'You broke Assolant... and he came back. It's a pattern.'

Alraune cocked an ear. She seized on Irene's observation.

'In your grand old days, it seems Angels didn't break them enough,' she said. 'Know who you don't see here? Any of *my* enemies. Thi Minh and I have put a lot of them down. You probably don't even know their names... Frank Braun, Dr Gilson, le Rat, Kilian Gurlitt. The ones we broke stay broken.'

Kate's hackles pricked at the younger woman's sneer.

Besides, she was wrong. The old days weren't always dainty, innocent and amusing.

Georges Du Roy wouldn't trouble them in this century, for a start. Kate shed no tears for him, or the other cut-up cut-ups of *le cercle rouge*. Few who'd met Clara Watson or Lady Yuki would think them more merciful than this century's Angels. Both filled graveyards by themselves. Clara took her own sweet time about it, giving individual attention to each of her enemies – and, Kate shuddered to recall, some of her *friends*. Many welcomed death as an end to pain.

But a dark light in the German girl's eyes disturbed Kate. An *unnatural* light.

If any Angel was ready for the next war – and the war after that – it was Alraune ten Brincken. Intelligence in her Diogenes Club file was vague and partial. One report averred she was seeded in a laboratory, grown from a culture like an Olympia of flesh. She was the Mandrake Maid. Identical sisters might be curled in embryo, nestled inside buds on a hardy potted vine. Ten Brincken wasn't a family name, but a *genus*. She was named for the Professor who *cultivated* her.

Falke jerkily approached Assolant and came to an awkward standstill. White fluid leaked from one of his knee-braces.

Kate realised the Black Bat must be the inventor of the frogman apparatus. If he'd concentrated on constructive uses of his inventions, he'd be recognised as a great man. He could help the lame walk and let men breathe underwater.

'The Fellowship has lost three more,' reported Falke. 'Many traps are set, all over the cellars. I must be given more resources.'

Kate's ears had pricked at the mention of traps.

Irene winked at her. They both knew who set traps in this building.

'It is imperative we bring in this Phantom,' said Falke. 'The Ascent cannot go ahead until he has been removed.'

Ascent? Another A.

'We have his women,' said Assolant. 'Without his cat's paws, he's nothing. A hollow mask.'

Kate knew that wasn't true.

If Assolant lined up the Angels and shot them, Erik would still prevail. She trusted it wouldn't come to that. She'd quite like to be on the prevailing team herself, rather than written off as a significant casualty.

What was the extent of this Fellowship? There must be more in it than Falke and Assolant. The Black Bat and the General were holdovers from the last century – like herself and Irene, she quietly admitted to herself. Falke was a genius and Assolant was cruel beyond reason, but neither could launch an attack on Unorna from the spiritual plane. They had to have a magician of their own.

So, some players had yet to show themselves.

'I believe Alraune has a point,' said Irene. 'So many of the Agency's old friends are here. One might almost think it a reunion. Do you figure all the folks Erik's given black eyes have a club or a society? And they've finally had enough of just bitching about him and set out to get their own back? By shutting us all down.'

'It's more like we're being swept aside or trodden on – an irritant in the way of huge plans,' said Kate. 'Nothing special, but annoying.'

'That's what I want on my tombstone, Katie. "Nothing special, but annoying".'

'I'm going with "Never Surrender". Though, at the moment, it seems we have.'

'Quiet, you!' said Rollo.

The little man had a knife in either hand.

'Are you our jailer now?' asked Kate. 'That's the best you can hope for in this company, I imagine.'

Rollo fingered a sharp, curved paring knife. Ideal for peeling apples, it would do just as neat a job on a face.

'You're not my prisoners, my Angels,' he said. 'You're my *reward*.'

Olympia, lurching a little as if her heart-clock were running down, laid a heavy hand on Rollo's shoulder. Steel fingers clamped tight. He turned and slashed at her face, scoring a line which didn't bleed, blunting his knife. She let him go and put her hands to her face. She pinched her wound shut and it healed over.

Rollo's mouth hung open.

'Don't you know,' said Irene. 'Angels never bleed.'

Rollo looked at his knife and tried to stick it in Olympia's chest. She caught his wrist and stopped his thrust. He strained, but she held him fast. The knife-point was inches away from her body. She kept hold and forced him to his knees, then wrenched his arm and made him drop the weapon. He yelped like a whipped dog. Mrs Eynsford Hill quietly snaffled the knife to go with the fork she'd stolen earlier. If she found a spoon, she'd have a dinner service.

None of Rollo's comrades made a move to help him. The foyer was so cavernous, underlit and crowded he could probably be killed without anyone paying attention. Olympia or Alraune would do the job – maybe even Irene. The American might easily take Alraune's sneer about 'the grand old days' as a challenge to show enough ruthlessness to keep up with this young, urgent, callous century.

The crowd stirred. Whispers went round. People shifted in half-scared, half-eager excitement. They reminded Kate of an audience who know a great star is about to make an entrance... or those flocking birds who sense a coming earthquake and fly off *en masse*.

Rollo didn't complain at his ill-treatment – as if he knew no one would listen.

Assolant and Falke looked to the staircase which dominated the foyer. The Paris Opéra often threw parties entirely on the steps. Kate had never seen a more impressive set of stairs under a roof.

Bare-chested Nubians with long white silk kilts and hats like lampshades formed rows on the steps. They raised trumpets and blew a discordant fanfare. Kate would have expected this sort of spectacle on the stage, not in the lobby.

Plumes of flame, reflected to infinity in the mirrors and polished gilt trim, puffed out of dragon-mouth mortars. More of Falke's ingenuity?

Someone shimmery appeared at the top of the stairs.

'Antinea,' went up the cry. 'Antinea, Antinea…'

Kate did not recognise the startlingly beautiful young woman.

The Queen of Atlantis wore a gigantic headdress of peacock feathers. Her sheer aquamarine sheath would have been too risqué for the Folies Bergère. She was decorated like a potentate's Christmas tree. More jewels hung off her than A.J. Raffles and Arsène Lupin could steal in their whole careers. Six little attendant girls with fish-masks and scaly leotards held a twenty-foot train.

'Oh no,' said Irene, 'not *her*!'

Kate looked to Irene for further explanation.

'As I live and breathe, Joséphine Balsamo!'

'Countess de Cagliostro?' asked Kate.

'Yeah, that's the hussy. *Another old friend.*'

VII

'**D**AMN IT, SHE'S still *young*,' said Irene, bitterly. 'She really is one of *those*.'

'Those?' prompted Kate.

'The frozen-in-time people. Not like you or I… No looking in the glass for grey hairs or tiny wrinkles... no worries about an extra glass or *petit-four* adding to the *avoirdupois*.'

The Countess de Cagliostro hadn't aged since the Affair of the Marriage Club, the best part of (cough) forty years before. Two thirds of Irene's life had passed since then. A few heartbeats for Jo Balsamo.

'You don't think she's *really* Cagliostro's daughter? She'd be over a hundred and fifty years old.'

'Didn't you read the stop press, Katie? Jo Balsamo doesn't claim that any more. Now, she's supposed to be *Antinea*. Eternal Queen of Atlantis. Which means she's been around for *thousands* of years. And has picked Paris as capital of her new Atlantean Empire.'

'Come on, Irene! She has to be a fraud!'

'Of course she is, but she's an *old* fraud... and doesn't look it. She's the same woman all right, the besom we saw off in the seventies. No mistaking those eyes. How does she do it? Smearing on a tincture of royal jelly and bee-venom? Maybe she was born that way, to age from birth to young womanhood and then *set*... like a pudding. Old as sin in her heart but fresh as a daisy in bloom on the outside.'

The store-room was cramped and mouldy. Water had got in, ruining a collection of *papier-mâché* animals. The Communards had used this part of the building as a jail. When the opera company took back the house, they didn't trouble to change locks or take out grilles in the doors. So it was easy to use the store-rooms as cells again.

Welcome to the Dungeons of Atlantis – don't mind the damp.

Rollo, the leering little beast with the bald head and the hairy wrists, had shoved them into three adjacent rooms. Elizabeth was in with Olympia (almost completely wound down). Thi Minh (jaunty as ever) and Alraune shared a cell with a pile of broken musical instruments. Irene and Kate were stuck with Unorna (still dead to the world).

'I wish she were awake,' said Kate, nodding at the witch.

'Do you?' asked Irene. 'Unorna is one of *them* too. Look at her face. You'd swear she was nineteen... but she was an Angel twenty-five years ago. With her, it'll be sorcery or alchemy. Face cream made from the fat of unbaptised babies. Baths of virgins' blood.'

Kate was doubtful.

'Unorna's not the only one in the Agency,' Irene continued. 'There's Olympia too. She *can't* change. If her face wore out or fell off, it could be repainted. She can be touched up like a picture.'

'Erik is supposed to keep spry with a potion stolen from the Shah of Persia,' said Kate.

When young and gay and foolish, Irene seldom thought about getting old. She'd heard the whispers that Erik could thwart the years but not pressed for details. Now, it was too late.

'The Lord of Strange Deaths is unageing,' said Kate. 'He has a philtre, too. Dr Nikola has been chasing the secret for a long time.'

More damned masterminds.

'There are others,' Kate continued, warming to the subject. 'Over a dozen different people have made convincing claims to be the Wandering Jew, tarrying till the Second Coming. Countess de Cagliostro is supposed to have been a lover of Saint-Germain, who swore he reached the age of five hundred by subsisting on a diet of sour milk, chicken breasts and gold flake...'

'At this point, I couldn't afford the chicken breasts.'

'There's the blue flame of Kôr, a lost city in the heart of Africa. Bathing in it apparently confers immortality, though it burns rarely... and I'm not sure how one goes about bathing in a fire. It's like drying yourself with a bucket of water. Féodor Dimitrius, a society doctor, charges handsome fees to reinvigorate rich old duffers with simian gland transplants. I wouldn't pay a quack to cut me open and sew in a slice of monkey-meat.'

Irene couldn't tell whether Kate Reed had made a special study or was just well-informed on curious matters which fell into the purview of the Diogenes Club. Possibly, the Irish woman was chattering to keep her spirits up.

'And vampires, of course, survive the centuries. They drink blood.'

'Didn't Falke use some sort of mechanical sponge in his vampire murders?'

'That doesn't prove there aren't vampires. The Diogenes Club have files on Mircalla Karnstein, Lord Ruthven and Count de Ville.'

'I'm sure they have a file on me too. Don't believe everything you read in it.'

Kate laughed, which struck Irene as peculiar even for her.

'Cough it up. What's funny, Katie?'

'Your Diogenes Club file. No one *reads* it. They look at the pictures.'

Irene knew which pictures she meant.

'They wouldn't be so eager if I posed for those studies now,' she said.

'Oh, I don't know... I'd say you were well-preserved.'

'Pickled, you mean. Like herring.'

Kate giggled now, less hysterically.

'Seriously, Irene – why does getting older burn you so much? Would you really wish to be like *them*? Antinea, Erik, Olympia, Countess de Cagliostro... even Unorna. Or Alraune, who's as strange a flower as the rest of them. They may not wither, but they're only half-alive – if that. Olympia's a *doll*, for Heaven's sake! If you had to wear a mask all your life, would you care if people thought you young or old?'

'I'd like to have the choice, Katie.'

Unorna turned over in her sleep. She was stirring, as if coming out of the spell. But didn't wake.

'Do you think she'll kill us?' Kate asked. 'Antinea?'

'No doubt about it,' said Irene. 'She's one of our *old friends*, like your General Assolant and Unorna's Doctor Falke – chewing over defeats for decades. If I held a grudge the way these jaspers do there'd be a sight fewer opera critics, crowned heads, great detectives and diabolical masterminds. I reckon we'll be the opening act for her coronation. At least we won't be burned at the stake. It'll be a water-themed death, for sure. Tied up in a slowly filling tank… weighted down and dropped in the Seine… or just chucked into that maelstrom where they were digging the Métro and sucked under. There are seven of us to get out of the way… eight, if they catch Erik.'

'*Can* Olympia drown?'

'Ever dropped a watch in a bowl of water? Olympia can *stop*.'

'Mrs Eynsford Hill can hold her breath a long time. All those exercises of the diaphragm. Alraune might be able to thrive in water like a lily. I think she photosynthesises.'

Now, Kate was being larkish.

'They'll have thought of all that,' said Irene. 'Look how elaborate this is. Antinea's Ascent has been a long time coming. She laid her plans and recruited her army and waited for rain. It's not about us… or even Erik. We're "other business". You know what they say: "We pass this way but once so if there's anyone you want to die a lingering death don't miss an opportunity to do them in."'

'Who says that?'

'Awful people like Jo Balsamo. Gack, how did it come to this? Is this what you expected when you turned Angel?'

'I'm not sure I really count. I wasn't with the Agency long.'

'Me neither, but I don't think that matters. Balsamo is making a Herodian point by wiping the lot of us out – the ones she knows and hates personally and the ones who came along and wore the wings after us.'

'I think that's why the Persian was murdered – to bring us together, as many of us as could get here easily.'

'That's how masterminds think. Sneaky and petty. Wasted cleverness.'

'After we're gone, she'll try to collect the rest – the ones who couldn't be here. She'll send assassins. If it's any comfort, I expect Lady Yuki will cut her head off for her. She's the Angel of the Sword.'

'I'm not ready to be avenged yet.'

Irene looked about the cell for any tools. She remembered Colonel Moran – Number Two to the late, unlamented Professor Moriarty – elaborating on the subject of getting out of tricky spots like this: 'If you're clapped in a cell, don't bother trying to pick the lock. Spoilsports who build jails always put time and effort into locks. You usually don't have a keyhole on your side of the door you can shove your stickpin into and scratch the tumblers. No, go for the *hinges*. No blighter ever bothers with hinges. Hit 'em with a hammer or handiest hammer substitute and they pop off. It don't matter how locked the door is, 'cause you can open it the other way. So much the better if you've been imprisoned by conscientious housekeepers who oil their hinges properly.'

A soggy *papier-mâché* elephant didn't seem a likely hammer substitute. And the hinges looked sturdy and unoiled.

'I'm the Angel of Truth,' Kate declared. 'I became a reporter because I saw we were surrounded by lies... or, worse, mysteries. I wanted to tell the truth, to expose the liars and solve the mysteries. Hard experience taught me it wasn't always possible or even advisable. Sometimes the truth won't be believed or would drive people mad or hurt the innocent. But I was addicted, by then... addicted to *finding out*. That's what brought me to the Diogenes Club, and the Opera Ghost Agency. If you find out a truth you can't in all conscience share, there's an obligation to do something about it. I won't be drowned like an unwanted kitten.'

Kate's little Irish face shone in the gloom. Irene wished she'd known her better – she could have used an Angel of Truth.

'Erik called me the Angel of Larceny,' she said. 'He was being facetious. Have you noticed how few people notice he's funny? Those pranks against the pompous. Cutting witticisms on black-edged paper. He was born with a smile, after all.'

'He ran away from the circus so he wouldn't be a clown,' said Kate. 'And came here in high seriousness. He could have haunted the Opéra Comique.'

Irene wondered about herself. What had Erik seen in her?

'After all, was I just a thief? I didn't think of it that way. I was what they used to call an "adventuress"... I wasn't a good enough singer not to be. And I certainly wasn't staying in New Jersey and marrying a civil engineer.'

'Didn't you marry a lawyer?'

'We don't mention him... the way we don't mention you not marrying Mr Charles Beauregard of the Diogenes Club.'

Kate goggled at her.

'Yes, Angel of Truth, I know the scores too.'

'Charles was married,' said Kate.

'Widowed,' corrected Irene.

'I knew his wife. Pamela. I wouldn't want to replace her.'

'Godfrey Norton replaced *me*.'

Irene had never acknowledged that in public. She hadn't mentioned her husband in years. Former husband.

God. She really had called him that.

The Persian and Erik had helped her make up her mind about him. No, her mind was already made up... they helped her settle on a course of action.

Desertion, it was called. That was what a truth-teller like Kate Reed would say instead of 'course of action'.

Godfrey Norton was happier without her. He *must* be. Everyone else was. The crowned heads of Europe paid her no mind any more. Great detectives and master criminals had fresher fish to fry. Once, she had been *the* woman... now, she was barely *a* woman. She was a thief after all. She had stolen her own life.

'I don't think we're supposed to get married,' said Kate. 'We are not wives and mothers.'

'We?'

'Angels. Adventuresses. Whatever you care to call us.'

'Christine got married – to a Count, too. They have grown-up kids who wish they'd hurry up and die so they can squabble about the family loot. A brood of de Chagny grand-brats run about too. Sophy Kratides, Angel of Vengeance, has a fatherless daughter. Moria Kratides – dangerous little minx. Elizabeth *is* married, though she tries not to be in the same country as Freddy Eynsford Hill. Ayda Heidari, Angel of Blood, married a Scotsman called Ferguson and settled down in Sussex. Thi Minh is engaged to Jacques d'Athys, the explorer who fetched her back from Indochina as if she were a gewgaw picked up from a market stall. I suppose he might die from tropic fever before he gets her to the altar.'

'Unorna had a lover, Israel Kafka,' said Kate. '*He* died. Still, look at her… as you say, she's beautiful. She must have had suitors.'

'I don't know, Katie. You try being called the Witch of Somewhere and see how easy it is to get a boyfriend.'

'Alraune has many admirers…'

'And they all fade away or are ruined,' said Irene. 'Like the enemies she mentioned. I think she gets her lovers and her enemies confused. That happens more than you'd think.'

'Not to me.'

'No, Katie. Not to you. You have found the perfect husband and, by some strange circumstance, have managed not to marry him.'

'That's a needlessly cruel observation.'

'You're Angel of Truth, remember. That quality is often needlessly cruel.'

'So, this – *adventuring* – is something we do *before* settling down in Twickenham to sew antimacassars and argue with nurse about baby's colic? Or *instead of*.'

'Or *after*. Erik has taken on widows over the years – Madame Lachaille and Madame Calhoun.'

'The Angel of Love and the Angel of Light.'

'Yes, them. I met Madame Calhoun. She wasn't an *official* widow. Her husband did the decent thing and disappeared from the face of the earth. One of those famous unsolved mysteries everyone lets lie. Before she tried settling down in her equivalent of Twickenham, Calhoun was La Marmoset, the greatest detective of either sex in Europe. Mistress of disguise. Never showed the same face twice. Escapologist, too. Pity she isn't with the Agency these days. She'd have those hinges off with a hairpin.'

She should have paid more attention to La Marmoset. The sleuth tried to tell her something and she wouldn't listen. Irene had a blind spot. Great Detectives put her back up. Preconceptions and prejudices could be fatal for those who lived as she had, flitting from caper to con and seduction to scheme.

'I'm an aunt,' said Kate, quietly. 'I *had* aunts and now I am one.'

'Aunts do not have adventures. If you are an aunt, it is incidental. You are an Angel.'

'I might have liked children,' said Kate.

'You might have not liked them too. Plenty don't...'

'Irene, do *you* have children?'

Unorna sat up straight, eyes wide open. And the subject changed, not too soon for Irene.

'Antinea is here,' Unorna announced.

'Slightly late with that announcement,' said Irene.

The witch was disoriented and unfocused. Irene offered her a nip from her flask, but Unorna said she wasn't thirsty.

Kate gave Unorna a précis of what had happened since she conked out.

The witch wasn't happy about it. She was intent on saying something.

'*One of us is not to be trusted. One of us is not who she seems.*'

That just hung there, annoying and ominous.

'You can't say that and not give names,' said Irene. 'Otherwise, it's worse than useless.'

'*One of us is not to be trusted. One of us is not who she seems.*'

'It is a pleasure to meet you,' Kate rattled off. 'I hope we shall be the best of friends.'

Unorna did sound like Olympia. Expressionless. A speaking box, not a person.

'None of us are to be trusted and none of us are who we

seem,' said Irene. 'That's who we are. It doesn't mean we can't trust *each other*.'

Kate was dubious. 'Unorna, what does that mean?'

The witch was still disoriented. 'I've walked pathways in dark,' she said, speaking for herself again. 'I walked for… a long time.'

'It's only been hours since you… fell asleep,' said Kate.

'For you. I've been to… well, somewhere in the dark. Somewhere purple. I've spoken with the shades of the departed. I was told… *one of us is…*'

'…not to be trusted, not who she seems,' said Irene. 'We got the wire.'

'Which shade? The Persian?'

Unorna shook her head. 'Pretty girl,' she said. 'Wore a man's hat.'

'Trilby,' said Irene.

Unorna frowned. She didn't know the name.

'One of the first Angels of Music,' said Kate. 'The Angel of Beauty.'

'Yes,' said Unorna. 'Her. She sang. Not with a human voice. She told me to tell you… *one of us is not to be trusted, one of us not who she seems*.'

Kate shrugged.

'Trilby wasn't very bright,' said Irene, putting it tactfully. 'Lovely girl, of course… but weak-willed, just the sort to fall under the influence of a mastermind. I don't see how death would make her smarter. Who knows what pull Antinea has with, ah, shades of the departed? If it were La Marmoset, I'd put more store by the message of doom. So far as I know, the Queen of Detectives isn't dead.'

Unorna didn't respond. She wasn't all here yet. Had she left something of herself behind 'somewhere in the dark'?

'More to the point,' Irene said, 'can you conjure up magic keys?'

Unorna didn't seem to hear that.

It didn't matter. The cell door opened.

'You have Olympia to thank,' said Elizabeth. 'She's become

self-winding… and can speak to locks. It's remarkable what her clever fingers can do.'

Alraune and Thi Minh peeked into the cell.

Unorna seemed about to repeat Trilby's message… but decided against it and kept quiet. Her wits were coming back. Good.

Thi Minh gestured, trotting as if on a horse, looking over her shoulder. She raised a dented trumpet to her mouth as if blowing an alarum. Irene gathered she meant something like 'the British are coming, the British are coming'.

A knife flew out of the dark and pinned the trumpet to the wall.

VIII

IN THE CORRIDOR, Unorna leant heavily on Kate and gestured with her free hand. Kate felt pressure in her ears. Dead electric bulbs flared and burst into tiny shards.

Rollo wasn't put off. He had another knife in his hand.

Unorna gestured again. Nothing. The witch was still woozy.

Kate couldn't help but worry about the message she'd brought back from her trance. But there wasn't time to puzzle it out.

Rollo raised the knife above his head, gripping the point. He was in no hurry.

Kate supposed Alraune could kiss the knife-thrower with poisoned lips… but it tended to take a week or two for her victims to waste away. They needed him downed well before that.

Mrs Eynsford Hill was knuckle-tapping the wall like a lunatic. Finally, she hit a section that sounded hollow as a drum. She poked the eyes of a plaster cherub and a door-sized panel slid open.

The English woman must have looked long and hard at Erik's architectural plans, to keep them in her head. She stepped through the secret door.

Rollo threw his knife. Serpent-swift, Thi Minh somersaulted in mid-air and kicked the flying blade off course. It thunked into a wall. Rollo was astonished.

'Into the labyrinth,' urged Irene.

Kate and Alraune helped Unorna through.

'Antinea will know where we are,' said Unorna.

'Who's a little ray of sunshine then?' said Irene, following quickly. 'Good news never stops rolling off the presses.'

Kate looked back into the corridor.

Olympia marched on Rollo, arms swinging. The knife-thrower recoiled in superstitious terror. The doll punched him in the stomach, and he bent over double – all the wind gone out of him. Thi Minh bounced off two walls and the ceiling like a triple cushion shot in billiards, and brought all her weight down on the torturer's head. He collapsed in a pained sprawl. The tiny acrobat tugged Rollo's knife-filled coat up over his head, wrenching his arms, pricking him with his own blades. He groaned and bled.

All very satisfying, but it wouldn't hold off the army of Atlantis for long.

The last of the Angels came into the secret passage. The panel slid shut behind them. Rollo's shouts for help were muffled.

Mrs Eynsford Hill – who, Kate remembered, was *not who she seemed* – struck a lucifer on the wall and lit a torch she took from a sconce. Chemically treated rags burned steadily, giving off much light, some heat and a foul smell. The English woman guided the Angels through a narrow, surprisingly undusty and non-cobwebbed passage to a coffin-sized dumb waiter.

'We have to go down,' she said. 'There are pulleys and levers.'

Irene went first.

Kate followed. Long seconds in the dark, confined as if buried, listening to the clanking of chains – not a pleasant experience. She imagined Erik posting himself around the building like a human *pneumatique* message.

In the basement, she waited as the others winched themselves down to the basement. Thi Minh and Olympia shared the lift, fit together like spoons in a case.

They had to stoop not to bash their heads on a vaulted ceiling. Mrs Eynsford Hill's torch left scorchmarks on the brick. Firelight reflected in murky water. A gold face seemed to bob just under the surface. A mask. Not even Erik's, but flotsam from the opera stores. Props and costumes floated all around. Items that looked like stone statues or metal armour were buoyant wood and paste.

This was how Kate envisioned Atlantis. A civilisation swamped.

Where they stood was once Erik's private dock. The flood had risen and the platform was under cold, shallow water. A step or two the wrong way and a careless person might plunge in over their head. Kate wore sensible if scarcely fashionable boots which kept the water out – but not the painful chill. Irene complained her shoes and stockings were ruined and she'd probably lose a toe or two.

'Better a toe than a head,' said Alraune.

No one argued with the German.

When the lagoon was low, this was a strange pleasure-boating lake. Erik would punt a gondola (scavenged from a production of Ponchielli's Venice-set *La Gioconda*) silently across still water to the house he'd hidden beneath the Palais Garnier when he was helping build the place. His own black chapel was here, a temple to his art.

An eerie wailing-whining came from all around.

'What in Hackensack is that?' asked Irene.

'It's his organ,' Kate said. 'Water pushing air through the pipes. The flood won't have done it any good.'

'It doesn't sound that much worse than *Don Juan Triumphant*,' said Irene.

Erik had been composing his oratorio for decades. From what Kate had heard, it was decidedly too avant-garde even for avant-gardistes. The piece sounded like bombs going off in a seal colony. Perhaps the 'mad genius' school of *fortissimo* dissonance would have a vogue in the wake of the continental war Antinea was sure to foment… if anyone with ears was left at the end of it.

'I suppose you don't like music from this century,' Alraune said to Irene. 'Mahler, Schönberg, Strauss.'

'I love Strauss,' said Irene. 'Those dear little waltzes.'

'*Richard* Strauss.'

'Oh, him. Teutonic noise-maker. Tunes you can't hum.'

The German shook her head and didn't take the bait. Had Erik been waiting for Angels who understood his music? Alraune had sung (and danced) Richard Strauss's *Salome* in Berlin – her audition piece for the Opera Ghost Agency. A person of a cattier nature might suggest she'd forgotten to stop playing the role when the curtain rang down. She was plainly *not to be trusted*.

Kate was now inclined to agree with Irene about Unorna's message from beyond. It was worse than useless. Antinea herself couldn't have done more to sew doubts among the Angels just as they needed to rely on each other.

So, was Unorna – or Trilby! – she who was *not to be trusted*? In which case, the pronouncement could be safely ignored.

'We shan't be able to get out through the sewers,' said Mrs Eynsford Hill. 'The water's too high. All the tunnels are flooded. We'll have to go up again. One of Erik's secret stairways is still passable.'

'How do you know which one?' Kate asked.

'Them rats,' said Mrs Eynsford Hill, nodding at a wriggling mass of the beasts. 'You can tell a lot from a rat, you can. Rats is clever, rats is quick…'

She was doing someone else's voice now. Someone who had better acquaintance with vermin.

Squeaking rats paddled towards a cave-like aperture, then scurried up steps inside.

'Rats are also small,' said Irene. 'We can't squeeze up drainpipes.'

Thi Minh made a 'speak for yourself' face. How could anyone know if she was *who she seemed* and *to be trusted*?

386

'That's no drainpipe, as you very well know,' said Mrs Eynsford Hill.

Kate had spent less of her time as an Angel in the opera house than the others. She had stayed in Madame Mandelip's *Hôpital des Poupées*, another of Erik's bolthole-cum-outposts. But she knew where the staircase lead.

Up to a mirror.

IX

DEAR OLD DRESSING Room 313 seemed smaller than Irene remembered. They had to hold their breaths to walk around each other.

At least she could change out of her wet shoes and stockings. And, while she was at it, the rest of her clothes. The day had not been kind to her ensemble.

'Some of Carlotta's dresses are still here,' said Alraune. 'They might fit you.'

'Ha ha,' Irene responded mirthlessly. 'Will you dress as Salome again? I heard that during the dance audiences begged you to put the veils back on again.'

'Angels,' rebuked Kate – who was being sensible.

'We're great pals, really,' said Irene, hugging the bony German girl, running fingers through her huge tangle of strangely scented hair. 'Darling, what do you use for shampoo? Some sort of healthy root?'

Alraune smiled at her.

'I shall keep my secrets,' she said.

Everyone except Kate and Olympia took the opportunity to change. Elizabeth came out from behind the dressing screen in an impractically chic pink dress with matching giant hat. A huge silk rosebud on her chest looked like an elaborate wound.

Unorna slipped into a monk's habit with voluminous hood

and sleeves. Thi Minh put on a sailor suit and straw hat. Alraune found a tailored jacket and skirt which suited her hipless, breastless shape. A knitted hat tidied away her hair and accentuated her plucked eyebrows.

Irene put on male evening dress, complete with red silk-lined black cloak, white gloves and top hat. The shoes were loose, but otherwise she was pleased.

Kate whistled, charitably.

'Find a mask and you could be a new Phantom,' she said.

'I wouldn't want to seem to be something I am not,' Irene responded.

Kate pursed her lips. None of the others picked up on it.

While the others dressed, Elizabeth wrote several pages of notes – with diagrams.

'She's set down what she saw of the Atlantean campaign plans,' said Kate. 'Antinea doesn't have that many supporters yet. Assolant hasn't got the whole army behind him. But he is holding strategic points. He's got the Fellowship of the Frog to surge up from beneath the waters. Grumbling malcontents will rally to the cause if it means an end to the Republic. Then, Antinea or Countess de Cagliostro or whoever she is can declare herself saviour of the country. She might as well call herself Joan of Arc Reborn or Betty Bonaparte and declare herself Empress-Queen-Pope of New Atlantis and settle in for a nice long tyrannical reign.'

'Can she be stopped?'

'If these papers get into the right hands,' said Kate, picking them up.

'How can we manage that? We're trapped in the walls of this house… like lady rats.'

Alraune spoke up. 'There's a way down from the roof. Erik often uses it.'

Irene was not afraid of heights, but did have a teensy-tiny fear of falling from them. Still, no one else in the room expressed qualms so she had to go along with it. Every gal for herself wasn't a slogan which would pass with Kate Reed.

'The roof is patrolled,' Irene pointed out.

'They won't be expecting us,' said Alraune, holding up one of Erik's lassos.

'We'll go up in small parties,' said Elizabeth. 'To attract less attention. If we look as if we're New Atlanteans and not hunted women, we should pass. I take it we all know the way to the roof?'

Everyone did.

Elizabeth, Unorna and Olympia went first.

'You look very handsome in tails,' said Alraune, flirting.

'Like your distinguished old rogue of a grandfather, perhaps,' said Irene.

Alraune was quiet. 'I don't have family... not like that.'

'You have family here,' said Irene. 'If not sisters, then aunts.'

Whatever the German girl had worked on women too. Irene wanted to make Alraune feel better, even though she wasn't sure she liked her. The strange creature was attractive – devilishly attractive. Not what was expected of an Angel, perhaps.

'It's what's special about the Agency,' said Kate. 'We don't just work together.'

Was the Irish woman broody? Earlier, she'd almost gone misty about the children she hadn't had.

Motherless Mandrake, meet Childless Angel of Truth... let's see how you get on.

Alraune squeezed Kate's hand. Then, the German girl left with Thi Minh.

'Interesting Angel, that,' said Irene.

Kate threw a cushion at her. Viciously.

Irene laughed at the unexpected attack. Kate's eyes sparkled behind her cheaters – not with humour, but the beginnings of tears.

'You can't help liking her, in spite of everything.'

'It's her musk. Be careful of feelings you can't help, Katie.'

Irene tossed the cushion back. It flew high. Kate reached for it, but missed.

The cushion struck a closet-catch and a door fell open. A slender white arm flopped out. A hand slapped the floor.

Kate quickly got over the shock. Irene's heart hammered.

Between them, they hauled the body – the *surprisingly heavy* body – out of the wardrobe. A woman in a ballet leotard, folded up to fit into the space.

Irene unwrapped a thick veil from around the head. A cracked china face showed – one green glass eye pushed in, the mouth a perfect, faded rosebud.

'It's Olympia,' said Irene.

The doll was limp, armature broken inside. Her works were stopped.

'If this is Olympia,' said Kate. 'Who's gone up to the roof?'

X

'I DON'T SUPPOSE YOU thought to pack a gun,' said Irene.

'We're not in the Wild West,' said Kate, looking askance at the American.

'I've toured the Wild West,' said Irene. 'They have fewer killings in Tombstone and Deadwood than Paris and London. Or parts of New Jersey, come to that.'

Kate hated to admit it, but Irene had a point. Going into battle clad in the armour of rectitude and bearing the sword of truth was all very well, but she'd have liked a Webley revolver to fall back on.

Olympia was *not who she seemed* – and *not to be trusted*!

'It is a pleasure to meet you,' she'd kept saying. 'I hope we shall be the best of friends.'

Indeed! Kate hadn't been imagining the smirk, then.

They'd treated Olympia as a useful machine – a dray horse, a tin soldier, a wind-up toy. Was someone inside, like the dwarf in the chess-playing Turk? Or was Fauxlympia another mannequin, substituted for their broken doll? A music box set to play a different tune.

Kate remembered the Surprise Symphony at the Persian's grave. Now, she detected the maker's mark of Dr Falke in that firecracker. He could run up a turncoat automaton too.

From Dressing Room 313, Kate and Irene hastened through corridors to the wings of the great stage. Workmen toiled by torchlight, erecting scenery that might pass for an Atlantean throne-room. A choir rehearsed something watery. Atlantis had a national anthem and it wasn't 'Oh I Do Like to Be Beside the Seaside' or 'Married to a Mermaid at the Bottom of the Deep Blue Sea'. Kate thought Antinea's Ascent was getting ahead of itself, but that was confidence for you...

They climbed fixed ladders to the flies. Kate's wrists hurt from pulling herself up, but she didn't complain – unlike some adventuresses she could mention. Irene muttered in pain on every rung.

'How do you do it, Katie?' she asked.

'Cycling and regular shuttlecock.'

'I'd rather fall.'

The other Angels had passed this way. High above the stage, a brace of Camelots hung upside-down from the rigging, gagged with their own caps and scarves. When Kate and Irene approached, the young men tried to get their attention with muffled cries – which became muffled groans when they realised they weren't rescuers.

'Thi Minh,' said Kate.

'Or Elizabeth,' said Irene. 'Alraune would rope them round their throats, not their ankles.'

Kate conceded the point.

'Olympia hasn't played her trick yet,' said Irene.

Kate chewed that over. The doll was waiting for something. A signal?

They were all dolls to someone. Mechanical chess pieces on pre-set courses, unwittingly playing to lose. Why so elaborate a stratagem? This wasn't just about a clean sweep of the Angels. Falke could have packed the automaton's corset full of dynamite and set her to detonate when they were all together. In the de Boscherville tomb or the Café de la Paix.

Irene found the trapdoor, which hung open. Kate was first through.

A filigree steel spiral staircase fed up inside a hollow column. Erik's route to the roof. Kate rapidly climbed stairs, turning round and round in the confined space, ignoring the creaking and wobbling. Irene, out of breath, kept up.

Water had trickled in and frozen. Gripping the guide-rail, Kate was grateful for her gloves. Footprints were crushed into ice on the steps.

'Nearly there,' she told Irene.

'Wonderful,' Irene responded, meaning something else.

The spiral staircase ended in a landing, with a door to the roof. Kate put her face up against a window, but it was frosted over.

'Hah, that's the last of you,' said a voice from the dark behind her. 'The grandmas.'

Irene turned to punch someone. Kate was more cautious.

Rollo had been waiting. His pate was scratched and bruised. His piggy eyes were bright and eager. He held a skinning knife.

Two frog-men were with him.

No, bird-men. Rubber suits and masks, but no air tanks. Instead, folded kite-wings were strapped to their backs. No flippers, but gloved talons.

Rollo gestured towards the door with his knife.

Kate pushed it open and stepped onto the roof. The Phantom's secret stairs came out behind the water tanks where, in summer, the corps de ballet liked to splash about. Someone had tried to carve an igloo out of ice blocks, but it had fallen in.

Sleet lashed Kate's face. Her specs fogged.

It wasn't snowing heavily, but up here the wind was worse – howling around the domes and statues and chimneys of the opera house.

Irene was shoved out after her. They clung to each other. Irene took Kate under her wing, wrapping her heavy cloak around them both.

Grandmas. That stung worse than the cold.

'Keep going,' said Rollo. 'Your carriage awaits.'

Kate supposed it was likely to be a tumbril.

Kate and Irene struggled along a cast-iron walkway. On a dome surmounting the Palais Garnier, a fig-leafless nude Apollo raised a golden lyre to the heavens.

'That's the tiniest penis I've ever seen,' commented Irene.

Kate giggled, though she'd rather scream.

'Make allowances,' she said. 'It is bloody cold.'

'Shush, you,' said Rollo.

They trudged around the dome, treading carefully to avoid falling over. It would be ignominious to slip and dash one's brains out on cast-iron before they even reached the scaffold, the guillotine or the ducking-stool.

Out in the city fires still blazed. Rescue work continued and skirmishes were decided in the dark. Did loyal army factions or the civil authorities yet recognise the Atlantean threat? Or were they still under the impression they fought only bad weather and disorganised looters?

The five Angels – Thi Minh, Alraune, Olympia, Mrs Eynsford Hill, Unorna - were on their knees, arranged atop the low wall at the edge of the roof. Alternating comic and tragic masks were fixed to the balustrade at the front of the building, and Angels were spaced between them. All the women were stripped of scarves, topcoats and hats. They looked out at Place de l'Opéra, hair whipped by the wind. All except Olympia shivered as if freshly soaked with ice-water. Unorna teetered alarmingly. Kate didn't suppose the witch could fly, with or without a broomstick.

'You've not been forgotten,' said Rollo. 'There are perches for you too.'

Kate and Irene were separated. Kate was roughly helped out of her coat. Irene handed her cloak to a bird-man as if he were an attendant. She fussed in her waistcoat pockets as if looking for a coin to tip him. She whirled her top hat away. It caught the wind, sailing off into the night.

Braziers burned all around the dome, casting some light but radiating little heat. The rooftop statuary – besides Apollo, winged ladies representing Poetry and Harmony and a pair of Pegasuses – was firelit. A canopied, presumably waterproof throne which resembled a sedan chair was a new feature. Snugly occupying this pretentious item of furniture was Queen Antinea. She wore armour pieces which resembled large seashells and shaggy white furs that might once have clad several polar bears. Her helmet had lobster claws and bobbing crustacean eye-stalks. Did the Balsamo woman really think she'd be able to rule a country dressed like that?

It would not do to underestimate her. She might be a fake Atlantean, but she was a real sorceress. At least the equal of Unorna, judging by the attack launched against the Witch of Prague on the astral plane. Her hat was very silly, however.

Assolant was here. And Dr Falke. A few evil-looking Jesuits and a nun with a disturbing glass-eyed fish-mask – if it was a mask – huddled with a fur-coated, top hat-sporting type Kate recognised as Favraux, the banker. A chorus of frog-men, bird-men and Camelots completed the whole Atlantean conspiracy. Favraux must be funding the coup – though he was the sort of financier who poured other people's money into risky ventures and kept his own fortune safe in a respectable bank.

A sloping frame was erected on one of the frozen-over vats, bearing one of Falke's contraptions – a bat-winged rocket. Was it to be fired at an opposing army or a strategic location?

This seemed more for show than tactics.

Rollo hauled Kate and Irene towards the balustrade.

Some of the Angels turned and saw them coming. Mrs Eynsford Hill had to pull Unorna back, to keep her from dropping over the edge.

Kate tried to shout a warning about Olympia, but a hairy hand clamped over her mouth.

'We've heard enough from you,' said Rollo.

Kate was hoisted up onto the wall with the rest, Irene to her left and Thi Minh to her right. The rim of the balustrade was broad enough for safety – unless wind, snow or trident-prod changed her balance. But she was unsteady. Her knees pressed on cold stone. It was like kneeling on black ice.

She didn't look down. The view across Place de l'Opéra was worrisome enough. People gathered. She saw them on the rooftops of other buildings, and down in the dark streets.

An audience for the executions? And then a coronation?

Antinea began a speech. Kate didn't bother to listen too closely. She got the gist. The Angels were being sacrificed to water the seeds of New Atlantis in blood.

Hoot and hosannah!

As she might have guessed, Rollo was up for doing the honours. He put away his knife and flexed his fingers.

This was a job for a shover.

Rollo walked along the path beside the wall, inspecting the Angels' backs.

'Who to pick, who to pick?'

The knife-thrower certainly had personal ill-feeling against Kate, an Angel during *l'affaire Guignol*.

But he passed her by.

Kate couldn't feel her face. She was perilously close to telling Rollo to hurry up and get on with it before they all froze to death.

'*Am stram gram, pic et pic et colégram…*'

She recognised the French version of the 'Eenie Meenie Miney Mo' choosing rhyme.

'*Bour et bour et ratatam,*' continued Rollo.

He was behind her again, fingers tickling her spine.

'*Am…*'

The touch was gone.

'*Stram…*'

He was behind Thi Minh.

'*Gram!*'

Alraune!

Rollo put powerful hands around Alraune's neck and shoved her over off the balustrade. He didn't let go. Dangling her in mid-air, he squeezed her throat.

Alraune choked and kicked.

XI

SUDDENLY, *HE* WAS there…
  Rising through a trapdoor no one had suspected.

Black cloak swirling like a dark cloud.

Mask pure white.

The Phantom of the Opera seized Rollo's coat-tails and dragged him away from the edge of the roof. The knife-thrower let go of Alraune…

…who fell, face calm, hands up, for *an instant*…

…until Thi Minh caught Alraune's thin wrist with one hand and hooked her other arm around a tragedy mask. The sudden weight pulled the acrobat off the ledge, but she kept hold of the mask – and Alraune. The stonework held. And Thi Minh's shoulders. With great strain, the tiny woman hauled her tall friend up until they were both safe. Breathing heavily, they lay on the roof.

Erik loomed, cloak like wings. Yellow eyes reflecting fire.

Kate and Irene got down off the balustrade and made themselves small.

Rollo couldn't get up. He convulsed, eyes bulging and bloody. Erik had pulled his coat tight like a strait-jacket, piercing him with his own blades. A dozen knives stuck through his ribs and into his soft insides. He coughed and died.

Antinea was still making her bloody speech.

Kate shouted 'Olympia!' at Erik and waved her hands like Thi Minh.

Olympia was *not who she seemed and could not be trusted.*

But it wasn't Olympia who leaped on the Phantom's back.

With a screech like a banshee, Alraune sprang up. She wrapped long, sinewy arms and legs around Erik's thin body from behind. She sank sharp teeth into the pale exposed flesh of his neck.

An Angel of Ill Fortune!

A fatal woman. All who cared for her died.

She was *exactly* who she seemed… and *not to be trusted*.

'Congratulations, Monsieur Erik,' said Antinea, clapping politely. 'So kind of you to join us at last. It is heartening to know something can always coax you from your rat-holes. We'd have searched the house for years and not laid hands on you. But you love your girls so. It's touching that such a monster is such a romantic.'

Erik's arms were pinned. He tried to shrug off Alraune but she clung like ivy, entwining tighter around him.

Kate understood this had all been to draw Erik out.

Alraune strongly argued for the diversionary theory that Fantômas was their enemy. Kate realised the traitor Angel had murdered the Persian herself. She'd have got close to him the way she got close to everyone – by being what they desired, one way or another. Mandrake was a weed, a parasite which killed its host. Kate had a sour burst of pity for Alraune – so soulless she could feel no friendship, no qualm, no shame. She had deceived Erik who, as Antinea said, was perhaps the deepest romantic of them all. A monster with a heart.

He must have watched them all along – through his many peep-holes. It had been the same at the *Théâtre des Horreurs* and in the Louvre, when he held back until the last. Only a direct threat to his protégées prompted him to step on the stage and act. Antinea understood him.

General Assolant walked over, pistol raised.

'You'll die last,' he said.

To Erik? Or to Kate? Hard to tell.

Assolant's arm shook in the cold. He couldn't get an aim until he was close. He'd never been in a battle, just administered head-shots to the fallen after his firing squad had done the heavy work of murder.

The General passed Mrs Eynsford Hill and fell back, dropping his gun.

His hand went up to his face. A knife and fork stuck out of it. More scars for the collection.

Murmurings among the chorus. Falke and Favraux sputtered.

Antinea raised her hand. She was intent on Erik and Alraune. Nothing else would mar her enjoyment of the Fall of the Phantom.

Olympia moved, striding towards Erik.

'It is a pleasure to meet you,' she said. 'I hope we shall be the best of friends.'

Alraune grinned like a fiend, teeth red. Erik seemed to relax, like a python's victim succumbing at last to the crushing coils. Blood seeped across his starched shirt-front and stained his perfectly tied white tie.

'It is a pleasure to meet you...'

The mannequin made a fist and punched Alraune in the face. The *pop!* of the German girl's nose breaking was like a pistol shot.

'I hope we shall be the best of friends.'

Olympia tore Alraune away from Erik and tossed the scrap of a girl off the roof.

She *wasn't* who she seemed, but she was *to be trusted*.

Kate stood, helping Irene up. The others scrambled around.

Unorna pressed her hand to Erik's wound and was sheltered under his cloak. Mrs Eynsford Hill tripped Assolant and kicked him when he was down. Thi Minh scooped up the General's pistol and fired a warning shot that tore Favraux's hat from his head.

Antinea was enraged. She swore violently in a language which wasn't Atlantean. It might have been Corsican or Sicilian.

Dr Falke, sensing the whole coup teetering, fiddled urgently with his bat-rocket. His armature hissed as he worked, as if he were steam-powered. His bird-men assisted, clumsily. They rushed through a process which should be carried out with more care.

Whatever the weapon was, it was about to be fired.

Kate, Irene and Olympia ran towards Falke's crew.

Antinea shouted.

Kate didn't even have an instant to wonder what she meant to do before she had her hands on Falke's backpack and started pulling wires. Irene got to his legs and twisted his metal braces.

The old man keened in frustration.

Olympia tossed bird-men the length of the vat. They crashed and skidded on ice. The fish-nun's mouth gaped and she barked like a seal, then ran off, scattering Jesuits and Camelots like a ball crashing through skittles.

A fuse fizzed. A clockwork whirr sounded.

'You're too late,' crowed Antinea.

Olympia – whoever or whatever she might be – threw herself onto the bat-rocket, shattering its works with her armoured body, smashing her head against the fuse. A small explosion broke the thing into pieces. A burning wing spun round and round across the ice like a runaway Catherine wheel. Fragments stuck into Falke's chest and he died, unable to fall. His locked metal braces held him in place, a slumped statue.

Olympia's head was on fire. She plunged her face into meltwater to extinguish the flame. She lay, breathing more like an injured person than an automaton, steam rising from her blackened mask.

Thi Minh, Erik, Unorna and Mrs Eynsford Hill fought bat-men and frog-men at close quarters. Everyone slid around on the roof, losing their footing. A bat-man toppled, wings torn apart by the wind, and screamed all the way down – which gave his comrades cause to distrust their equipment.

Irene boxed Favraux's ears and administered several kicks to his upholstered trousers.

Kate took the pages Mrs Eynsford Hill had written and gave them to Erik.

'It's her plan,' she said, nodding at Antinea.

Behind his mask, Erik chuckled. He crumpled the pages up and tossed them over his head – where they caught light and burned with a purplish magnesium flare. Answering flares rose from rooftops all around... Cheers sounded from across the square, then across the city.

The rooftops were swarming.

White dots appeared in the dark... on the roofs and in the square below, and the streets feeding into Place de l'Opéra.

'The Grand Vampire has opened his roost,' said Erik.

Kate had forgotten the persuasive power of the Phantom's voice – that suave purr with strange glottals as he compensated for his ruin of a mouth... deep, beautiful, perfectly cadenced speech... reassuring and all-encompassing as if directed precisely into her soul... unearthly, inspiring, terrifying.

Erik had brought them all in with just a voice.

'And *Les Vampires* hold the rooftops of Paris,' he continued. 'Fantômas is abroad tonight, and Judex the Avenger... and the Angels you couldn't net, Lady Yuki and Riolama and Elsie Venner... and others, old friends and foes united with us against you... Irma Vep, Rouletabille and Belphégor. Everywhere, your allies are confronted and checked and beaten. The company of the Opéra have pulled down your gaudy throne and tossed your choir into the street. Gendarmes and *apaches* together are trouncing your Camelots du Roi. Your traitors in the army have been rooted out and will be cashiered. Your frog-men and bird-men are routed. This is not your city. It never will be.'

Explosions and alarms sounded. But also songs – 'La Marseillaise', of course, and 'Auprès de ma Blonde', but something else too... a section from *Don Juan Triumphant*, voiced by people who *understood*, who believed in phantoms.

Kate saw what the white dots were. Masks!

Luminous, greenish-white masks. Worn by men and women in black cloaks and hats. A hundred phantoms – a thousand! ten thousand! – marched against the armies of Atlantis. Erik had his own plan, a game inside the stratagem laid against him. He had gulled his tricksters and surrendered to draw them into a trap. He was of the opera, after all. This was not a political coup, but a theatrical coup –

a mastermind's master-stroke. A final flourish when all seemed lost, and the curtain rung down to thunderous applause.

Kate cheered for the Phantom.

Antinea rose from her throne.

She was alone now – allies dead or fled or useless.

But she had one final move.

She flung off her furs. A set of fish-scaled wings popped out of her armoured carapace.

She threw herself into the air and screeched across the roof, claw-gauntlets out. She would tear off the Phantom's mask... and his head!

Erik pushed Unorna aside and grabbed Antinea's arms, holding her talons away from him. The Queen's impetus lifted them both up and over the balustrade.

Kate stopped breathing as they hovered in space. Antinea's wings flapped, once – then failed! Fabric ripped.

They plummeted, each firmly gripping the other, picking up speed, cloak and wings in a ragged tangle...

There was a splash as they fell into the flooded Métro works. The current whirled and eddied around the deep pit. For a moment, an arm thrust up out of the water, holding up a mask... then it was sucked under.

Erik and Antinea were gone.

XII

EVENTUALLY, THE WATERS receded, the lights burned again and damage was assessed. Kate sent informative articles about the disaster to *The Clarion* and a confidential report about everything else to the Diogenes Club. Periodicals were filled with photographs of Paris under water, which also appeared on popular postcards. When over, the flood seemed a strange dream. People needed pictures to remind themselves the Eiffel Tower once stood in a lake.

Commissions of enquiry probed How the Flood Happened. Editorials suggested What Should Be Done to Prevent the Flood Happening Again. Wrecked businesses and the temporarily – or permanently – homeless demanded assistance and compensation. Supplies of disinfectant were distributed, and battalions of concierges and housewives set about Making the Smell Go Away. Looters were tried and convicted quietly, to protect them from angry citizens who couldn't find the silver coffee pot left behind when they were forced to abandon home. The courts also welcomed a new breed of *blagueurs* – chancers who put in bogus insurance claims for non-existent lost property. By Mardi Gras, the Seine was down around the Zouave's ankles. Paris managed a modest celebration – though the Prefect of Police banned confetti-throwing, for fear of blocking just-unclogged drains.

Few remembered New Atlantis. Casualties of the aborted coup were written off as flood victims. General Assolant was awarded another medal, for stalwart service during the late emergency (he had been wounded, after all), then quietly transferred to a post where he could do no more harm. Other conspirators returned to respectable life, shaken and afraid of consequences – but scarcely ashamed or even dissuaded from trying something similar again. Immediate threats were quashed, though. The Fellowship of the Frog disappeared, and many wrote them off as a myth. The Camelots du Roi were lauded for their patriotic spirit.

The Opéra season resumed with a gala performance to raise funds for flood relief. Reigning divas shared the stage with performers called out of retirement for the occasion. Irene Adler appeared low on the bill, singing 'Hello! My Baby (Send Me a Kiss by Wire)' – and received offers from cabarets and variety halls to perform again. The haughty sniffed that Tin Pan Alley wasn't opera. Kate supposed Irene didn't care. Carlotta joined Margarita da Cordova in the 'Flower Duet' from *Lakmé*. The former prima donna was note-perfect for the first half of the song, then croaked pathetically like a frog… while the chandelier above the auditorium shook alarmingly.

Was the house now haunted by the *ghost* of the Phantom?

Everyone looked to Box 5, which was – genuinely – empty. Modest obituaries had appeared. Everyone knew Erik was dead, but few wished to speak of him.

After the gala, a small, elderly fellow with a sad face approached Kate in the lobby. He plainly knew her, though she couldn't place him. He said it was shocking what passed for entertainment these days and argued earnestly for stringent censorship. Only when he moved on did she realise who he was. She'd never seen his face, but the voice couldn't be mistaken. Jacques Hulot... Guignol! He'd shut the *Théâtre des Horreurs* because of competition from the flickers.

Later that night, Kate attended another reception, under the opera house.

The lagoon was low. Repairs had been made.

She joined Irene, who still wore her gala dress, among the women on the dock. Her old friend Yuki was here, but not Clara Watson. Yuki passed on a rumour that Clara had installed herself as absolute ruler of a fearsome tribe inhabiting an ancient jungle temple in the Protectorate of Cambodia. The Japanese Angel had duelled frog-men in Montmartre. Mrs Eynsford Hill introduced a chittering, endearing creature as Riolama. The bird-girl had harried Camelots in Bercy, fending them off while the dynamos of the power station were started up again.

Irene also had a guest. A black-veiled, newly widowed Countess de Chagny. Her husband caught his death of a chill while protecting his estates from a swarm of bedraggled Parisian flood refugees. Kate had a sense of occasion at meeting the first Angel. Irene talked over everything Christine said.

Irma Vep, spectacular in a sheer black leotard and batwing cape, represented *Les Vampires*, who had come out of the flood quite well. On the principle that the drowned can't pay protection money, the Grand Vampire had ordered his legions to contribute to life-saving efforts.

Kate recognised many of the company – but by no means all of them. Here was Hagar Stanley, the Romany genius, casting a valuer's eye over everyone present... Elsie Venner, the whatever-she-was – more terrifying even than the late, not-to-be-mentioned Alraune ten Brincken... a repaired Olympia, up on her points and whirling like a figure atop a music box... dark, sombre Sophy Kratides, with her impish four-year-old Moria... the modern dancer Lavinia King and the ragtime gal Trudy Evans... the physicist Marie Curie and the alienist Sabina Spielrein... anarchists and princesses, and anarchist princesses... girls from the corps de ballet and the chorus who might yet show talents... smart young women who typed, bicycled, drove automobiles and demanded the vote... mature ladies who'd discovered aptitudes for detection, violence, disguise and daring. Angels all. Or potential Angels.

If there was still an Opera Ghost Agency.

A lantern moved across the subterranean lake. A gondola approached.

A masked, cloaked figure stood up in the boat. She wore a plumed hat.

La Marmoset, Queen of Detectives, Mistress of Disguise.

She had been Erik's Secret Angel throughout *l'affaire Antinea*, holding herself rigid and unblinking, looking out through Olympia's glass eyes, marking Alraune's moves. The German girl had thought too little of the doll. Balsamo, her mistress, had thought too much of the Angels, wasting her cunning on vengeance rather than committing fully to her Ascent.

Had Erik known what might happen – to La Marmoset and to himself?

A woman who seldom showed her true face was burned beyond recognition. Under her mask, she wore bandages. One of her eyes was stained yellow.

Erik was gone – though his body, like Jo Balsamo's, had not been found. To stay open for business, the Opera Ghost Agency needed a new Phantom...

...and a new Persian. Irene was averse to staying in one place too long. A young composer called Berlin wanted her to be first to sing his new song 'Alexander's Ragtime Clarinet' – which Kate was sure no one would ever hear again, even if he did pay attention to Irene and change the title to 'Alexander's Ragtime Band'. It fell to Unorna – the Witch of Paris, now – to take over the Persian's table at the Café de la Paix. Monsieur Gustave ensured there was a fresh cloth on it every morning.

From among this crowd of women – former and present Angels, and women who had not yet heard the call – La Marmoset would choose three.

Kate had not left her name in the ring. She was needed at home. Charles's cipher telegram outlined a series of baffling crimes which required the attention of the Diogenes Club. Objects of little value stolen from impossible places. He didn't say as much – in a telegram, how could he? – but she knew he missed her.

Kate was already thinking. Who would – indeed, who *could* – steal an ordinary thimble from the Queen's sewing room at Windsor Castle? An empty inkwell from inside the most secure vault of the Bank of England? And, most disturbing of all, a cigar-cutter from the Inner Chamber of the Diogenes Club itself?

Paris should be safe without her. Enough worthy candidates were ready to move into Dressing Room 313.

Thi Minh, survivor of the last trio, was a shoo-in...

Mrs Eynsford Hill was willing to return to the lists.

Maybe Irma Vep was inclined to transfer from *Les Vampires*...

If that was how the Agency was configured, Kate had confidence in it.

Irene was interested in the selection, but eager to get away. What was it she had to get away from... or get away to? It couldn't just be a song. Even as it wasn't just a cigar-cutter that recalled Kate to London.

The gondola reached the dock. The Phantom stepped out.

'Ladies,' she began...

NOTES AND ACKNOWLEDGEMENTS

RANDY AND JEAN-MARC Lofficier commissioned an earlier draft of the first 'Angels of Music' novella for their anthology series *Tales of the Shadowmen*; Mike Chinn reprinted it in *The Alchemy Press Book of Pulp Heroes 2*. Stephen Jones took 'Guignol' for his *Horrorology* collection. Thanks to them for the support and encouragement – and, of course, to Cath Trechman, Angel of Editing, at Titan. Thanks especially to Pierre Bouvet, for pointers on French language and Paris landmarks.

I first read an abridged translation of Gaston Leroux's novel *The Phantom of the Opera* in an anthology called *The Ghouls*, and the full book as Volume 34 of The Dennis Wheatley Library of the Occult (Sphere) in 1975. For *Angels of Music*, I've relied on *The Essential Phantom of the Opera*, annotated by Leonard Wolf, and a 2004 variant translation of the novel by Randy and Jean-Marc Lofficier from Black Coat Press. During work on this novel, I watched all the available film versions of *The Phantom of the Opera* – none perfect, all interesting. It's a property that has evolved since Leroux published it, with each adaptor adding something new or emphasising something different. I still see Lon Chaney's face behind every Phantom mask – but there's a real Scenes We'd Like to See moment at the end of the 1943 Claude Rains film where Christine (Susanna Foster) walks out on both her smothering suitors and decides being an opera star is better than a stifling marriage, even to someone who doesn't have to wear a mask.

Naturally, I recommend George du Maurier's *Trilby*; Arthur Conan Doyle's 'A Scandal in Bohemia', 'The Greek Interpreter' and 'The Sussex Vampire'; F. Marion Crawford's *The Witch of Prague* (another Dennis Wheatley Library of the Occult volume); Albert W. Aiken's 'La Marmoset, the Detective Queen; or: The Lost Heir of Morel'; Fergus Hume's *Hagar of the Pawn-Shop*; Bram Stoker's *Dracula*; Octave Mirbeau's *Torture Garden* (and Oscar Méténier's stage adaptation); the *Lady Snowblood* films; Guy de Maupassant's *Bel-Ami*; Colette's *Gigi*; George Bernard Shaw's *Pygmalion* (especially with Shaw's Preface and Notes); W. H. Hudson's *Green Mansions* (and Epstein's Riolama statue – still in Hyde Park); H. H. Ewers' *Alraune*; E.T.A. Hoffmann's 'The Sandman' and Offenbach's *Tales of Hoffmann* (and the Powell and Pressburger film, with Moira Shearer's definitive Olympia) and Louis Feuillade's *Fantômas*, *Les Vampires* and *Tih Minh* (thanks to Yung Kha for putting me right on how that should be spelled).

Among many books consulted (not to mention the Internet), I found especially useful stuff in Richard J. Hand and Michael Wilson's *Grand-Guignol: The French Theatre of Horror*, Jeffrey H. Jackson's *Paris Under Water: How the City of Light Survived the Great Flood of 1910*, Susan Kay's *Phantom*, Randy and Jean-Marc Lofficier's *Shadowmen* and *Shadowmen 2*, Jess Nevins' *Encyclopedia of Fantastic Victoriana*, Piers Paul Read's *The Dreyfus Affair* and Graham Robb's *Parisians: An Adventure History of Paris*.

Other Angels – Claire Amias, Chiara Barbo, Saskia Baron, Liz Beardsworth, Lauren Beukes, Anne Billson, Jamie Birkett, Prano Bailey-Bond, Susan Byrne, Pat Cadigan, Cat Camacho, Hayley Campbell, Katharine Carroll, Simret Cheema-Innis, Sarah Cleary, Ellen Datlow, Meg Davis, Sarah Douglas, Val Edwards, Jennifer Eiss, Angela Errigo, Manon Fargetton, Mélanie Fazi, Jo

Fletcher, Amanda Foubister, Kathy Gale, Ellen Gallagher, Lisa Gaye, Jane Giles, Lydia Gittins, Georgina Hawtrey-Woore, Jen Handorf, Nicole Helfrich, Susannah Hickling, Roz Kaveney, Leigh Kennedy, Grace Ker, Roz Kidd, Vivian Landau, Amanda Lipman, Maitland McDonagh, Maura McHugh, Cindy Moul, Silja Mueller, Helen Mullane, Julia Newman, Sasha Newman, Violet Newman, Helen O'Hara, Katya Pendill, Marcelle Perks, Sarah Pinborough, Rhianna Pratchett, Jenny Runacre, Deborah Salter, Alice Scarling, Hayley Shepherd, Lynda Rucker, Martina Seesto, Mandy Slater, Sylvia Starshine, Catriona Toplis, Sara Tracy, Lisa Tuttle, Kat Wearne, Miranda Wood, Ally Wybrew.

ABOUT THE AUTHOR

KIM NEWMAN IS a novelist, critic and broadcaster. His fiction includes *The Night Mayor*, *Bad Dreams*, *Jago*, the Anno Dracula novels and stories, *The Quorum* and *Life's Lottery*, all currently being reissued by Titan Books, *Professor Moriarty: The Hound of the D'Urbervilles* published by Titan Books and *The Vampire Genevieve* and *Orgy of the Blood Parasites* as Jack Yeovil. The critically acclaimed *An English Ghost Story*, which was nominated for the inaugural James Herbert Award, and most recently, *The Secrets of Drearcliff Grange School* are also published by Titan Books. His non-fiction titles include the influential *Nightmare Movies* (recently reissued by Bloomsbury in an updated edition), *Ghastly Beyond Belief* (with Neil Gaiman), *Horror: 100 Best Books* (with Stephen Jones), *Wild West Movies*, *The BFI Companion to Horror*, *Millennium Movies*, *BFI Classics* studies of *Cat People* and *Doctor Who*, and the forthcoming *Video Dungeon*, a collection of his popular *Empire* magazine columns of the same name.

He is a contributing editor to *Sight & Sound* and *Empire* magazines, has written and broadcast widely on a range of topics, and scripted radio and television documentaries. His stories 'Week Woman' and 'Ubermensch' have been adapted into an episode of the TV series *The Hunger* and an Australian short film; he has directed and written a tiny film *Missing Girl*. Following his Radio 4 play 'Cry Babies', he wrote an episode ('Phish Phood') for Radio 7's series *The Man in Black*.

Follow him on Twitter @annodracula. His official website can be found at

WWW. JOHNNYALUCARD.COM

THE SECRETS OF DREARCLIFF GRANGE SCHOOL

By Kim Newman

A week after her mother found her sleeping on the ceiling, Amy Thomsett is delivered to her new school, Drearcliff Grange in Somerset.

Although it looks like a regular boarding school, Amy learns that Drearcliff girls are special, the daughters of criminal masterminds, outlaw scientists and master magicians. Several of the pupils also have special gifts like Amy's, and when one of the girls in her dormitory is abducted by a mysterious group in black hoods, Amy forms a secret, superpowered society called the Moth Club to rescue their friend. They soon discover that the Hooded Conspiracy runs through the school, and it's up to the Moth Club to get to the heart of it.

'Kim Newman stands among speculative fiction's finest, and his new book is no less impressive than the best of the rest of his writing...I had a hunch it would be wonderful and it was.'
Tor.com

'I can see myself re-reading this book time and again.'
Fantasy Book Review

AN ENGLISH GHOST STORY

BY KIM NEWMAN

The Naremores, a dysfunctional British nuclear family, seek
a new life away from the big city in the sleepy Somerset
countryside. At first their new home, The Hollow, seems to
embrace them, creating a rare peace and harmony within the
family. But when the house turns on them, it seems to know just
how to hurt them the most – threatening to destroy them from
the inside out.

'Immersive, claustrophobic and utterly wonderful.'
M.R. Carey, *New York Times* bestselling author of
The Girl With All the Gifts

'Thoroughly enjoyable, master storytelling.'
Lauren Beukes, bestselling author of *Broken Monsters*

'Deserves to stand beside the great novels of the ghostly.'
Ramsey Campbell

'An intoxicating read.'
Paul Cornell, bestselling author of *London Falling*

AFTER THE CURTAIN

HIS CELL WAS (ironically) called Box 5.

It was literally a box – with a corrugated iron lid, instead of a door. Tropic rain fell in through an open grille in the lid. Or else burning sun made his wet rags steam. They let him keep his mask so they wouldn't have to look at him. If it ever occurred to them how susceptible his pale skin was to sunburn, it would be taken away.

The Governor would occasionally sit by Box 5, reading aloud from the Paris papers, which arrived in this harsh corner of the world six weeks after publication. Many shows had closed by the time he heard what the critics thought of them.

On this island, France kept its monsters.

Balaoo, the trusty who helped keep inmates in line, was a shambling ape with the rudimentary power of speech. He was crueller than the guards. To show he was a man, he had to be worse than any beast.

On his first escape attempt, he merely scouted out the compound, peeking into cells. He was curious about his fellow prisoners.

Some of the finest families in France packed their disgraces off to *l'Île des Monstres*. The Marquis de Coulteray, who drank blood, as if that were anything special… Reginald de Malveneur, who tore at the bars and howled when the full moon shone down.

One cell bore the name Maximus Leo. Inside was a severed hand, nailed to a board but still wriggling. Even he was minded to stay away from that.

Up to her neck in swamp-water, he found a claimant to the Throne of Atlantis.

He took no pleasure in that.

They caught him before dawn, as he expected.

Balaoo whipped him, but he was used to pain. He had lived with pain all his life.

Back in Box 5, he closed his eyes and willed the rattle of rain to sound like *Idomeneo*. Electra – Christine Daaé – singing '*Tutte nel Cor vi Sento Furie del Cupo Averno*'. 'I Can Feel you All in My Heart, Furies of the Dark Hell'. In his mind, he explored the building he had made his home – had rarely left for forty years – summoning up the tiniest detail.

He heard the rustle of dresses. Smelled powder and rosin. Sensed the anticipation of an audience. The thunder of applause. His heart swelled. His skull rang with music.

A bucket of filth was tipped in on him. Gibbering laughter interrupted his reverie.

Still, he hoped for a deliverance. He trusted in Angels.

The occupant of Box 5 smiled. Without lips, he had no choice.